FIND
HER
ALIVE

D1335320

30128 80472 835 5

BOOKS BY LISA REGAN

FIND
HER
ALIVE

LISA REGAN

Bookouture

Published by Bookouture in 2020

An imprint of Storyfire Ltd.
Carmelite House
50 Victoria Embankment
London EC4Y 0DZ

www.bookouture.com

Copyright © Lisa Regan, 2020

Lisa Regan has asserted her right to be identified
as the author of this work.

All rights reserved. No part of this publication may be reproduced,
stored in any retrieval system, or transmitted, in any form or by
any means, electronic, mechanical, photocopying, recording or
otherwise, without the prior written permission of the publishers.

ISBN: 978-1-83888-230-3
eBook ISBN: 978-1-83888-229-7

This book is a work of fiction. Names, characters, businesses,
organizations, places and events other than those clearly in the
public domain, are either the product of the author's imagination
or are used fictitiously. Any resemblance to actual persons, living or
dead, events or locales is entirely coincidental.

In Loving Memory of Jennifer Jaynes
I will miss your words.

CHAPTER ONE

Before the incidents started, Alex's father used to take him out into the woods on adventures. That's what he called them, but Alex soon discovered that his father's idea of adventure was sitting on a log or laying in the brush all day, staring through a pair of binoculars at birds. Still, his father, Francis, wasn't nice to Alex very often, so whenever he took him out into the woods, Alex made sure to pay attention. He made sure to act interested and to do everything that his father said as soon as he said it and exactly the way he said to do it. After one adventure during which Alex had worked very hard to be very good, he was rewarded with his own pair of binoculars. They weren't as big or as nice as the ones his father carried, but Alex enjoyed mimicking his movements, staring through them at hawks and falcons and owls. Those were the birds his father was most interested in. Raptors, he called them.

"They're birds of prey," his father told him. "Hunters. They have amazing eyesight. They can spot their target from way up high in the sky. They wait for just the right moment, and then they strike! They're very intelligent birds."

Alex wasn't sure what made them intelligent, but he knew that intelligence was important to his father. It was a word he used a lot. He didn't like people who weren't intelligent, and Alex lived in fear of being deemed not intelligent by his father. That was why he carried around a notebook and pencil just like his father did. At six, he had just learned to read and write, so he couldn't write lots of words in his notebook like his father did, but he drew pictures of the birds they watched.

One day they were out in the woods, standing beside a clearing, and his father spotted a large raptor in the sky. It was so high up, Alex couldn't tell what kind of bird it was, but his dad assured him it was a hawk. "Watch this, son," he told him.

He reached into a satchel he'd brought with him from their house and brought out a snake. Alex recoiled, falling backward over a branch on the ground. His head knocked against a nearby tree. "Ow," he cried.

His father stood several feet away, frozen, with the wriggling snake in his hand, and glared at his son. "Get. Up!" he snarled.

Alex scrambled to his feet. He reached behind his head and felt something damp. His fingers came away bloodied. He dared not point this out to his father, who was waiting for him to get back into position, his face getting more and more red with fury with each second that passed.

"Sorry Dad," Alex muttered, stepping up beside his father again. He looked out into the clearing, then up at the sky even though the movement sent a white-hot streak of pain down his neck. The hawk flew closer to the treetops.

"Watch," his father said. He tossed the snake into the middle of the clearing. Immediately, it began writhing and wriggling away in the opposite direction. Suddenly the hawk was there, only a few feet away, its thick talons pointed downward like spears, its gloriously large wings spread wide. It snatched the squirming snake from the grass and flew effortlessly back into the sky.

Alex's father watched with wonder as the bird receded from view.

Alex felt a warm stickiness slide down the back of his neck. "Dad," he said quietly. "I think I need a bandage."

He touched the back of his head again and this time, when he brought it forward to show his father, his entire palm was covered in blood. His father looked down at him, his look of awe transforming into one of disgust. For a long moment, he stared down at Alex, his lip curled in a sneer. Then he shook his head, huffed, and walked away. Momentarily dumbfounded, Alex watched him go. He had already covered quite a bit of ground when he turned and spat the words back at his son, but Alex heard them as clearly as if he'd shouted them into his ear.

"Stupid boy."

CHAPTER TWO

A cold, wet nose nudged Josie's arm. Then came the mournful whine. When she didn't respond to her Boston Terrier's efforts to get her out of bed, he jumped up onto the covers and began to sniff her ears and the nape of her neck. "Trout," she groaned, rolling over to face him. A pair of soulful brown eyes stared back.

He huffed at her and sat down, his smooshy black and white face a study in seriousness, his ears perfect steeples. Without even moving his mouth, he emitted another small whine. She rubbed beneath his chin.

"What time is it, buddy?" she asked sleepily, although she didn't even have to look at her bedside clock to know that her alarm was due to go off in ten minutes—at least, on a work day it would be, but today she was off. In the six months since she and her live-in boyfriend, Noah Fraley, had rescued Trout they'd developed something of a routine. The dog woke them just before their alarm went off, Josie would let him out, feed him, and then the three of them would go for a brief jog before the humans got ready and went off to work. Even on days off, Trout was persistent about keeping to their routine.

Josie and Noah both worked for the city of Denton's police department—she as a detective and he as a lieutenant. Denton was nestled in the mountains of central Pennsylvania, spanning approximately twenty-five square miles. In the central area of the city where the retail establishments, police headquarters, post office, and Denton University were located, the streets and buildings were grouped closely together in a predictable grid pattern except for the sprawling city park. The rest of the city was spread out over rural wooded areas, accessible by ribbons of single-lane winding roads. Although Denton was a small city, it was no stranger to crime, and the police department stayed busy.

Josie rolled over and nudged Noah's shoulder. "Time to get up," she told him, getting only a grunt in response.

"Come on," she added.

"Put the coffee on, would you?" Noah mumbled.

Josie threw her legs over the side of the bed. Excitedly, Trout jumped down, his rear end wiggling as he ran toward the bedroom door. Josie turned her alarm clock off and padded out into the hallway and downstairs. Twenty minutes later, Trout was fed, both Josie and Noah had consumed one quick cup of coffee, and then dressed in their running clothes. Josie knelt on the foyer floor, trying to coax Trout's trembling body into his harness while Noah went upstairs to get his phone.

"We do this every morning, buddy," Josie murmured as she tried to snap the harness across Trout's back. "You know you have to keep still while I get this on."

Trout couldn't contain his excitement. He jumped up to lick her face, and the harness fell half off him. Josie laughed which made him hop around, his little rear end wriggling until he bumped the foyer table. The table was small. It didn't take much to knock it out of place. Trout knocked into it again, and it slid a few inches across the floor. Two sets of keys and a pair of sunglasses clattered to the floor.

"Shit," Josie said, snatching up the sunglasses before Trout accidentally stepped on them, relief flooding through her.

Noah jogged down the steps. Seeing Josie with the sunglasses in her hand, he said, "Your sister still hasn't come back for those? She's probably got another pair by now."

Josie placed them back on the table, along with their keys, and tried once more to wrestle Trout into his harness. "Noah, we're talking about Trinity here. Do you have any idea how much those sunglasses cost? Do you even know what brand those are?"

He knelt on the floor and pointed to the area in front of him. Dutifully, Trout scampered over and sat down, letting Noah secure harness, leash, and collar with ease.

"Traitor," Josie muttered.

Noah said, "Why would I know what brand Trinity's sunglasses are?"

Josie rolled her eyes as they made their way out the front door and took off in a slow jog down the street with Trout leading the way. "They're Gucci, and I'm guessing they cost at least three hundred dollars, maybe more."

Noah stopped in his tracks, pulling Trout up short on his leash. The dog looked back at them curiously, his ears pointed. Noah said, "Who would pay three hundred dollars for a pair of sunglasses?"

Josie took the leash from his hand and they started moving again. He caught up with her. She replied, "A news anchor for a major network morning show, that's who. She's a celebrity. She can afford three hundred-dollar sunglasses."

Noah shook his head. "Is she still co-hosting? When's the last time you heard from her?"

Josie felt a kernel of discomfort at her core, like a jab in her stomach. "A month ago," she said quietly.

"So you don't even know if she's still holed up in that cabin or if she went back to New York City?"

"I think she's still on her self-imposed retreat," Josie said. "She hasn't talked with our parents or our brother in weeks."

"She's fighting with everyone, then?"

Josie sighed. "No, just me."

"You ready to tell me what happened?"

Josie jogged a few strides ahead of him. "Not particularly."

Trout stopped to sniff a telephone pole, and Josie paused as well. She felt Noah's gaze boring into her before she looked up at him.

His hazel eyes were serious. "Josie, I know this rift between you and Trinity has been bothering you. Just tell me what happened. You might feel better if we talk about it."

"I don't think so," she said. "Besides, you were there for most of it."

Noah raised a brow. "Yeah, I came in from working an overnight shift. I said a few words to her, and she freaked out. Then I took Trout for a walk. I have no idea what went down between the two of you, but when I came home Trinity was gone. You've been miserable ever since."

"I haven't been—"

Noah held up a hand to silence her. "I know you don't like to hear it, but you've been off. Not yourself. I can see you're trying to wait her out, and that's fine, but while you're doing that, let's just talk about it. Maybe I can help."

Finished with the telephone pole, Trout pulled at his leash and they followed, on the move once more. "You can't help," Josie said. Her cheeks burned as she thought of the last time she'd spoken with Trinity. "I'm not waiting her out. She hasn't responded to any of my calls or texts. She's freezing me out."

"Then maybe you should just take her sunglasses to her. Show up at her cabin and make her talk to you again."

"I can't do that."

"So what, then? You're just going to keep wallowing, leaving her overpriced sunglasses on the foyer table so you can be reminded of your misery indefinitely, and not even try to patch things up with her?"

That was my plan, she wanted to say, but remained silent, edging ahead of him as they rounded the block.

"Josie."

She slowed and met his eyes. "You really want to know what happened?"

CHAPTER THREE

One Month Ago

Josie woke before Trout for once, turning to find the dog fast asleep on Noah's side of the bed. Any time Noah worked the night shift without Josie, Trout slept next to her. She knew Noah didn't want them to get into the habit of letting the dog sleep in their bed, but Josie enjoyed being able to reach over and stroke his soft, warm fur. Sunlight streamed through the bedroom windows. She scratched between Trout's ears. "Time to get up, buddy."

Downstairs in the kitchen, Josie's twin sister, Trinity Payne sat at the table, her laptop open before her. Without giving Trinity a second glance, Trout ran to the back door to be let out as Josie turned the coffeemaker on, taking a moment to study her sister.

Rarely had Josie seen her anything less than camera-ready. Usually, even when she was just out of bed, she had a sort of glamorous television glow about her. But now she wore sweatpants and mismatched socks. Her lithe frame was dwarfed by an NYU sweatshirt. Josie had often joked that Trinity's black hair was so shiny, a person could see their reflection in it. Now it was greasy and thrown up into a ponytail that looked like Trinity had started and forgotten to finish. No make-up on her face, she wore bright red earbuds and chewed her lower lip as her fingers pushed around the laptop mouse.

Josie poured two cups of coffee and fixed them—both she and Trinity took their coffee the same way—and walked around the table to stand beside her. She set Trinity's coffee next to the laptop and then tugged an earbud from her sister's ear.

"Ow," Trinity said, shooting Josie a look of annoyance. She moved to take the earbud back, but Josie whipped the other one from Trinity's head and then pulled them completely from the laptop.

Trinity's voice got high and squeaky. "What are you doing?"

Josie motioned to the laptop screen. "You're watching that again? Trinity, this has to stop."

On the screen, the clip played. Now that Josie had removed the earbuds, the sound filled the kitchen. It was the end of a segment that the network had run on a young woman in Arkansas who had made the news for getting twenty-two scholarships to the best schools in the country. As the piece wrapped up, the screen cut back to Trinity and her co-anchor, Hayden Keating. They sat side by side at a round table, smiles plastered across their faces. "What a remarkable young lady," Hayden commented. "With a very bright future ahead of her."

"The sky is the limit for her," Trinity agreed. "She obviously has her pick of any school in the country. It's kind of ridiculous that she applied to twenty-two schools, don't you think?"

The first time Josie had seen the clip she hadn't noticed the tension that froze Hayden's face, but now she'd seen it so many times that the slight stiffening of Hayden's jaw, his gritted teeth and forced smile were painfully obvious. "Ridiculous?" he scoffed. "I think it's wonderful."

Trinity smiled and waved a hand as if in dismissal. "Oh, it is wonderful. I'm just saying, a young woman that smart and talented could have just chosen her top pick and applied there, rather than spending all that money on application fees for twenty-one schools she's not going to attend. How much are application fees these days? They were very expensive when I went to college. I can only imagine how much they've increased."

A few painful seconds of dead air followed. Then Hayden cleared his throat and began to read from the teleprompter. "Up next, we'll check in with our meteorologist for an update on the weather."

Josie reached across Trinity and moved the cursor to pause the clip. "You need to let this go," she said.

"Let it go?" Trinity said. "That comment is going to cost me my career." She stood, her chair scraping across the tiles of the kitchen. Pacing, she went on. "I can't believe it. One stupid comment and my life is over."

"I'm sure it's not that bad," Josie said. "What you said—it wasn't even that terrible. I've heard news anchors say some pretty inappropriate things. Comments that were racist or mean-spirited. What you said wasn't even offensive."

Trinity stopped and stared at Josie. "Not offensive? Do you have any idea the backlash that the network got for what I said? I even apologized on air and issued a statement, and people are still enraged."

"It will blow over," Josie said. "It was two weeks ago."

"Two weeks is the longest I've been off the air since I became co-anchor, Josie. I'm out. Hayden told me. Barring a miracle, the network is going to replace me. They're already trying to woo Mila Kates. They've been after her for months. Now they have an excuse to get rid of me and offer her some ridiculous amount of money to take my place." She groaned and stared at the ceiling. "I can't believe I said that. I can never use the word ridiculous again."

Josie sat at the table and sipped her own coffee. "Mila Kates?" she said. "I thought she was on a cable network."

"She is," Trinity answered. "But she had that stalker, don't you remember? He showed up armed while she was doing a story at a charity benefit for sick kids and threatened to kill everyone if she didn't leave with him. She defused the situation and calmed him long enough for the police to come and take him down."

"Oh yeah," Josie said. "I remember seeing it on the news. That was months ago."

"But it changed everything," Trinity said. "It was a huge story, and it was *her* story. That stalker story was for her what the Denton vanishing girls case was to me five years ago. It put me on the map. I got my job because of that story."

"And your network sent you here to do a story on the five-year anniversary of when that case broke," Josie pointed out. "They didn't fire you."

Trinity arched a brow. She waved an arm around the kitchen. "Do you see any producers or camera people here? Yeah, they sent me to do the story. I did the piece and sent it in a week ago. My crew went back to New York City but here I am. They haven't called me back, and they're not going to."

Josie stopped herself from trying again to convince Trinity that the network would call her back. Her sister was most likely right, and Josie didn't think that baseless reassurance was going to help. Instead, she said, "Trinity, you can get a job at any network. In just the last five years, you've covered some of the biggest cases in the country. You even broke some of them yourself."

Trinity pointed a finger at Josie. "No, *you* broke them. Then I got the story. I don't have my own story."

Now it was Josie's turn to raise a brow. "I seem to remember both of us being the actual story not so long ago. I did that damn episode of *Dateline* for you. I didn't want to, but you insisted."

When Josie and Trinity first met, roughly six years ago, Trinity had been a national correspondent for the network. After a source fed her bad information, the network banished her to Denton's local news station, WYEP, where she worked as a roving reporter. After a year at WYEP, Trinity had been instrumental in helping Josie expose the depravities and the criminals behind the famous Denton missing girls case. That story had propelled Trinity to her current position.

Back then they hadn't even known they were related. They'd simply been police officer and reporter—often at odds with one another. In fact, Josie couldn't stand Trinity; she was ambitious to a fault and always underfoot, sniffing around for the scoop on a big story. Qualities Josie later came to appreciate. Two years after the missing girls' case, human remains were found behind the trailer park where Josie had grown up. The labyrinthian case surrounding those remains ultimately led the women to find out that they were long-lost sisters. At three weeks old, Josie had been snatched from her family and raised just a few hours away from her twin by an evil and abusive woman. The woman who kidnapped Josie set the Payne family home on fire leading both authorities and the Paynes to believe that Josie had perished in the fire. The reunification of the Payne family after thirty years, together with the fact that Josie and Trinity had not only known one another before finding out they were related, but worked together on high-profile cases, was television gold. With such a scintillating past, and Trinity's willingness to share it on air, she firmly cemented her place as co-anchor for as long as she chose to hold it.

Until now.

"Oh please," Trinity said. "The news cycle is like twenty seconds now. No one cares about our long-lost twin story anymore."

Josie bit back a remark about her using their traumatic history to advance her career. "Trinity, you're good at what you do. Maybe you won't stay with this network, but you'll find a home elsewhere. Things will work out. I'm sure of it."

"Yeah, they'll work out for Mila Kates. I'll be lucky to get my old job back at WYEP."

"Really, Trinity," Josie said. "You're overreacting."

"Am I?" When Josie didn't answer, Trinity splayed her fingers across her own chest. "I need something big. Bigger than the missing girls' case. Bigger than Mila Kates. Not some case you solved that I can piggyback on. I need to get the story myself, and it can't be just any old story."

"I thought there was some rule that journalists should never be the story, anyway," Josie said.

Trinity rolled her eyes. "Oh sure. That's what they teach you in school, but that's not necessarily true anymore. Look at Mila Kates. Look at that guy who worked for our biggest competitor. He wrote a book on how his own bosses tried to kill one of his stories for a year and now he's famous."

Josie did remember that reporter. "But he was covering something very explosive. It was about sexual harassment in the entertainment industry, wasn't it?"

"Yeah."

"So, if he was covering a small-town bake-off, he wouldn't be famous. He needed a good story."

"So do I!" Trinity exclaimed. "I need something that all of the networks would kill for, figuratively, of course. Something no one has ever done. I have to do something. Something really…"

"Desperate?"

Trinity glared. "Ambitious. Explosive."

Josie didn't like the sound of it, or the look in Trinity's eyes. It wasn't ambition. It was despair.

"I think your career is going to be fine," Josie told her. "Your body of work stands."

Trinity pointed at her. "You're wrong. You probably think I'm crazy, but I'm not, Josie. Everything I've worked for is in jeopardy."

"You made one off-hand comment, Trin. Celebrities have come back from worse."

A scratch sounded from the other side of the back door. Trinity reached over and let Trout in. He trotted past her and over to Josie, nudging at her hand for a pet. Josie stroked the soft hair behind his ears.

Trinity walked back around the table and sat by her laptop. Her fingers worked to bring the clip up once more. As it started to play, Josie reached across her and snapped the laptop closed. "Enough," she said. "Stop obsessing. Go for a run. Take a shower. Do something to clear your head."

Trout startled them both with his high-pitched barking. A second later, over the din, they heard the front door open and close. "It's just me," Noah called.

Trout raced into the foyer. Josie heard Noah greet him as the dog's nails clicked on the hardwood floor. Then Noah appeared in the kitchen, his tousled brown hair sticking up every which way and dark circles gathered beneath his hazel eyes. In his hand he held a small box wrapped in brown paper.

Glancing at the clock, Josie said, "What are you doing home early? Rough night?"

Trout danced around between the two of them, letting out small barks until Noah reached down with one hand and petted him again.

"Gretchen came in early. We had reports of a big off-campus party. Went up there, and the kids scattered. Spent all night rounding up the underage drinkers."

Satisfied, Trout went over to the corner of the kitchen where his food and water bowls lived and dragged his empty food bowl over to Josie. Keeping an eye on Noah, Josie said, "Always fun. How many of them are education majors?" She filled Trout's bowl and set it back down for him.

Noah smiled. "You mean how many of them begged us not to book them because it would ruin their future teaching careers? Fourteen."

Josie shook her head. "What's that?" she asked, pointing to the box in Noah's hands. It was no bigger than his palm.

He looked down at it and then back up at Josie and Trinity. "It was outside. It's addressed to Trinity."

Trinity held out a hand for the box, and Noah smiled. "Is this your way of telling us you're moving in? Getting mail here?"

Trinity pushed her coffee cup aside, setting the parcel down and beginning to unwrap it as she answered. "I'm not getting mail here."

Noah said, "That's the second box this week."

"Oh, well, I had my assistant ship me some things from my office. Where was I supposed to have them delivered?"

There was an edge to her voice. Noah put both his hands in the air. "Relax," he said. "I'm just messing with you. It's fine." Then he grinned and Josie knew his next words were meant to be taken as a joke. "By the way, I love what you've done with the guest room..."

But Trinity wasn't looking at him. She was looking inside the box. Her face paled. She set it aside and picked up her mug, downing the rest of her coffee.

"Where did you find this?"

"I told you. It was outside."

"There's no postage on it," Trinity said. "Where was it exactly?"

Josie glanced over Trinity's shoulder to see that there was indeed no postage, nor was there a return address. "What is it?" Josie asked. "What's inside?"

Trinity picked up the box and clutched it to her chest. "Nothing important. I'm just curious because it came with no postage. Where was it, Noah?"

Noah said, "It was in the mailbox at the end of the driveway. You know, where we normally get our mail?"

Trinity used her free hand to scoop up her laptop. She looked at Noah, eyes suddenly ablaze. "You have a problem with me staying here?"

Josie said, "Trin, he was joking."

"Was he?" Trinity snapped, turning on Josie. "Why was he snooping in my room?"

"I wasn't snooping," Noah said. "I just happened to walk past the other day when the door was open."

Trinity hugged both her laptop and the small box to her. Taking a step toward Noah, she challenged, "You don't want me here."

"That's not true," Noah protested.

A second passed in silence. Trinity stared at him, almost as though she was trying to decide something. She said, "I know when I'm not wanted."

"What are you talking about?" Noah said. "Don't be ridiculous."

Josie cringed at his accidentally terrible choice of word, knowing it would send her sister over the edge. Trinity's cheeks flushed. Her mouth pressed into a thin line. Trying to defuse the situation, Josie said, "Trinity, you know you're always welcome here. Please—"

But before she could finish, her sister stormed out of the room. Josie and Noah listened as her feet pounded up the stairs. When the guest room door slammed, Trout looked up from his breakfast, startled. He looked back and forth between them, eyes wary, ears pointed, until Josie said, "It's okay, boy."

Noah held up both hands. "I'm sorry. I really was joking."

"I know," Josie said. "She's just having a rough time."

Noah's brow furrowed. "Is she going to be okay? She's kind of all over the place."

"You don't say," Josie said with a sigh. She glanced at the microwave clock. She would have to start getting ready for work soon. "I'll go talk to her. Can you take Trout for a walk?"

Noah followed her into the foyer where he grabbed Trout's leash, the dog racing after him. Josie walked up the steps, her feet heavy. She had never seen Trinity like this. For a moment, she wondered if she should call their mother, Shannon. She had over three decades' experience dealing with Trinity – a significant amount more than Josie – and all the ups and downs that life brought. But Trinity hadn't gone home to their parents' house to lick her wounds. She'd come to Josie. She heard Trinity moving around inside the guest room as her hand gripped the doorknob.

"Trinity?"

She pushed the door, but it didn't open.

"Go away," Trinity yelled.

Josie pushed at the door again, realizing there was something on the other side that was preventing her from opening it. "Did you block the door?"

More noises came from the room. The shuffling of papers, the sounds of muted thuds. Was she throwing her clothes around? Finally, the door swung open and Trinity stood before her, face ashen. Her blue eyes were wide with anger and something else.

Before Josie could put her finger on it, Trinity said, "I'll be out of your way in a few minutes."

"Trinity, really," Josie said. "You're overreacting. You can stay here as long as you want. You know that. Noah was joking."

"What is it they say about jokes?" Trinity shot back. "There's always some truth behind them?"

Josie opened her mouth to speak again, but the state of the room behind Trinity stopped her cold. Her suitcase lay on the double bed, open, and piled full of clothes and shoes. A letter box sat on the dresser across from the bed, pages spilling out of it. Another letter box lay on its side on the floor, papers and other items—what looked like clothing, jewelry and office supplies bursting out of it. The television that Noah had mounted on the wall over the dresser was covered in colorful Post-it notes. Plastered across the cream-colored walls were papers and photographs. Josie tried to take it all in, but her mind couldn't process it all at once. She pointed to a series of photos taped to the wall behind Trinity. "Is that a skeleton?"

Trinity turned away from her and scrambled across the room, tearing the pages from the walls and stuffing them into the letterbox on the dresser. "Never mind," she told Josie.

Josie took a step into the room, nearly tripping over a Louis Vuitton stiletto. "This looks like a war room. What is all this?"

Trinity continued to rip the pages from the walls before Josie could get a read on what they were about. She thought she recognized pages from an autopsy report and some from what looked like a police report. She tried to read some of the words before Trinity snatched them away and stuffed them into the box. The words "psychological profile" flashed before her as Trinity took down the last of them, leaving small flags of torn paper in her path. Next, she went to the television and began to attack the Post-it notes. Josie only had a chance to read a few of the notes before those too were relegated to the overstuffed letter box.

Symmetry?

Mirror killings?

OCD?

"Trinity," Josie said. "What the hell is all this?"

Trinity slapped the lid onto the box and went to the other box, stuffing its contents back inside before righting it. "I told you. None of your business."

"Is this your big story? The story that's going to get you back in the good graces of the network?"

Trinity didn't answer as she scoured the floor for strewn shoes and clothes, tossing them into her suitcase.

Josie folded her arms across her chest and regarded her sister seriously. "Trinity. This looks like a murder case. Is that what it is? You're trying to solve a cold case? Why don't you get some sleep? You need it. You've been up all night. When I've finished my shift, you can bring your box downstairs and we'll go through it together."

Ignoring her, Trinity stuffed her feet into the Louis Vuitton stilettos and dragged her suitcase off the bed. It hit the floor with a loud thud. Josie stood resolute in the doorway, giving Trinity a once-over. "You're going out like that? Sweatpants and stilettos? You are still a celebrity, you know. Are you driving back to New York like that?"

"Not New York. There's nothing there for me now. It doesn't matter what I look like or how I dress now. Nothing matters anymore."

"Where will you go? Home to Mom and Dad?"

"Are you crazy? No. I'll rent a place. Somewhere out of the way. A cabin in the woods or something. I need to be alone."

"I don't think this is the best time for you to be alone," Josie said. "Please, just stay here, get some sleep, and we'll figure this out together."

"That's easy for you to say, isn't it? Everything always works out for you. The great Josie Quinn. I'll just let her swoop in and fix all my problems."

Josie felt as though she had been slapped. "What are you talking about?"

Trinity pointed a long, manicured nail at her. "You always land on your feet, don't you? Your whole department was turned upside down and somehow you ended up as chief. Then you lost that position and yet you still ended up with a job. You always solve your cases. You always get your man. It must be nice to be so perfect."

Josie said, "You think I'm perfect?"

"You're famous and loved by everyone. You've got a great career—no matter what happens or what you do—a beautiful home and a fantastic boyfriend. You've got everything. This house is always full of people. Friends, colleagues, family. People who shouldn't even like you—like Misty, your late husband's girlfriend—yet, they're here for you. No one is here for me. Not one person."

With each word, Josie felt as if Trinity had snapped a small but critical bone inside of her. Still, she managed to eke out the words, "I'm here for you."

"Oh sure, you're here for me now. What about my whole entire life? Where were you? I needed you. Things could have been different if you'd been there, but you weren't."

A flare of anger ignited in Josie's stomach. "You know that wasn't my fault."

"But it doesn't change anything, does it?" Trinity cried. "You were never there. I was alone. Now you've got the perfect life, and I've got nothing. The one thing I cared about—the only thing I ever cared about—has just been taken away from me. You don't even get it. My own sister. My twin. But how could you understand?"

Josie pointed back at her sister, mirroring her. "You weren't alone, Trinity. You had our whole family. You know what I had? A closet. I was in hell. Actual hell. You grew up in a beautiful home with two loving parents and a sweet little brother. You never wanted for anything. You always had money. You always had food in your stomach, a roof over your head." She pulled back the hair on the right side of her face and pointed to the long, faded scar that ran from her ear to just under the middle of her chin. "No one ever held you down and tried to cut your face off, did they? You don't want to play who had the worse childhood with me, because I will win."

Dropping her gaze to the floor, Trinity walked over and pushed Josie out of the way, staggering into the hallway as she pulled the heavy suitcase along behind her.

At the top of the steps, she turned back to Josie. "Did you ever think that maybe we should have just left things alone? Sure, we have DNA in common, but that doesn't make us family. We weren't meant to be sisters, not really."

"Trinity—"

"It's true. You didn't even like me before we found out about our DNA. You hated me."

"There was a time that I disliked you, yes," Josie admitted. "But that was before I really got to know you—"

"But you don't know me, not really," Trinity said. "How long have we been 'sisters' now? Three years? What do you really know about me?"

"I—I—" Josie stammered.

"What's the worst thing that ever happened to me? Besides losing my anchor position, obviously."

Josie racked her brain. Trinity was right. The things she knew about her were superficial. They'd never had the chance for the kinds of conversations where they'd spilled their guts and divulged every detail of their lives. Then again, Josie never had those conversations with anyone.

"The worst thing that ever happened to you was when you got demoted from the network morning show back to WYEP after that source fed you bad information."

Trinity put a hand on her hip. "Wrong. What's the *best* thing that ever happened to me?"

Josie said meekly, "Getting your anchor position?"

Tears gleamed in Trinity's eyes. When she spoke, her voice cracked. "Wrong."

With a sinking heart, Josie trailed behind her sister as she lugged the suitcase outside to her red Fiat convertible and jammed it into the passenger seat. Trinity went back into the house twice to get her letter boxes and her purse. She positioned the boxes precariously between the suitcase and the dash with her brown Gucci purse tossed into the box on top. Josie pleaded with her to stay, to talk about things, but Trinity ignored her.

As she turned the ignition and the Fiat roared to life, she rolled the window down and looked at Josie one last time. "We're not sisters, Josie. Not really. I think it's time we stopped forcing something that was never meant to happen."

CHAPTER FOUR

"Wow," Noah said as they let themselves back into the house. "I didn't know it was that brutal. I'm sorry."

In the foyer, Josie extricated Trout from his leash and harness. He trotted off to the kitchen for a drink of water. Noah pulled her in for a hug. "You haven't talked to her since?" he asked into the top of her head.

Josie let her cheek rest against his chest and mumbled, "No. I called and texted a bunch of times, but she never responded."

He released her and they trudged upstairs to shower and dress. In the bedroom, as he stripped off his T-shirt, Noah said, "Did you talk to Shannon?"

"Of course. Several times. She tried to smooth things over, but Trinity wasn't having that. She said she didn't want to talk to me or see me. Or anyone, actually. I found out from Shannon that she had rented a cabin."

"She stayed around here, though," Noah pointed out. "That's got to mean something."

"I don't think so, Noah. I've never seen her like that, and the worst part is…"

She couldn't bring herself to say it, even to him.

"What?"

She sat on the edge of the bed and closed her eyes so she wouldn't have to see him watching her. "She's right. I don't know anything about her. Not really. I never asked."

"What is there to know?" Noah said.

Her eyes snapped open. "Noah, really."

He held out his arms. "I'm serious. So you find out you're sisters. Were you supposed to sit down and catalog every single thing about one another that you missed? You two spend a lot of time together given both your busy schedules. You've fully immersed yourself in the family. What else did she expect of you? Did she ask you about every little detail of your life?"

"She didn't have to. Much of it became public knowledge, unfortunately."

He sat beside her, slinging an arm across her shoulders and pulling her in tight to him. "I think she's been overdramatic about all of this. Obviously, she was upset about losing her anchor position. You know how she is about her career."

But I don't know why, Josie thought. What made Trinity that way?

Noah went on, "For someone like Trinity, losing this co-host position is like a death in the family. She's unmoored now. She doesn't know what to do with herself. She lashed out at you because you're closest to her. She's had a month at her cabin retreat to figure out who she is without this job. Maybe it's time you just went up there and talked to her."

"If she wanted to talk to me, she'd respond to one of my texts or calls."

"Maybe she's embarrassed by the way she acted. Maybe she needs you to make contact first."

"I don't think so," Josie said.

"There's only one way to find out," Noah said. "She's already not talking to you. What do you have to lose? Take the sunglasses. Go out to the cabin. Tell her you want to be her sister."

"I don't even know where the cabin is."

"Don't make excuses. Shannon's got the address, doesn't she?"

Josie said nothing.

"Grab a shower. I'll make breakfast, and then you go see her."

"What if she slams the door in my face? Or worse, she doesn't even come to the door?"

Noah stood and smiled down at her. "Then you'll try again tomorrow."

The Whispering Oaks Cabins had been around as long as Josie could remember. They were usually used by hunters or fishermen at this time of year—late March—and occasionally, in the summer, families rented them. High up in the mountains, the area seemed remote but was really only a half hour from the city. A stream ran through the various properties as well as several hiking trails. A rutted gravel road snaked up the mountain, leading to the driveways of each cabin. There were ten in all. Trinity, Shannon had said, was staying in number six.

Josie bounced along in her Ford Escape until she found the driveway marked with a faded waist-level wooden sign with the number six on it. She turned, following another narrow gravel path until Trinity's red Fiat Spider came into view, its front end pointed in the direction Josie had come. The cabin was small with faux log-siding the color of smoke and a bright red aluminum roof. It had a narrow porch just big enough for two wooden rocking chairs. Its door was bright red with a wicker wreath hanging on it, complete with fake, brightly colored spring flowers. It was quaint and inviting, and the exact opposite of Trinity's style. How had she managed to stay in a place like this for a whole month? Josie wondered. A voice in the back of Josie's head reminded her of Trinity's accusation that she'd never really known her at all.

With a sigh, Josie parked beside the Fiat, grabbed Trinity's sunglasses, and got out. As she walked past the Fiat, something in the passenger's seat caught her eye. Trinity's suitcase was visible through the passenger's side window. On top of it was her purse. A Gucci purse to go with her Gucci sunglasses. Noah would have a stroke if he knew how much Trinity had paid for the purse. Josie had been with her in New York City when she bought it and had felt nauseated watching Trinity hand the cashier her credit card.

Trinity was leaving. Josie wondered if she'd gotten her anchor position back. She had been watching the morning show all month, hoping to hear that the network was planning Trinity's return, but all she'd seen was a string of temporary co-hosts who fell short of filling Trinity's shoes. There was no mention of Trinity other than that she was "out on assignment". Nor was there any mention of the now-famous Mila Kates taking over her anchor seat. It was a strange coincidence that Trinity was leaving the very day that Josie worked up the nerve to come see her.

Josie's feet felt heavy as she climbed the porch and knocked on the door. "Trin?" she called.

No answer. She looked into the window beside the front door, but the white curtains blocked her from seeing inside. "Trinity?" she called again. She knocked again, louder this time. Nothing.

Pressing her ear against the door below the wreath, she listened for any sounds from inside but heard nothing. She tried the door-knob. Surprisingly, it turned easily in her hand. She put Trinity's sunglasses in her pocket and pushed the door open, calling for her sister again. A musty smell hit her as soon as she crossed the threshold. It was nearly ten a.m. and the sun was bright overhead. No lights were on inside. Josie called for Trinity again but got no answer. Her heart did a double-tap. Her hand checked for her service weapon, but it wasn't there as it was her day off. There was no reason to think she needed it to visit Trinity. The cabin, quaintly decorated in dark red and brown, was clean and orderly except for the dust covering every surface. Josie quickly checked the one bedroom and the tiny bathroom. Both were empty, neat, and covered in dust. Turning back to the main living area, Josie couldn't stop the creeping sense of dread dragging its icy fingers up her spine. On the kitchen table was a note written on what looked like a page torn from Trinity's planner:

Mr. P, Thanks for the rental. The place is lovely. I know I only stayed for a week, but you can keep the deposit. I don't expect a refund. I hope you find everything in good repair. If there are any issues, please call me. Trinity.

Below that was her cell phone number. Next to the note was a single key on a keychain in the shape of a bear with the words *Whispering Oaks 6* printed in white across it. Josie's eyes scanned the note again, landing on the words: *I know I only stayed for a week.*

"A week?" she muttered.

That would mean Trinity had left three weeks ago. But she hadn't. Her car was sitting outside the cabin with her suitcase and purse inside.

Josie raced back out to the driveway, rounding the driver's side of the Fiat. Without touching the car, she leaned over and peered inside. Keys dangled from the ignition. In the center console, beneath the dash, at the level of the gear shift, was a small opening where Trinity usually kept her phone. Josie's heart stuttered when she saw the phone there.

She reached out to fling the door open but stopped herself a fraction of a second before she touched the car. The police officer in her wouldn't let her contaminate any fingerprint evidence that might be left on the outside of the car. Her hand trembled as she snatched it back.

She turned around, eyes panning the grass and the trees beyond it, then the driveway. She walked out past her own vehicle to the perimeter of the property, searching for footprints or any sign of Trinity. Had she walked off into the woods? Had someone come onto the property and taken her? If so, had they simply dragged her into the forest, or had they driven off with her? The gravel driveway would make it near impossible to get casts of tire tracks. And, she realized, even if there were tire tracks, Josie had just driven over them.

She rounded the back of the cabin. The first thing she saw was a clearing with two Adirondack chairs bracketing a fire ring made from an old tire rim. Against the back of the cabin was a rack filled with firewood. No way had Trinity been making a campfire out here. She wasn't the woodsy type. Josie's eyes were drawn to the fire ring. Old ash and pieces of burnt logs lay tamped down inside of it. It looked as if it hadn't been used in a long time. Josie looked up from the fire ring toward the trees at the back of the property. On the ground, about a foot from the treeline, something white caught her eye. She took two steps forward and froze. Her mind couldn't quite process what she was seeing. The grass was a few inches tall. It hadn't been cut in some time although they were just entering spring after a cold winter so the grass wouldn't be growing very fast during this time of year. The landlord had probably had it cut just before Trinity moved in, a month earlier.

She forced her feet to move another step. Her throat constricted, and she worked hard to push the air in and out of her lungs. Arrayed on the grass before her were bones. Human bones. Not left there or dumped, but arranged.

Displayed.

A rib cage and spine made up the centerpiece of whatever it was that Josie was staring at—some kind of symbol? Remnants of some kind of satanic ritual? Surrounding the rib cage and spine were smaller bones. Some clinical part of her mind recognized those as the tiny bones of the hands, fingers, feet, and toes. Intermingled with those were the clavicles. At the bottom of the circle, pointing from the outer edge toward Josie's feet were longer bones. *Arm bones*, the cool investigator in the back of her mind whispered, because they were too small to be leg bones. Beneath those bones were the skull and pelvic bone. The empty eye sockets of the skull stared back at Josie, making her chest feel tight. She tore her eyes away from it and looked toward the upper right-hand side of the circle, where the leg bones lay, angled away from Josie.

A violent trembling took over her body. Her feet turned and tried to carry her away, but her shins knocked against one of the

Adirondack chairs and she went flying over it, tumbling toward the back of the cabin. Her head smacked against the rack of firewood and some of the logs toppled into her lap. She closed her eyes and tried to slow her breathing. There was a calm, firm voice in the back of her mind—the one that gave her orders when her body shut down from fear or panic. The police officer inside her. *Take out your phone*, it told her. *Call for back-up.*

It went on like a mantra until she opened her eyes, pushed the logs off her body, and fished her phone out of her pocket. *Breathe*, the voice said as she punched in her passcode. *Just breathe.*

Noah answered on the third ring. "Hey," he said. "I'm glad you called. I can't find Trout's heartworm—"

"Something's wrong," Josie said, cutting him off. "I need you here. I need the team."

Noah's tone turned serious. "Josie, are you in trouble? What's going on?"

"B-b-bones," she stammered.

"What? Josie, what's happening? Where's Trinity? Is she there?"

Her voice was a whisper. "I think she's dead."

CHAPTER FIVE

Noah started with simple questions that Josie could answer easily with just one or two words. Was she inside the cabin? No. Was she at the front or the back? Back. Was anyone there with her? No. His voice was an anchor, steadying her, keeping her from being swept away on a choppy tide of panic. Bit by bit, he pulled the information from her. In the background, she was vaguely aware of the jingle of his keys, the slam of a door, his car roaring to life. He was on his way.

"You're saying she left a note for the landlord three weeks ago. Her car is packed with the keys in the ignition and her phone in the console but she's not there," he recapped.

"Th-there are bones. Remains. I think it's—I think it's her. Oh God, Noah."

His voice didn't waver, "Josie, right now I need you to get in your car and go back down to the main road. We'll meet you there."

Josie shook her head even though he couldn't see her. "I can't." Her legs felt paralyzed. She didn't want to stand up because then she would see those empty eye sockets again. She already knew she wouldn't be able to look away.

"Get in your car," Noah repeated. "Meet us at the main road."

She said nothing.

"Please, Josie, listen to me," he went on. "You're in the middle of a crime scene. You know that it needs to be preserved. That means you need to leave until we can get the Evidence Response Team out there."

Crime scene. Evidence Response Team. These were words she recognized. Concepts that made sense even in her shock-addled brain. "Okay," she said, hefting herself off the ground and averting her eyes from the display on the other side of the fire ring.

"Are you going back to the car?" Noah asked.

"Yes," she mumbled. She was unsteady on her feet but slowly, she made her way back to the front of the cabin to her car. "I'm at the car," she told him once she reached it.

"Good," he said. "Get in. Drive to the end of the driveway. We'll be there as soon as we can."

He hung up. Josie sat in the driver's seat, the phone still pressed to her ear. Her breath came fast as her eyes tracked from the cabin to Trinity's vehicle. Even as her body became overwhelmed by emotion—fear, panic, shock; making her skin crawl, her scalp tingle, and her heart thunder in her chest——the police officer in her was going over the details she had managed to take in while she was at the back of the cabin. An image of the garish display flashed through her mind.

Her investigator's brain worked to remember everything she knew about human decomposition. If Trinity had been taken on the day she'd intended to leave, and killed that same day, that meant that three weeks had passed. That wasn't enough time for her body to decompose to the point of being skeletal, Josie told herself. Right? She tried to remember everything she'd learned from her time on the job about how long it took for a body to skeletonize, but the knowledge wouldn't come into focus. She would need the county medical examiner, Dr. Anya Feist. She thought about calling Noah back, but that was stupid. Her team would know to alert Dr. Feist.

Shaking the morbid thoughts out of her head, Josie pocketed her phone and started her car. Her mind raced so fast, it was dizzying. There was a war within her—sister versus police officer. Emotional versus clinical. Never had she felt so torn in those two different directions.

She barely remembered driving back out to the main road but there she was, seated in her vehicle, white-knuckling the steering wheel when Noah and Detective Finn Mettner pulled up in Mettner's car, with two patrol units in tow. Their lights flashed blue and red through the canopy of trees that shielded the gravel road from the sun. Detective Mettner had been with the Denton PD for several years before being promoted from patrol to Detective two years earlier. Since taking on the new role, he had seen his share of difficult cases—including taking the lead on Noah's mother's murder. Dedicated and thorough, he was a valuable asset to Denton's investigative team.

Josie watched him and Noah emerge from the vehicle and jog over toward her car. Noah opened her door, extending a hand to her. She took it and let him guide her out of the car. Mettner said, "Hummel and the Evidence Response Team should be here in five minutes. We'll wait for them to secure the scene before we go up. Dr. Feist is on her way as well. Once we start moving, stay off the driveway. If there are any tire tracks, I want to get them."

"I already drove up there," Josie croaked. "I probably destroyed whatever was there."

"There might still be something," Mettner assured her. "If there is, Hummel will find it."

CHAPTER SIX

Alex's favorite time of day was when his mother, Hanna, went into her studio to work. Not only did she let him come inside, but she often sought him out and asked him to help her. He set up her canvases and paints, retrieved brushes and glue, and any other items she needed while she worked. After his adventures in the woods with his father, Alex was very good at sitting still for a long time. While Hanna worked, he sat on a stool behind her, watching and listening to her as she hummed. It was always a variation of the same song. He'd never heard words to the song, but he'd heard her hum it so many times, he could carry the tune in his sleep.

She was putting the finishing touches on a new painting when she said, "Alex, dear, where is your sister? I think she'd like this one."

He felt his throat tighten. Was she serious? "You-you mean... ?" His voice was barely a squeak. He couldn't even get it out. He hadn't spoken her name in almost a year. No one ever said it anymore. Sometimes he wondered if he had imagined her. He tried again, only getting out the first syllable.

Hanna's eyes narrowed, and the name froze in his throat. She gave him a meaningful look and her tone grew cold. "I don't know who you're talking about."

"Oh," he breathed.

She kept her eyes locked on him. "Where is Zandra?"

He shifted on the stool. "Dad says she has to stay away because she's sick."

Hanna frowned. "Still? She's been locked away for days. Why don't you check on her?"

"I can't," he said. "You know the rules."

Paintbrush in hand, she turned and looked at him. "Right," she said. She took a moment to touch a long cut on her painting arm, her fingers tracing over the dark scab. "Well, your father makes the rules. Although, Alex, it would be nice to be able to have both of my children in the studio again."

"I'm sorry," he said, although he wasn't sorry for what had happened to her, only sorry that he hadn't been strong enough to stop Zandra.

He cast his gaze downward, but he could feel her eyes on him. He heard her drop the paintbrush into a cup. Then she knelt in front of him, staring up at him. She seemed smaller now that he was almost eleven years old. "My son," she said. "Look at me. You have to help your sister, do you understand?"

He nodded.

She looked behind him, toward the door, and then back into his eyes. "I worry, Alex, that your father will get… carried away with his punishment if these incidents with Zandra continue."

"I understand."

"Do you?"

But he didn't have a chance to answer. The sound of the front door slamming shut made them both jump. Hanna squeezed his hand and whispered, "Quickly, get downstairs to your studies."

Before he could hop off the stool and scurry into the hall, Francis's heavy steps sounded on the stairs. A moment later, he filled the doorway. "Hanna, what's he doing in here? Aren't you working?"

She smiled. "Yes, I've been working all morning. What do you think?" She turned and presented her latest painting with a flourish.

He raised a brow. "It's very good," he said. "But it's missing something." Zeroing in on Alex, he said, "Get downstairs. Let your mother concentrate."

Alex moved toward the door but Hanna said, "Alex was helping me. He's fine. Let him stay. He's not a bother. Maybe he can help me find what's missing."

"He's a stupid boy, Hanna," Francis snapped. "You're an accomplished artist. Don't be ridiculous."

Alex slipped past his father into the hallway before either of them could argue over him anymore. As he flew down the steps, he heard his father say, "You go back to work. I'll check on Zandra."

CHAPTER SEVEN

Josie, Mettner, and Noah stood beside their vehicles and waited for the Denton PD Evidence Response Team to arrive. In spite of the stillness and natural beauty all around them, Josie couldn't stop her thoughts from spinning out. Luckily, Mettner took out his phone, pulled up his note-taking app, and started firing off questions. Josie gave him a rundown of everything that had happened in the last six weeks, except that she didn't elaborate on anything she and Trinity had said to each other before Trinity stormed out of Josie and Noah's house, only saying they'd had an argument.

"You haven't heard from her in a month?" Mettner asked, face bent to the screen as he tapped notes into his phone. "What about friends or family members?"

"Our mother," Josie said. "Shannon Payne. She was still in contact with her after Trinity cut me off. We should also talk to my dad and brother. Oh, and Trinity's assistant. I know they were in touch when Trinity was staying with us."

Josie rattled off the phone numbers she knew by heart and looked the others up in her phone. She added, "But could you wait to talk to Shannon? Let me tell her first?"

"Of course," Mettner said. "Let's try to get a handle on what we're dealing with here first."

"Mett," Josie said, reaching out and touching his forearm. His eyes jerked up toward her. He shot Noah a quick glance before returning his gaze to her. Josie swallowed over a lump in her throat. "What I saw up there—"

"Remains," he said. "Noah told me. We'll handle it."

"No," she said, tugging on his arm. "Not just remains. This is something we haven't seen before."

Mettner opened his mouth to speak, but the sound of wheels on gravel swallowed his response. Two Denton police SUVs pulled in behind the line of vehicles already present. Officers Hummel and Chan got out of the first SUV. Two more members of the ERT got out of the other one. Hummel popped the hatch on the back of his vehicle and the four of them immediately started donning their Tyvek suits and removing equipment needed to process the scene. Mettner jogged over to brief them. Hummel handed him a Tyvek suit and he pulled it on. Josie stayed at her vehicle and watched as they began their ascent up the driveway with Mettner and one of the other uniformed officers in tow, walking on the edges of the gravel, looking for tire tracks, careful not to disturb anything that might be evidence.

Josie felt Noah's hand on her shoulder and looked up to see his hazel eyes swimming with concern. "It might not be her," he said.

"I know," she said, hoping he was right.

Noah glanced at the driveway. "You want me here with you or up at the scene?"

"I don't want you to see that," Josie said. She pressed her eyes closed, willing the memory of the bones to flush from her brain, but it wouldn't. It would always be there. It would haunt her nightmares for years, she knew.

Noah said, "I'm going to see it no matter what, Josie. You know that."

"Then go," Josie told him, opening her eyes. "I'll wait here for Dr. Feist and call Shannon."

He gave her shoulder a squeeze and went over to Hummel's vehicle to suit up. A few moments later he was gone. A couple of uniformed officers stood along the road like sentries, prepared to keep any passers-by or other curious tenants away should they drive up the road. One stood at the edge of the driveway with a clipboard in hand. He would log people in and out of the crime scene as they passed.

Josie took out her phone again to call Shannon. At this time of day, she'd be at work. She was a chemist with a large pharmaceutical company called Quarmark. Josie imagined her standing in a lab at that moment, swathed in a white coat, overseeing some experiment with safety goggles covering her eyes. Or maybe she was in her office, reviewing lab results. Josie was about to blast a crater of destruction right into her normal day. She didn't want to face Shannon. Not yet. She could barely process what was happening. Had someone really taken Trinity? Had Trinity let them? Were those her bones behind the cabin? How was that possible? Before her reluctance got the better of her, she found Shannon's name in her contacts, and pressed the green call icon beneath her mother's name.

Shannon answered after two rings, her voice sounding light and happy. It was a punch to Josie's gut. "Hi honey, what's going on?"

Josie knew from experience that ripping the Band-Aid off swiftly was the best way to deliver bad news. "Shannon, something's happened to Trinity."

Silence. Josie heard Shannon's breathing grow labored. "Please don't tell me—please, don't—is she… is she…"

"We don't know," Josie filled in quickly. She couldn't tell Shannon about the bones. Not yet. They didn't know for sure that they belonged to Trinity, and Josie wasn't about to tell her family anything she didn't know with complete certainty. "I came to the cabin to try to talk to her. Her car is here. All of her things are packed up and inside it. But she isn't here."

It took several seconds for Shannon's breathing to slow to the point where she could speak again. "Then she walked off. She's in the woods or down by the stream. Maybe she went to talk to someone in one of the other cabins. I'll call her—"

Josie cut her off. "Her phone is inside the car. She left the landlord a note three weeks ago saying she was leaving. Shannon, when was the last time you were in contact with her?"

Another beat of silence. Then Shannon said, "I'm not sure. I'd have to look at my texts, maybe my call log. It's been a few weeks. Things have been crazy at work with my team trying to perfect this new cancer drug. The last time I spoke with her, she had just moved into the cabin. She told me everything was fine. She just needed time to unplug, she said. She was going to stay there."

A few weeks.

Josie closed her eyes, willing the police officer in her to take over. Who else had regular contact with Trinity? Definitely their father, Christian and younger brother, Patrick. She opened her eyes, and when she spoke, her voice sounded strangely calm and confident. "Shannon, this is really important. I need you to contact Christian and Patrick, and find out when they last had contact with her. Can you do that for me?"

"Of course. Josie, what are you not telling me?"

"We don't have all the information yet. My team is at her cabin now—" she stopped speaking before the word processing came out, instead using the words, "looking around. We're doing everything we can to find out what happened to her."

"Do you—do you think someone took her?"

"We simply don't know at this point."

The phone was silent except for Shannon's ragged breathing. Josie used two fingers to squeeze the bridge of her nose, willing the tears gathering behind her eyes not to fall. She tried out the word she'd only used once or twice before with Shannon. "Mom."

A muffled cry came over the line, as though Shannon had clamped a hand over her mouth to try to stop it.

Josie went on, "I will do everything I can to find out what happened to her."

"What happened to her? What are you saying, Josie? Because if she's dead—oh my God. You know I can't do this. I can't do this again. I can't lose another child. I know we found you, but I lived with that loss for thirty years. I know Trinity is a grown woman, but I can't go through this again. I just can't, I—"

"I know," Josie said, talking over her mother, hoping to stave off Shannon's rising hysteria. "Shannon, I am being honest with you. I don't know where she is or what happened to her. My team is working on it. Right now, I need you to talk to Dad and Patrick and then I need all of you to meet me at the Denton Police headquarters. There are questions about Trinity I can't answer. I'll need your help."

"Of course."

CHAPTER EIGHT

Josie heard more tires over gravel as she hung up on Shannon. The medical examiner, Dr. Anya Feist's white pickup truck bounced along the rutted road. She parked behind the ERT vehicles and hopped out, waving to the uniformed officers and striding in Josie's direction. The sight of the doctor, who had worked so many cases with Josie and her team, had a calming effect on her. Dr. Feist tucked a strand of silver-blonde hair behind one ear as she approached.

"You don't look so good," she told Josie.

"You don't need to check my pulse," Josie told her. "I can already tell you it's racing."

Dr. Feist put her hands into her jeans pockets. "Mettner called me. He told me…" she trailed off.

Josie said, "I need you to look at the remains. I need to know… if it's her."

"We'll need dental records. That's the fastest way to do this. You know that DNA testing can take weeks. Months, even."

"I know. Her dentist would be in New York City. I can get in touch with her assistant and find out who she saw there."

Dr. Feist nodded. Silence descended between them. All around them, Josie heard the sounds of insects, birds, and a light breeze filtering through the trees. Finally, she said, "Doc, how long does it take for a human body to decompose to the point that it's skeletonized? It's years, isn't it?"

Dr. Feist stared at her, eyes narrowing. "There's no easy answer to that, Josie. You know that. Soil, vegetation, sunlight, temperature—all of those things factor in. It could be months or years."

"But not days or weeks?"

"Not typically days, no, although I'm sure there are exceptions. It's possible for it to happen in weeks. There are circumstances in which a body could be skeletonized in a short amount of time, especially in cases where insects or animals are able to disturb the body. A lot of conditions would have to be just right in order for a body to decompose to that point that quickly, but again, you know this already."

Josie tried and failed to smile. "I needed to hear it from you."

Dr. Feist nodded. "I'll suit up and go have a look. Do you want to come have a look with me?"

Josie suppressed a shudder recalling the remains. She didn't want to see them again, but she owed it to her sister to find out what was going on. "Yes," she answered.

"Will they let you on the scene?"

Josie said, "I don't know."

Dr. Feist smiled at her. "What is it you say? Sometimes it's better to ask for forgiveness than permission. Let's go."

Once they were properly suited up, they had the uniformed officer log them into the scene. Then Josie followed the doctor up the driveway, both of them staying to the side. They passed two ERT members taking casts of some of the tire tracks where the gravel had worn down to mud. Trinity's car came into view, the late morning sun beating down on its shiny red frame. A uniformed officer stood at the side of the cabin. He gave Josie a mock salute as she and Dr. Feist approached. "They're around the back, boss."

In the back, Noah and Mettner stood staring down at the bones in the grass while Hummel finished taking photos. When Noah looked up at Josie, she saw the pallor that had come over his features. She hung back while Dr. Feist picked her way over. Mettner's cell phone rang. He answered it, pressed it to his ear, and stepped away from the scene as Dr. Feist knelt beside the bones. Noah walked over to Josie. "This can't be her," he said. "No way would her body have decomposed this quickly."

"We don't know that," Josie choked out. "Dr. Feist said there are some conditions in which it can happen."

"It's definitely a female," Dr. Feist called out. "The skull has a smooth, vertical frontal bone and a more rounded chin than we'd expect to see in a male. The mastoid process—this small, conical bone behind the jaw where the neck muscles attach—it's very small. Much smaller than that of a male."

Noah and Josie moved closer.

Dr. Feist pointed to the pelvis. "See how the opening of the pelvic girdle is broad and round? That's typical of a female. The pubic arch, here at the bottom where the two sides come together, is wide, greater than ninety degrees, all of which is to allow for childbirth, as both of you know."

Noah's hand wrapped around Josie's upper arm just as her knees buckled. She leaned against him to stay upright but continued to stare at Dr. Feist, who went on, "Whoever this is, she didn't die here. The grass underneath is pristine. If this body had decomposed here, the ground would not look like this. When a body decomposes, the fatty acids leak into the ground and leave a greasy residue. This body decomposed somewhere else and then someone brought these bones here."

"Can you tell how long they've been here?" Noah asked.

"Normally, I'd say a few hours," Dr. Feist said. "Only because out here, in the woods, this little arrangement here wouldn't last longer than that."

"What do you mean?" Noah asked.

"Animals would have found these bones and carried some of them off or at least disturbed them," Josie put in.

"Exactly," Dr. Feist said. "Bodies left out in the elements, exposed, are usually subject to scavenging. Out here, there are all kinds of animals that would be interested in a decomposing body. There's not much left of this one that would be of interest to scavenging animals but that wouldn't stop them from investigating." She leaned over, one of her gloved fingers hovering over the rib cage. "Actually, it does look like something got to these bones." She beckoned them closer. Noah kept a careful hold on Josie's arm, and they took a few more steps together. Dr. Feist pointed to the two lower left ribs where it looked as though pieces of fibrous material clung to the bones. "See this? This is soft tissue that wasn't entirely removed from the bones. See how the bone looks frayed? That's usually from scavengers picking the soft tissue off the bones."

Josie thought she might be sick.

Dr. Feist kept talking. "This body was definitely exposed to scavengers during decomposition, but that didn't happen here."

Noah said, "You said 'normally' you'd say a few hours. You think these remains have been here longer than a few hours?"

Dr. Feist nodded. She shifted her weight and pointed to the arm bones. "Yes, but only because they've been pinned down."

"What?" Josie said.

Dr. Feist reached down and tugged something from the ground. It was metal, about ten inches long, pointed at the end that went into the ground with a clear plastic piece on the top of it. "Steel tent stakes," Dr. Feist explained. She held the stake in one hand and with the fingers of her other hand, she pinched a clear string that attached to another stake on the other side of the bones. "Fishing line. Someone tied one end to each stake and then used it to keep the bones tied down to the ground."

"Fishing line?" Noah said.

Josie's throat was dry. "So it doesn't interfere with the way the display looks. It doesn't distract from… this."

Dr. Feist said, "Someone spent some time over this."

"Even with the stakes, a determined animal would be able to make off with some of these bones, don't you think?" Noah said.

Dr. Feist laid the stake back onto the ground. "Sure, but like I said, there's not much left on these bones to entice them."

"How long?" Josie asked. "How long have they been out here?"

Dr. Feist stood. "You know I can't say with certainty, but knowing what I know about bones and animals and this area, I'd say no more than a day or two."

"Can you tell how long the victim has been dead?" Noah asked.

"That's a little more complicated. Since the body didn't decompose here, we don't know what kind of temperature or condition it was left in during the decomp process. To estimate the time of death, we generally rely on being able to determine the temperature of the environment in which the body decomposed, ideally going back as far as two months, as well as whether conditions were moist or dry. We rely on the presence of insects and bacteria in the soil. We also know that scavengers and extreme heat can accelerate decomposition considerably. Oftentimes, we can tell a lot by any personal items found along with it. Without any of those contextual clues, I can't really say how long this victim has been dead. I might need to consult an expert in forensic taphonomy to give you any idea at all."

"Forensic taphonomy?" Noah repeated.

"It's the study of how remains decompose and fossilize," Dr. Feist said.

Hummel, who had been standing nearby listening, said, "We'll take those stakes in for analysis. Maybe we can get a print or a partial print. We'll definitely check for manufacturer and which stores sell them."

"Thanks, Hummel," Josie said.

He nodded. "I'll get Chan out here to get these remains transferred to the morgue. You want to have a look inside?"

CHAPTER NINE

Josie was about to say that she'd been inside, but Noah was already steering her away from the bones, around the cabin and through the front door. She did feel as though she could breathe better away from the crime scene. They were looking around when Mettner walked in.

"I talked with the landlord. He hasn't heard from Trinity since they signed the rental agreement. Her lease was up this week. He hasn't been up here and hasn't had any complaints. Four of the other properties are rented right now. I called in some extra units to go around and canvass those cabins, see if anyone heard or saw anything unusual."

"Good call," Noah said.

"Our family is on their way to the police station," Josie said. "They'll meet us there, but our mother, Shannon, already told me she hasn't heard from Trinity in a few weeks."

Mettner frowned. "I'm betting the rest of them won't have heard from her either. Her phone is in the console of her car, as you know. She was getting ready to leave and someone showed up here. That's what it looks like."

"Or someone was here with her," Noah suggested. "Regardless; someone took her. We'll need her dental records. The doc also said the remains were brought here from some other location."

"I'll have Hummel print this place," Mettner said. "Especially since the door was open. Although nothing in here looks disturbed."

Josie looked around again, something pricking at the edges of her mind. "Her car too," she said.

"You think someone touched the car?"

Josie walked over to the door and looked out into the driveway. "Her keys were in the ignition. She had already gotten into the car."

"Unless whoever took her made it look that way," Noah said.

"Why would someone do that?" Mettner asked.

Josie studied the red Fiat Spider. "She was already in the car," Josie said. "Her phone is where she always put it. When she left our house last month, she positioned her suitcase and purse exactly like that, except for—"

She broke off and looked at Noah. As if reading her mind, he said, "The boxes."

Mettner looked up from the note-taking app on his phone. "What boxes?"

"She had two boxes with her when she left our house," Josie said. "Document boxes. She loaded them into the car when she left, put them on top of the suitcase, and put her purse inside one of the boxes."

Mettner said, "There're no boxes in the car or in this cabin."

"Maybe the person who took Trinity took the boxes, too," Noah said.

A sense of deep foreboding gathered in Josie's stomach. "There's a locked trash bin on the side of the cabin. Someone needs to check it."

Mettner stepped out of the cabin momentarily to speak with a member of the ERT. Josie watched as he pointed to the side of the cabin where the trash bin was located. When he came back in, he asked, "What was in the boxes?"

"I'm not sure," Josie said. "Documents, photos, what looked like personal effects. It looked like a cold case file of some kind." She turned to Noah. "You said her room looked a mess. Did you get a look at anything she had hanging on the walls or scattered around?"

"I'm sorry, Josie. I didn't see much more than you did. I just happened to walk past one day, and her door was cracked. I just glanced inside. I didn't want to invade her privacy, so I didn't go in. From what I could see, there were some photos of what looked like skeletal remains."

"I saw that, too," Josie said.

Mettner said, "Like the kind of remains we've got out back?"

"I'm not sure," Noah answered. "All I saw was a photo of a torso, and it was just a quick glance."

"So it could have been a close-up of the rib cage," Mettner said. "With all the other bones arranged around it just like out back but not actually shown in the photo."

Noah nodded. "It's possible, yes."

"I saw that photo as well," Josie added. "I also saw a few others—leg bones, a pelvis, some smaller bones—but they were all close-up photos, and I only got a quick glance. I would remember if she had a photo showing something like what's out back."

Mettner said, "Where'd she get those boxes? Did she bring them with her from New York?"

"I'm not sure," Josie said. "I think so."

Noah said, "I'm pretty sure one of those boxes came from her assistant. Remember Trinity said she had her assistant mail stuff to the house. We should talk to her. She could tell us what was in at least one of the boxes."

"Yes," Josie said. "That's a good idea."

Hummel rapped on the cabin door, beckoning them. Josie stepped outside with Mettner and Noah in tow. "Chan checked the trash bin," Hummel said. "Bunch of microwave meal boxes, various food wrappers, crumpled paper towels, coffee grounds…"

"I want to look," Josie said. "To see if there's anything I don't think Trinity left."

Hummel pointed in the direction of the trash bin. "Be my guest."

But there was nothing unusual in Trinity's trash. There wasn't much there as she had only spent one week at the cabin. When Josie and Hummel returned to the front of the cabin, Noah asked, "No documents? Photos?"

"Nothing," Josie said.

Hummel led them over to Trinity's car and used a gloved hand to open the driver's side door. "We'll need warrants, but we'll definitely pull whatever prints we can from the car. As you can see, there are no obvious signs of a struggle. No blood, no scratches or damage of any kind to the interior of the vehicle. At least at first glance."

Josie peered inside. Besides the suitcase and purse crammed into the passenger's seat, the car looked pristine, as though Trinity had just driven off the lot. Josie knew she rarely had a chance to drive it. She usually kept it in a garage just outside of New York City. She used public transport or cabs to get around inside the city. The only time she drove it was when she visited Josie or her parents and brother two hours from Denton and not every visit. If the weather was bad or she thought she'd have to venture too far from her family's homes, she would rent a car. Josie had often wondered why she'd even bought the damn thing. She was surprised that Trinity had braved the gravel roads leading to the cabin with her prized Fiat.

Hummel said, "We've got to impound it, take it for secure processing. The tow truck is on its way."

Josie knew this meant they'd tow the car to Denton's police impound lot where they had two car bays that were accessible only to the police. They were used specifically for processing vehicles. The secure indoor environment made it easier for Hummel's team to do their job and less likely that anything would be lost or overlooked.

"Print the inside, too, would you?"

"Will do," Hummel replied. "We've got Trinity's prints on file as elimination prints from an earlier case, so we'll be able to identify those."

"Okay," Josie said. She motioned toward the purse and suitcase. "Hummel, Trinity was working on something before she left. I'm not sure what, though, I'd like to have a look at her phone and laptop when you've finished processing everything. I'm assuming her laptop is packed away in her suitcase."

"We can dump the electronics—we'll make sure we get a warrant for them—but you know that if we try to get latent prints from the outside of the phone or laptop we'd have to use the cyanoacrylate fuming, right?"

"Cause they have non-porous surfaces," Josie replied, seeing where he was going.

"Yeah, so if we use the cyanoacrylate to develop latent prints, it will more or less destroy the electronics."

"Right," Josie said. Cyanoacrylate was basically superglue. Fumes from it reacted with the moisture in latent fingerprints to produce a visible, white film which formed over the ridges of the print that could then be photographed. The problem was that the white material was sticky and near-impossible to remove from any surface it was developed on. "I think her phone has a case on it. Just remove it and see what you get from the case. If the laptop is somewhere deep in her suitcase, I don't think you need to try to pull prints from that. Whoever took her left her phone so they weren't concerned with Trinity's electronics."

Hummel closed the driver's side door. The rumble of a large truck sounded from the direction of the road. A moment later, a flatbed tow truck lumbered into view. Hummel waved to the driver, who spent several minutes getting the truck into position to haul away Trinity's car. Then he hopped down from the truck and pulled on a pair of gloves before approaching the car.

"Hummel," Josie said. "I need everything you can get as soon as you can get it."

He nodded. "You got it, boss."

CHAPTER TEN

Alex stared at his mother's unfinished painting. The one his father said was missing something. She hadn't worked on it in days. She was having one of her dark times. That's how he thought of them; when she stayed in her darkened bedroom for days on end. Sometimes he wanted to creep inside and try to coax her back out, but his father forbade it. Alex had watched her stand in front of the painting for hours each day, brooding over what it was that Francis found wanting. He, too, had studied its abstract whorls and lines and splashes. To him, it looked the same as the last several paintings she had sold that had made Francis so proud of her. Yet, she hadn't finished it.

He went back into the hallway and listened. Francis was out tending to his duties. Zandra, as usual, was locked away.

She had told him that she hadn't meant to hurt their mother, but that wasn't true. It had given her some kind of thrill. Alex knew it. He had been aware of the look on her face as their mother bled. It was the same expression Alex had seen on their dad's face the day the raptor flew down from the sky and snatched the snake away. A sort of wonder. Admiration. Almost… joy. The first few times Zandra did it, their mother scolded her but didn't tell Francis. But the last time—the time Zandra had sliced Hanna's arm so badly that she needed stitches—their mother had called their father on the telephone. "We've had an incident," she'd said. Then she'd looked at Zandra with regret. As though she was sorry for what was about to happen to her.

Shaking the memory from his head, Alex made his way down the steps and outside. An hour later, he had gathered enough feathers to complete the painting. He used his mother's hot glue gun to fix them onto the painting until it looked like wings were emerging from a fusion of color beneath. He was surveying his work when he heard a gasp from the doorway. He turned to see Hanna standing in her shift, one hand covering her heart.

"Oh Alex," she murmured. "It's beautiful. It's exactly right, isn't it?" She stepped forward, admiring it. "Wait until your father sees this!"

Wordlessly, Alex unplugged the glue gun and shuffled toward the door.

"Honey," she called after him.

"Yes, Mom."

"Thank you. Let's just not tell your father, okay? For now?"

"Sure."

CHAPTER ELEVEN

Josie, Noah, and Mettner sat at their desks in the second-floor great room at Denton PD headquarters. Chief Bob Chitwood stood before them, his thin arms crossed over his chest. Beneath gray stubble, his acne-pitted cheeks grew pinker with each fact that the detectives relayed about Trinity's disappearance. Wisps of his white hair floated over the top of his scalp as he turned his head from Mettner to Josie and back. When they finished recapping what little they knew, Chitwood pointed a finger at Mettner. "This is your case. Quinn and Fraley can assist, but you're the lead." Chitwood aimed his finger at Josie. "You. Stay on the sidelines, you got that?"

"Sir," Josie protested. "It's my sister."

"I know that, Quinn. That means you're too close. This is Mettner's case, understand? He calls the shots."

"Yes, sir," Josie said, relieved he wasn't going to send her home or forbid her from having any involvement at all.

"When Detective Palmer gets here, she can run secondary. But Quinn," he added in a warning tone, "your sister is a celebrity. The minute the press gets wind of this, they're going to be on us like flies on crap. They'll want interviews and comments. I don't want to see your face on TV unless Mett says so. You got that?"

Josie nodded. Chitwood gave her a long, appraising look, one of his bushy white brows kinking upward before he turned toward Noah. "You stay out of it too, you got that, Fraley?"

"Chief—" Noah began but Chitwood cut him off.

"Don't want to hear it, Fraley. You assist Mettner and Palmer. That's it."

Noah didn't respond, watching silently as Chitwood walked back to his office and slammed the door behind him. Mettner picked up the receiver of his desk phone and started dialing. "I'm going to contact the network in New York, see if I can get in touch with Trinity's assistant first thing," he said.

Noah added, "Ask her about Trinity's dentist, would you? We need those dental records before the close of business today if possible."

Josie looked at her cell phone. It would be a couple of hours before Shannon, Christian, and Patrick arrived from their hometown of Callowhill. She couldn't move forward with the investigation—or help Mettner move forward with it—until the ERT had something, or at least until they released some of the contents of Trinity's car. She thought about making some calls as well, but who else was there to call? Trinity wasn't married or even dating anyone, to Josie's knowledge. She didn't have any friends.

Or did she?

In the two weeks that Trinity had stayed with Josie and Noah, Josie couldn't remember her speaking to anyone besides their parents, her assistant, and her other coworkers. Josie had never heard her talk about any friends. Trinity had colleagues, contacts and sources, but not friends. When Josie visited her in New York, they were never joined by anyone else for meals or outings. Josie had always just assumed that Trinity wanted time alone, but maybe it was because there was no one else she could invite. When Trinity visited Josie, they were often joined by Detective Gretchen Palmer, Mettner, Josie's friend Misty, and Josie's grandmother, Lisette. Even without Trinity staying with them, Josie and Noah's house was busy and often filled with family, coworkers, and friends.

Who did Trinity talk to besides Josie and Shannon?

A small stab of guilt pierced Josie's heart. She should know this. Trinity was her twin sister. Sure, they'd only been reunited three years ago, but still, if Josie was the person closest to Trinity, she should know the people Trinity held the closest. Trinity's words came back to her like little daggers. Was it true that they were never meant to be sisters?

"Boss?" Mettner said.

Josie looked up from her now-darkened phone screen to see Mettner looking at her quizzically. From his desk, Noah stared at her as well, hands frozen over his keyboard.

"What?"

"You okay?" Mettner asked.

"Yeah, sure. Why?"

"Mett was just talking to you," Noah said. "You were in a trance."

Josie glanced back and forth between them before addressing Mettner again. "I'm sorry. What did you say?"

"Trinity's assistant texted us the name and number of her dentist. Noah's working on a warrant for her records right now." As if on cue, Noah's fingers lowered to the keyboard and started clicking away.

"That's great," Josie choked out.

"Jaime—that's the assistant's name—also says she only sent one box, but she doesn't remember what was in it. She thinks it was some old stuff from a reporter who used to work at the network."

"Did she know the name of the reporter?'" Josie asked.

"She'll look through her email for the name. She's going to check with a few other people at the network to see if Trinity had any contact with them in the last few weeks, and she'll be here in a few hours."

"Great. I think. That will blow the lid off this case, though. You know they're going to do a story on it."

"We'll deal with that later," Mettner said. "It's not the worst thing for the public to know Trinity is missing. It could generate leads. For now, we've got our own work to do."

He sounded just like her. Josie couldn't help but smile. "Got it," she said.

"Was your sister dating anyone?" Mettner asked.

"No. Not that I know of."

"Did she break up with anyone recently?"

"No," Josie said. "I don't think so. She always said she didn't have time to date. Her career came first."

Now that Josie thought about it, in all the years she had known Trinity, she'd never heard her talk about dating anyone at all, even casually.

Noah, finished typing up his warrant, stood up from his desk and stretched his arms overhead. Across the room, the ancient ink jet printer whirred to life. Noah retrieved the pages and returned to his desk. He gave Josie an appraising look. "I've got to get this signed by a judge, but first I'll go downstairs and get you some coffee," he said.

"Thanks," Josie said.

After Noah left, Mettner went on asking questions, and Josie tried to answer as best she could. However, her lack of knowledge about her own sister was painfully glaring. She was relieved that Mettner kept his eyes on his phone as he tapped away, using his favorite note-taking app to record her answers and any notes of his own for follow-up later.

A hand squeezed her shoulder and Josie looked up to see Detective Gretchen Palmer, her face fixed in a grim look of sympathy. "Fraley just brought me up to speed," she said.

Josie nodded, loving Gretchen for saying nothing more than that. There was nothing she could say to reassure Josie that they would locate Trinity safe and unharmed. There was only the work, the investigation, and Josie knew that Gretchen would throw her whole self into that, as would Mettner. Gretchen had come to the department four years earlier, hired by Josie when Josie was interim Chief of Police. Before joining Denton PD, Gretchen had been a homicide detective in Philadelphia for fifteen years. She was one of the finest investigators Josie had ever known and had become a good friend over the years.

Gretchen placed a steaming mug of coffee in front of Josie. "Fraley said to give this to you. He went to get his warrant signed."

"Thanks," Josie said. "Did you see the photos?"

"Not yet. I just heard it was pretty bad."

"Creepy as hell," Josie corrected, taking a long swig of her coffee.

Her desk phone jangled. She snatched it up, barking "Quinn" into the receiver.

"Boss," said Hummel. "We're finished."

"What've you got?" Josie asked, ignoring the look Mettner shot her.

There was a moment of hesitation. Then Hummel said, "It's easier if you come out here to the impound lot and take a look for yourself."

CHAPTER TWELVE

Josie followed Gretchen outside to the municipal parking lot at the back of the police headquarters. The moment the spring air hit their faces, they were crowded by a half dozen reporters, holding out cell phones and recording devices and shouting questions. It had been less than an hour since Mettner contacted Trinity's network and spoke with her assistant. News traveled lightning fast in the media world.

"Is it true that Trinity Payne was abducted?"

"Who was the last person to speak to Ms. Payne?"

"Is there any chance that Ms. Payne's disappearance is a ploy for her to get her anchor position back?"

The words were a splash of ice water down Josie's back. She turned and scanned the reporters until she found the man who had shouted the question. He held out his phone, waiting anxiously for her response. She saw from his press badge that he was from one of Trinity's network's competitors. Josie met his eyes. She opened her mouth to respond but felt Gretchen's hand clamp around her upper arm, wrenching her toward the car.

"No comment," Gretchen shouted as she hustled Josie away.

The reporters crowded the car the moment they got into it, but Gretchen fired up the engine and expertly maneuvered around them and out of the parking lot. In the passenger's seat, Josie seethed.

Gretchen said, "Ignore it. They have no details right now so they're trying to make a story out of nothing. It's just spin."

"Spin that's hugely insulting to my sister," Josie muttered, staring out the window.

"You have to let it go, boss. When we get to the impound, I'll text Mett and let him know he's got to get a handle on them. This story is only going to spread. By the time we get back, there will be twice as many reporters out there."

Josie nodded but remained silent for the remainder of the ride. The impound lot was in a sparsely populated area of North Denton along a thin ribbon of road that was bordered by forest and an occasional house. It was gated and guarded by an officer sitting inside a small booth at the entrance. Gretchen flashed her credentials and the gate lurched open. She weaved through two rows of cars until she came to the far back right of the lot where a plain, cinderblock building stood. On the right was a single dark blue door, solid and unwelcoming. To the left were two garage doors, also blue, their windows white laminate so that no one could see through. Hummel's ERT vehicle sat just outside, and Gretchen pulled in beside it.

The blue door was unlocked. Josie followed Gretchen inside to a small office where Chan sat at a desk, a laptop in front of her, furiously typing. She glanced up and gave the detectives a nod before returning to her work. "Hummel's inside," she said.

They moved through the next door which led to a utilitarian room outfitted with aluminum shelving that housed any and all supplies they might need for processing a vehicle as well as a large stainless-steel table which held Trinity's suitcase and purse. On the wall across from the table was a large window where they could see into the first garage bay. Josie could see Trinity's Fiat Spider, its doors open. Hummel stood nearby, still in his Tyvek suit, booties, and gloves. Only his skull cap was missing, his red hair sticking out in every direction. He held a clipboard and pen, taking down notes. Gretchen rapped lightly on the window and he turned, waving them in through the door which was only a few feet away from the window.

Josie felt her stomach go into freefall when they entered the chamber. This was real. Trinity was missing—possibly dead—and her beloved convertible had been picked over by Josie's own Evidence Response Team. She held back a shiver as she stepped toward Hummel.

Gretchen already had her notebook out.

Hummel said, "Don't worry. It's all been processed. You don't need to suit up."

"What've you got?" Gretchen asked.

Hummel looked past her to Josie. "Boss?"

"What is it, Hummel?" Josie said.

He motioned for her to come around to the driver's side door. "We got prints from the inside and outside of the car. They'll take some time to be run through AFIS."

"That's not why you called me here," Josie said as she walked up to the open door.

Her heart pounded as she stared at the driver's side door panel, just above the handle. The interior of Trinity's Fiat Spider was upholstered in black, so Hummel had used fluorescent fingerprint powder to dust for latent prints. The bright yellow powder had illuminated some fingerprints, but that wasn't what Hummel wanted her to see.

A hastily scrawled message stretched across the panel. It was one word. A name, actually.

Vanessa.

Her heart thumped so loudly, Josie worried that Gretchen and Hummel could hear it. She put one hand against the side of the car to steady herself. A tremble started in her legs and worked its way upward until her fingers drummed against the car's cool red metal. She snatched her hand back to her chest, willing her body to settle.

If Hummel noticed her reaction, he didn't let on. He pointed to the panel. "Fingerprints 101, right? Your fingers leave oil residue. Even if you don't leave a clear print, if you try to draw something with your finger, it might show up. I didn't see it until I dusted."

Trinity had covered enough crime stories to know that it was the moisture from a person's skin that left fingerprints behind. Someone with exceptionally dry skin wouldn't leave as crisp and defined a fingerprint as someone with oily or sweaty fingers. Trinity also would have known that the ERT would process the inside of her car, particularly since her keys had been left in the ignition—it made for suspicious circumstances. Before she got out of the car, she had used a fingertip to hastily scrawl the name onto her door panel. Whoever took her wouldn't have seen it. In fact, no one would ever know it was there unless they used magnetic fingerprint powder or cyanoacrylate fuming to check for prints.

Below the name were some squiggly lines and shapes—almost as though she had attempted to write something else but perhaps hadn't had time.

Hummel said, "Who's Vanessa?"

Josie stared at the letters as the thundering of her heart slowed incrementally. "Me," she replied. "I'm Vanessa."

"I don't understand," Hummel said.

Gretchen stepped up beside Josie, using her phone to snap a few pictures of the door. "That was the boss's given name when she was born," she explained to Hummel. "She was kidnapped at three weeks old, remember? Her parents thought she died in a fire but she had actually been taken."

Hummel grimaced. "Right. Sorry, boss. I forgot. Well, I didn't forget, I just—"

Josie put up a hand. "It's okay, Hummel."

"But you were raised as Josie," Gretchen said. "Trinity knew you as Josie for years before you found out you were sisters. You never changed your name to Vanessa. Did she call you that in private?"

Josie shook her head. "No. Never." *Vanessa never existed,* she almost said.

Hummel used the cap of his pen to scratch his temple. "Then why would she write Vanessa inside the door of her car?"

Again, Josie felt a strange and piercing sense of grief and frustration. They were sisters. Twins. Yet, Josie was astounded by how little she really understood about Trinity. "I have no idea," she told him.

Gretchen knelt beside the open door, putting her reading glasses on and examining the door panel up close. She pointed to the lines beneath the name. "What do you think this is that she was trying to write underneath?"

"I don't know," Hummel said. "It doesn't look like letters."

"They almost look like symbols," Gretchen said.

Josie studied the shapes, but she couldn't make sense of them either. Regardless, she understood that this was a message, and it was meant for her. "Do you mind if I get in?" she asked Hummel.

"Go for it," he said. "We're finished with the car."

Josie sat in the driver's seat and put her hands on the wheel, imagining herself in Trinity's position. "Hummel," Josie asked. "Did the car start?"

"No. The battery was dead, and the car was out of gas."

That meant that Trinity had not only been sitting in the car with the keys in the ignition, but she'd turned the car on. She'd probably been about to put the car in drive and pull away when something stopped her. Another vehicle pulling into the driveway, blocking her way? Josie worked through the scenario in her mind. Trinity would have stayed in the car, waiting to see who emerged from the other vehicle. Wouldn't she? Was she curious? She hadn't been expecting anyone, since she was leaving. Only a handful of people even knew she was at the cabin. Had she recognized the vehicle? Probably not, Josie thought. Was she afraid? Surely she would have at least been apprehensive when a strange vehicle pulled unexpectedly into the long drive to cabin number six. She was there alone with no one even in shouting distance should the person pulling in mean to harm her. She would have watched the person—or persons—getting out of their car, approaching hers. But she couldn't have flung open the door to confront them. Otherwise she wouldn't have been able to leave Josie the message. Once she was out of the car, she didn't get back in. Josie was certain of that. Had she been able to get back into the car, she would have taken off, tried to get away, or she would have used her phone. Josie had seen Trinity send off lengthy texts to her assistant in a matter of seconds.

To Hummel, Josie said, "Did you check the phone yet?"

Hummel shook his head. "We got a warrant for its contents, but it will take a few days for us to get into it."

"Technically, I'm her next of kin. I can give you permission."

Gretchen said, "Her parents are next of kin, boss."

"They can give you permission," Josie said.

Hummel said, "I figured that. Charged it up. Tried to get into it. It's password-protected."

"Shit."

But if Trinity had sent a text to anyone she knew with a cryptic or alarming message, Josie would surely have been notified by now. The message inside the door was for Josie, so it stood to reason that if Trinity had had time to send a text, she would have sent it to Josie. Through the windshield Josie could only see the back wall of the evidence room, which was painted white cinderblock.

In her mind, she visualized the driveway to the cabin again. It sloped slightly downward and the way Trinity's car was positioned when she found it, there would be little room to maneuver around another vehicle. The person in the other vehicle must have gotten out and approached Trinity. Josie assumed the person who took Trinity had arrived in a vehicle and not on foot—otherwise it would have been far too difficult to control Trinity and also take two document boxes from the scene. He or she would have come to the driver's side door first. Did Trinity recognize him or her—or them? Was there more than one person? Or did the driver have a gun in his hand? Josie's mind tried to work through the scenarios. There were no signs that Trinity had fought or tried to run.

Yet, she had known she was in trouble. Once she saw the driver, she knew she had only seconds to do something—anything. She used her fingertip to write the name *Vanessa* on the inside of the door. "Hummel," Josie called. "Can you stand in front of the car?"

He nodded and walked over toward the hood of the Fiat, moving back toward the garage door. Josie pulled the door closed and let her own fingertips linger over the fluorescent letters, tracing the letters in the air. She watched Hummel's face as he slowly walked toward the door. Josie opened it when he reached her. "Could you see what I was doing?"

"Not really. I mean this car is low to the ground and I'm six foot so I could see you were doing something but mostly it looked like you were fumbling to find the handle or something. Of course, we're on level ground here, not at an angle like at the cabin, but I think on the angle the car was positioned there, it would have been even more difficult for me to see what you were doing—if I could see it at all."

Trinity's phone was in the console. She could have reached for it, but she didn't. Josie wondered what time of day Trinity had tried to leave. "Hummel, were the headlights turned on?"

He shook his head. "Nope."

So it had been daylight when Trinity got into the car three weeks earlier. Even in daylight, the kidnapper would have clearly seen her head bent to the screen had she attempted to use her phone. She could have drawn the letters on the door panel without ever looking away from him.

What was she trying to tell Josie by evoking that name?

Before Josie had a chance to consider it, Hummel said, "There's one more thing I want you to see. Come into the other room."

CHAPTER THIRTEEN

Josie and Gretchen followed Hummel back into the room beside the garage. Hummel walked over to a set of shelves and changed his gloves, snapping on a fresh pair and tossing the old ones into a garbage bin. At the stainless-steel table, he flipped open Trinity's suitcase and spoke as he riffled through it. "I'll have Chan catalogue the items. It's mostly clothes, shoes, purses, toiletries, make-up, hair care products, and then we've got a laptop and charger." One gloved hand reached inside the mesh pocket on the inside of the flap and came up with a small box wrapped in brown paper.

Josie said, "That came for Trinity the day she left our house. Noah found it in our mailbox and brought it in."

Again, she saw the neat, block print in black marker spelling out Trinity's name and Josie and Noah's address. No return address. No postage. At one end, the wrapping had been torn where Trinity had looked inside. Gingerly, Hummel reached inside and pulled out a small black box, like the kind jewelry came in.

"Where was that?" Josie asked.

"Just where you saw it—in her suitcase."

"What's inside it?" Gretchen asked.

Hummel set aside the larger box with its torn wrapping and then pried open the smaller one, revealing a bed of black velvet with a single French-style hair comb resting in it. Gretchen immediately took out her phone and snapped a few photos of it while Josie stared. It was a strange color between tan and cream, delicate, smooth, and shiny. Another image of the strange array of bones behind Trinity's rented cabin flashed in her mind. "Oh good God," she said. "Do you think that's—do you... ?" Her throat seized. She sucked in several deep breaths, trying to get her vocal cords to work again. Hummel and Gretchen waited patiently. Finally, she managed, "Is that made of bone?"

Hummel set it down on the table and peered at it. "I don't know. We can send it to the lab. You think this is from whoever left those remains? You think he was stalking her or something?"

"It's unusual," Josie pointed out.

Gretchen said, "People do make jewelry and hair accessories from bone, although it's usually from tortoise shells or antlers."

Hummel said, "This may be animal bone. Like I said, we'll ask the lab to test it."

"There was only one?" Josie asked.

"Yeah, that's all that was in this box. I mean if there was another one, it's not here or in Trinity's car or in the cabin."

Gretchen said, "Have them analyze the packaging as well." She turned to Josie. "Did she mention anything about a stalker to you? Did she get any other unusual packages?"

Josie sighed. Her mind felt clouded. She needed another coffee. "She never said anything about a stalker. The only other package that I know of that she received at our house was from her assistant. She's on her way here but Mett already confirmed with her that she mailed Trinity a package to our house prior to this one arriving. This one, however, didn't come by mail. It had no postage. Someone had to have dropped it off. Also, right after she looked inside it, she took off."

"I thought you said she had an argument with Noah."

"She did," Josie answered. "Sort of. But she really didn't start arguing with him until she had looked inside the package. She was already worked up before that because we were discussing her problems with her network. I thought when she freaked out on Noah she was just overreacting. I didn't think the box had anything to do with it. But now... I don't know."

Gretchen nodded. "You said Noah found it in your mailbox. You've got one of those cameras, don't you? Those Ring cameras?"

Josie felt a jolt. "I do!" A few years earlier she had had surveillance cameras installed around her house after a robbery. It was an old system that she could only access using her laptop. When Noah moved in, they switched over to Ring cameras which they could set to alert their phones if there was any motion detected. Josie didn't remember getting any unusual notifications the morning Trinity took off. Then again, it might not have picked up any movement at the mailbox since it was at the end of their driveway and the motion detection range didn't extend that far. She took her phone out and opened the app, pulling up the Event History and going back a month. Gretchen watched over Josie's shoulder. On the screen, the app showed fourteen events on that date. Most of them were of Josie and Noah leaving and arriving throughout the day as well as Trinity going in and out of the house to retrieve her things and then leaving.

"There's nothing else here," Josie said.

"Doesn't it have footage of the entire day?"

"Not going back thirty days," Josie said. "It only keeps history of the events, which is whenever the motion sensors picked something up."

"Your motion sensor doesn't go off when someone accesses your mailbox?"

"No," Josie said, pulling up the motion settings on the app. She pointed to the screen which showed her front stoop, driveway, front yard, and then the street beyond. A blue haze hung over the area in front of the stoop, just barely reaching the fenders of hers and Noah's vehicles. "See this? That hazy area is where the motion detection starts. You have to walk all the way up to it in order to set off the camera. When we first installed the camera, we had it set to pick up motion all the way out to the street but then every time a car drove past, or one of our neighbors walked their dog, our phones were going off. It was all day long."

Gretchen said. "It's a long shot, but I can have some units canvass your neighbors to see if they saw anyone suspicious lingering around the last six weeks."

"Thank you," Josie said.

Gretchen made a quick call while Josie continued to stare at the comb. Had Trinity known the person who left it for her? Why hadn't she said anything? Would she have had any idea that it might be made of bone? Even if she hadn't, Josie couldn't remember ever seeing Trinity wear a French hair comb before. This one wasn't Trinity's style at all. It was simple—Trinity preferred simplicity in her clothing and even in her home décor—but it lacked the elegance that Josie usually associated with her sister. Maybe Josie didn't know as much as she should about Trinity, but she knew the comb was not something Trinity would ever purchase for herself—or wear even if she'd received it as a gift.

Was Josie right in saying that it was the package, and not Noah's ill-timed joke, that sent Trinity spiraling out of control and storming from the house? But if that was the case, why would she feel the need to leave? What did the package mean?

"We need to take a serious look at the stalker angle," Josie said. "We should talk with people she worked with at the network to find out if she mentioned or reported anything or anyone unusual or menacing."

Gretchen looked over at Josie and nodded. Hummel said, "A stalker would make a lot of sense. Maybe there will be something on her phone or laptop. Chan already did a dump on the laptop. She'll give you the drive with all of its contents when you leave. Take her phone as well. Dr. Feist has the remains over at the morgue."

"Thanks," Josie said. She turned to Gretchen. "Let's stop over there now."

CHAPTER FOURTEEN

Denton's city morgue consisted of a large windowless exam room and one small office presided over by Dr. Feist. It was housed in the basement of Denton Memorial Hospital, an ancient brick building on top of a hill that overlooked most of the city. The smell hit them before they even entered the exam room—a putrid combination of chemicals and decay. Inside the room, Dr. Feist stood next to a stainless-steel autopsy table, arranging the bones from the cabin into a loose facsimile of a skeleton. A large, movable light shined down on them. The skull's empty eyes stared at Josie once more, somehow less creepy here in Dr. Feist's clinical domain, but still disturbing. She felt a pang thinking about how a human being could be reduced to just a pile of off-white jigsaw pieces like this. A table full of bones; incomplete, small, and sad.

Was it Trinity? Was this all that was left of Josie's dynamic force of a sister?

Josie looked up to see Dr. Feist staring at her. "As I told you at the scene, this is a woman. She's over thirty, based on the fact that all of her growth plates are fused, including the medial aspect of her clavicles."

Gretchen said, "You mean the end of the collarbone that goes into the shoulder?"

"Right," said Dr. Feist. "As you will recall, the long bones in the body have three parts: the diaphysis—that's the shaft—the metaphysis, which is the part where it widens and flares at the end—the knobby end—and then the epiphysis, which is basically the end cap of the bone or the growth plate. In children, there is a gap between the epiphysis and the metaphysis but in adults, the epiphysis and the metaphysis are fused together."

Josie said, "So, in adults, the knobby end of the bone fuses with the cap on the end of it."

"Right. The clavicles are the last to fuse and that happens between nineteen and thirty at the latest. In this woman we see that fusion. I actually think she may be much older than thirty." Dr. Feist moved to the head of the table, her gloved fingers hovering over the top of the skull. She indicated very faint traces of squiggly lines running from front to back of the skull and also horizontally across the back of the skull.

"See these cranial sutures? They're openings in the skull that remain open and stretch as our brains grow from birth to adulthood. Some close in childhood but these two that you see here—well, you can barely see them since they're closed now—usually they're open well into adulthood. This one running along the center of her skull from front to back is the sagittal suture, and this one running across the back of the skull is the lambdoid suture. Both are almost completely closed which doesn't normally happen until between ages thirty and forty, although sometimes the sagittal suture can remain open into the fifties."

She moved down to the pelvis, pointing to the planes of the large curved bones. "Examination of her pelvis indicates she likely had children. When the pubic bones separate to allow the baby to fit through, the ligaments pull away from the bone and can sometimes cause scars. I see some pitting scars here which are sometimes an indicator of that. Again, it's not an exact science, but it's a good indicator."

With each word, Josie felt a spasm of relief until her limbs felt weak and jelly-like.

Gretchen leaned over, peering at the pubic bones, glasses sliding down to the end of her nose. Josie, too, leaned forward to get a closer look. "The bone looks almost spongy," she noted.

Dr. Feist nodded. "That's another reason I believe she is over forty, possibly in her fifties. When a person gets into their forties, the pelvic bones take on a more porous look."

Josie said, "This woman can't possibly be Trinity. She's had a child and she's much older."

Dr. Feist replied, "I believe so, yes, but I would prefer to wait until I've got Trinity's dental records before confirming that definitively."

Josie thought she might need to sit down. So profound was her relief that every inch of her body felt unsteady. Yet, the longer she stared at the bones, the more that relief receded, leaving her back in a state of high anxiety. Trinity could still be alive, but the woman before them was not. Somewhere she had loved ones—a child or children. Surely, they were looking for her, wondering what had become of her? Josie ached with the thought of the devastation that lay ahead of them.

Gretchen asked, "Can you determine her race?"

Dr. Feist moved back toward the skull. "I'm not a forensic anthropologist, but I can make an educated guess based on what I know and what I've seen in my career."

"Which is what?" Josie coaxed.

"I would say that this is a Caucasian female based on the narrow nasal opening and the fact that the nasal bridge is so pronounced and high up on the face. Also, if you look at the eye sockets—"

Josie had to force herself to look at them again.

"—they're quite circular but their margins are squared. That's consistent with Caucasoid skulls."

Josie looked away from the skull once more.

With a nod, Gretchen said, "Let me call Noah and see if he's gotten anywhere with the warrant for Trinity's dental records."

As she walked off into the hallway, Josie asked, "Can you tell how this woman died?"

Dr. Feist frowned. "I'm afraid I can't. There is no evidence of trauma. No fractures of any kind. No damage from bullets. Her hyoid is intact. If she had been strangled, I'd expect to see damage to the hyoid. Although that's not one hundred percent accurate as an indicator. She might have been strangled without her hyoid being damaged. She could have asphyxiated—that wouldn't cause visible trauma to the bones. I don't see any marks that indicate that she might have been stabbed, although it's possible she was stabbed, and the damage was to the soft tissue only. At this advanced stage of decomposition, there's no soft tissue left for me to make that determination."

Josie said, "So right now all we know is that this is a Caucasian woman, likely in her forties or older, who has probably had children. What about distinguishing characteristics? Individual characteristics?"

Dr. Feist frowned. "I'm afraid there's nothing."

Gretchen returned to the room, her phone in hand. "Dr. Feist, check your email. Noah got Trinity's dental records."

"That was fast," Dr. Feist said, walking over to the stainless-steel counter to open her laptop.

If Noah had been there, Josie would have hugged him. She was certain his doggedness had procured the dental x-rays in record time. It often took several days for the police department to obtain the necessary records or images to move their cases forward.

A few moments later, Dr. Feist's screen showed images of Trinity's dental x-rays side by side with those that had been taken of the woman on the autopsy table. Josie and Gretchen crowded in on either side of the doctor, studying the images. Dr. Feist pointed to several places on the mystery woman's x-rays where posts had been placed into her root canals to hold crowns in place. "Trinity doesn't have this many crowns and hers are on the top. None on the bottom." She turned and met Josie's eyes, a grim smile on her face. "This woman is not your sister."

Tears stung the backs of Josie's eyes. There was a chance of getting Trinity back alive.

Gretchen said, "If they're not Trinity's remains, whose are they?"

CHAPTER FIFTEEN

Alex sat on the bench next to the front door, itchy in the stiff suit his parents had made him wear. Zandra had wanted to wear a puffy, glittery pink dress with matching pink bows in her hair. There had been quite an argument over her choice, which their parents had won. Francis chose the outfit, and that was that.

From upstairs Alex could hear his parents talking. Moments later, his mother descended the steps wearing a silky red dress and heels, her long brown hair swept back from her face. She looked like a movie star. A few minutes later, his father came down, dressed in his only suit. He looked at Alex. "This is a big night for your mother," he said gravely. "There will be some very important people at her art show this evening. If she sells just one piece, it could mean financial security for our entire family. Do you understand?"

Hanna placed an elegant hand on Francis's arm. "You don't need to worry about Alex, not tonight."

"Somehow, I find that hard to believe," he told her. Turning back to Alex, he said, "If you don't keep your sister in check, you'll be sleeping in the yard for a month, do you understand?"

Hanna's brow furrowed. "Really, Francis, it's going to be fine. Alex and Zandra know how important this night is for our family. Alex will do everything he can to make sure things go off perfectly. He has a stake in it, too, you know."

She gave Alex a conspiratorial smile.

Francis frowned. "What are you talking about?"

"The painting you love so much? The one you said should be the centerpiece of the show? Alex finished it, not me. The wings were his idea. He collected the feathers and arranged them on the canvas. Amazing, isn't it? Perhaps he'll be an artist like me."

Alex expected Francis to be as delighted with this news as Hanna was delivering it. Instead, his dark eyes flashed with fury. He whirled on Hanna. "You let the boy finish your painting?"

Hanna took two uneven steps back, away from him. "It doesn't matter. Everyone loves it. Besides, we're the only ones who know."

Francis pointed a finger at Alex, but kept his gaze on Hanna. "You let this stupid, awful boy destroy the very centerpiece of your show? Are you out of your mind?"

Her lower lip trembled. "I think you're overreacting," she said.

Francis pulled at his tie. "We're not going."

A tear slid from the corner of Hanna's eye. "We have to go. They're expecting us. There are going to be over a hundred people there. Francis, it's one painting. No one will know."

Francis stormed upstairs. Hanna gave Alex a weak smile before running after him.

An hour later they were all in the car, headed to the gallery. The moment they walked into the building, people converged on Hanna, praising her work and asking her questions about individual pieces. Francis disappeared in the crowd.

It took nearly an hour for Hanna and Alex to work their way through the throngs of Hanna's admirers to the painting they'd created together. Hanna clamped a hand over her mouth. A woman beside her said, "This is an interesting piece, Hanna. It has an unfinished look about it, doesn't it?"

Alex looked up at his mother. Tears spilled from her eyes, over the hand covering her mouth. Without a word, she ran off, leaving him standing in front of the naked canvas.

All of the feathers were gone.

CHAPTER SIXTEEN

Josie pointed to Dr. Feist's laptop. "Do you mind if I use this?"

Dr. Feist closed out her tabs and waved Josie over. "Be my guest."

With Gretchen peering over her shoulder, Josie pulled up the website for NamUs, the National Missing and Unidentified Persons System, and logged in. She selected Pennsylvania and searched, turning up a total of 438 missing persons in the entire state listed in the NamUs database.

Gretchen said, "She might not be listed in NamUs. She might not even be from Pennsylvania."

"True," Josie conceded. "But it's a good place to start."

Dr. Feist looked over Josie's other shoulder and gave a low whistle. "That's a lot of missing people to sort through. This could take a while."

"No, it won't," Josie said. "We'll sort by sex, age, and race. Thanks to you, we've got some parameters to work with. Here we go."

Together they studied the list. There were nine Caucasian females between the ages of forty-five and fifty-five currently listed in the NamUs database as missing. One by one, Josie clicked on them and she and Gretchen read the details. Four of them had been missing for decades.

"We have no idea how long this woman has been dead," Gretchen pointed out. "We'd have to check out every single one of these."

"First things first," Josie said. "Let's cross-check to see if any of these women's dental records have been submitted to the National Dental Image/Information Repository. If we can get dental records for comparison, we can start narrowing down our list." She glanced back at Dr. Feist. "Do you mind?"

"Not at all. The sooner this woman is identified, the sooner her family can begin to have closure."

Only four of the nine women were listed in the NDIR database, their dental records having been uploaded so that Josie, Gretchen, and Dr. Feist could review them. When Josie pulled up the dental x-rays for the third woman on their list and placed them side by side with the images that Dr. Feist had taken of their victim, Dr. Feist slapped the counter excitedly. "That's her!"

"Are you sure?" Josie said, peering at one set of images, then the other, and back again. But as she looked more closely, she could clearly see the similarities for herself.

Gretchen reached across Josie and clicked back to the details of the missing woman's case. "This can't be right," she said.

Dr. Feist said, "That's a match. What's her name?"

"Nicci," Josie read off. "Nicci Webb. Age forty-five."

Gretchen said, "But she only went missing a couple of weeks ago. Seventeen days ago to be precise."

"Only a few days after Trinity went missing," Josie pointed out.

"True," Gretchen said. "We'll have to see if there's a connection. But seventeen days? This can't be Nicci Webb."

The three of them turned and stared at the remains on the autopsy table.

Dr. Feist said, "It's not impossible for a body to decompose that quickly, but as I told Josie, the conditions would have to be right. Extreme heat, insects, scavengers… like I told Josie at the scene, the body didn't decompose behind the cabin where it was found. We have no idea of the location or conditions in which her body decomposed." Turning back to the laptop, she reviewed the x-ray images once more. "This is a match," she added. "I'm sure of it."

Josie glanced at Gretchen. "We could contact the detective in charge of the case and tell him or her we have a possible match, and go from there."

Gretchen said, "That report says she was from Keller Hollow. That's almost an hour from here, on the other side of Bellewood. They don't have their own police department. Too rural. They rely on the state police."

Josie clicked on the report again to find the name of the officer who had submitted Nicci Webb's dental records. "The investigating officer is Detective Heather Loughlin."

Gretchen smiled and took out her phone. "Perfect."

They'd worked with Heather on several cases. She was thorough, fair, and no-nonsense. Gretchen put the call on speakerphone. Heather picked up after three rings. "Detective Palmer," she said. "What can I do for you?"

Gretchen said, "We found some... remains here in Denton. The dental images Dr. Feist took match up with a missing woman in the National Dental Image Repository. Nicci Webb."

There was a beat of silence, then a long sigh filled with disappointment and sadness. "You sure?"

From over Gretchen's shoulder, Dr. Feist piped up. "I've been staring at them for the last half hour. It's a match."

"Shit," Heather muttered. Then, "Send me what you've got. I'll call you back in fifteen minutes."

Dr. Feist emailed the x-rays to Heather and the three of them waited in silence. While Gretchen fired off a text to Mettner letting him know about the ID, Josie looked over the NamUs report for Nicci Webb. It didn't contain many details—her age, height, weight, and town she lived in. Under 'last seen' it simply said: Keller Hollow. That could mean anything. Had she disappeared from her home or from somewhere else in the small town? Josie studied the photo, wondering how forty-five-year old Nicci Webb had come to be gruesomely displayed behind Trinity's rental cabin. The photo showed

Nicci from the waist up, wearing a red sweater with a multi-colored scarf wrapped round her neck. It looked as though someone had cropped other people out of the rest of the picture. Nicci sported shoulder-length brown hair shot through with gray and glasses over a narrow nose and thin lips. Her smile looked slightly strained.

Josie used her phone to search various social media outlets for Webb. She found a Facebook account, but its privacy settings were so strict that Josie could only view her profile picture which showed her face up close. Her brown hair was pulled back with a black headband and her smile was slightly wider than in the NamUs photo, but it still didn't quite reach her eyes.

Gretchen said, "Does she look familiar? Do you think Trinity knew her?"

"No," Josie said. "I've never seen her before. Trinity never mentioned her, but it's entirely possible they knew one another, and I didn't know about it."

"Once we have the laptop dump and get her phone unlocked, we can see if Nicci Webb is one of Trinity's contacts or if there's any evidence there that they knew one another."

Josie said, "We should also ask Trinity's assistant. Nicci might have been a source of some kind for one of Trinity's stories."

Gretchen's phone rang and she answered, putting it on speakerphone. Heather's voice filled the room. "That's my missing person," she said, words filled with resignation. "You mind telling me where you found her?"

Gretchen quickly gave her a rundown of the situation. The only thing she left out was the fact that the bones had been arranged in a strange and disturbing tableau. Josie knew that that was a detail better discussed in person. As if reading Josie's mind, Gretchen told Heather, "There are a few other details, but we'd rather discuss those in person."

"Of course," said Heather. "Can you ladies meet me in Bellewood in an hour? There's a gas station at the edge of town, right before the road that leads into Keller Hollow."

"I know it," Josie said. "We'll see you soon."

As soon as they hung up, Gretchen called Mettner to let him know what was going on. They thanked Dr. Feist and headed to their vehicle. Gretchen drove, stopping for takeout cheeseburgers before taking the twisty back roads to Bellewood, the Alcott County seat. Josie thought she had no appetite until the smell of the burgers filled the car. She hadn't eaten since breakfast and it was after four in the afternoon. She thanked Gretchen before scarfing down the food. Once she finished, she turned toward the window, watching the gorgeous mountain scenery flash past, her mind working to make some kind of connection between Trinity and Nicci Webb.

There was none. Josie hoped they would find one. Perhaps that connection would help them locate Trinity—before Trinity met the same gruesome fate as Webb.

At the Gas 'N Go station on the east side of Bellewood, Detective Heather Loughlin waited, leaning up against the side of her unmarked Chevrolet Tahoe with a cup of coffee in her hand. She wore black slacks and a polo shirt under a light jacket with the State Police logo emblazoned next to the left lapel. Her blonde hair was pulled back into a ponytail, and she offered them a grim smile as they got out of their own vehicle.

"I'm happy to see you, but not under these circumstances," she told them. "Tell me what you couldn't tell me over the phone."

Josie let Gretchen do the talking. She watched Heather's face transform from cool professionalism to shock when Gretchen showed her the photos of Nicci's remains as they'd been found behind the cabin. "Sweet lord," Heather muttered.

Josie stepped forward. "Nicci Webb wasn't involved in anything… satanic or ritualistic, was she?"

Heather shook her head. "No, not at all. She was a regular parishioner at the Episcopal church in Bellewood."

Josie said, "What can you tell us about her?"

"She was a sixth grade schoolteacher in Bellewood. She lived in Keller Hollow for well over twenty years. Raised her daughter here. Daughter's name is Monica. She's twenty-one, lives with Webb. Monica has a two-year-old daughter. Nicci's husband died of a heart attack six years ago. She drove out to the cemetery to tend to his grave almost three weeks ago, which is something she does regularly, and no one saw her again. When she didn't come home, the daughter tried calling her. No answer. The daughter drove to the cemetery. Found Webb's vehicle there with everything left inside: purse, phone, keys in the ignition. It was like Webb just got out and walked away."

Josie felt a shiver along her spine. Just like Trinity—Nicci Webb had left everything behind and vanished into thin air. "There was nothing left behind at the cemetery, right?" Josie asked Heather. "Nothing unusual or… alarming?"

Heather gave a dry laugh. "If you mean some kind of sickening display like what you guys found, no. Nothing. Believe me, I would have led with that. Part of the problem with the investigation was that it looked like she just walked off. That's what everyone thought. Her daughter searched the area, found nothing, and so she called us in. We did some searches, didn't turn anything up. Monica said that Nicci sometimes got depressed, especially after her husband passed, although she never sought professional help. For a while I thought maybe she had gone off and killed herself, but we never did find any evidence. Brought in the K-9 unit, they found her scent, but it didn't go anywhere."

Josie said, "Which usually indicates that the person got into a vehicle."

"Exactly," Heather agreed. "We checked into every person Nicci knew. She doesn't have a very wide social circle. Everyone checked out."

"What about the cemetery?" Gretchen asked.

"It's small and rural. No cameras. It's maintained by a couple in their eighties who live in Bellewood. They take care of the grass-cutting and other needs using their own equipment."

"So unless someone else was inside the cemetery that day with Nicci, no one would have seen anything," Josie said.

Gretchen said, "Someone was inside the cemetery with her, obviously. No one saw them."

Heather nodded. "We talked with everyone in Keller Hollow. As you probably know, there are only about four hundred people who live there, but between Monica and my people, we got to everyone. No one remembers seeing Nicci that day. No one remembers seeing any other vehicles arriving at or leaving the cemetery. We asked Bellewood PD to talk to people in their community. They put some stuff up on social media. We got no leads."

Josie asked, "There was no one she was feuding with? No troublesome boyfriends or ex-boyfriends?"

"No," Heather replied.

"How about Monica?" Gretchen asked. "You said she's got a two-year-old daughter. What about the father?"

"He's in the air force," Heather replied. "Deployed. They're not married but they have a good relationship. I did check out all of Monica's known associates though just to be thorough. No one sent up any red flags."

Josie motioned toward Heather's Tahoe. "You asked us here."

Heather nodded. "I've got to give Monica the death notification. She's going to have a lot of questions. Since her mother's homicide was in your jurisdiction, you should meet her."

"Of course," Josie said.

CHAPTER SEVENTEEN

Heather drove them down the long, wooded, two-lane road that led to Keller Hollow. They passed the cemetery on the way there, and just as Heather had said, there wasn't much to it. It wasn't gated. It was merely a plot of land that had been carved out of a forested hill, its headstones lined up neatly in rows. A single asphalt road split the middle of it, leading up and over the crest in the hill. As they drove past, Heather said, "Mr. Webb is buried up on the other side of the hill. You couldn't see Nicci's vehicle from this road which means that anyone who drove in after her and approached her wouldn't have been seen from the road."

Keller Hollow appeared, a small collection of houses nestled along the rural route. Heather pulled into the driveway of a small, two-story house with blue siding and black shutters. Beside them were two other vehicles—both sedans, one red and one silver. As they got out, Heather pointed to the silver car. "That's Nicci's car. We did process it but didn't find anything. The other car is Monica's. She's usually home. She's taking online college courses. Plus, with a toddler and the cost of childcare, it's tough for her to get out of the house much."

They stepped onto a porch that was littered with brightly colored toddler toys: a play lawn mower, a cozy coupe car, and a plastic ice-cream stand complete with plastic ice-cream cones in all flavors imaginable. Before Josie could take it all in, the creak of the screen door drew her attention. A young woman stepped out, holding a little girl on her hip. Both had dark hair, pale skin, and narrow noses like Nicci Webb.

"Monica," Heather greeted her.

Monica's blue eyes traveled from Heather to Josie and Gretchen and back. She drew in a deep, stuttering breath, and said, "She's gone, isn't she?"

Heather's face was drawn with sympathy. "Can we go inside?"

Wordlessly, Monica led them inside the house. More toys were scattered across the living room. The furniture was well worn, as was the tan carpet. Family photos hung from the walls. Most were of a family of three—Monica stood circled protectively by her parents at various ages, bracketed by a much younger Nicci and her husband. He was taller than his wife, barrel-chested and bearded with kind eyes and a wide smile. His own expression held none of the strain that his wife's did. Then he disappeared from the photos, eventually replaced by Nicci's infant granddaughter.

Josie tore her eyes from the photos to take in the rest of the room. Houseplants sat in each corner and on the end tables. Everything in the room except the toys looked very old, and yet the place felt homey and warm. A blanket had been spread on the floor, with various dolls on it. Monica set her daughter down on it and handed her a sippy cup. "Annabelle," she said, a tremble in her voice. "Mommy has to talk to these ladies, okay? Why don't you sit here and play and watch TV for a while, okay? I'll put on your favorite show?"

Annabelle pointed to the television and cried out, "*Paw Patrol*."

Monica kissed her cheek and smiled back, even as a tear sneaked down her face. "You got it, baby."

Once Annabelle was fully engrossed in *Paw Patrol*, they all sat down—Gretchen and Josie on the couch and Heather and Monica on the love seat. Heather made introductions while Monica twisted her hands together in her lap. "Just tell me," she said. "Just tell me where you found her."

Heather said, "Your mother's remains were found near a rental cabin in Denton."

Monica closed her eyes for a moment, sucking in several deep breaths. "Remains?"

Gretchen cleared her throat and when Monica opened her eyes again, she said, "She was badly decomposed, I'm afraid. We weren't able to determine her cause of death or even how long she's been dead, but we estimate that she probably passed away shortly after she went missing."

"She didn't go missing," Monica said.

Josie said, "You're right. Someone took her, Monica." She glanced at Gretchen. She knew they couldn't disclose the bone display. Not at this stage in the investigation. Not that she wanted to tell Monica about the ghastly way her mother's bones had been displayed. "But we're not sure where she was killed. It was clear from how clean the scene was that her remains had been brought from another location and placed there."

Monica's brow furrowed. "You said Denton? I don't think my mom's ever been to Denton."

Gretchen said, "Well, that's kind of why we're here. We need to know if she had any connection there."

Monica shook her head. "No. None. Wait, you said it was a rental cabin. She wasn't renting it, was she?"

"No," Josie said, "She wasn't the one renting it. It was Trinity Payne."

"You mean the reporter? The one who used to be on the morning show? The one who just went missing from—what the hell is going on here?"

Josie asked, "Are you aware of any connection between your mother and Trinity Payne?"

"No," Monica replied. "None. I don't understand. What does Trinity Payne have to do with my mother?"

Heather said, "Trinity Payne went missing a few days before your mother did in the same way that your mother vanished. Her vehicle and all her personal belongings, including her phone, were left behind. Your mother's remains were found not far from where Ms. Payne went missing."

Monica's face paled slightly. "You mean there's a serial killer loose?"

Josie said, "It's far too early to make that assumption, Monica. We're just looking at any possible connections between the two cases."

Monica pointed at Josie. "I recognize you now. You're that cop. Trinity Payne's twin sister. I saw you on *Dateline*."

Josie nodded. "That's right. Are you absolutely sure that your mom didn't know Trinity?"

Monica swiped at another tear and laughed. "I'm positive. She didn't know anyone famous. No offense, but she didn't even watch that network." Her gaze drifted to Annabelle who was still riveted to the television.

Gretchen asked, "Had your mom ever had any contact with anyone from the press for any reason?"

"No. Never. She lives—lived—a quiet life. We were—we were happy." Her voice cracked and she stood up. Again, she looked at Annabelle, then back to the three women. "I—I—"

Heather said, "Take a moment, Monica. We'll keep an eye on Annabelle."

Monica fled toward the back of the house but not before they all heard a strangled sob escape from her throat. Heather got onto the floor and sat near Annabelle, who hadn't yet realized that her mother was no longer in the room.

"I hate this," Gretchen muttered when they heard the back door slam.

"Me too," Josie said. "But we're going to find the person who did this. No matter what we have to do."

When *Paw Patrol* finished, Heather picked up the remote control and streamed another episode. Josie stood and smoothed her pants with sweaty hands. Then she went in search of Monica.

CHAPTER EIGHTEEN

Josie found her way to the kitchen. Like the living room, the furniture and appliances seemed old and well-used, but there were small homey touches that made it feel welcoming, like the cheery blue and white curtains on the windows, the brightly colored highchair at the head of the kitchen table, more houseplants, and a wooden sign on the wall that said, *I love you even when you're HANGRY*. Josie pushed through the back door into the yard and gasped when she emerged onto the patio. Tall vinyl fencing encased the yard, but all along the inside of the fencing someone had affixed copper wire, twisting it into ornate designs which Josie quickly realized were in the shapes of trees. The branches of each tree reached upward and out from the fence, reaching toward the center of the yard. Dangling from each branch were faux jewels and polished stones.

From a chair nearby, Monica said, "My mom made this."

"It's beautiful," Josie breathed, and it was. It was unlike anything she had ever seen.

She tore her eyes away to look at Monica who studied the copper trees, three horizontal lines creasing her forehead. "Yeah, it is," she said. "I forget how… unique it is because I see it every day. She's been working on it bit by bit most of my life. Adding stuff, subtracting stuff. My dad called it her garden, but he wasn't being mean. He loved this. He wanted her to make things and sell them, but she hated that idea. This was just for her, she said."

Monica's nose and eyes were red and swollen from crying. In her hand, she clutched a balled-up tissue. She rocked back and forth in her chair. "I don't know what I'm going to do without her."

Josie said, "You'll finish school. You'll raise your daughter. You'll live."

Monica met her eyes. "That sounds very much like something she would say."

Josie walked over, found another patio chair and pulled it closer to Monica, angling it so she was facing her. "I'm very sorry for your loss. There's nothing anyone can say or do to make this hurt less, but I do promise you that I'll do everything I possibly can to find the person who did this to your mother and put him away for life."

Monica nodded.

Josie continued, "Is there anyone we can call for you?"

"No," Monica said. "No one. I mean, I have friends, but I'll call them. My dad's family lives in California. I hardly ever see them. Mom didn't have anyone."

"No siblings? What happened to her parents?"

"She never knew her father, she said. He was never in the picture. Her mother was largely absent, according to her. Then she died when Mom was fifteen."

Thinking of what Heather had said about Nicci's occasional struggles with depression, Josie said, "That must have been difficult for her. What happened to her after her mom died?"

"She ran away," Monica said. "She didn't want to go into foster care. She said she stayed in a shelter for homeless youth for a while, until she aged out."

"Was that around here? In Bellewood?"

"No," Monica answered. "I think in Philadelphia. She never talked about it other than to say it wasn't great, but it wasn't horrible. Eventually, she got a job and a shitty apartment. Started taking college courses to get her teaching degree at Temple University. That's where she met my dad. He got a job at the courthouse in Bellewood and they moved here. They were together until the day he died."

Josie said, "What was her maiden name?"

"Cahill," Monica answered.

"Detective Loughlin mentioned that your mom would become depressed at times. Was that even before your dad passed away?"

Monica nodded. "Yeah, my whole life. It wasn't often. Sometimes she'd just get into these funks. She would stay in bed for a few days, cry a lot, not eat. My dad used to take care of her, and he'd always tell me just to let her be, that she was 'going through something' although he never said what."

"Did you ever ask her?"

"Once, right after I moved back in here when Anabelle was first born. I asked her why she had those episodes and she wouldn't tell me. She said it was none of my business."

"What do you think they were from?" Josie asked.

Monica shrugged. "I don't know, but one time when I was a teenager and my dad was still alive, I heard him trying to comfort her, you know? He had left their bedroom door cracked and I could hear them. She kept saying, 'I could have done more,' and my dad said, 'You did everything you could.' I was too scared to ask about it. Even when I was an adult. I mean, that one time I brought it up with her; I told her I'd overheard that whole thing. That's when she said it was none of my business. I just thought it must have something to do with before she met my dad or when she was a kid or something."

Josie thought about Trinity and the week before she went missing, when she was still staying with Josie and Noah. "Monica," she asked. "Did your mom seem out of sorts or anything before she vanished?"

"In what way?

"More stressed than normal? Anxious? Did she act unusual in any way?"

"No, not at all."

"Did she receive any unusual items before she disappeared? Anything in the mail?"

"No, why?" Monica asked, one brow kinking with suspicion.

"My sister—Trinity—received a white hair comb in the mailbox a few days before she was abducted. It could be nothing. Maybe it has nothing at all to do with her abduction but I'm just—"

"Grasping at straws?" Monica said with a dry laugh. "I've been doing that for the last seventeen days. Going over every tiny detail of my mom's life, trying to figure out if there was any clue as to what happened to her, no matter how obscure. When you don't know what's important, everything is important."

Josie smiled and nodded, thinking that Monica should go into law enforcement. "Exactly," she said.

"My mom didn't receive any unusual packages before she was taken, and she never wore hair combs."

"Thank you," Josie said. "Is there anything else you think I should know about your mom?"

"She was a good mom," Monica said, a fierceness to her tone. "A great mom. I know we talked about her being down sometimes, but she was happy, especially after Annabelle came and we moved back in. She took my dad's death so hard. When Annabelle was born, things got so much better. Good lord, how am I going to do this?" She looked toward the back door. "Annabelle keeps asking where Nanny went. I don't know what to tell her. Shit."

More tears streaked her face and her rocking increased. Josie knew there was nothing she could say. There were no answers, no comfort she could give. The road ahead of Monica and her little girl was thorny and fraught with grief. Josie sat with her until she composed herself, and stood up, ready to go back inside. Before they went in, Josie handed her a business card. "My cell number is on there. Call anytime. Day or night."

Monica studied it before putting it into her back jeans pocket. "Thank you."

Josie said, "Now I've got to get to work."

CHAPTER NINETEEN

They arrived back at Denton PD headquarters after seven in the evening to find the press crowding both the front and back entrances of the building. Two WYEP vans sat out in front of the building. Several reporters milled around on the sidewalk, converging on any police officer who entered or exited. There was no chance of them sneaking in unnoticed. Gretchen kept one hand firmly wrapped around Josie's arm as they waded through a sea of shouting people and into the back entrance. They took the stairs to the second floor, where the desk phones were ringing off the hook. Noah and Mettner were seated at their desks, receivers pressed to their ears. Josie's phone buzzed with a text. It was her friend Misty.

I just heard. Let me know if I can do anything. I'm here for you.
Josie ultimately settled on a simple reply: *Thank you. I'll keep you posted.*

Misty immediately responded with a heart emoji.

Noah hung up his desk phone and gave her a quizzical look. She held out her phone so he could read the text exchange. "The press has gone insane over this," he said. "We've been fielding calls almost since you left."

"What are we telling them?" Josie asked.

Mettner hung up as well and said, "That Trinity is missing, and that foul play is suspected given the fact that although her phone and purse were found inside the car, other personal items were taken. We're keeping Nicci Webb's remains under wraps for now." He looked around at all of them. "That means no one mentions them or Webb to anyone who is not on the Denton PD staff—everyone got that?"

They nodded. Noah said, "You'd better spread the word. Don't want any of these patrol guys going home telling their wives and their wives telling their… you get the idea."

"I'll handle it," Mettner assured him. "This is delicate, but I want to try to use the press coverage to our advantage since there's no avoiding it. WYEP already ran a few spots as breaking news. They've got it up on their social media pages. I'm going to have to do a press conference at some point, but for now, let's just keep working the case. What did you guys get from Detective Loughlin?"

Gretchen and Josie sat down at their desks. Gretchen gave him and Noah a rundown of everything they'd learned about Nicci Webb and her disappearance. She also recapped their meeting with Monica Webb, concluding with, "Heather's going to send over a copy of her investigative file, although she says she doesn't think there's anything in there that will be helpful to us."

Mettner furiously typed notes into his phone as Gretchen spoke. "We'll have to see if we can find a connection between Trinity and Nicci Webb on Trinity's end," he muttered.

"Yes," Josie agreed. "Did you talk to Hummel?"

Mettner nodded. "He told us about the message in the car and the comb, yeah. He uploaded photos to the file. Also, I got in touch with Trinity's co-anchor, Hayden Keating, as well as one of her producers."

"That's great," Josie said. "Did they say anything? Have they heard from her recently? Did they know what she was working on?"

Mettner stopped typing into his phone and shook his head. "No. They haven't heard from her in over a month. They didn't have anything to offer. But they're sending out a crew with Keating. They'll be here in a few hours. We can talk more with them then."

"What about the canvassing?" Josie asked. "Of the other occupied cabins?"

"I'm sorry, boss, but it didn't turn anything up. Only four of the other cabins were occupied. No one heard or saw anything. None of those people even knew that number six was occupied."

"What about the tenants?" Josie asked. "Did they all check out?"

Mettner said, "Well, two of them are families and they all alibied each other. The other two cabins are occupied by single men here for fishing season. They don't have alibis, but they let our officers look around inside and out of the cabins and nothing turned up."

"Let's do background checks on all of them," Josie said. "Even the families."

"You got it, boss." Mettner said, making another note in his app.

Gretchen asked, "Did someone canvass Josie and Noah's neighborhood to see if anyone remembers seeing someone putting something in their mailbox last month or lingering in the area?"

Mettner nodded. "I had a couple of guys out to do that. No one remembers seeing anyone or anything suspicious or out of place."

Josie frowned. "I'm not surprised. That was a month ago."

"We've still got a lot of leads to run down," Mettner reminded her. "I want to have a look at the contents of Trinity's laptop. You think you could figure out the password to her phone?"

"I can try," Josie said. "But our mom might have a better idea."

Mettner asked, "You think your family could shed some light on why she wrote *Vanessa* inside the car?"

"Maybe," Josie said.

Noah stood and came around the desk, gently touching Josie's arm. "They're here. Your parents and brother. They've been downstairs waiting a long time. Sergeant Lamay put them in the conference room. I sat with them for as long as I could, until Mett needed me. They'll want to see you."

CHAPTER TWENTY

She let Noah lead her toward the stairwell. She had questions for Shannon, but the thought of seeing her family filled her with dread. They still didn't feel like her family. Not exactly. Josie knew the Paynes loved her, and like her, they longed to have back the thirty years they'd lost. They had tried very hard to become a part of Josie's life over the last three years, and Josie had tried to be as open to them as she possibly could. They'd spent a great deal of time together. Shannon made weekly trips to see Josie, driving the two hours back and forth to accommodate Josie's busy work schedule. Still, when Josie heard the words "your family" there was only one person she instantly thought of.

"Noah," Josie said quietly. "I need my grandmother."

She was grateful he didn't ask questions. Instead, as they emerged from the stairwell onto the first floor and walked toward the conference room, he said, "I'll call her and ask her to be ready in fifteen minutes. Then I'll run over to Rockview and pick her up."

She gave his arm a squeeze before stepping through the conference room door. Her brother, Patrick, who was now college-age and attending nearby Denton University, slouched in a chair, scrolling on his phone. His shaggy brown hair fell across his face, obscuring his eyes as his head bent to the screen. Christian, tall and thin with salt-and-pepper hair, paced back and forth along one wall. Shannon sat in a chair at the center of the long table, her elbows resting on its glass top, her head resting in her palms. She looked up when Josie entered, then sprang from her seat and raced over, pulling

Josie into a hard embrace. Josie hugged her back, trying to push down the emotions that rose to the surface while in Shannon's arms.

Pulling back, Shannon studied Josie's face. It still gave Josie a shock sometimes to see her mother. The resemblance between them was strongest with Shannon. They had the same porcelain skin, blue eyes beneath long lashes, and long black hair that sometimes looked brown after a summer spent in the sun, only Shannon's was now streaked with gray. Josie and Trinity were twins, but Trinity had always looked different from Josie. As a television news reporter, Trinity always radiated glamour with her heavy make-up and her shiny, perfect hair that never seemed to suffer no matter the weather. The resemblance had always been there, of course, but Josie had just thought it was a coincidence. Meeting Shannon for the first time, however, had been extremely jarring. Just like Josie, Shannon looked like a stripped-down version of Trinity.

Christian walked over and gave Josie a brief hug. Patrick watched intently from the other end of the room. Shannon said, "Have you heard anything?"

Josie swallowed over the lump in her throat. "No, I'm sorry. Nothing. It seems that you were the last one to hear from her and that was three weeks ago. There's something I need to ask you."

She took out her phone and pulled up the photo of Nicci Webb she had taken from the woman's Facebook profile. "Do you recognize this woman?"

Shannon and Christian studied it. Patrick walked over and peered at the photo as well. One by one, they shook their heads and answered no.

"Who is she?" Shannon asked.

Josie pocketed her phone. "Her name is Nicci Webb. Her remains were found near Trinity's cabin."

Shannon splayed a hand over her chest. "What? What do you mean 'remains'? You found her… her body?"

Christian's voice was husky, as though he was trying to hold back a wave of emotion. "Are you sure it was this Webb woman and not your sister?"

Josie held up her hands, gesturing for them to calm down. "Yes, we found Webb's body behind Trinity's cabin. It was badly decomposed. We can't tell how she was killed, but we believe she was murdered, given the fact that she disappeared almost three weeks ago from her hometown which is located over forty miles from here, and her remains were found here." Josie didn't mention the fact that her bones had been pinned down in some sort of sick display. Not only did she not want to go there with them, but Mettner, as the lead detective, had forbidden it. "The remains definitely belong to Nicci Webb, a forty-five-year-old sixth grade teacher from Keller Hollow. The medical examiner confirmed her identity using dental records."

Christian sagged with relief.

Shannon said, "You're saying that someone took Trinity and then left someone else's body behind at the cabin?"

Josie nodded, grimacing. "Yes, it appears that way."

"But why?" Shannon asked. "Why would someone do that?"

"We don't know at this point," Josie answered. "We're trying to find a connection between Trinity and Webb, if one exists. We are still doing everything we can to locate Trinity. There is something else I need to discuss with you."

She told them about Trinity's hidden message inside the Fiat.

Christian said, "Why would she write 'Vanessa'?"

"We were hoping you guys might be able to tell us," Josie replied.

Christian and Shannon looked at one another, then turned to Patrick, who shrugged. Looking back at Josie, Shannon said, "Honey, I'm sorry but we don't know why she would do that. She never called you Vanessa. She always referred to you as Josie. I mean, that's who you are—Josie."

Josie felt some of her anxiety ease. She hadn't expected her mother to understand this, and she felt heartened by Shannon's words. "Give it some thought," Josie said. "Maybe it will come to you. Let me text Gretchen and ask her to send me the photos she took of the inside of the door."

She fired off a text to Gretchen and then she addressed the Paynes again. "We've got a warrant out for the contents of her phone, but it could take a while for us to get permission to get into it. Things would move faster if I had your permission for us to go through it. You're her next of kin."

Christian said, "Of course. Whatever you need to do."

"Thank you," Josie said. "Her phone is pin protected. Do any of you know it, by any chance?"

Christian and Shannon looked at one another, faces drawn. Shannon said, "I don't."

"Did you try her birthday?" Christian asked.

"We can," Josie said. "But I don't think she would use something that easy. Her birthday is public knowledge, especially after our long-lost-twin story went public. It would be too easy for someone to figure out if they got their hands on her phone. She's a celebrity, so privacy is important to her personal security."

Patrick said, "It's the day you two were reunited."

The three of them looked at him. He placed his phone on the table and shook the hair from his eyes.

"How do you know that?" Shannon asked.

Patrick rolled his eyes. "Cause she told me. She had a virus on her phone the last time she was home. She asked me to help her get rid of it. I had to do a factory reset and then download all her contacts, reinstall apps, all that stuff. Anyway, I told her I had to reset the pin. She put it in and then she said, 'that's the day Josie and I were reunited.'" He met Josie's eyes. "That was a big deal to her, you know?"

Josie's heart skipped a beat. "I know," she said. "It was a big deal to me, too."

She thought of the questions that Trinity had asked her before she left Josie's house. *What was the best thing that ever happened to me? What was the worst thing that ever happened to me?*

Christian said, "The day you two were reunited? You knew each other for years before we found out the truth."

"Right," Josie said. "But we found out in March three years ago." Turning to Patrick, she asked, "Do you know if she meant the day we were rescued in the forest or the day we got the DNA results?"

"Don't know," Patrick said. "Which one felt more significant to you?"

A shiver worked its way up Josie's spine. She remembered the first time they'd talked about it—about the possibility. They'd both been tied up, prisoners of a madwoman. Shortly after that, Trinity had been marched out into the woods to be executed. A neighbor had helped free Josie so she could go after her sister. "The day in the forest," she said. "But I don't know the exact date."

"Would it be in your police reports?" Christian asked.

"Yes," Josie said. "Good idea." Her phone buzzed. It was Gretchen, sending the photos of the message Trinity had left on the car door. Josie pulled one up and showed them. No one spoke.

Finally, Christian said, "What's that underneath the name?"

"We don't know," Josie said. "Maybe she started to write something else but didn't have time?"

There was only silence. No one hazarded a guess as to what Trinity had been trying to communicate with the strange symbols.

"There is one more thing I'd like you to see." She pulled up a photo of the comb and showed them. "This was dropped off at my house in the early morning hours before Trinity left. That was a month ago. It came in a box wrapped in plain brown paper with her name written on it. She opened it and looked inside right before she left. I didn't know what was in the box until our

Evidence Response Team found it in her suitcase. Obviously, we'll have it processed, but I'm wondering if it holds any significance to any of you?"

They all studied it. Finally, Patrick said, "It looks familiar."

Shannon and Christian turned to him. Shannon gave him a wavering smile. "Familiar? You know this isn't your sister's style at all, right?"

He shrugged. "I didn't say she'd wear it. I just said it looks familiar for some reason."

"Where have you seen it or something like it before?" Josie asked.

He met her eyes. "I really don't remember."

Christian said, "Son, this is important. If you've seen this comb before, we need to know."

Patrick took a step back. "Dad, I just told you, I don't remember."

"Your sister's in trouble, Pat," Christian continued.

"You're not listening to me, Dad," Patrick shot back. "You think I'm not worried about her?" He pointed to his chest. "You think I don't care? I'm closer to her than you guys."

Josie lowered her voice, making her tone soothing. "Patrick, when were you last in touch with Trinity?"

He glared at his father. "A little over a month ago. It was right before she rented the cabin, but she was still staying at your house. She met me at the café on campus."

They hadn't even invited her. That was Josie's first thought, which was silly and childish given the circumstances. Still, as if reading her mind, Patrick said, "You were at work. She was really upset, you know, about her work situation and all. I think she just needed company."

Shannon said, "What did you two talk about?"

"Just stuff."

Josie noticed a vein throbbing in Christian's forehead. His words came out through gritted teeth. "What. Kind. Of. Stuff?"

Josie stepped between father and son before Patrick could respond, before the situation could escalate. She'd never seen this kind of tension between the two of them before. To Patrick, Josie said, "Did she say anything about someone following her? Someone stalking her? Did she indicate that she was worried about anything? Besides losing her place at the network, that is?"

"She just said that she thought she was onto some big story—that she thought she could make contact with a major source—but it fell through. She was pretty disappointed. She said it would be bigger than the Mila Kates stalker story."

"Did she give you any idea what the story was?" Josie asked.

"She didn't want to talk about it. I asked her but she would only say it was some kind of cold case."

Shannon interjected. "What kind of cold case would be more sensational than the Mila Kates stalker story? That happened in real time."

Patrick said, "I don't know, but she said she wouldn't only solve it, but she'd be part of it. I didn't really get what she was saying, but whenever I asked a question, she just told me to forget it since it wasn't going to happen anyway."

"Her research was in the boxes that she had with her," Josie told their parents. "They weren't in her car or in the cabin. We're operating under the theory that whoever took her also took the boxes. Her assistant might be able to help us with what was in at least one of them. She's on her way here now."

Josie turned toward the conference room door. Christian filled the space where her body had been, eye to eye with his son. "Why would Trinity be telling you all these things?"

"Christian," Shannon said, her tone a warning.

"Because I'm her brother," Patrick said, exasperated.

"But you're just a—" he broke off.

"Christian, that's enough," Shannon said.

Patrick's face flushed. "Just a kid? Is that what you were going to say, Dad?" He said the word 'dad' with sarcastic emphasis.

"This is not the time," Shannon said, looking back and forth between them.

"I'm an adult now, Dad," Patrick told his father. "Not that you would know, or care."

With that, he stomped out of the room.

Immediately, Shannon whirled on her husband. "What were you thinking? Our daughter is missing, and you're choosing now to pick a fight with Patrick?"

"I wasn't picking a fight," Christian exclaimed.

"You were."

"You know what? I need to make some calls." He stormed out, heading in the opposite direction to Patrick.

Alone with Josie, Shannon hugged herself. Tears streamed down her face. Josie walked around to the far end of the table and picked up a box of tissues which she handed to Shannon.

"I'm sorry about this," Shannon said, pulling a tissue from the box and dabbing her eyes. "They haven't been getting along... well, pretty much since Pat hit puberty."

"It's okay," Josie said.

"There are fourteen years between you girls and Patrick. When Patrick was a boy, we used to have problems with Trinity talking to him about adult subjects, letting him watch movies that weren't appropriate for his age, giving him books he was too young to read."

Josie laughed. She could imagine Trinity doing this, and she had noticed from the start that Trinity had a very special bond with their little brother. It hurt her heart a little that she didn't have the same relationship with him. She barely had any relationship with him. He'd been a teenager when Josie came into their lives. It was tough finding common ground with Patrick. But Trinity had a shared history with him. "Patrick's right, though," Josie told Shannon, "They're very close."

"I know. They always were. Trinity adores him. She was so excited when we told her we were pregnant. She couldn't wait for him to arrive. She helped me with him and as he got older, she did more and more with him. She always—" Shannon didn't finish.

"What is it?" Josie said.

Shannon used another tissue to swipe at the fresh tears spilling down her cheeks. "She always wanted a sibling. We never kept you a secret from her, and she felt cheated by your… death."

"No one ever told me that," Josie said.

"Well," Shannon said, sucking in a deep breath. "Why would we? Remember how overwhelmed we all were when we were reunited? Instead of trying to catch up on lost time, I was the one who suggested we should start from where we are, wasn't I?"

CHAPTER TWENTY-ONE

Josie told Shannon that they could all go back to her and Noah's house to wait for news, but she insisted on staying at the station house for the time being. Josie assured her that they could remain in the conference room as long as they liked. She went back upstairs to the great room, excited to see Mettner at his desk, scrolling through some documents on his computer.

"What've you got?" Josie asked as she approached.

"This is the dump from Trinity's laptop." Mettner sighed, his finger clicking the mouse repeatedly. "There's a lot of stuff on here. I mean, a lot. This has got to be notes and research on every story she ever did."

"Emails?" Josie asked.

Mettner said, "Those weren't saved to the laptop, so no, but if she's logged into her email on her laptop, and we can get it open, you could probably just open the browser or the app and access it."

"Did you try to get into it?"

Mettner stopped scrolling and looked at Josie. "It uses facial recognition to open it."

Josie smiled. "I can help you with that."

"First help us get into her phone, would you?" Gretchen said. "We had to charge it since it was dead. There should be enough juice in it now for you to go through it." She stood and retrieved Trinity's phone from her desk, handing it over to Josie.

Josie placed it next to her keyboard while she used her computer to access the police reports from the Belinda Rose case from three years ago. That was the case during which they'd been reunited. The exact date, which Trinity used for her passcode, would be in the reports. It took a few minutes of sifting through the file to find the date that she and Trinity had first discussed the possibility that they were sisters. March 23, 2017. Josie picked up the phone and typed in 03232017. Incorrect passcode. She tried a few more variations before hitting on the correct one: 32317. The screen came to life, its wallpaper aglow with a photo of Trinity sitting in her spot at the morning anchor desk at her network. The photo had been taken from an angle, so Trinity wasn't looking directly at whoever had taken it—probably her assistant. Instead, she smiled confidently at a studio camera beside a teleprompter. Her back was straight, her legs crossed at the ankles. She wore a tight-fitting, muted pink, peplum dress with matching pale pink stilettos. As ever, her hair and make-up were perfect.

Most people might have thought that Trinity was self-absorbed for having a photo of herself as her cell phone wallpaper. She could come off as self-centered, Josie knew, but if you looked more deeply, you'd understand it was merely her ambition that made her seem that way. It was her drive, pure and simple. In the past six weeks, Trinity had been in freefall, with not just her job at risk, but her identity. This photo was Trinity in her element, at the top of her game. It was her reminder that she had been there once, and she could get there again. Even if she didn't believe it.

The phone and text icons had several notifications hovering over them. Josie ignored them and searched Trinity's contacts first, looking for Nicci Webb's name. It wasn't there. She then pulled up the call history and scrolled back a month, finding incoming and outgoing calls from Shannon and Jaime, Trinity's assistant. There were two calls to her co-anchor, Hayden Keating and two calls to someone listed in her contacts simply as Drake. The last call to him had been only days before Trinity packed up and left the cabin. Josie didn't recognize the name. She closed the call list and opened Trinity's texts.

There were text messages going back four months between her and Drake, most of them brief and to do with when and where to meet. There was a single message from Trinity to Drake a week before Trinity left the network for Denton that hinted at the nature of their relationship. *Last night was fantastic.* Minutes later, Drake had answered: *Let's do it again soon.*

Had Trinity been seeing someone?

Josie hadn't seen Patrick on her way back up to the second floor. She had no idea if he was still in the building or if he'd gone back to campus, so she texted him: *Did Trinity ever mention a guy named Drake?*

His response came back seconds later: *No, sorry.*

She found Shannon and Christian in the conference room and asked them, but neither of them had ever heard Trinity mention someone by that name. Back upstairs, she ran Drake's phone number through one of their databases, coming up with his full name, age, and address. Drake Nally, thirty-seven years old, a resident of New York City. She tried looking up more information on him but found nothing of use.

"You got something from the phone?" Gretchen asked.

Josie told Gretchen and Mettner what she'd found. "I'm going to call him," she said. "See what he can tell me. It may be nothing, but at this point, every angle is worth looking at."

Mettner nodded. Josie used Trinity's phone to call. On the sixth ring, a man's voice answered. "Trinity," he said. "I haven't changed my mind."

For a split second, Josie considered trying to impersonate her sister to find out what he hadn't changed his mind about, but as quickly as the thought flitted through her head, it was gone. Instead, she said, "Drake Nally? This is Trinity's sister, Detective Josie Quinn."

A beat of silence.

"I know who you are," he said. "She talks about you all the time. Why do you have her phone? Is she okay?"

"Have you watched the news at all today, Mr. Nally?"

"No, I've been in meetings all day. Why? What happened? Is she okay?"

"How do you know Trinity, Mr. Nally?" Josie asked.

He made a noise of frustration. "Agent Nally."

"I'm sorry, what?"

"Special Agent Nally. I'm an FBI agent with the New York field office. I know who you are, and I know what you're trying to do here, so let me save you some time. Trinity and I met last year while she was covering a story. We've been seeing each other, sort of, for the last few months. You didn't know who I was which means she didn't tell you about me. If you're calling me on her phone to get information from me then something bad has happened to her. I'd really like to know what."

Josie took a deep breath. "If you know what I'm trying to do, then you know I'm going to need to verify your identity before I give out any information."

His tone was one of barely controlled rage. "My SAC is Erin Bacine."

"Give me a minute," Josie said. "In the meantime, turn on the news."

She put the phone on mute and set it on her desk. It took fifteen minutes to confirm with Drake's Special Agent in Charge in the FBI New York field office that he was, indeed, who he claimed to be. When she picked up Trinity's phone again, unmuted it, and said hello, Drake answered, "I saw the news. Text me the address of your station there. I'll be there later tonight."

"Agent Nally," Josie said. "I really need you to answer some—"

"I know," he said. "You'll have a chance to ask your questions, but this is something we need to discuss in person. I'm on my way."

Then he hung up.

CHAPTER TWENTY-TWO

Josie stared at the phone for a long moment after Drake disconnected. He wasn't just coming to the station house because he had been in some kind of relationship with Trinity. This was something else altogether. She checked the time on her phone. It was after eight in the evening and he was driving straight to Denton. "This is something we need to discuss in person," had never sounded so ominous. She updated Mettner and Gretchen. Then, using Trinity's phone, she texted Drake the address of Denton police headquarters. She jumped when she felt a hand on her shoulder.

"It's just me," Noah said.

Josie looked up at him and tried to smile.

"Lisette's downstairs in the conference room with Shannon and Christian. Your brother went back to his dorm room."

Josie stood. "Thank you. I'll go see her."

"You might want to wait," Noah said. "Mett, Gretchen? Trinity's assistant just arrived. She's down in the lobby. I told Sergeant Lamay to put her in interview room one."

The two detectives stood, Gretchen grabbing her notepad and pen and Mettner his phone. "You guys want to watch on the CCTV?" Mettner asked. "I don't want all four of us in there. She's not a suspect, we just need to ask her some questions. Less is more in this case, I think."

Noah gave him the thumbs-up. He placed a palm on Josie's back and they followed their colleagues down the hall, stepping into the small anteroom next to interview room one where a large television screen showed a young woman with long blonde hair, smartly dressed in skinny jeans, knee-high leather boots, and a matching brown cashmere wrap sweater. She had perched on the edge of the table inside the room, her head bent to her phone, manicured fingers tapping away at its screen. Josie had only met her once, a year earlier, and she had been far too hungover to retain any details about the woman other than that she was probably in her twenties and that Trinity likely overworked her. At the time, Josie had been following a lead on a homicide case, had met up with her ex-fiancé and gotten drunk. Trinity had driven deep into the mountains to get Josie back, bringing her assistant along to drive Josie's vehicle back to Denton.

Gretchen and Mettner stepped inside the interview room and the woman strode confidently toward them, extending the hand not holding her phone toward Gretchen first and then Mettner. "Jaime Pestrak," she said. "The other officer told you I'm Ms. Payne's assistant, right?"

"He did," Mettner said. "Thank you for coming. Please, have a seat."

He made introductions for himself and Gretchen and the three of them sat at the table. Jaime kept her phone on the tabletop, occasionally responding to notifications as Mettner took her through a number of questions.

"How long have you worked for Trinity—Ms. Payne?"

"Three years."

"Is she the only person you work with at the network?" Gretchen asked. "Or are you assistant to some of the other anchors?"

Jaime lifted her long blonde locks from her shoulders and fluffed them. "Just Trinity."

"When is the last time you were in contact with her?" Mettner asked.

They had already established the last calls and texts between Trinity and her assistant from Trinity's phone, but Mettner was covering every base. "It was like a month ago. She emailed me. By the way, I found the name of the reporter whose stuff she asked me to ship to her. Codie Lash. She used to have Trinity's job."

Gretchen asked, "Did Trinity replace her?"

Jaime gave her phone a quick tap and swipe. "No. Codie Lash was before her time. Besides, she was murdered."

In the CCTV room, Josie and Noah looked at one another. Josie took out her phone and Googled 'Codie Lash anchor'. Pictures of a woman in her forties with short brown hair and a thousand-watt smile filled the screen. Beneath was a long list of headlines, all of them reporting the same thing: *Award-winning Journalist Codie Lash Murdered on Her Way to Charity Gala.*

Josie clicked on the first link and quickly skimmed the article while Mettner and Gretchen continued asking Jaime questions. There was a grainy black and white video of Codie and a man being confronted by another man in a hoodie on a sidewalk. It looked as though a surveillance camera from across the street had captured the incident. Josie squinted at her screen, but the attacker's face wasn't visible, and the video cut off before any physical contact between the mugger and the Lash couple took place.

"How was she murdered?" Mettner asked. "Do you know?"

"I'm not sure. I really didn't know anything about her except what I just told you."

According to the news article Josie had clicked on, Lash, along with her husband, had been killed during a mugging in New York City six years earlier. Jaime had probably still been in high school. No wonder she didn't remember or even care to know the details.

Jaime continued, "Trinity asked me to see if any of her personal effects were still around at the news station. It took some digging, but I found a box of stuff from when they cleaned out her office after she died. Apparently, no one came to claim her things and whoever worked with her back then couldn't bring themselves to throw her stuff away, so it was just in storage in the closet of one of the dressing rooms."

"Trinity asked you to send her that box?" Mettner confirmed.

"Yeah. I don't know why, though. I didn't ask. She probably wouldn't tell me anyway. She was always afraid of getting scooped if she was onto something she thought might be big. Even after she became anchor, she was like that."

"Do you remember what was in the box?" Gretchen asked.

"Just a bunch of old stuff. Some awards she won, a sweater, some of her old notes, some hair stuff, a pair of shoes. Random stuff."

"Besides notes, were there any documents of any kind? Any photos?"

Jaime shook her head. "I don't think so. Oh, well, there was a picture of her and her husband in a frame. I mean, I guess it was her husband. I'm not really sure."

"You sent the whole box to her?" Mettner said. "There wasn't anything in particular that she was looking for?"

"She never said," Jaime replied. "She just wanted whatever I could find."

"Do you have any ideas of your own about what she might have wanted with Codie Lash's old stuff?" Mettner asked.

Again, Jaime's attention was diverted to her phone. Tap, tap, tap, scroll, tap. Then she turned back to Mettner and Gretchen. "What does Trinity ever want with anything? A story. She's all about stories. Even now with the anchor position—I mean she's the co-host, she doesn't really have to chase stories, but it's like she's obsessed. Like she's always afraid they're going to take it away from her. Well, I guess they are now."

"Because of what she said about that college kid?" Gretchen probed.

"Yeah, and because the network is trying to get Mila Kates. You know who she is, right?"

They knew because Josie had told them. Nodding, Mettner said, "Trinity was working on a story about Codie Lash? If there were awards in her personal effects and she used to be co-host of the morning show, she must have been pretty accomplished."

Gretchen added, "I remember her. She was very successful and well-loved. It was pretty tragic when she was killed."

Mettner said, "Was Trinity doing a story on her life, or on her death?"

Jaime shrugged. "I don't know. Like I said, she probably wouldn't have told me anyway. She's a good boss, but she's really nuts about her stories."

Gretchen tapped her chin with the cap of her pen, a small frown on her face. "She didn't trust you? Her own assistant?"

Jaime rolled her eyes. "She didn't trust anyone! She probably trusted me most of all, but not enough to let me in on whatever she was working on at any given time. She even had this stupid code she wrote in that only she could understand so that if someone did see her notes, they'd have no idea what they said."

"Secret code?" Mettner asked. "Did it look like random lines and squiggles by any chance?"

"Yeah, pretty much."

Josie stood, ready to race into the interview room, but Noah put a hand on her forearm. "They'll show her the photo," he said.

On the screen, Gretchen pulled her cell phone out, put her reading glasses on, and found the photo of the inside of Trinity's door. She turned it toward Jaime. "Look under the name. Like that?"

Jaime peered at the photo, lips turned downward. "Yeah, that's it."

"Do you know what that says?" Mettner asked her.

"The code? No. I never knew what the hell she was writing when she used that. I used to tease her that she was writing in hieroglyphs. It was like some kind of shorthand or something."

"Something she made up herself?" Gretchen asked.

"I don't know, but knowing Trinity, probably. Wait, was that from inside her car?"

"Yes," Mettner said. "When our Evidence Response Team used the fluorescent magnetic powder to lift latent fingerprints, they found this."

Jaime pointed to the photo. "You know Vanessa is her sister, right? Well, her real name is Josie but when they were babies, their parents named her Vanessa."

"We're aware," Mettner said.

"Is Josie here?"

Gretchen turned and looked at the camera, nodding subtly. In seconds, Josie was inside the room, standing before Jaime.

"Hey," Jaime said. "You look better than the last time I saw you."

"Thanks, I think," Josie said. "Jaime, how long was Trinity using her secret code to take notes?"

"As long as I've known her."

Josie took out her phone and pulled up the photo of Nicci Webb. "Do you recognize this woman?"

"No, I'm sorry. I don't. Who is she?"

"Her name is Nicci Webb. Does that name sound familiar?"

"No," Jaime answered. "What does she have to do with Trinity's disappearance?"

Josie ignored the question and asked another of her own. "Did Trinity ever talk about someone called Drake?"

"The FBI agent? She didn't talk about him much, but I know they were hot and heavy for a while."

"How do you know that?" Mettner asked.

Another eye-roll. "I'm her assistant, remember? I have access to almost everything in her life."

"Does Trinity have any friends who might know what she was working on?" Gretchen asked.

"Friends? Trinity didn't have time for friends. You were either family, a coworker, or a source."

Josie placed a palm on the table and leaned in toward Jaime. "Besides the Codie Lash materials, did Trinity ask you for anything else since she came here?"

"No."

"She had another box with her. We think it held documents. Do you have any idea what they might have been?"

"No, sorry."

"She said she was working on some huge story. Did she talk to you about that?"

"No, but she's been pretty out of contact with me since the network banished her. Like I said, she only contacted me to ask me to get her the Codie Lash stuff."

Gretchen said, "Jaime, did Trinity have a stalker?"

"None that I know of."

"We believe someone took Trinity," Mettner said. "We also believe that whoever that person was also took the box of Codie Lash's possessions as well as the other box that Trinity had with her. Do you have any idea who might have abducted her? Any idea who would be interested in what she was working on?"

Jaime's eyes diverted to her phone. Tap, tap, tap. Scroll, scroll, tap. A sigh. "I have no idea. Maybe she didn't tell you, but she was about to lose her job. Hayden told me she was out. I don't know why anyone would even care what she was working on."

"You've been very helpful, Ms. Pestrak," Mettner said. "We appreciate your coming all the way out here to speak with us especially this late at night."

"I'll be staying at the Eudora Hotel if you need me. You have my number," Jaime replied.

"Why did you come?" Josie blurted out.

Gretchen said, "Detective Quinn."

Jaime stared at Josie, confusion drawing a vertical line between her eyebrows. "Trinity's my boss. I thought I should be here. She might need me when you guys find her."

"But you just said she was out of a job. If that's the case, she wouldn't need you anymore, would she?" Josie said.

"She'll get another job, no problem," Jaime said. "She's really talented and driven as hell. I've met Mila Kates, you know. She's kind of an asshole, and she's not nearly as smart as Trinity."

Gretchen, perhaps picking up on the discomfort that Josie felt with the young woman, who hadn't yet shown any concern for Trinity's well-being, said to Jaime, "Trinity was abducted. Aren't you worried about her?"

Jaime looked past Gretchen and locked eyes with Josie. "You probably think because she's just a news anchor, she's not as tough as you, but she's just as badass as you are. The person dumb enough to kidnap her is the one I'd worry about."

CHAPTER TWENTY-THREE

In the stairwell, Josie told Noah, "Trinity's tough, no doubt, but she can't fight. Maybe if she took off one of her stilettos and used it to stab her attacker in the eye, but other than that, I'm not sure Jaime's technically correct."

Noah grimaced. "That's a nice visual. Thanks for that. Jaime was right about one thing: Trinity is smart. Any way she can find to stay alive, she's going to do it."

They emerged onto the first floor and headed toward the conference room. Inside stood Lisette Matson, leaning heavily on her walker as she spoke with Shannon and Christian. She turned as they entered, jerked her walker around and moved over toward Josie, nudging Noah out of her way. Her soft gray curls bounced as she moved, and her blue eyes gleamed as she smiled at Josie. She reached out a gnarled hand and Josie took it.

"Thank you for coming," Josie said softly.

"It's better than sitting around with all those old blue rinses at Rockview," Lisette said.

Josie couldn't help but laugh. "Gram, I'm pretty sure you're one of the oldest in that place."

"Mentally, I'm still in my twenties, dear." Lisette knew better than to ask Josie how she was holding up or to offer too much comfort. Lisette knew Josie better than anyone in the world. She knew that what Josie valued most in that moment was to maintain her focus so she could best help her team locate Trinity. "I hear you've got half decent coffee here," Lisette added. "Why don't you show me where?"

Josie managed a small smile for her grandmother. "Come on," she said. "The break room is just down the hall. Noah can bring

Shannon and Christian up to speed on what we just found out from Trinity's assistant."

She shuffled along beside Lisette until they came to the break room which was also a functioning kitchen complete with a sink, refrigerator, several appliances, and a long table surrounded by several chairs. It was empty but Josie smelled freshly brewed coffee before they crossed the threshold. Lisette seated herself at the table while Josie prepared their drinks.

She sat across from her grandmother, pushing a mug toward her. Lisette said, "This shows real growth, you know."

"What's that?" Josie asked, sipping from her own mug.

"That you sent Noah to get me. That you wanted me here for moral support. Usually when there's some kind of incident, I'm the last to know. I'm proud of you, Josie."

"Thanks."

Before the moment could become too fraught with emotion, Lisette got right to business. "Do you have any idea who took your sister?"

"No," Josie admitted. "I don't know Trinity that well, Gram. Yes, we're sisters, and we've spent as much time together in the last three years as we could manage given both our careers, but Gram—"

"You know her well enough, Josie."

Josie lowered her voice. "No, I don't. I know how she takes her coffee. I know her favorite restaurant. I know she weighs less than me, but she eats like an NFL linebacker. I've been to her apartment. I know she values her career above all else. Those are the things I know about her. That doesn't add up to much. Do you realize, I don't even know what kind of childhood she had?"

Lisette sighed. "A happier one than you."

"Well, yeah," Josie said. "That's always been my assumption, but how do I really know for sure? I never even bothered to ask her."

"Shannon and Christian are good people," Lisette said.

"I'm not suggesting they aren't. Trinity… we all know she's ambitious… but Gram, she's even more closed-off and isolated than I am."

Lisette laughed. "I'm glad you realize that about yourself. Like I said, growth."

"I'm serious, Gram. In all the time I've known her, Trinity's never had a boyfriend. Never even dated anyone. Today I find out she was seeing an FBI agent for the last few months. She never even told me."

"Maybe it's not serious," Lisette argued. "Maybe she didn't want to start telling people until she knew it was going somewhere."

"It's not just that. Trinity literally has no friends. None. What kind of person has zero friends?"

Lisette reached across the table and covered Josie's hands with one of her own. The warmth and familiarity of her grandmother's touch soothed some of Josie's frayed nerves. "She has you, Josie."

Guilt from her last exchange with Trinity washed over her. "I don't think I count as a friend."

"Don't you? It was your name she wrote on her door just before she was taken. That's what Shannon and Christian told me."

"Not my name," Josie said. "She wrote Vanessa."

"Because she was trying to tell you something, dear. Point you in a direction. It would have been far quicker to write Josie than Vanessa, wouldn't it? There's something she wants you to see, Josie. What does Trinity know about you?"

Josie swallowed, her mouth dry. "She knows how I take my coffee. She knows my favorite restaurant, what my house looks like, who all my friends are, my boyfriend. She knows my romantic history, mostly because she was there after Ray died and when Luke and I broke up—as a reporter, not as my sister. She knows that I have—that I've had—a drinking problem. She knows that I value my career…"

"She knows that you're exceptional at what you do, Josie. She knows you'll follow the trail. She knows you've solved cases before by following the most unlikely clues. She trusts you to find her."

Josie fought to keep her voice from cracking. "I don't think I can."

"Nonsense. Think, Josie. Why Vanessa? What is she trying to tell you?"

Josie shook her head. "I don't know. I really don't, Gram."

"What does the name Vanessa evoke, Josie?"

"I don't know. The abduction? Our family? The past?"

"Which of those is most relevant here?" Lisette prodded.

"Gram, I don't know. The abduction, I guess."

"Because she was being abducted? Too easy. What else does the name Vanessa evoke?"

Josie felt like she was playing a game for which she didn't even know the rules. "The past?"

"She's pointing you in a direction, Josie. Toward the past. Probably quite far back."

"But we didn't even know each other far back in the past."

Lisette frowned. Trying a different tack, she said, "Do you have inside jokes? I know you've only been officially sisters for three years now, but surely you've developed some ways of communicating with one another that are unique to the two of you. Lots of friends have a shorthand of sorts."

"What did you say?"

"Shorthand," Lisette repeated. "An abbreviated way of communicating with one another that only the two of you understand."

"We don't, but Gram, when I was small, before you took the job at the jewelry store, you were a secretary, weren't you?"

Lisette's eyes widened. She pulled her hand away from Josie and wrapped both palms around her coffee mug. "Josie, are you okay?"

Something had been niggling at the back of Josie's mind since she, Gretchen, and Mettner had interviewed Jaime Pestrak. "This is important, Gram."

"We're talking about Trinity, dear."

"I know. This is about Trinity. How many years did you work as a secretary?"

Lisette shrugged. "Oh, decades. I started while I was still in high school. That was back in the fifties."

"Before computers," Josie said.

Lisette laughed. "Before any technology, really, unless you count typewriters."

"You used shorthand to take notes, didn't you? To transcribe meetings?"

"Why yes, we did," Lisette said. "It took weeks to learn it. There were two systems at the time: Gregg and Pitman. I learned Gregg. I used it all the way up until the late nineties. They still taught it in a lot of high schools then, too. The ones out here in rural Pennsylvania, at least. Then came lots of new technology. Shorthand went out of fashion."

"Do you remember it?" Josie asked, a spiral of excitement shooting from her stomach straight to her head. She took out her phone and searched for the photo of Trinity's door panel.

"I'm sure I do," Lisette said. "I'm not sure how well I could write it with my arthritis, but I used it for forty years. I could probably remember it. I bet the library has a few books on it if I needed to refresh my skills. But Josie, what is this all about?"

Josie turned her phone toward Lisette. "Under the name. Is that shorthand?"

Lisette took the phone from Josie, holding it in both of her hands which now shook. She stared at the photo. "I believe it is. It sure looks like Gregg shorthand to me."

Josie's heart felt like it might spring right out of her chest. "What does it say? Can you read it?"

"It says, if I remember my shorthand, 'read my day.'"

"Read my day?"

Lisette's brow lifted. "That can't be right, but I think it is. She must have misspelled or forgotten some letters."

"Read my day," Josie murmured.

"It could be dairy."

"No," Josie said. "Not day or dairy. Diary."

CHAPTER TWENTY-FOUR

"Shorthand?" Shannon said, eyes wide.

She stared across the conference room table at Josie and Lisette. Beside her, Christian reached over and rested a hand on her shoulder. He said, "Trinity learned shorthand from my mother when she was twelve years old."

Shannon glanced at him. "Oh wait, I remember that now. It was when your mom got sick, wasn't it?"

Josie didn't know much about her biological grandparents. Shannon's father had died of heart failure only three years before Josie found out about the Paynes, and her mother was in a skilled nursing facility for residents with advanced Alzheimer's. Josie had met Shannon's mother once, but the woman had no idea who her own daughter was, let alone the significance of Josie having been reunited with Shannon and her family. Both of Christian's parents were deceased. His father had served as a marine in the Vietnam War and died in combat. His mother raised him on her own, working as a paralegal for a large law firm to support him and his younger sister. She had passed of cancer decades earlier.

Christian looked at Josie. "Your grandmother, my mom, she got lung cancer when Trinity was in the sixth grade. She moved in with us so we could care for her. They treated it as aggressively as they could, but the cancer was too advanced. The doctors gave her a year to live. She made it eighteen months. She and Trinity were very close, especially during the last year of her life."

"I had no idea," Josie croaked.

Shannon added, "Trinity used to come home from school and spend the entire afternoon and evening sitting in her room with her."

Christian's eyes shone with tears. "She was very devoted to her. I know it meant a lot to my mom."

Beneath the table, Josie felt Lisette's hand slip into hers and squeeze.

"Trinity didn't want her to be alone," Shannon said. "I mean, she wasn't alone, we were there with her, but…"

Christian looked at his wife, whose eyes were now on the table. He cleared his throat. "Trinity had a hard time in school. Socially. Especially that year."

Shannon met her husband's eyes. "Your mother was her only friend during that time."

Christian pursed his lips and nodded. Turning back to Josie, he said, "They played cards and board games. Trinity would put on these little dance numbers for her to try to make her laugh. They watched television together. My mom taught her how to do her make-up."

"And taught her shorthand," Josie filled in.

Christian laughed. "It was their secret code. They used to leave little notes for one another that only they could understand."

Josie felt a piercing ache in her chest. She knew how much a grandparent could mean to a young girl. If it hadn't been for Lisette, Josie would never have survived her childhood. The woman who had posed as Josie's mother had been cruel and abusive. Lisette had fought to get custody of Josie and had done everything in her power to protect her. The day Josie finally, permanently, went to live with Lisette had been one of the best days of her life. It had been a turning point. Lisette and Josie had also played cards and board games. Lisette had taken Josie on many adventures: sledding, roller skating, beach vacations, amusement parks, Broadway musicals, museums. Although they hadn't had a literal secret code, they'd enjoyed certain rituals like picking each other wildflowers and leaving them in the vase in Lisette's foyer for one another, belting out the U2 song 'Beautiful Day' together whenever it came on the radio, and going out for ice-cream whenever one of them had a particularly bad day—whipped cream and sprinkles were required. Josie couldn't even imagine what might have happened to her if she had lost Lisette as a young girl. Emotionally, she had already been on precarious footing. That kind of devastation would have derailed her life entirely.

"Then your mom died," Josie said softly to Christian. "And Trinity was alone."

Shannon and Christian looked at one another again. Shannon reached up to where his hand rested on her shoulder and covered it with one of her own.

Lisette said, "That must have been devastating for her."

Shannon nodded. "It was. She struggled badly for a long time."

"We had to get her a therapist," Christian agreed. "We even considered home-schooling her."

Josie asked, "She was having trouble in school? With the other kids?"

"Yes," Shannon said. "No matter how many times we met with the principal or threatened legal action against the other kids who messed with her, it just continued. It got worse after her grandmother passed."

"It?" Josie said. "You mean bullying?"

Christian said, "Yes, she was bullied badly."

It was hard for Josie to imagine. Trinity was one of the most savagely confident people she knew. She worked in an industry that daily put her under a microscope. Josie had seen some of the derisive and downright nasty comments on social media directed toward Trinity at times, criticizing anything and everything: her weight, her skin, her teeth, her hair, her clothes, her shoes, her laugh, the tone of her voice. There was no end to the demeaning and cruel online commentary. Yet, Trinity had always been flippant about it. Sometimes she even read comments out loud to Josie and laughed at them. "It's just the nature of this business," she would say when Josie got upset about what people had written. "I just focus on my fans, and I have a lot of wonderful fans."

"She was bullied badly, but she went into a profession where every little thing about her would be under scrutiny and she would be subject to bullying and harassment on a daily basis," Lisette observed, as if reading Josie's mind. Under the table, she gave Josie's hand another squeeze.

Shannon gave a little laugh. "I know. It always seemed strange to me, too. But it was kind of like her giving every person who ever bullied her the finger, wasn't it? She becomes a journalist and ends up on the highest rated morning show in the country."

"She met that reporter, though, remember?" Christian said.

"What reporter?" Josie asked. "Codie Lash?"

"No, that wasn't her name," Shannon said, "It was some local correspondent. Trinity was fourteen, I think. She found some... remains in the woods. Because it was such a small town, a reporter came to interview her. She was completely enamored of the woman. It was after that she decided to be a reporter."

"Remains? Human remains?" Josie asked, trying to keep her voice level.

Shannon waved a hand dismissively. "It was the body of a hunter who had gone missing the year before, an older gentleman. It was very sad. He must have gotten lost because when Trinity found him, he was curled up around his rifle. His clothes were still in pretty good shape and his wallet and hunting license were there."

No connection, Josie thought. "What was Trinity doing when she found him?" Josie asked.

"She was volunteering at a nature preserve at the time," Shannon explained.

Christian laughed. "Volunteering? No, she was doing community service."

"Hard to imagine Trinity *volunteering* for much," Josie agreed. "Community service for what?"

"She got into a fight with a girl at school," Christian said.

"No, not a girl from her school," Shannon said. "It was someone from a different school."

"Oh, right. Well, it's not important. They both got in trouble. There were criminal charges brought against both of them, but our attorney made an out-of-court arrangement for her to do community service, and she had to go to therapy although she was already seeing a psychologist at that point because of everything else: losing my mom, the school stuff and—"

He broke off and his face went ashen.

"And what?" Josie said.

Christian looked at Shannon. "*Vanessa*," he said.

Shannon's hand flew to her chest. "Oh my God. I can't believe I forgot."

"Forgot what?" Josie asked.

Shannon shifted uncomfortably in her seat. "After your grandmother died, Trinity became kind of fixated on death."

"Understandable," Josie said. "She was so young."

"But she became fixated on *you*," Christian said.

"Me?"

"Well, not you, specifically because we thought you were dead, but the idea of you," Shannon explained. "She kept asking questions about you although there wasn't much to tell. You were only three weeks old when you were taken from us. Then she…"

Christian took over. "She started telling people she had a twin sister. She said you were away at boarding school. Sometimes she told people you were in a foreign exchange student program."

"Oh God," Josie said.

"That was one of the reasons we had to get her into therapy," Shannon said. "But the therapist said it was her way of processing her grief and that we should let her work through it."

"Did the therapist, by any chance, suggest she keep a diary?" Josie asked.

"Letters," Shannon said. "She told Trinity to write letters to you."

"Do you still have them?" Josie asked.

"We might," Shannon said.

"We have a bunch of Trinity's stuff in the attic," Christian said. "She didn't have room for it in New York City, but she didn't want to part with it either."

"I need you to go home and see if you can find those letters or any sort of diary she might have written at that time. I need you to do it as soon as possible," Josie said.

"We'll do it," Shannon said. "But Josie, why on earth would Trinity want you to read a bunch of letters she wrote to you when she was in high school? What does that have to do with her going missing now?"

"I don't know," Josie said. "But it's the only clue we've got. I have to see where it leads."

CHAPTER TWENTY-FIVE

Alex eavesdropped on his mother's side of the phone call from the end of the hall. He watched as one of her bare feet tapped against the wooden floor. Her free arm was clutched against her stomach, swathed in a hard cast that ran from her hand to just below her elbow. When she hung up, a grin stretched wide across her face. She beckoned him to her and took one of his hands, twirling him around. "Dance with me!" she exclaimed. "I've just had the best news! Just wait until your father gets home."

But Alex doubted that any news would make his father happy. Not after the latest incident. Once again, Alex had earnestly assured his mother that he had tried to stop Zandra before she knocked her off the back deck. But he hadn't gotten there in time, and Zandra had let their mother scream for a very long time while she stared at the bone protruding from the skin of her forearm. Looking at Hanna now, he realized that the sight of her latest injury—of the sharp, jagged end of her bone—had made him feel like dancing. But he couldn't tell anyone that. They wouldn't understand.

Zandra was locked away again, and now Alex had to sleep out back in a shed his father had built—even in the freezing cold.

When Francis came home, Hanna told him how someone had bought almost her entire collection; how they wouldn't need to worry about money for a very long time. Alex expected fury from his father for some reason, but he was jubilant. Happier than Alex had ever seen him. Hanna danced through the foyer with Francis that night as well. They had a bottle of wine and let Alex eat a second helping of dinner before Francis sent him out back for the night.

In the morning, Alex waited by the back door for his mother to wake up and let him inside. She sang as she cooked breakfast, sashaying around the kitchen in her bare feet. She served him bacon and eggs, and he shoveled it into his mouth. His father didn't acknowledge him when he came into the kitchen. Instead, he went over to where Hanna stood by the stove, cupped her rear end with his hand and kissed her neck.

He sat across from Alex, and Hanna served him coffee. The spoon clinked around inside the mug. Francis said, "Hanna, you left a mess in the bedroom."

His voice was low but taut, like a string about to snap. Hanna froze and turned slowly to him, a puzzled look on her face. "What?"

He drew each word out. "You. Left. A. Mess. In. The. Bedroom."

"Oh, well, I'll clean up after I make breakfast."

Francis said, "Hopefully no one will trip and fall over the clothes you left on the floor before that."

"Clothes on the floor?" she said. "You sure were in a hurry to get them off last night."

"You didn't make the bed," he added. "And your make-up and hair ties are all over the dresser."

With a flustered sigh, Hanna threw her spatula down and stomped out of the room. Alex counted her footsteps on the stairs. Francis said, "Boy, keep an eye on that bacon, would you?"

Alex walked over to the stove, picked up the spatula and pushed the greasy meat around inside the pan. He had never cooked bacon before. He had no idea how to do it or when it would be done so he kept pushing it around. After a few minutes, Francis said, "Isn't it done?"

"I—I don't know," Alex stammered.

Francis's chair scraped across the tiles as he stood. "Stupid, stupid, *useless* boy," he muttered. He pushed Alex out of the way and then held his hand out for the spatula. "Give me that, boy."

But Alex didn't want to. He didn't want to give his father anything anymore. He was tired of yielding to him and his arbitrary demands. He held fast to the handle of the spatula.

"Boy," Francis said, his voice rising. "I said, give me that!"

He seized the flat part of the handle, trying to snatch it from Alex's hand. With a grunt, Alex began to wrestle him for it. With each push and pull, Francis grew more frustrated. Finally, he reached up, snaked a hand behind Alex's head and pushed with all his might. Alex's face slammed into the sizzling pan of bacon. A scream ripped from Alex's throat as he scrambled away from the stove. His face was on fire. He ran to the kitchen sink and let the water run cold before thrusting his head beneath it.

It didn't help.

By the time his mother came back into the room, led by his screams, Francis was again seated at the table, calmly sipping his coffee and reading the newspaper.

CHAPTER TWENTY-SIX

While Shannon and Christian drove the two hours back to their home in Callowhill to find Trinity's letters, Josie brought Lisette home with her, and freshened up the guest bedroom so that Lisette could stay with them for the time being. It was ten at night, and poor Trout had been alone all day, so she took him for a run and fed him, checking her phone every few minutes to see if there was any word on Trinity. There wasn't.

On her way back to the station house, Mettner called to let her know that Special Agent Drake Nally had arrived. "I'll be there in ten minutes," she told him.

"We're in the conference room. We'll wait for you."

Josie nearly forgot to put her vehicle in park after pulling into the municipal parking lot. She sprinted through the crowd of shouting reporters stationed at the back door and up to the first level. The conference room door was open. Around the table sat Gretchen, Mettner, and Noah together with Drake. Josie took in his dark brown eyes, neatly trimmed goatee and charcoal-colored suit. When he saw Josie, his face flushed. His lips moved as though to speak but no words came out. He stood up, and Josie saw he was tall and rangy, every bit the imposing federal agent except for the shock on his face. Drake walked around the table and extended a hand, finally managing to find some words.

"Sorry," he said. "You just… you look exactly like her. When she's not all made up, I mean."

"Thank you for coming," Josie said. "I assume the team brought you up to speed on all the developments. Not that there's much to report. We've got far more questions than answers."

He nodded and motioned to a thick file on the table in front of where he'd been sitting. "They did. I'm sorry I couldn't talk to you about this over the phone but it's a lot to… get into."

Josie looked at Mettner pointedly, mentally asking if he'd told Drake about the remains. He gave a brief shake of his head. Mettner was still keeping that detail close. Since Drake was here as a civilian, and not as an FBI agent, there was no need to tell him any details about the investigation that they deemed sensitive.

"What's in the file?" Josie asked, turning back to Drake.

Drake remained standing while Josie sat down between Gretchen and Mettner. Noah sat across from her, next to Drake's chair.

Drake pulled the file closer to him and placed a large palm over it. "In a minute," he said.

Mettner spoke up. "With all due respect, Agent Nally, you're not here in your official capacity. You're here as a known associate of a high-profile citizen who was abducted from our town, so we're going to be the ones asking questions."

Drake's lips were a thin line. Josie could see the barely perceptible movement of his jaw as he ground his teeth together. He removed his hand from the file, pushed it toward Mettner and sat down, adjusting his suit jacket and tie. He said, "I will answer any questions you have, but I need to know one thing before we start. The news reports state that some personal items may have been taken from Trinity's vehicle along with her. May I ask what those were?"

"Why?" Josie asked. "Why do you need to know?"

"Because she took something from me, and I have a right to know if that thing was one of the items taken during her abduction."

Mettner didn't open the file. Instead he pushed it over to Gretchen. She put on her reading glasses and opened it up. Josie glanced at the contents and saw the familiar layout of an autopsy report.

Mettner told Drake, "Two letter boxes. One of them had the personal effects of the late news anchor, Codie Lash, which Trinity's assistant had shipped to her from New York. We don't know what the other box contained."

Drake let out a long sigh and rubbed his hands over his face. His shoulders slumped.

Noah said, "I'm guessing you do know what was in it."

"It was a file. A very large file. Trinity had compiled it over the last two months. She was obsessed. It was a story she wanted to tackle. A serial killer."

Gretchen turned more pages in the file until she came to some photographs of a skeleton—except that it wasn't a normal skeleton. "Mettner," Gretchen said, the tone of her voice higher than normal.

Josie had to grip the arms of her chair to keep from jumping out of it. Gretchen flipped through more of the photos. All of them were the same. Torso in the middle circled by small bones. The bones of the arms together at six o'clock with the pelvic bone sitting at their knobby ends, along with the skull, and the leg bones at two o'clock. In one of the photos, the pelvic bone and skull were at the two o'clock position, at the ends of the leg bones instead of the arm bones.

"Mett," Josie said.

She pressed her back into the chair so that he could lean across her and see the photos for himself. Drake opened his mouth to speak, but Mettner held up a hand to silence him. He glanced at Noah, who stood, walked around the table and stared at the photos. A moment later, his hand settled on Josie's shoulder. He looked at Drake. "What is this?"

"That's the serial case I was just talking about. The Bone Artist."

Josie said, "Why does that sound familiar?"

Drake replied, "He was active in Pennsylvania beginning in 2008."

Gretchen said, "One of his victims was found in Philadelphia, but it wasn't my case. Someone on day shift caught that one, but the FBI swooped in and took over. That was the last I heard of it.

I had my own caseload. I never heard anything about it after that. There was a task force, although they never caught the guy."

A muscle ticked in Drake's jaw. "The Philadelphia victim was a thirty-three-year-old guy named Kenneth Darden. He lived in a suburb. Left his house after dinner for a late doctor's appointment. His car was in the doctor's parking lot, but he never made it to the appointment and never made it home."

"No cameras in the doctor's lot?" Mettner cut in.

"Nope. Not back then. Not in a low-crime suburb. Exactly thirty days after he disappeared his bones were found arranged on the bank of the Schuylkill River in Philadelphia."

"Arranged?" Josie said. "Like these photos?"

Drake held a hand out to Gretchen, and she gave him a stack of photos. He riffled through them, plucked out a color photograph, and handed it to Josie. She stared at an eerie facsimile of the scene she'd found behind Trinity's cabin that morning. "The case was covered on the news from time to time, but they never showed… this."

"These were never made public. There were some witnesses who saw the bones who talked about it, but no photographs were ever released."

Noah asked, "They were all like this?"

Drake said, "Always. The torso—rib cage and spine—is always in the center with all the small bones from the hands and feet as well as the clavicles circling it. The arm bones are at six o'clock and the leg bones are at two o'clock. The only difference is that sometimes the pelvic bone and skull are placed near the arm bones and sometimes they're near the leg bones. Sometimes the positions of the pelvic bone and skull are reversed."

Josie pulled another photo from the file in front of Gretchen, also of a set of human bones arranged just as Drake described them, this time in what looked like an abandoned gravel lot. "What's the difference? Why does he put them in different places?"

"We don't know," Drake said. "A lot of theories have been developed over the years as to why, but none of them have helped us get any closer to this guy. We've had teams study the arrangements trying to figure out what they mean. It's definitely ritualistic but no one has been able to come to a definitive conclusion. I can get you those reports if you'd like to read them, but I'm not sure that the meaning behind these displays will help us find the killer."

Mettner looked over Josie's shoulder. "How many victims in total?"

"Four," he answered. "Darden, in Philadelphia, was the third victim."

"What was their cause of death?" Gretchen asked.

Drake replied, "We don't know for certain."

Mettner asked, "None of the bones indicated stabbing or shooting or trauma of any kind?"

"No," Drake said. "We just know all the victims were abducted and killed in even-numbered years. In 2008 it started with Anthony Yanetti. Then in 2010 he killed Terri Abbott; in 2012, Kenneth Darden and then in 2014, Robert Ingram. All in the state of Pennsylvania. With every single one of them, exactly thirty days after they went missing, their bones turned up somewhere else arranged like that."

Josie thought of the Post-it notes she'd seen in Trinity's room before she'd torn them down. One of them had said OCD. Many serial killers had rituals—that didn't mean they had Obsessive Compulsive Disorder, but she supposed it was possible that the Bone Artist suffered from it. Even-numbered years; exactly thirty days between abduction and staging of the remains—Josie could see why Trinity had raised the possibility of OCD.

Noah reached down and tapped a finger on the photo in front of Josie. "Thirty days? It's our understanding that that's not long enough for a body to decompose that badly."

Drake said, "There are ways."

For a moment, Josie's heart stuttered before going back to its regular rhythm. She thought of Nicci Webb, missing for only seventeen days and reduced to a skeleton. She noted the name *Abbott, Terri* at the top of the photo. With her finger, she traced the woman's rib cage. "There's frayed material here, on her rib cage." She pointed to the femur bones. "And here as well. That's usually an indicator of scavenging, isn't it? Could animals accelerate the decomposition of a body if they… got to it?"

She looked up from the photo. Drake held her gaze for a long moment. As tension filled the room, she resisted the urge to tug at her collar. "There were some studies done at a body farm in Texas," he said quietly. "Scavenger birds—specifically black vultures—in a great enough number, say a gathering of about twenty to thirty—can reduce a body to skeletal remains in as few as four hours."

Josie's throat felt painfully dry. When she spoke, her voice cracked. "He leaves his victims outside? Exposed to the elements until they're picked clean?"

"That's what we think. Four different experts have examined the remains and opined that the victims were reduced to skeletons by avian scavengers over a relatively short period of time. Except for Anthony Yanetti, the first victim; there were no indicators of rodent or canid scavenging."

Gretchen said, "The first victim's remains were exposed to other animals in the wild then."

"That's what we believe, yes."

"We," Josie said. "As in the FBI?"

"Yes. The task force was disbanded in 2018 after the Bone Artist failed to kill for a four-year period. He's been inactive now for six years total."

Josie and her team exchanged a few looks. Drake didn't miss it. "What?" he asked. "What is it?"

"Any idea why he stopped?" Noah asked, ignoring his questions.

"None," Drake said. "We used to think that a serial killer who stopped killing was either dead or in prison. Of course, the Bind Torture Kill, or BTK Killer, threw that whole theory on its head. He started killing in the seventies, then took an eight-year break before killing three more people. His last murder was in 1991, and he was inactive until 2004 when he contacted the media again. He was out there living a perfectly normal life all those years."

"Didn't the Bone Artist contact the press as well?" Gretchen asked. "I think I remember seeing that on the news."

"Yes," Drake confirmed. "It was right before his last victim was found. The press had dubbed him the Boneyard Killer, but he didn't like that. He wrote to several reporters demanding to be called the Bone Artist. We were never able to trace him through any of those communications though."

Josie asked, "Was Codie Lash one of those reporters?"

"No," Drake said.

"Why was Trinity obsessed with this case?" Mettner asked.

Drake sighed and gave his head a little shake. "She thought she could 'make contact' with him."

Josie looked down at Terri Abbott's remains, staged like some kind of obscene art installation. *Oh Trinity*, she thought. *What have you gotten yourself into?*

CHAPTER TWENTY-SEVEN

Hanna ran a brush across the palette of skin-colored powder and then swiped at Alex's face. "Close your eyes, my love," she instructed. The make-up brush tickled his forehead, nose and the side of his mouth. "Okay," she told him when she'd finished.

He opened his eyes and watched her facial expression as she surveyed her work. "Much better," she assured him, but he could see fine lines at the corners of her eyes, a tightening in her cheeks when she pursed her lips.

"You can barely see the scar," she told him. A moment later, she said, "Zandra, darling, don't you think the make-up works well? You can barely see Alex's scar?"

Zandra met her mother's eyes. "I guess."

Hanna stared at her. "Zandra."

"What?"

"It's really important that we don't have any more incidents."

Zandra said, "You're joking, right?"

Hanna looked stricken. She threw the make-up brush onto the vanity with a clatter. "This is no joke. You cannot hurt me anymore. Alex tries to stop you, but he can't and then he gets punished. So you have to stop, do you understand? Restrain yourself. I don't want Alex sleeping in the shed like a dog. I don't want you locked away."

Zandra looked up at Hanna defiantly. "Then do something about it."

Alex saw Hanna's hands trembling as she fisted them at her sides. He stood up.

"Hanna," came a voice from the doorway. "What's going on here?"

The tension in the room was so thick and all-encompassing that none of them had heard Francis come into the house and up the steps. He leaned into the bedroom, watching them.

Hanna put her hands on Alex's shoulders and turned him away from the mirror. "Nothing," she said. "Everything's fine. We were just spending time together."

He took another step inside and folded his arms across his chest. "You know that the children can't be trusted. They shouldn't be in here."

"Zandra has promised not to hurt me again. They've both promised to be good."

"They're lying, Hanna."

She dropped her hands from Alex's shoulders and stepped in front of him, as if shielding him from the accusation. "I'm right here, Francis. I'm watching them."

A sneer curled his upper lip. "The way you were watching Alex the day he nearly burned his face off?"

Alex felt Hanna's whole body quiver—with rage or regret, he couldn't tell—but she said nothing.

"Zandra," Francis said. "Go back to your room."

CHAPTER TWENTY-EIGHT

Josie felt a cloying sense of dread overtake her as she watched Gretchen sift through the Bone Artist file Drake had brought, making piles for each of the four victims across the table. Josie said, "Four victims, multiple jurisdictions, a task force. This can't be the entire file."

"It's not. Those are just the highlights."

Noah said, "Trinity had access to all this?"

Josie noticed a vein in Drake's forehead bulge. "There's no way you would have let her view classified FBI files," she said.

"I'd lose my job, get into legal trouble," Drake agreed.

"But she found a way, didn't she?" Josie went on. "You're not even here for her, are you?"

Drake said nothing.

"Agent Nally?" Mettner prompted.

"Whatever she managed to take or copy from the FBI files, you don't want it going public," Josie accused. "Because if it ever got out that she had tricked you or stolen some information from you while you were dating, your career would be over."

The vein in Drake's forehead pulsed.

Josie kept going. "You said the photos were never released to the public. What else? The expert reports? Autopsy reports?"

His voice was so quiet, Josie strained to hear it. "Everything we had," he said. "Cleared suspects, the investigation, all of it. That's what I believe. There were things she talked about that she could only have known if she'd had access to the files."

"That's what you were fighting about," Josie said.

"How do you know we were fighting?"

"Because when I called you, you thought I was her, and you said, 'I haven't changed my mind.' You didn't ask her how she was, you didn't say it was good to hear from her. What was it that you didn't change your mind about?"

"Helping her," Drake said. "She wanted to solve the case." His eyes flitted to the table, a half smile curling one side of his mouth. "This woman—she thought she could solve a cold serial case that an entire task force and the FBI hasn't been able to solve."

Josie fought her own smile. "Of course she did. That's Trinity. But she's not wrong. Sometimes a fresh set of eyes makes all the difference. There was a blogger in Minnesota who helped solve the abduction case of Jacob Wetterling twenty-seven years after his kidnapping. She had help from law enforcement, of course, but it was her work that led to the perpetrator."

Mettner said, "Why would Trinity think she could make contact with him? What did she see that no one else did?"

"I don't know," Drake said, "She wouldn't tell me."

That was classic Trinity, Josie knew. She'd never tell Drake without some assurance that she wouldn't be shut out of the investigation.

"She had some kind of theory," Drake explained. "But I don't know what it was."

"What did she ask you to do?" Gretchen asked.

"She wanted to draw him out into the open, and I could arrest him, she said." He rolled his eyes. "It sounded like some kind of press stunt which could and would most likely go down in flames."

Noah said, "You weren't willing to take the chance."

Drake turned to him. "That's not how these things work. You guys know that. If she had a lead or a theory, she should have just told me and let me take it from there."

Josie said, "That's not how Trinity operates."

"No shit."

"How did she even become fixated on this case in the first place? Why this killer?" Gretchen asked.

Drake rubbed a hand over his face. "Right after we started seeing one another, she had some spat on the air with a correspondent. This was probably four months ago. The correspondent was doing an ongoing true crime segment. He chose a geographical area each week and prepared a segment on killers in those areas who had never been caught. That particular week, he did a piece on serial killers in the Northeast which included the Bone Artist. His theory was that the Bone Artist and a couple of the others in the report were dead or in prison and that was the end of it. Trinity thought that that was just an easy way out and argued that just because a serial killer was inactive for a period of time didn't mean that they were no longer a threat. She said maybe some of these guys were smart enough to know when they had to take a break in order not to get caught. Anyway, she was all fired up about it. I guess she got a talking-to by the brass although the viewers liked it. They saw it as her being a 'hard-hitting' journalist. But at the time, she was pretty bent out of shape. We talked about it over dinner, and she played the whole thing for me. I told her that actually, the going theory *was* that the Bone Artist was dead or in prison. She asked how the hell I'd know that, and I told her it was my file."

Josie raised a brow. "Trinity might have liked you, but she wouldn't get that obsessed with a cold serial case just because you had the file."

"Well, she got obsessed with it. She was miffed that I didn't side with her on the whole thing. I think she was trying to prove me wrong."

"Initially," Josie said. "But the deeper she got into the case details, the more she became convinced she could solve the case. Then when she got banished here to Denton after her on-air faux pas, she thought she might use the whole thing to get back in the limelight."

Mettner said, "Do you know how she planned on making contact with him?"

"I have no idea," Drake said.

Noah asked, "When the Bone Artist contacted the journalists back in 2014, how did he do it?"

Drake said, "Letters."

"Postage?" Noah asked.

Drake replied, "No postage. We're still not sure how he got them into the mailrooms of the networks, but there were far too many people in and out of those buildings all day and all night long for us to pinpoint any suspects after the fact."

"Did he ever leave them packages?" Josie asked.

"No."

"But he dropped the letters off in person without being seen or noticed by anyone," Josie said.

Drake nodded.

Noah said, "The Bone Artist has Trinity."

Drake smiled. "There's no way the Bone Artist took Trinity. This was a wild goose chase that she was on. That's not my concern. My concern is that whoever did take her has a whole lot of classified information."

Gretchen said, "Lieutenant Fraley is correct, Agent Nally. The Bone Artist took Trinity."

"The Bone Artist is dead," Drake said.

Mettner took out his phone, tapped, scrolled and held it out for Drake to see. "This photo was taken this morning behind the cabin Trinity had rented."

Drake stared at the photo, his face rapidly losing color. "My God," he mumbled. "This isn't—this can't be right. This isn't possible."

"You think it's a copycat?" Noah asked.

"No, I—I—" Drake stammered. "It can't be. The public never saw the displays. No one has, except the responding officers and task force."

Josie said, "He's got her. He took her."

Drake rubbed his hands over his face, recovering some of his composure. "What did he use to hold the bones down?"

Mettner said, "Tent stakes and fishing line. Our Evidence Response Team already checked out the stakes. They're a generic Walmart brand. Could have been bought anywhere in the country. Fishing line could have been bought at any store that stocks fishing supplies."

"My God," Drake said again. "Is that—is that—"

"It's not Trinity," Noah said. He filled Drake in on all they knew about Nicci Webb and her disappearance.

"This isn't right," Drake said. "Seventeen days—he's never left someone on display after only seventeen days, it's always thirty—and he took Trinity *and* Webb? That's not his pattern."

"But that's what happened," Noah said.

"We have to go through your files," Gretchen said to Drake. "We need to see everything that Trinity saw so we can figure out how she contacted him. If we can figure that out, maybe we can find him."

"Can you get us what we need?" Josie asked.

Mettner said, "We'll make an official request."

"The Bone Artist is my file. It was assigned to me as a cold case after the last agent working on it retired. I can get you what you need."

"Thank you," Josie said.

"But there's one thing you need to understand," he added. "You said that Trinity went missing three weeks ago. If he took her... I mean his pattern is all out of whack, obviously, with this Webb woman, but still, this guy, he always leaves the remains on day thirty. She could already be—"

"We know," Noah said, cutting him off. "But that changes nothing. No matter what happens, we're going after this guy with everything we have."

CHAPTER TWENTY-NINE

"Take us through it," Mettner told Drake. "The entire case, piece by piece."

Drake looked at each of them. "We don't have that kind of time."

"Condense it, then," Noah said. "But you'd better start telling us what you know, and what Trinity would have known. The sooner we know what she knew, the sooner we find her and the Bone Artist."

Drake raised a brow at Noah. "No offense, but we've been after this guy for over ten years. You have any idea how many law enforcement officers and other experts have been over this file? You think I'll give you a presentation on this case and you'll just figure it out? When no one else could?"

Gretchen said, "Why not? Trinity figured out enough to make contact with this guy."

"Whatever our Evidence Response Team turns up on Trinity's abduction and Nicci Webb's murder might help as well," Mettner added.

Drake shook his head. The fingers of his right hand tapped on the table. "You think your team's going to turn something up that the Federal Bureau of Investigation hasn't?"

Josie stood up, gathered the remains of the file in front of Gretchen, walked over to Drake, and slammed it onto the table in front of him. His flinch was barely perceptible, but Josie saw it. She leaned down, her face inches from his. "What I think is that every second you sit here questioning our competence, is one more second we could have spent finding my sister. I don't care how long you've been after this killer or how many people failed to find him in the past. Right now, we have a case to solve. It's as simple as that. We've got a lot of work to do, so if you're not going to help us, then shut up and get out of my stationhouse. I'll get in touch with your SAC. I'm sure she'll be happy to lend any assistance she can on this."

Josie moved aside and held her arm out, gesturing toward the door. Slowly, Drake stood, smoothing the lapels of his jacket. "You're just like her," he said quietly.

He picked up the file and moved past her, but he didn't go to the door. Instead, he circled the table and walked over to the large whiteboard at the back of the room. He put the file on the table and opened it, spreading out reports. He motioned toward Gretchen's neatly organized piles. "Do you mind?"

She slid them over to him. He plucked the dry erase marker from the whiteboard ledge and uncapped it, listing dates, names, and brief notes as he spoke.

"We didn't know this was a serial case until the third victim, so the first two cases were handled by local departments. It wasn't even clear they were connected until just before the third victim went missing."

Drake tapped his marker against the board where he had written Anthony Yanetti, 2008. "This guy was a truck driver. Forty-one years old. Wife and one kid. He lived in Newtown, Pennsylvania."

"That's in the southeastern part of the state, right?" Mettner asked.

"Yeah," Josie said. "A couple of hours from here."

Drake continued, "He delivered furniture for a local store. He was out delivering. He made a stop at about eleven a.m., left that stop, and drove off to his next destination. Except he never made it. The customer called the store to complain when he didn't show. No one could get in touch with him. A few hours later, his truck was found on a rural road outside of Newtown. Keys still in the ignition. Wallet, phone, lunch all still in the truck. It was like he pulled over, got out, and never came back. Thirty days later, some guy working in a salvage yard finds bones arranged on one of his back lots in King of Prussia, roughly thirty-five miles from where he went missing. That was treated as a homicide in that jurisdiction. He was identified using dental records."

Drake picked up a set of photos and passed them around. This set included close-ups of each bone group, like the ones both Josie and Noah had glimpsed in the guest room when Trinity stayed with them.

Noah said, "You said earlier that the killer struck every two years. Are we talking to the day? Two years from the abduction or from the staging of the bones?"

Drake drew an arrow from the name Anthony Yanetti to the name Terri Abbott. "The victims are always abducted in March and their bones are always found in April, usually early April. It's two years to the month."

Josie tried to suppress the shiver working its way through her body. It was nearly April. "The exact dates don't matter?" she said.

"They don't seem to matter, no. He doesn't leave the remains every April fifteenth or anything like that. Terri Abbott, a twenty-eight-year-old day care worker from Pittsburgh, was walking home from a pre-season Pirates game. Her last known contact was a phone call with her roommate during which she told the roommate she was walking across the Roberto Clemente bridge."

Mettner said, "Did you find her on any cameras?"

Drake shook his head. "It was too crowded. Too many people. We couldn't isolate her. Her phone and purse were found in the gutter on the other side of the bridge, so we think she did make it across."

Josie's throat was dry. "Then thirty days later…"

"Her bones were found in the parking lot of an abandoned steel mill outside of Pittsburgh. Some foundation had bought it up, and they were planning to put an art installation there. That's how her bones were found."

Gretchen frowned. "How does he ensure that the bones are found on the thirtieth day if he's leaving them in remote places?"

"Hand-delivered notes." Drake riffled through the pages in the file until he came up with two photos. Both showed a regular piece of white copy paper with the same block writing Josie had seen on the package Trinity had received. One simply said: *Please check the back lot immediately. Urgent.* The other said: *There's a problem at the mill. The installation cannot go ahead. Please check the parking lot immediately.*

Josie and her team passed them around as Drake continued, "The first one was taped to the front door of the salvage yard office, left there overnight, we assume after he left the bones. There weren't any cameras on the exterior back then or in the back two lots. The second one was left in the mailbox of the artist who had been chosen to do the installation."

Noah asked, "No prints on the paper?"

"Nothing. We analyzed the paper and the ink he used. Every little thing. It all led nowhere. That's the thing. He leaves nothing behind."

"Except the bones," Josie said.

"Right. But other than that, he's never been caught on camera. He's left no prints, no shoeprints, no tire tracks, no DNA. He's a ghost."

CHAPTER THIRTY

"A ghost didn't take my sister," Josie said, "We've got something else. A comb."

Drake raised a skeptical brow. "What? Like a hair comb? How do you know it's his?"

Noah said, "He left it in our mailbox addressed to Trinity."

Mettner took out his phone and pulled up a photo of the comb that Josie had sent him earlier in the day, "We believe it's made of bone. It can't be a coincidence that Trinity was neck-deep into this case and then had this delivered to her anonymously."

Drake stared at the photo. "You can't be serious."

"Where else would it come from?" Josie asked.

Mettner swiped to the photo of the packaging.

Drake said, "Did you send all of that for analysis?"

"Of course we did," Gretchen interjected.

"You won't get anything. He's too careful. The comb? You won't get anything from that either."

Josie said, "If we're right, and it's made of bone, we need to know who it came from. We can do DNA testing, run it through CODIS."

"That's not going to help you find this guy," Drake argued.

Josie held his gaze. "The four victims in your file—were there any bones missing?"

"No, but—"

"That means there could be other victims out there. Victims we don't know about yet. Besides that, we've got a new victim. Between Nicci Webb's murder and Trinity's abduction, there may be a way to track this guy down."

"He never leaves clues behind," Drake argued.

"But it's an avenue we can't ignore," Josie said.

When Drake didn't respond, Mettner said, "You told us about the third victim, Kenneth Darden. He disappeared in 2012 from Paoli, thirty days later his bones showed up in Philadelphia."

"Right," Drake replied, looking away from Josie and resuming his recap of the Bone Artist case. "Those were in a very public place, so he didn't need to leave any notes."

"Yeah," Gretchen said, fingering a photo of Darden's remains with a river in the background. "That particular area on the bank of the Schuylkill River sees a lot of traffic. Joggers, bikers, walkers, rowers, homeless people. You name it. Also, there were no cameras there back then, so that was smart."

Drake said, "The 911 call on that one came in at five-thirty in the morning."

The door to the conference room opened and they all turned to see Hummel standing there with a laptop in his hands. "Boss," he said, addressing Josie. "Thought you'd want this. It's Trinity's."

"Thanks, Hummel," Josie said. She took the computer from him and sat back down. To Mettner and Gretchen, she asked, "Were there any documents on here about the Bone Artist?"

"No," Mettner replied. "Which was not surprising given what her assistant said. If she was that worried about getting scooped, she wouldn't leave notes on the computer."

"I'll check the emails," Josie said, opening the laptop and powering it up.

"Sorry for the interruption," Mettner told Drake. "Please, tell us about the fourth victim."

Drake nodded and continued, "The fourth victim was a thirty-seven-year-old stockbroker named Robert Ingram. He lived in East Stroudsburg—the upper east side of the state of Pennsylvania. His wife drove him to the train station and dropped him off for a meeting in New York City that day. He never made it inside the station. Thirty days later his bones were found arranged on the Bloomsburg Fairgrounds."

The laptop screen came to life, showing a photo of a French villa. The small eye beneath the camera began scanning for Trinity's face. The words *Looking for You* flashed beneath it. Josie leaned in and kept still. The eye focused on her. Then it disappeared and the words *Welcome, Trinity Payne* popped up before the home screen appeared.

Mettner said, "East Stroudsburg? That's almost a hundred miles from Bloomsburg. Why so far?"

"We don't know," Drake admitted. "There doesn't seem to be any pattern to where he leaves the bones."

"Except places where there are no cameras," Noah said. "I've been to the Bloomsburg fairgrounds. When the fair isn't going on, they're empty. There aren't any cameras there, and the area is pretty large. Was a note left for someone that time so the bones could be located?"

"No. He left them in a part of the fairgrounds where they could easily be seen from Route 11 or the overpass going to Route 42. Someone spotted them as soon as the sun came up."

Trinity's home screen showed a photo of the entire Payne family in front of a Christmas tree. Josie recognized it from the year before, only about four months ago. The sight of it pained her now. She had the same photo printed out and framed in her and Noah's living room. She pulled up Trinity's email app and started trawling through her inbox while she listened to her team and Drake discuss the Bone Artist.

Gretchen said, "So this guy is careful enough to not be caught on camera taking people, careful enough to stage their remains where there are no cameras, but takes the risk of delivering notes. He always leaves the bodies in April exactly thirty days after he's taken them, but there's no pattern at all to where he leaves them. I mean, those first three victims were found relatively close to where they went missing but the last one was very far from where he went missing."

"What about the victims themselves?" Noah asked. "Any commonalities? Did any of them know each other or have mutual friends or acquaintances?"

Drake shook his head. "Nothing." He went through more photos in the file until he came up with photos of each victim. All of them looked as though they'd been pulled from the victims' social media profiles. "They have no friends, family or acquaintances in common. Nothing job-related in common. They don't even look alike, other than they're all Caucasian. We even had their medical histories compared. There's nothing. We believe that the victims are chosen for convenience. The killer sees an opportunity to abduct someone where there are no cameras or witnesses or, as with Terri Abbott, in such a crowded place that no one would notice her going off with him."

"So he's not choosy," Mettner said. "He doesn't have a type."

Josie found nothing in Trinity's emails to indicate she had ever known or come into contact with Nicci Webb. Nothing in her email was unusual or sending up any red flags. It was all work-related. There were three emails exchanged between Trinity and her assistant three months earlier where she asked Jaime to see if the network had ever done any pieces on unsolved serial cases. Jaime had later sent her links to segments about the Zodiac Killer, the Alphabet Murders, the Tylenol poisoning and the Freeway Phantom. It looked as though the only link Trinity had clicked on and viewed was the one for the Alphabet Killer. Josie clicked on the link as well. She muted the video segment but quickly read the transcript below it. The killings had occurred in the 1970s in Rochester, New York. The three victims' first and last names all started with the same initial. Josie saw that Trinity had only visited the site once. Her search history didn't turn up any more links for the Alphabet murders, only the Bone Artist and several news stories about Codie Lash's murder. Josie kept skimming Trinity's emails. The email exchange between Trinity and her assistant regarding Lash's personal effects was exactly as Jaime had described it. There was no clue as to why Trinity had wanted the items.

Josie sighed and closed the laptop. They had nothing.

CHAPTER THIRTY-ONE

Josie turned her attention back to Drake and the team as they continued to review the Bone Artist file. Noah said, "Also there's a break in the geographical pattern. Three victims on the eastern side of Pennsylvania and one on the western side. Why?"

Drake said, "We really don't know."

Josie thought about the Post-it notes she had managed to glimpse in her guest room before Trinity had torn them down. *OCD? Symmetry? Mirror killings?* She said, "Are you absolutely sure there haven't been any other Bone Artist cases on the western side of the state?"

"None," Drake answered.

Trinity had been looking for patterns just as they were now. As if reading her mind, Noah said, "That one outlier, the killing in Pittsburgh, was a woman. The other three victims were men. Today's victim was a woman. Don't serial killers usually stay with one type of victim?"

"There are always exceptions but yes, usually serial killers have a type."

"Why, then?" Josie asked. "Why would he go all the way to the other side of the state for his next victim and choose a woman? It couldn't be a copycat because by that point you didn't even know you had a serial killer on your hands."

Drake said, "That's right. Terri Abbott was the second victim. We think perhaps he meant to zig-zag the state and alternate the sex of his victims, but for some reason, with the fourth victim, Robert Ingram, he took a man instead of a woman."

"What would make him break his pattern?" Josie pressed.

"Some kind of personal stressor," Drake offered. "Or he may have had to change his plans based on his ability to get away with it. Perhaps Ingram was a more convenient victim. Perhaps he meant to head west again but logistically he wasn't able to do it, so he took someone on this side of the state. We have no way of really knowing why he changed his pattern—if his pattern was indeed to alternate male and female victims and east and west of the state."

"You're assuming he has patterns because of the thirty-day thing," Mettner pointed out. "The ages of the victims are disparate. Their socioeconomic status. Some have kids and some don't."

"True," Drake said. "For every pattern we can establish, there are other things that aren't done according to a pattern. Other than the way the victims are taken, like vanishing into thin air, and the way their bones are staged exactly thirty days after they go missing, there aren't any similarities."

Mettner said, "He could be trying to throw us off by breaking that pattern with Nicci Webb's murder."

Noah said, "Were there ever any viable suspects?"

Drake pulled out another report. "The short answer is no."

"How is that even possible?" Mettner asked.

Drake didn't answer. Instead he said, "We concentrated our search on funeral home workers, orthopedic surgeons, hunters, taxidermists, anthropologists, archaeologists, orthotists, prosthetists, artists, and art students in the eastern area of the state. We even looked at coroners and medical examiners. We found a couple of odd birds, for sure, but no one who looked good for these killings."

"What about ornithologists?" Josie asked.

"I'm sorry, what?" Drake said.

"Ornithologists. Bird experts."

Drake stared at her.

Noah said, "You said he uses avian scavengers to accelerate decomposition. It makes sense that it could be someone who knows a bit about birds."

"There are carrion birds all over this state," Drake said. "Driving here, I saw at least two dozen groups of them feeding on roadkill. You don't have to be a bird expert to know what scavenger birds do."

"It's still worth looking into," Gretchen said.

"Did you check veterinarians or veterinarian techs?" Josie went on.

"Why would we?" Drake asked.

"Because you've obviously covered the bone angle, which makes sense. Look for someone who works with bones or is around bones or has some affinity for bones. Or look at artists, cause this guy thinks he's an artist. But none of those produced any suspects. If you know he uses animals to accelerate decomposition, the next logical step would be to look at people who work with animals."

"We looked at hunters and taxidermists," Drake repeated.

Josie said, "Makes sense. What about anyone who worked at a zoo? Or even someone on the state game commission? They're in charge of collecting and disposing of roadkill."

Drake said nothing.

Mettner tapped a note into his cell phone. "We'll look into those as well."

"How about large properties?" Josie asked. "He would need a large enough property to leave a body out for days or weeks for the vultures to get to it without drawing attention."

Drake took a packet of pages out of the folder and slid them across the table. "These are all the property owners we checked out. We went halfway across the state. No red flags."

Josie remembered something she had seen among Trinity's things when she was cleaning out the guest room. "What about the psychological profile?"

Drake sifted through the pages left in the file until he came up with the report. "Caucasian male, mid to late thirties. That was based on the sophistication of his crimes—being able to abduct adult individuals without leaving any evidence or being caught on camera; being able to accelerate the decomposition of the bodies using avian scavengers without drawing attention to his activities; and being able to stage the remains, again, without getting caught. We also believe he has at least some college education. Make no mistake, this guy is smart. He's probably got a higher than average IQ. He can likely function just fine in society, but he is a loner. Other people may grate on him."

"Why?" Noah asked.

"Because he's got an inflated sense of self," Josie remarked.

Drake nodded. "Exactly."

"What makes you think that?" Mettner asked her.

Josie said, "Because he felt the need to contact the press. It wasn't enough for him to kill. He wanted people to understand how smart he is, how clever, how sophisticated. He wanted people to see that he was getting away with it."

"That's what our profiler believed," Drake said.

Gretchen said, "The messages he sent to members of the press show he wanted to control his own story, especially the way he wanted to be known as the Bone Artist and not the Boneyard Killer."

"Thinking of himself as some kind of artist definitely tracks with the inflated sense of self," Mettner agreed.

Noah asked, "Who in the press did he contact?"

Drake answered, "A handful of anchors from most of the network morning shows."

"The position Trinity holds now," Gretchen said. "Or used to hold."

"Right," Drake said. He fished through the pages of the file again until he came up with a large color photograph. He slid it across the table so they could all view it. Black, block letters filled a piece of copy paper, the writing just like on the packaging Trinity had received and the notes the killer had left at the steel mill and junkyard. Gretchen shifted her reading glasses on the bridge of her nose and read it out loud:

Ladies and Gentleman: This is the murderer you call the Boneyard Killer. It's true I have done evil things. The devil inside me has grown strong. Not even I can stop him now. The police can't stop him. They have never caught me. They won't catch me. No one is smart enough to stop what is happening. Now the devil has grown bored. He wants a new game. I invite you to play. If you signal me on air, you can save a life. The next victim is ready. Will you save? Yours in life and death,
   The Bone Artist

Mettner gave a low whistle. "Is this guy trying to tell us he's batshit crazy?"

"Hardly," Drake said. "These guys like to make themselves out to be out of control or overcome by some otherworldly force because, like Detective Palmer said, they're trying to control the narrative. By saying all the heinous things they did are the result of some monster or evil, they seem more sympathetic or even innocent. 'It wasn't me, it was the devil.' H.H. Holmes, a serial killer out of Chicago in the 1890s said he had the devil in him—just like this guy. Dennis Rader, the BTK killer in Kansas said there was a monster in him. It's all meant to manipulate their own image. These killers know exactly what they're doing, and they enjoy it."

"He's gotten away with it for years and now he wants to play a game?" Noah remarked.

Josie said, "Because he thinks he's smarter than anyone else. He gets satisfaction out of this. He's outwitted the police all this time. They're not worthy opponents. Contacting the press, playing his 'game' is another way for him to flaunt what he sees as his high intelligence."

Drake nodded. "That's right. Except that no one played his game. The members of the press who received this letter turned them over to the FBI immediately."

Gretchen pointed at the top of the letter where someone—presumably an FBI agent—had handwritten *Received by male anchor at CBS on April 3, 2014*. She said, "You didn't think you could save the victim? By having one of these anchors pretend to play his game?"

Drake sighed. "Engaging this guy like that, with him holding all the cards and making all the rules, was deemed too risky by both the bureau and the networks. No one on the task force really believed he would let a victim go. That was confirmed five days later when the remains of Robert Ingram were found. He never had any intention of letting Ingram go. In fact, we believe that Ingram was already dead when he sent those letters."

Mettner raised a brow. "What was the signal, anyway? He never even said."

"Exactly," Drake agreed. "It was just a stunt to try to engage the press. The press didn't bite, and he stopped killing. Until now."

"Why did he start again?" Mettner asked to no one in particular.

Drake said, "Because Trinity drew him out."

"Trinity drew him out," Gretchen said, "But he was killing long before she made contact, and he would probably have killed again even if she hadn't made contact. For all we know, he's been killing nonstop since 2014 but not putting any of his victims on display, so no one is the wiser."

Josie could tell by the look on Drake's face, as though he'd been slapped, that he didn't like this idea—because it was likely true.

"The psychological profile—what else does it say?" she asked. "Besides him being an almost forty-year old white male with some college and a higher than average IQ? Does it mention the possibility that he has a job that involves driving? He'd have to, wouldn't he? His victims are all over the place."

"Yes," Drake said, turning his attention back to Josie. "We believe his job involves him driving but with very little oversight, which he will prefer because he won't like having a supervisor. He'll always believe he is smarter and better qualified. He likely drives a pretty nondescript vehicle but one that could accommodate his activities, so a van or a pickup truck but likely an older model, nothing that would draw a great deal of attention. Also, he is someone who is quite comfortable outdoors and with animals."

Drake pushed the report across the table to Josie. "Look, you can read that yourself, but none of it has ever helped us find this guy."

Josie's cell phone rang. Everyone stared at her as she pulled it out of her pocket. "It's Shannon," she said, hyper aware of everyone's gaze boring into her as she swiped Answer.

"Josie?" Shannon said. "You there?"

"Yes, what's going on? Are you still in Callowhill?"

"We are. Is there any word?"

Josie's eyes were drawn to the photos spread across the table. The ghastly displays that the killer considered art. Her stomach turned. "No word," Josie said. "My team is still running down leads. Did you find the letters?"

"No, I'm sorry. We've got the whole attic turned upside down. There's nothing here. Christian checked our old things as well, thinking maybe one of us kept them since they were part of her therapy, but they're not here."

"What about the therapist?" Josie asked. "Maybe we can get in touch with him or her."

Silence filled the line. After a beat, Shannon said, "That's not possible. We had the same thought, so Christian Googled her. We were just looking for her phone number. We figured we'd call her as soon as her office opened, but all we found was her obituary."

"Oh God."

"I'm so sorry, Josie. She wasn't very young when Trinity saw her. Apparently, she developed ALS—Lou Gehrig's disease—in her later years and died of complications from that. What do we do?"

"I guess just come back then. You can stay with me. Lisette's in the guest bedroom, but we can figure something out. I—"

She broke off. Lisette's words from earlier whispered in her ear. *You know her well enough, Josie… she was trying to tell you something, dear. Point you in a direction.*

"Josie?" Shannon asked, her voice reedy.

"I'm here," she replied quickly. "Shannon, the letters that Trinity wrote to me for her therapist—were they in shorthand?"

"Well, no. The therapist read them. They were like a homework assignment."

"Did you ever read them?"

"No. Trinity asked her therapist if she could keep them private from us. She said it was bad enough that she had to show them to the therapist. Neither one of them shared them with us, but we thought Trinity kept them. Why?"

"I need to come there."

"Josie," Noah said. "It's 11:30 at night."

Ignoring him, she told Shannon, "Stay there, would you? I'm going to drive down. Try to get some rest. Sleep, if you can. I'll see you soon."

"Boss," Gretchen said when Josie hung up. "You need to rest as well."

Josie stood up. "I'll sleep when I get there, okay? I promise. There's something I need to do."

"Will someone tell me what letters you're all talking about?" Drake asked.

Josie said, "Mett can fill you in. I'll be back as soon as I can."

"Josie," Noah said. "I'll go with you."

"No," she said, even though she wanted him to go with her, badly. "I need you here with my grandmother and Trout." She looked at Mettner. "I need to tell Shannon and Christian about the Bone Artist."

Mettner held her gaze. "That's your call, but it has to stay out of the press."

Gretchen said, "Mett and I will stay on. We'll start running down leads."

Mettner looked at Noah. "You go home and get some rest, too. We'll call you both if anything develops."

Josie was reluctant to leave. She wanted to run down every lead herself, but she knew that wasn't possible. Her team would not let her or Trinity down—that she knew with absolute conviction. For now, she had to follow the trail Trinity had left for her. She pointed to the Bone Artist file, now spread out across the conference room table. "Just one thing: I'd like to take a copy of that with me."

CHAPTER THIRTY-TWO

Alex shook the snow from his boots at the back door and knocked three times. Hanna opened the door with a smile. A blast of hot air engulfed him. Almost immediately he began to feel uncomfortable and sweaty. He'd grown so used to being outside and cold, now the stifling inside of the house bothered him. But he needed to eat. He sat at the table in front of a plate of food that Hanna had prepared for him.

"Mom," he tried. "There haven't been any incidents in a long time. I've helped with Zandra, keeping her from hurting you. Things have been good. Plus, she's twelve years old now. She's more mature. I was just thinking that maybe… maybe things could change."

"Well, your father…" She drifted off and, in that moment, he hated her for never standing up to Francis.

The front door scraped open. Alex listened as Francis stomped the snow from his boots in the foyer and took his coat, hat, and gloves off. He tromped into the kitchen, giving Alex a brief glare before sitting down at the dinner table. While Hanna served him dinner, he talked about his day, the weather, the imbeciles he had to deal with in his work. When he finished, she served him coffee and then she went into the other room and came back with a stack of papers which she placed in front of him.

"What is this?" Francis asked.

"An Agreement of Sale for the property behind this one. One hundred acres! I'm going to buy it."

He paged through the document. "Why would you do that?"

"Because we always wanted property of our own. This is our chance."

"You expect me to keep up with one hundred acres?"

"No, I—"

"There's not even a house on the land!"

"Well, we could build—"

"No," he said. "This is a stupid idea."

He pushed the pages away from him and stood up. When he reached the doorway, Hanna said, "I wasn't asking you. It's my money. I can buy the land if I choose. We're not married. I don't need your permission."

Alex felt a shockwave punch through the room. Francis turned back to her and pointed a finger in her face. "You know why I could never marry you. These children—"

She cut him off. "They need a legacy. Something for when I'm gone."

He walked over to the table, picked up the Agreement of Sale and tore it in half. "If you want to keep your precious children, you'll never speak of this again."

CHAPTER THIRTY-THREE

Callowhill was a small town two hours east of Denton. Town, Josie thought, as she drove through its streets in the early hours of the morning, was a strong word for Callowhill. It had one main street where the essentials were grouped together: a police station, post office, library, gas station, fire house, pharmacy and an urgent care center. The rest of the town was spread across the two square miles of rolling hills and small mountains surrounding the town center. The Paynes lived in a large faux-brick luxury home situated on four acres of land. A narrow, single-lane road led to their driveway. Josie knew there were additional houses along the road, but she rarely saw any neighbors when she visited.

She pulled up in front of the three-car garage, parking next to Shannon's SUV, and made her way up the walk to the front door. They'd given her a key the first time she visited, but she still couldn't shake the feeling that she should ring the doorbell. As she did every time she visited, she paused at the front door and looked around. She could have grown up here. She *should* have grown up here. What would it have been like if she hadn't been torn away from her family just after birth? What would *she* be like?

What would Trinity be like?

As the thoughts whirled through her mind, Christian opened the front door. "You okay?"

Josie gave him a weak smile and stepped inside. "Sorry," she said. "I'm just… tired."

He waved her through the cavernous, marble-tiled foyer into the kitchen, where Shannon sat at their island countertop, a cup of coffee in hand. Josie took a good look at her parents. They clearly hadn't slept. Christian's salt and pepper hair was greasy and in disarray. Stubble covered his face, and large bags hung beneath his bloodshot eyes. He looked smaller somehow in a pair of sweatpants and a T-shirt. Josie was so used to seeing him in suits. Shannon wore cotton pajamas. Her hair was pulled back in a ponytail. Dark circles gathered beneath her eyes. Her nose was bright red from crying. To Josie, it seemed she had aged a decade in mere hours.

Here she was, about to shatter them once again with her news.

Shannon met her eyes, set her mug onto the countertop, and whispered, "Just tell us."

Josie stood in place, her feet concrete blocks. "We believe that Trinity was abducted by a serial killer."

The words hung in the air for several seconds. Then a strangled cry escaped Shannon's throat. She clamped both her hands over her mouth, as if she were trying to stop more sound from coming out. Christian stood behind her, wrapping his arms around her and pressing his face into the top of her head.

Josie took a step forward, and with the most clinical detachment she could muster, gave them a brief summary of the reasoning behind her team's theory that the Bone Artist had Trinity and what little they knew about him, careful not to say anything that would devastate them even more. She already knew that one or both of them would Google the Bone Artist in private, and that would be enough to ratchet up their anxiety to life-threatening levels.

Shannon wept silently as Josie spoke. Christian remained calm until Josie finished and then leaned on his wife, sobbing. Josie watched them dissolve. Part of her wanted to go to them, collapse into their collective embrace and let all her own grief and fear loose. They were her parents, after all. But she couldn't do that. The moment she gave in to those crushing feelings, the moment she stopped driving forward, all would be lost. Trinity needed her.

Whether she wanted to be Josie's sister or not, Josie was going to do everything she could to find her.

After a few moments, Shannon and Christian's tears subsided. Shannon snatched a napkin from the holder in the center of the countertop and handed it to her husband before taking one for herself. As she dabbed her eyes, she said, "You came here to tell us this?"

"Not just that," Josie said. "I need to look through Trinity's things myself."

Christian said, "Josie, if those letters were here, believe me, we would have found them."

"Not the letters. She had a diary. That's what her message said. *Read my diary.* Not my letters. She wrote it in shorthand, not just because she was pressed for time in the seconds she had between this guy pulling into the cabin's driveway and coming to her car to take her, but because she was trying to tell me something. The diary—wherever it is—is written in shorthand. Whatever was in it, she didn't want anyone to read it."

"Honey," Shannon said, "There's no diary either. We would have called you right away if we found a whole diary filled with shorthand."

"She's hidden it somewhere," Josie said.

"Where?" Christian asked.

Somewhere only I would know to look, Josie thought. Even as the words filled her mind, she thought of how absurd that assertion was—Trinity had accused Josie of not knowing her at all the last time they spoke. Why would Trinity think that Josie, and Josie alone, could figure out where she'd hidden her high school diary?

"I don't know where," Josie said. "I just know I have to look."

Christian guided her upstairs. The door to the attic, a panel with fold-out stairs affixed to it, was open. Scattered all over the long hallway were boxes. Some of them had been dumped onto the floor. Others sat open, their contents in disarray. Christian stepped over piles of clothes, CDs, paperback books, VHS tapes, shoes, and various other items. He pointed to the door of Trinity's bedroom. Josie knew that since Trinity had moved out years ago, they'd cleaned it out so that it was basically a guest room now. Still, Josie knew that Trinity stayed in that room whenever she was home. "You can have a look," Christian said.

Josie stepped into the room to see that Shannon and Christian really hadn't left any stone unturned. The mattress was off center, the drawers of the nightstand hung open, the closet door was ajar, the sheets and towels on shelves inside of it were disheveled.

"Do you need help?" Christian asked.

"No," Josie said. "Thank you."

He left her. She spent several minutes studying every corner of the room, trying to think where Trinity would have left a high school diary. Josie took a thorough look around, even testing the edges of the wall to wall carpet to make sure there weren't any places it peeled back, before deciding that, as an adult, Trinity wouldn't have hidden any diary in here. In fact, the last time Trinity probably handled the diary was when she was in high school. Working on that assumption, Josie went back to the hall and began to methodically search the boxes as well as the items that Shannon and Christian had already removed from them and left scattered on the floor. She checked the compartment of every jewelry box, cosmetic bag, purse, even inside shoes. Any item that had a compartment, no matter how small, Josie deconstructed.

She found nothing.

Nothing except the realization that she and Trinity, despite being raised hours apart in two very different environments, and despite how different they were as adults, had had very similar tastes as teenagers. Trinity had many of the same CDs, movies, books, and even clothes that Josie had liked as a teen. Josie hadn't been able to afford nearly as much as Trinity had collected, but she had certainly admired and enjoyed many of the same things.

They'd both worn skinny jeans and listened to an eclectic range of music which included albums by Nelly Furtado, Jennifer Lopez, Matchbox 20, Leanne Womack, and Rascal Flatts. Tears stung the backs of Josie's eyes as she wondered if Trinity had ever sung along with the same anthems of Josie's teenage years, felt the same escape in Nelly Furtado's 'I'm Like a Bird' and reassurance in Jennifer Lopez's 'I'm Gonna Be Alright'. They'd both also had the same pink and turquoise caboodle—a large plastic cosmetics case that kids their age were crazy over in the early 2000s. Josie had given her own away ages ago. With a stab of nostalgia, she opened Trinity's to find two dried up tubes of body glitter which made her laugh in spite of the situation. She had liked most of the things that teenagers at that time liked, but she wouldn't have been caught dead wearing body glitter. She searched the compartments, but they were empty.

She found a silver-plated trinket box and flipped it open to find a Tiffany's charm bracelet. Josie touched it reverently. It seemed so big and chunky now with its silver chain links and huge heart-shaped charm announcing: *Please return to Tiffany & Co.* Many of the wealthier girls in Josie's school had had these. She had coveted them all through high school, but she knew they were expensive, and Lisette was hardly rich. She set it aside and moved on to a new bin of Trinity's belongings, this one containing the movies Trinity had collected during high school.

Shannon's voice startled her from her thoughts. "No one even watches VHS tapes anymore," she said, pointing to a pile of movies from the early 2000s in Josie's lap. "I'm not even sure you can sell them on eBay as vintage. I'll have to tell her to just get rid of them when she—"

She broke off and covered her eyes with one hand. Josie pushed the movies aside and stood up. Gently, she pulled Shannon's hand away from her face. "When she gets back," Josie finished for her. "She can go through these things when she gets back. Look at these movies—these were my favorites at that age, too:

Miss Congeniality, Return to Me, Erin Brockovich, Notting Hill, Shakespeare in Love."

Shannon smiled. "She loved to watch movies. She'd sit for hours in her bedroom and watch movie after movie. I think it was a good distraction for her."

Josie held up one of the tapes. "This one was my favorite. *Frequency*. Do you remember it?"

"I think so," Shannon said.

"It was about a police detective who is able to communicate with his late father over a HAM radio during the aurora borealis. Somehow, they could talk to one another thirty years apart and change both their futures. I loved it because my dad—"

The rest of the sentence died in her throat, choked by a sob.

Shannon took the movie from her and placed it on the pile on the floor. She stroked Josie's hair. "Because your dad died when you were six and you wished you could change that?"

Josie couldn't speak so she merely nodded. The woman who had taken her from the Paynes when she was only three weeks old had been seeing Lisette Matson's son, Eli, on and off at the time. She returned to him after a long break-up and told him that Josie was his daughter. He had raised Josie until the age of six when he was killed. Eli had been a wonderful father—the only father Josie had ever known—and Josie had missed him terribly her entire life. It wasn't until decades after Eli's death that Josie found out Christian Payne was her real father. Even knowing the truth, it was difficult to think of Eli as anything but her dad.

Shannon pointed to another VHS tape. "*Erin Brockovich* was Trinity's favorite."

A small laugh escaped Josie's mouth. "I'm not surprised."

"Josie," Shannon said. "It's almost eight a.m. You haven't slept. Noah called me."

"He wants me to rest."

Shannon smiled. "And eat something."

"That sounds about right." Josie knew he hadn't bothered calling her to urge her to rest and eat because he knew she wouldn't listen to him.

"I'll make you breakfast and then you can sleep. Did you find what you were looking for?"

Josie looked at the detritus all around her. It was like a mall from the early 2000s had exploded in Shannon and Christian's hallway. "No," she croaked. "I don't think it's here."

She stared at the mess a beat longer before Shannon took her elbow. "Leave it," she said. "Come down to the kitchen."

CHAPTER THIRTY-FOUR

Josie sat at the island countertop watching Shannon cook up an omelet. Christian sat across from Josie, laptop open, Googling the Bone Artist, his face taking on a greenish hue as he read. "I'm not sure that's a good idea... Dad," Josie said.

He looked up at her, his entire face suddenly alight. As with calling Shannon "Mom", she'd only tried out "Dad" with him once or twice before. The euphoric joy and desperate hope that washed over both their faces whenever Josie called them Mom and Dad always made her uncomfortable. It wouldn't undo the past, nor would it fill the void her thirty-year absence had left. Josie knew this. Her entire life had been a parade of harsh truths and a nonstop roller coaster ride of even harsher realities. She just wasn't sure the Paynes knew it. She didn't want to be a disappointment to them.

As if sensing her discomfort, Christian looked away and when he looked back, his expression had sobered. "I know," he agreed. "But I have to know. I can't help myself. More information is always better. I mean, it's not—not for my mental state—but usually the more information I have on any particular subject, the better I feel."

"I'm kind of like that, too," Josie said. In fact, her need to know things, to unravel mysteries and put puzzles together often put her in peril.

"Trinity was the same," Shannon remarked over her shoulder. "When her grandmother was sick, she researched everything there was to find about lung cancer. We didn't think it was healthy, but there was no stopping her."

Christian gave a sad little laugh. "Remember, she thought you could develop a drug that would save her?" he said to his wife.

Shannon turned the heat off on the stove. She wiped a tear from her eye. "Oh yes. That was a low point for me as a parent—her realizing that even though I was a chemist with a major pharmaceutical company, I couldn't save her grandmother."

"Her realizing that her parents couldn't save the day was the devastating part," Christian said.

"At least you were there," Josie said. "A safe place for her to fall, comfort when she was heartbroken."

"I'm not sure we were any help to her at all," Shannon said with a sigh. She used the spatula to transfer the omelet from the pan to a plate and set it in front of Josie. She hadn't eaten since the night before, and still had no appetite, but she took the fork Shannon offered and dug in. She needed all the fuel she could get to continue searching for her sister.

"Those years after Mom died were brutal," Christian agreed.

"So you said," Josie said. "But she turned out just fine."

"Did she?" Shannon asked. "She has no friends. This past couple of months has been the roughest—even worse than early on in her career when that source fed her bad information on a story and got her kicked off the morning network show. She's got no one but us. We thought she'd got past all the bullying and relational issues in middle and high school but maybe she didn't."

"It doesn't matter now," Christian said. "What matters is getting her back alive."

Josie asked, "She didn't have a best friend in high school?"

"No," Shannon said. "It was always very sad. We would want to take her places and we'd suggest she invite a friend to go with us, but there was no one. All the other girls had paired off, but she was just alone, all the time. Any time she tried to make friends, it fizzled."

"Remember that one girl?" Christian asked. "Her family was on vacation at the beach at the same time as us the summer before Trinity's freshman year of high school?"

"The parasailing girl? Of course I do. That bitch." Shannon looked at Josie. "This girl was in Trinity's class at the middle school. She was going to the same high school. She hung out with Trinity the entire week we were at the beach. We took them parasailing together and they had a blast. I thought it really bonded them since it was a pretty intense experience. Trinity was on top of the world. For the first time in a couple of years, I had hope for her. She had a friend finally. Someone her own age to do things with. As soon as we got back to Callowhill, the girl acted like she didn't exist."

"I think it's called 'ghosting' now," Christian said.

"It's called being a terrible human being," Shannon spat. "Then and now. I even called her mother, tried to set up some get-togethers but she blew me off as well. Trinity spent the rest of the year wondering what she had said or done wrong."

Josie's heart ached for her twin. "That's terrible."

Christian shook his head. "No, that's not terrible. After what happened to her during freshman year, that really wasn't so bad."

Shannon wiped more tears from her eyes. "You'd think after all these years, that dumb high school stuff wouldn't bother me anymore, but it still does."

"What happened?" Josie asked.

Shannon moved to the kitchen sink, searching the cabinet above it until she found teabags. She heated water in a kettle on the stove as she spoke. "It started with this purse she found at a thrift shop in Philadelphia. It was an eighties-style thing—patchwork with lots of different colors and patterns. She loved it. God knows why, but she was so thrilled with it. It was unlike anything anyone else had, she said."

"Because it was from twenty years before her time," Christian said.

Shannon shook her head. "That shouldn't have mattered. She liked it. It was a bag. Well, she took it to school, and it was like blood in the water to those horrible kids. Immediately they started making fun of her, calling her 'ugly bag lady.'"

"How creative," Josie said.

"Yes, well, they were never very smart, those kids," Shannon said. "Then they said she couldn't afford a real bag and started calling her 'Poorhouse Payne' and that pretty much set the tone for the entire year."

Christian said. "Trinity couldn't understand why they would make fun of her for being poor when we clearly weren't. We tried to explain that wasn't the point—these kids were being cruel for cruelty's sake."

Shannon chimed in. "We told her it was unacceptable for anyone to make fun of another person because of their socioeconomic status, and that if they weren't calling her 'Poorhouse Payne', they'd find something else to tease her about."

In her mind, Josie catalogued the handbags she'd found among Trinity's things upstairs. "What happened to the purse?"

Shannon poured hot water into a mug and dipped a teabag into it. "She threw it away. Before she even left school. She was mortified. I marched her right back down to school to pick it out of the trash because I wanted her to keep taking it to school to prove a point—"

Christian smiled. "Which was that those kids could shove their taunts right up their asses, although I believe my wife used much stronger language back then."

Shannon went on, "But when we got there, all the trash bins had been emptied. There were about a hundred trash bags in the dumpster. Trinity's day had already been horrific, I didn't want to make it worse by making her dumpster dive for the very thing that had made her the object of such ridicule."

Josie could just imagine if anyone from school had seen that. Poorhouse Payne dumpster diving with her own mother? The rumors and verbal abuse would be relentless. "Good call," she told Shannon.

"We told her to ignore them, to keep her head held high, that it didn't matter. They were just being cruel for no reason and who would want to be friends with people like that, anyway?"

All things that well-meaning parents told children who were being bullied, Josie knew, but which rarely helped in any situation. Then again, what else was there to say or even to do?

"The next day," Shannon continued. "She took one of my very expensive bags from my closet without telling me and wore it to school."

Josie flinched. Although she and Trinity had had similar tastes in high school, their personalities couldn't have been more different. If it had been Josie who'd endured all that abuse over a vintage eighties bag at fourteen, she would have made the loudest and most obnoxious bully wear it as a hat by the end of the day, and then she would have paraded that person around so all of his or her cronies knew not to mess with her anymore. Then, she would have saved up for an entire collection of vintage eighties handbags and taken a different one to school each day of the week, daring anyone to make fun of her.

She couldn't help but wonder if she'd been like that because she wasn't raised by Shannon and Christian. Had her own shitty child-hood given her some grit she might not have developed otherwise? Shaking the thoughts from her head, she focused on her parents. "What happened after that?"

Shannon put the mug of tea in front of Josie. "Chamomile," she said. "It will help you sleep."

Christian said, "The kids said she stole it. One of them took it from her and said they were going to turn her into the main office for stealing. She said it was her mother's, and then a group of about four of them destroyed it."

"Ripped it to shreds," Shannon said.

"My God."

"It was bad," Christian said. "We decided enough was enough and got the principal involved. Shannon even called the police."

"Over a bag?" Josie couldn't help asking.

Shannon shook her head. "Not over the bag. I didn't care about the bag. These kids forcibly ripped this bag from Trinity's body and destroyed it. Can you imagine walking down a city street and someone coming up to you, tearing your purse from your body and then shredding it right in front of you? That's not acceptable behavior. We wouldn't tolerate that kind of behavior as adults in a world that has consequences. Why should we let high school kids get away with it?"

"True," Josie conceded.

"Imagine these kids going into the workforce thinking they can act like this? That they can do whatever they damn well please and nothing will happen to them? Assaulting people verbally and physically, destroying other peoples' property? Grown-ups have to respect the rules of a civilized society, why shouldn't high school kids have to do the same?"

"Shan," Christian said.

She waved a hand in the air. "Okay, okay, I'll get off my soapbox now. Sorry."

"It's okay," Josie said. "What happened after that?"

Christian said, "Well those particular kids were disciplined, and they didn't dare come after Trinity again—not physically—but they turned everyone else in the school against her. Don't go near Poorhouse Payne or she'll call the cops and say you did something to her. That sort of thing. She still had issues. Lots of them, including getting into a fight with a girl from another school during a school trip. That's what led to the whole community service thing."

"But she never found her place in high school," Shannon said. "It was hell from beginning to end. I still wonder if we should have home-schooled her. If we did the wrong thing by forcing her to go there every day."

"I don't know," Josie said. "It might have prepared her well for the job she has now. She works in a pretty cutthroat industry—and she's exceptionally good at what she does."

"Maybe," Shannon said. "Sometimes in life you just never know if you're doing the right thing when you're actually doing it."

CHAPTER THIRTY-FIVE

The first time Alex saw the black vultures was on one of his adventures with his father. He often mistook them for hawks when they flew high overhead. It was only when they glided closer to the ground and he saw the black underside of their great wings that he knew they were vultures. His father told him to ignore them. "Dirty scavengers," he called them. "They don't even have nests. They roost on the ground and in abandoned buildings."

Alex didn't see the problem. In his mind, the vultures were the intelligent ones. There was no waste. They fed on things already dead. They were twice as large as most of the other raptors that his father seemed to worship.

"Ugly, stupid things," Francis called the scavengers. He did whatever he could to ensure they didn't come onto the land, but there was too much wildlife. Inevitably, a deer or coyote or smaller game like a rabbit or raccoon would die and they would descend on the corpse, picking it clean with savage efficiency.

This was what Alex found awe-inspiring.

He liked to go out by the rocks and leave them a gift—there was no shortage of carcasses in the woods. Then he waited for the vultures to arrive. There was plenty of time since he'd been banished from the house other than mealtimes. One day he was watching them scavenge a red fox when he heard a noise behind him. Expecting Francis, he whirled, on guard for insults and ready to be shooed away from the activities of the "stupid, dirty scavengers," but it was Zandra.

"What are you doing here?" he asked.

"I'm exploring."

"No," he said. "How did you get out?"

"I told her what he was doing in that room."

Alex felt a wave of disgust wash over him. He swallowed. "What room?"

"I know you're not that stupid," she said. "My bedroom."

He said nothing.

She picked up twigs that had gathered in the cracks of the rocks and tossed them toward the group of vultures, but they were undeterred. They maintained singular focus. When they were doing their work, very little could disturb them. Alex particularly liked this about them.

Zandra said, "That's really disgusting."

"No, it's not."

"Yeah, it is. It's gross."

She couldn't see the beauty, not just in the majestic black birds, but in the art of scavenging. He didn't respond.

A moment later, she spoke again. "I want to be outside, with you."

"You can't be," he said. "You hurt mother. I'm supposed to stop you. Sometimes, I don't really want to. Sometimes I want to let you... do bad things."

"You do?" she asked.

He shrugged. "I have bad thoughts."

"About Mom?"

"About everyone," he whispered.

"Even me?" she asked.

"Yes."

"Like what?"

He looked away from the scene unfolding before them where one of the vultures had just loosened a small bone, flying away with it. Alex said, "I want to know what you look like without skin."

CHAPTER THIRTY-SIX

Josie didn't think she'd be able to sleep, especially after the revelations about Trinity's childhood. No wonder Trinity was the way she was—ambitious, driven to a fault, and almost callous in her pursuit of stories. By all accounts and from the photo albums that Josie had pored over that morning, Trinity's early childhood had been idyllic whereas Josie's had been straight out of hell. By high school, when Josie went to live with Lisette and her life was finally getting on track, Trinity had descended into her own special sort of hell. As Josie lay in the guest room, blackout shades drawn, she wondered why Trinity had never told her any of this. Then she realized it was the same reason that Josie never talked willingly about the woman who had kidnapped and raised her. Those horrors were in the past and that's where they belonged. Josie had no desire to revisit them, not for anyone. Still, as she drifted off to sleep, her heart was heavy with regret for all the conversations she'd never had with her sister.

When she woke three hours later, her phone showed that it was just after one in the afternoon and she had two missed calls from Noah. Josie called him back before she even had a chance to blink the sleep from her eyes. "What's going on?" she asked when he answered. "Any news?"

"Not yet," he said. "I'm sorry. But Drake made some calls and got the evidence taken from the scene at the cabin forwarded to the FBI lab and expedited since this is now a serial case. I don't know what kinds of strings he had to pull, but having all this stuff analyzed sooner rather than later can't hurt."

"What about the prints from the cabin, Trinity's car, and her phone case?" Josie asked. "Have they been run through AFIS?"

"Yeah, but no hits. There are some unknowns from both the car and the cabin, but we can't be certain that any of them belong to the killer. No prints on the packaging from the comb except mine and Trinity's. They're still analyzing the rest of the packaging and the comb but that's going to take longer to process. Also, Drake's got agents checking out the leads you suggested—ornithologists, veterinarians, game commission officers—Mettner gave them a list."

"Did you sleep?" Josie asked.

"A few hours."

She stood up and peeked into the hallway. The smell of food cooking wafted upstairs. "I think Shannon is going to try to feed me again before I come back."

"Let her. We'll be here."

Josie hung up, used the bathroom, and headed downstairs. In the kitchen, she found Christian at the stove instead of Shannon. "Your mother's in the attic, putting things away," he told her. "I'm surprised you didn't hear her."

"I was pretty tired," Josie said.

A moment later, Christian slid a dish with pasta and roasted vegetables in front of her. "Eat," he said. "I've got to make some calls since I won't be going to work for the time being. You okay here?"

Josie nodded. As soon as he was gone, she went to her bag and took out the copy of the Bone Artist file she had brought with her. The first thing she did was tuck the copies of the photos into the back of the file. If Shannon or Christian walked back in, she didn't want them seeing those. As she ate, she thumbed through the autopsy reports, DNA profiles, victim profiles, trying to see what Trinity had seen that had unlocked the case for her. She had to have put something critical together if she was able to make contact with the killer, especially after law enforcement had been looking for him for over a decade.

But nothing stood out to her.

She went back to the psychological profile, reading it more carefully. Someone—she assumed Drake—had written in the margins and at the end: *craves attention and validation for his intelligence; wants to feel important; employ Supercop strategy?* Josie made a note to ask Drake about that later. She read through the profile twice, trying again to view things through Trinity's eyes. Nothing stood out. She finished her meal and washed the plate in the sink. Returning to her seat, she kept still and strained to hear Shannon and Christian in the house. Christian's voice carried easily from his first-floor study—he was still on the phone. A few thumps from upstairs assured her that Shannon was cleaning the hallway. Confident that they'd both be engaged for a few more minutes, Josie took a deep breath and pulled out the photos she'd hidden earlier. She steeled herself, realizing too late that it wasn't the best idea to eat just before viewing them. She took another deep breath. Forcing her eyes to focus on the remains marked as Robert Ingram's, she tried to think clinically about this instead of emotionally. She needed to remove the element of horror and try to think like the killer. He wasn't horrified by what he did. Most serial killers enjoyed their work. This killer in particular not only enjoyed his work but was trying to make a statement. But what kind? He deemed himself an artist. These garish displays were art to him. Symbolic of something. Josie reached down into her bag and took out her notebook and pen.

She began to draw the shape of the display, starting with a circle, like a clock. Inside that circle she drew another circle to represent the torso. Where six would be, she drew a line representing the arm bones, then more shapes at the end of them to match the skull and pelvic bone. She went to draw a line from two o'clock where the leg bones had been arranged and stopped suddenly.

"What the hell?"

She turned a page in her notebook and started again with the circle, drawing a line downward from six o'clock and then another line crossing it.

She riffled through the photos until she found Terri Abbott's remains. In that display the pelvis and skull had been placed in a reverse position at the end of the leg bones which were at two o'clock. Josie turned another page in her notebook and drew a new circle, this time with a line outward from the two o'clock position and a line at the end of that—not a line, she realized. An arrow.

She sat back in her chair and stared at her crude drawings. Symbols. Female and male.

Closing the file, she took out her cell phone and called Noah.

CHAPTER THIRTY-SEVEN

He answered on the second ring. "You okay?" he asked. "You on your way back?"

"I'm leaving soon," Josie told him. "Where are you? Are you with the team?"

"Gretchen went home to sleep but Mettner and Drake just got here. They grabbed a few hours of sleep this morning. What's going on? Did you find the diary?"

"No," Josie said. "Not that. But I think I figured out what the displays mean. Get the photos out, would you?"

"Hold on."

She heard him moving around, talking, gathering Drake and Mettner. She heard footsteps pounding down stairs, a door creaking open, papers rustling. Then Noah came back on the line. "Okay, we've got the photos. I'm going to put you on speakerphone."

There was a beep and then Mettner and Drake greeted her. She plunged ahead. "The photos of the male victims, look at them. The skull and pelvic bones in those are on the bottom, at the six o'clock position."

"We see that," Mettner said.

"Cover up the leg bones at the two o'clock position. Pretend they're not there. All you've got is a circle with a line extending from the bottom and another line crossing it."

Someone gave a low whistle. Then Drake said, "It's the symbol for female."

"Yes," Josie said. "Now look at Terri Abbott's, the only female victim, the pelvic bone and skull are near the top, at the two o'clock position."

"Got it," Noah said. "If we cover the bones at the six o'clock position, we've got the symbol for male. Holy shit."

"They're symbols. Male and female," Josie said.

Mettner asked, "But why does the female victim get the male sign and the male get the female sign?"

Josie thought about Trinity's Post-it notes. Symmetry. Something about symmetry. But what? Wouldn't it make more sense for the males to be marked with the male sign and the female to be marked with the female sign?

"I don't know," Josie said. "But this is something."

There was a long silence. Then Drake said, "This is brilliant, Detective Quinn, and it's very likely you're right about these being male and female symbols. Unfortunately, this doesn't get us any closer to finding this guy."

Josie slumped in her chair. He was right.

"But," Drake added. "I'll talk to my contact in the Behavioral Analysis Unit and see if they can make any sense of it or if they can think of a way to use this in our investigation."

"Thanks," Josie said, feeling defeated. "I'm going to head back in a few minutes. I'll see you then."

She packed up her things, said goodbye to Shannon and Christian, who promised to follow her back to Denton later that day, and got into her vehicle. As she drove a series of tree-lined rural roads out of Callowhill, her exhausted mind worked through what she'd just figured out. Had Trinity figured it out as well? Surely, she had. If so, where had that led? How had she gotten from the male/female symbols to drawing the killer out of hiding after so many years?

She tightened her hands on the steering wheel as the road narrowed ahead of her. To her right was a drop-off leading to a ravine and to her left were trees as far as the eye could see. A moment later, on her left, a truck came into view. It had been backed into a break in the woods on the shoulder of the road. Its white cab jutted out from the trees. Dirt covered the bottom of the door and someone had used a fingertip to write the words *Wash Me* in it. Josie gave a little laugh as she passed. From the corner of her eye, below the words, something else caught her eye. A symbol.

She was already well past the truck when its significance registered.

He likely drives a pretty nondescript vehicle but one that could accommodate his activities, so a van or a pickup truck but likely an older model, nothing that would draw a great deal of attention.

Her mind worked quickly through the possibilities. Could she be right? Or was the stress of the case and her lack of sleep making her crazy? Josie shook her head, as if to reorder her thoughts. It couldn't be a coincidence, she decided. Everything that came next felt like it took hours, but in reality was only a matter of seconds. She spun her vehicle around and gunned it, heading back toward the truck. Using the voice command feature in her Ford Escape she dialed Noah. Before he could say anything, she said, "Noah, I think I've got him. The Bone Artist."

"Josie, what? What are you talking—"

"Listen to me, there's not much time." She rattled off her location as best she could estimate it. "Looks like a white Chevrolet pickup truck. Older model."

Before she could say anything else, a man stepped out of the woods and got into the driver's side of the truck. He didn't see her. He was tall, maybe six feet, dressed in jeans and a flannel shirt. Brown hair peeked from beneath a baseball cap pulled low over his face. He looked up just before she reached him, and they locked eyes.

"He's here," Josie said. "And his face—there's something—"

The man punched the gas and his truck lurched forward, spraying grass and mud behind it. He aimed directly for her, his front-end plowing into the front passenger's side of Josie's car. The impact jarred her, jerking her body to and fro. Her head smacked against the driver's side window. Stars appeared before her eyes. Her hands clutched the wheel, trying to gain control of her SUV, but she couldn't. The man continued to accelerate, his truck pushing her car all the way across to the other side of the road. Josie was vaguely aware of the impact as her car was crushed against the guardrail. Metal screamed against metal. The truck kept coming. Her car tipped, rolling down the ravine, glass popping and smashing. Her seat belt tightened across her chest, knocking the air from her lungs momentarily. She landed upside down, her car suspended between two large trees.

Everything around her seemed hazy. The windshield had shattered. Glass was everywhere. She tried to move. Her fingers reached for her seat buckle, punching the button to release her, but it wouldn't work.

Noah's voice floated from somewhere inside the vehicle, only adding to her disorientation. "Josie," he shouted. "Josie! Are you okay? Josie!"

"Acc—accident," she rasped.

His voice receded after that although she could hear him talking to someone else in the background, barking orders. "Stay where you are," he said into the phone once more. "Help is on the way."

Through her disorientation, her mind tried to tell her something very important. He was there. He was close. *He tried to kill you.* She sucked in a breath and blinked rapidly, setting off a firestorm in her eyeballs. Pricks of pain exploded across her corneas.

"Don't touch them," said a male voice as she reached for her eyes.

Panic stiffened every muscle in her body. She couldn't open her eyes. The pain was too unbearable. She put her hands out as if to ward him off. Her voice was high-pitched when she spoke. "Get away from me. Don't touch me."

She sensed him coming closer. There was a grunt and then she felt and heard her door open. Her body recoiled but the man's voice stayed calm. "You've got glass in your eyes," he said. "Don't rub them and don't blink."

A scream erupted from her body, and her arms and legs flailed when she felt his hands on her, tugging and pulling. Then there was a click and she was in freefall. Seconds later, she landed with a thud on the forest floor. Arms slid under her knees and shoulders and lifted her. Her body jostled against him as he carried her. He froze when Noah's tinny voice came from above their heads. "Josie! Josie! Talk to me."

Her body lowered and she felt the ground beneath her once more. She opened one eye slowly in spite of the pain, but he was a blur walking away from her. She tried to stand but dizziness assailed her, and she fell to her knees.

"Wait," she gasped. "Wait. My sister."

He stopped but didn't turn around. Her hands searched for her shoulder holster, tried to remove her gun, but the damn holster wouldn't unsnap. Or her fingers were shaking too hard. "Where is she?" Josie asked him. "Where's Trinity?"

No answer. No movement. Her eyes burned.

"Is she still alive?" Josie asked. "Please, tell me if she's still alive."

He started walking again. Josie crawled after him, desperate as her only link to her sister receded from view. "Wait," she screamed, tears streaming down her face, the burning in her corneas an inferno now, her vision a strange, misshapen kaleidoscope. "Take me with you! Take me with you!"

The footsteps stopped. His shape loomed ahead of her, a blur on the steep incline of the ravine. His words floated on the air, across the seemingly interminable distance between them. He said, "Not yet."

CHAPTER THIRTY-EIGHT

Josie crawled to the top of the ravine, to the shoulder of the road, using her hands to guide her and trying not to blink or to think about her fiery eyes. It seemed like hours until she heard a vehicle speeding down the road. She wanted to open her eyes, to see who it was. Help? Or was he back? Would he take her with him? Take her to Trinity? Moments later, she heard the squawk of a police radio and relief flooded through her. Hands lifted her. Questions were fired at her. She did her best to answer, but she could barely concentrate because the pain was so intense. Every part of her body hurt, especially her neck. Still, she did her best to give them a description of the vehicle and of the man.

"His face," she said. "There's something wrong with his face."

A man's voice said, "What? Like a scar?"

"No. Yes. Sort of." What had she seen? It had been so fast. Had it only been a shadow or the angle from which she'd seen him when he first looked up and saw her? "A burn mark, I think, on the left side of his face. Red."

"Got it. Let's go."

They took her to a hospital. Hands probed her. She was wheeled to and fro. X-rays and CT scans were taken. A gentle nurse flushed both her eyes again and again, water pouring over her entire head like a cold, painful baptism. Eventually she heard familiar voices. Noah, Gretchen, Shannon, and Christian. She wanted to talk to them, to reach for them, but the doctors kept them at bay. Next came rounds of eyedrops and a doctor prying open her eyelids and tweezing out tiny splinters of glass. Then she was in a bed, an IV in the crook of her arm. She heard Noah's voice again and then an unfamiliar voice saying, "She's got a concussion and some bruising. We got all the glass out of her eyes. She was lucky—she only sustained corneal abrasions which should heal well with proper care. She's had a pretty traumatic day though. We'll let her rest a bit."

A moment later, Josie felt the familiar feeling of Noah's hand sliding into hers. She fought the overwhelming fatigue creeping into every inch of her body, but it was too heavy. Squeezing Noah's hand, she fell into a deep sleep.

Night had fallen outside of her hospital room when she woke. Noah snoozed in a chair next to her bed. Blinking against the dim light in the room, she tried to sit up. Her body felt like it had been put through a triathlon. The muscles in her neck and back felt stiff and achy. "Noah," she said, her voice coming out as a broken whisper.

He jolted awake, leaping from his chair and leaning over the bed. "I'm here. You scared the shit out of me. You okay?"

She blinked several times, relieved that his face came into focus above her. "I'm fine. My eyes feel like someone poured sand into them."

"Yeah, they'll feel that way for a while," he said. "The doctor gave me drops for you to put in them for two weeks—that should help."

"Did you—did you get him?"

She could tell by his eyes that they hadn't. "I'm sorry, no. Callowhill is small. They didn't have the resources to rescue you and put on a full-scale search for this guy. We called in the State Police, but so far they've got nothing. There's a statewide APB out for an older model, white Chevy pickup."

"With front end damage," Josie said. "He rammed right into me."

Noah's head reared back. "*He* did this to you?"

She started to nod but pain shot up the back of her neck into the base of her skull. She gasped and closed her eyes until the pulsating beats of agony subsided. When she opened them again, Noah stared at her curiously.

"His truck was backed into the woods so I couldn't see his license plate. I thought I saw something on the passenger's side door, though. It looked like, like—"

"Like what?" Noah asked.

But her mind was fuzzy as she tried to bring what she had seen into relief. "Shorthand," she said finally. "Like the kind in Trinity's car."

"Maybe I should have the doctor come back in," he said, his brow furrowed with concern.

"No," Josie said. "Just listen." She explained about the *Wash Me* message written in the dirt on the side of the truck and how she'd seen what looked like shorthand below it. She'd been well past the truck by the time the significance of the symbol and the nondescript older model pickup truck dawned on her.

"Why was he in Callowhill? He must be stalking you," Noah said.

"Me or Shannon or Christian," she said. "It's hard to say. Is Patrick still at school in Denton?"

"He's staying at our house with Lisette but yeah, he's there and he's safe."

"I don't know why the Bone Artist was here in Callowhill," Josie said. "But he knew who I was. I turned around and started driving back toward him. As soon as he saw me…"

"If this guy has a television, or the internet, he'd know that Trinity Payne has a twin sister," Noah said. "So yeah, he probably knew right away it was you."

"He came after me. No hesitation. Ran me off the road, and then… My car," Josie said. "The seat belt—was it cut?"

"Yeah," Noah said. "What did you use to saw yourself out?"

"Not me," she said. "*He* cut me out."

"Josie, I'm a little worried now. Your head—"

"I know, I know. I have a concussion, but I'm telling you this is what happened. He came down to the car. He cut me out. He was carrying me and then your voice—the hands-free phone app was still on in the car. When he heard it, he put me on the ground and started to walk away. I asked him where Trinity was and if she was still alive and he wouldn't tell me anything."

"He was talking to you?"

"Yes," Josie said, a shiver working its way through her entire body. "But then he heard you. He must have thought first responders would get there too quickly. He didn't want to take the chance, so he left."

Noah was silent for several seconds. Then he said, "You can't be alone after this. Do you understand? Not until we get this guy."

"I'm fine," Josie said even as a steady pounding started in her head.

Noah smiled and smoothed a lock of hair away from her face. "I know, you're always fine. Why do you think he wanted you? Did he say anything?"

"I don't know," Josie admitted. "He didn't say anything."

"This doesn't fit with this guy's pattern though," Noah said. "To take two people so close together—three if you count Nicci Webb."

"I know." She needed more time to think it over. In that moment, her thoughts were still muddled. She looked around the room. "They admitted me? When can I leave?"

"Tomorrow. They want to keep an eye on you. Frankly, I think they should."

She took a look around the room. A television had been affixed to the wall opposite her bed. Two reporters sat at a news desk. On a screen behind them was a photo of Trinity. Beneath it were the words: *Network Anchor Abducted.* The volume was set low, but Josie could still hear the reporters discussing the case.

"Am I in Callowhill?"

"About twenty miles away. This was the closest hospital. Tomorrow you'll be released, and you'll come back to Denton with me, Gretchen, Shannon, and Christian."

She knew she couldn't argue. Not only was she in no position to fight them, but she was in pain and exhausted. The television screen cut to Hayden Keating standing outside of the Denton Police station, talking into a microphone with an intense look of concern on his face. He kept referring to Trinity as "my partner" even though she hadn't shared the anchor desk with him in two months. Josie shook her head, sending a spike of pain up her neck into the base of her skull. She turned back to Noah.

"Did you guys talk to Hayden Keating?"

"Yeah," Noah answered. "He came to the station. He didn't know anything useful. He asked more questions than we did."

"Mettner's still working the case?"

"Yes, with the assistance of the FBI. Gretchen is out coordinating with Callowhill PD and the State Police to see if we can find this guy or his truck." He took out his phone and fired off a text. "I'm letting her know about the front-end damage. You said he had a burn on his face?"

"I think so. It all happened so fast. He had a hat pulled low, but there was something going down the left side of his face. Dark red or something. Before I had a chance to get a good look at it, he was ramming into me like a maniac. When he came down to the car, there was glass in my eyes. I couldn't see. I'm sorry."

"Don't be. You did great. Now get some rest. I'll wake you if there's any news."

CHAPTER THIRTY-NINE

They walked back to the house. The kitchen was cold and dark. No Hanna. No dinner cooking on the stove. In the foyer, Alex saw why. Francis's body lay in a crumpled heap at the bottom of the steps. One of his legs was twisted at an unusual angle. For a moment, Alex thought he was dead. A pool of blood circled his head like a halo, and he wasn't moving. Alex peered hard at him, trying to see if his chest was rising and falling, but he couldn't tell. Then Francis blinked. Alex jumped back. Zandra giggled. Her laughter went on for several minutes. Alex looked over to see Hanna sitting barefoot on the steps. Her elbows were on her knees and from one hand dangled a metal bar which Alex recognized as a leg from one of her easels.

When Zandra's laughter stopped, Hanna looked over, as if noticing Alex for the first time. Her eyes were wider than he'd ever seen them. With the bar, she pointed toward Francis. "He wasn't like us," she said.

Alex walked over and tried to take the bar from her, but she clutched it to her chest. "No," she said. "They'll think you did this. You'll be in trouble. They'll make you go away. I did this for you, do you understand?"

"No you didn't, you selfish bitch," Zandra said as she walked over to Francis and stared down into his face. She let a long string of spit drip from her puckered lips into one of his eyes, and giggled some more.

Hanna ignored her. Her eyes pleaded with Alex. "He wasn't like us, do you understand?"

"No," Alex mumbled.

Zandra kicked Francis in the ribs. "He's not our father, dummy. That's what she's trying to tell you. He wouldn't marry her because she had two bastards."

Alex looked to Hanna for confirmation. She nodded. He tried to remember a time when Francis had not been in their lives, but he couldn't. Francis had always been their father.

"I'm sorry," Hanna whispered.

"Save it for the police," Zandra said, now sounding bored. "I'm going to get something to eat."

CHAPTER FORTY

As Noah promised, the next day Josie was discharged. He and Gretchen drove her back to Denton with Shannon and Christian following. Josie wanted to go back to the stationhouse, but no one would let her. She needed rest, they said. Rest, rest, rest. No amount of rest was going to bring Trinity back. Noah left her at home and went back to the station to join the rest of her team. Sitting on her living room couch with Lisette on one side and Trout on the other, Josie tried for hours to recreate the shorthand symbol she had seen on the side of the Bone Artist's truck. Each time she attempted it, Lisette studied it and frowned, uttering an, "I'm not sure, dear." When Josie's head hurt too badly to keep her eyes open any longer, she gave Shannon and Christian her library card and asked them to go to Denton's local library to see if they could find a book on Gregg shorthand.

Josie swallowed some ibuprofen dry and sprawled out on her bed with her eyes closed. Sleep wouldn't come, only thoughts of Trinity and the case. In her head, she went over the Bone Artist file again and again. What had Trinity seen that Josie couldn't? What was she missing?

Symmetry. Male. Female. Symbols. Games.

Her eyes snapped open. She was overlooking a major piece of what Trinity had been studying. Creeping downstairs, she saw Trout cuddled up beside Lisette on the couch. Shannon and Christian were still out. She managed to get to the kitchen to retrieve the bag that Gretchen had gotten out of Josie's mangled car before they left Callowhill. Josie carried it upstairs and into her bedroom. She fished out the Bone Artist file and spread the pages out on the bed, searching for the notes that the Bone Artist had sent to members of the press in 2014 before his last victim was found and he went off the radar.

She lined the notes up next to one another. All of them had been delivered within the same week, addressed to different anchors. There were three major broadcast networks in the United States with popular morning shows. The Bone Artist had delivered a note addressed to a male and female anchor at each of the three networks. Except the network that Trinity worked for. Only a male anchor had received a letter at Trinity's network, not a female anchor. Josie found the photo of the envelope that note had come in and read the name: *Hayden Keating.*

Trinity's co-anchor.

The Eudora was the nicest hotel in town, so it was likely he was staying there. A brief text exchange with Trinity's assistant confirmed this. Josie started to get dressed, trading sweatpants for jeans, and a T-shirt for a Denton PD polo shirt. She strapped on her holster and found a light jacket in the closet. She ignored the dizziness that nearly knocked her to the ground when she bent to put her shoes on. She pocketed her cell phone and spent ten minutes looking for her keys before she remembered that she had no vehicle. Her Ford Escape had been totaled in yesterday's accident. She would have to wait for a check from her insurance company and then go shopping for a new car.

She sank back onto her bed with a groan. Then she called Gretchen, quietly explaining what she wanted to do. "Boss," Gretchen said, lowering her voice. "You know it's my ass if I take you out on the town. You scared the hell out of everyone here. Noah will kill me if he finds out."

"I'm not asking to go out on the town," Josie said. "I'm asking you to take me with you on one interview. You're secondary on this case. You'll have to do the questioning anyway. I'm just asking to ride along."

Laughter filtered through the line. "Sure, and if I don't let you ride along?"

Josie sighed. "Gretchen, don't make me walk to the Eudora Hotel. It's a few miles from my house."

Gretchen matched Josie's sigh. "Fine. Meet me outside in fifteen minutes."

"Around the block from my house," Josie said. "If my parents get back before you get here, I'm busted."

True to her word, Gretchen pulled up a block over from Josie's house fifteen minutes later. Josie got in and thanked her. Gretchen drove off, pointing to a large Komorrah's coffee cup in the console. "Drink that. It might help your headache."

"How do you know I have a headache?" Josie asked as she picked up the cup.

"Because you have a concussion, that's how," Gretchen said. "Now drink. As soon as we're done, I'm taking you home."

"Thank you," Josie said. She sipped from the cup, the taste and smell of the coffee making her feel somewhat restored.

"You sure about this?" Gretchen asked.

"Codie Lash was Hayden Keating's co-anchor when the Bone Artist sent notes to all the networks. He sent a note to the male and female hosts of each national network morning show—except at Trinity's network, where only Hayden Keating received one. That makes an uneven number of notes. I don't think he really likes uneven numbers."

"You mean because he only kills in even numbered years?"

"Right."

"And he sent five letters to the press instead of six?"

"Yes. It's off-balance, off-pattern."

"Is it? He took Nicci Webb, Trinity, and then tried to take you. That's three people. It's uneven. That's off-pattern. How can we know what his pattern is at all now?"

"But Trinity provoked him," Josie said. "She's the break in the pattern."

"Nicci Webb's remains were found seventeen days after she went missing, not thirty. That's off-pattern as well," Gretchen argued.

Josie sighed and rubbed her temples. "He's off-pattern now, yes, but I'm talking about six years ago when he was at the height of his known activity. He had a strict formula then. Even numbers were important to him so why would he send the male and female hosts of the other two networks letters but only send a letter to the male host of the final network?"

"Codie Lash got a letter."

"That's what I think," Josie agreed. "Why else would Trinity be looking into her?"

"You think Hayden Keating knew that Codie Lash got a letter and didn't tell the police?"

"I don't know," Josie said. "It seems unlikely but then again, she was killed in a mugging gone wrong a couple of weeks after the press received their letters. Maybe he didn't think it was relevant. Or maybe he didn't know. We'll find out."

"We have to be careful with him," Gretchen said. "Mettner still doesn't want the press to know that the Bone Artist is involved. If we give this guy any indication that there's a connection between Trinity and the Bone Artist, he's going to run with it."

"Got it," Josie said.

CHAPTER FORTY-ONE

At the Eudora, Josie let Gretchen do all the talking. The concierge rang Hayden Keating's room, talked with him for a brief moment, and then had one of his colleagues guide them to Keating's room on the tenth floor. Hayden Keating was in his late fifties, barrel-chested with thick, wavy gray hair and the straightest, whitest teeth Josie had ever seen. She'd seen him on television dressed in bespoke suits hundreds of times. Now he stood before them in a pair of faded jeans and a salmon-colored button-down shirt that was partially open, revealing springy gray chest hair. He gave them his most serious look, the one he used when he read news from the teleprompter about natural disasters and other tragedies. "Ladies," he said. "Welcome. Please, come in and have a seat."

His room was equipped with a small table and chairs. The three of them gathered at the table. Josie thought she heard water running. The door to his bathroom was closed. Was there someone else staying with him? Or was her concussed brain playing tricks on her?

Hayden asked, "Has there been any news about Trinity?"

Josie turned her attention to him and folded her hands in front of her on the table. "I'm sorry, but no. Nothing yet."

He looked disappointed. Josie wondered if it was because he was genuinely worried about Trinity or because any news would make him look good when he reported it on television. Probably the television thing.

Josie heard the distinct sound of the water in the bathroom being shut off. Then came sounds of rustling from behind the closed door.

Definitely not her imagination. She exchanged a quick glance of acknowledgment with Gretchen. If Hayden noticed, he didn't let on.

Gretchen took out her notebook and pen, slid her reading glasses on, and looked at him. "Mr. Keating, we're looking into all the things that Trinity was working on before she was abducted."

He laughed. "Working on? Trinity wasn't working on anything. Listen, I don't know how to say this, and I probably shouldn't because it's confidential." He looked pointedly at Josie. "I don't want to upset you, but—"

"The network is replacing Trinity with Mila Kates," Josie filled in.

He looked surprised.

Josie smiled. "It's our job to find things out, Mr. Keating. Trinity wasn't working on anything for the network. We think maybe she was trying to develop a story—something that would have a lot of appeal to viewers—that she could pitch to the network in a bid to save her job. Either that or she would use it as leverage to get a position at another network."

He smiled. "That sounds like her." He looked over his shoulder toward the closed bathroom door. "Well, if you already know, then you won't mind…"

"Mind what?" Josie asked.

"Darling," he called. "Join us, would you?"

The bathroom door swung open and there stood a woman in a thick, white terrycloth robe, toweling her short blonde hair dry. She sauntered toward them in her bare feet, her blue eyes locked on Josie. "Wow," she said. "You do look quite like her, don't you?"

Josie had to remind herself to close her mouth.

Hayden said, "This is—"

"I know who this is," Josie snapped.

The woman extended a hand to Gretchen. "Mila Kates," she said. "You are?"

"Detective Palmer. We're here to talk to Mr. Keating."

Mila leaned a hip into Hayden's shoulder and slung an arm across the back of his neck. "Do you have any leads?"

Josie felt her face flush. She gripped the handles of her chair, ready to push herself up, primed to explode. Gretchen placed a gentle hand on her wrist, a reminder to keep her anger in check. A tight smile spread across Gretchen's face. "Miss Kates, I'm sorry but we're not at liberty to discuss the details of an active investigation. Did you know Trinity?"

"Oh, not well. We would run into each other from time to time at different functions."

Josie said, "Hayden didn't introduce the two of you?"

The two looked at one another, smiling. When they looked back at Josie and Gretchen, they had matching expressions of discomfort. "We haven't gone public with our relationship yet," Hayden said.

Gretchen said, "That must be tough."

They both nodded.

Keeping the note of accusation out of her voice and instead choosing a tone of deep concern, Josie said, "It must have been really difficult for both of you after Ms. Kates' stalker confronted her on live television."

Hayden looked up at Mila, eyes shining with unshed tears. "It was very hard," he admitted. "I wanted to go to her, but the press coverage was so intense—obviously—so I had to keep my distance."

Mila touched his cheek, gazing down at him so lovingly that Josie felt her stomach lurch. "And all I wanted was to see you and I couldn't. Not until things died down."

Mila Kates' stalker had made her national news long before Trinity's job was in jeopardy. Picking up on Josie's line of questioning, Gretchen asked with the perfect note of innocence, "Was it Hayden's idea to bring you over to his network? So you wouldn't have to be separated?"

The motion was barely perceptible, but Josie noticed it: Hayden nudged Mila away from him just slightly. He cleared his throat. "Why don't you get dressed while I finish up here?"

She raised a brow. "I thought I'd hear what the detectives have to say about Trinity's case."

Hayden smiled. "Darling, you just heard them say they can't discuss it."

She folded her arms over her chest and glared at him.

He added, "Trinity was my co-anchor for years. I'm well-equipped to answer any questions about her."

Wordlessly, Mila turned on her heel and stalked off to the bathroom, slamming the door behind her. Hayden let out a sigh and gave one of his on-camera megawatt smiles. "You have to understand," he said quietly. "I've been with the network for decades. Far longer than Trinity. She's talented. She can get an anchor job anywhere. I wouldn't have requested that the network bring Mila in if I didn't think Trinity would land on her feet."

Josie's heart thundered in her chest. It took everything in her not to fly across the table and wrap her hands around his pompous throat. She felt the pressure of Gretchen's fingers on her arm. Calm. She had to stay calm. Strangling the back-stabbing bastard in front of her was not going to get Trinity back. They needed information from him. She took a deep breath and a moment later, Gretchen released her arm.

Ignoring Hayden's admission, Gretchen said, "As we told you, Trinity was working on something before she was abducted. We believe that one of the stories she was looking into was the Codie Lash murder."

His features went slack. "Codie Lash. Wow. Well, any story on Codie would be gold. She was successful, beloved, and tragically murdered. They never solved the case, did you know that?"

"We're aware," Gretchen said. "Were you and Codie close? Trinity's notes indicated she was particularly interested in the few weeks before Codie's death. Do you have any idea why?"

"Codie was in line for a humanitarian award, I remember that. She was actually on her way to a charity gala with her husband when they were both killed. I didn't see her much before she died even though we were on air together. There was a—" he broke off. "I'm not sure I can say."

Josie, having regained as much of her composure as she could gather, leaned forward and touched Hayden's hand in exactly the same manner she'd seen Trinity do countless times on air. "Whatever it is, it will stay between us. We're just trying to do everything and anything we can to find Trinity."

He looked at her fingers which lingered on the top of his hand. With his other palm, he patted them. Josie worked hard not to recoil. "Of course," he said. "It has nothing to do with Trinity anyway. It was a long time ago. There was this serial killer back then. I won't say which one because I was never supposed to talk about it. He sent a letter to me at the network. He wanted me to play some kind of sick game with him on air. I turned it over to the FBI immediately, of course."

Gretchen said, "Wow, that must have been frightening."

"It was unsettling, yes. Anyway, there was a flurry of meetings and such with the network brass and the FBI."

"Codie didn't get a letter?" Josie asked.

"No. She would have turned it over right away."

Gretchen said, "Did you have people who went through your mail before it got to you?"

"No," Keating said. "We opened everything ourselves. Letters and packages were rare anyway—still are. Now everything is email or social media messages."

"Did Codie know about your letter?"

"Of course. She was my co-host. We were together all the time. She was in on all the meetings."

"Meetings?" Gretchen coaxed.

"Well there was talk of me engaging with this… killer, as per his letter. There were a handful of agents in the Bureau who thought they could safely draw him out. Ultimately, the network attorneys and my own personal attorney felt it would be too risky for me. Without a consensus, the whole thing fell flat."

Josie asked, "What did Codie think of the whole thing? She would have been on the air with you if you'd gone forward with trying to draw him out."

"She didn't think there was any harm in it. In fact, she believed I should do it because it might save lives."

"You didn't think you could save lives?" Gretchen asked.

"It wasn't up to me. It was up to the attorneys, the network. Besides, it was all a joke. The killer did kill again shortly after that. Then Codie died and, well, life goes on, doesn't it?"

Josie had to bite her lower lip to keep something snide from coming out. This man had used his clout with the network to get rid of Trinity, pouncing on one of her mistakes to ensure her exit so that he could bring his much younger girlfriend into a position she hadn't even earned. His actions had caused a domino effect that ultimately led to Trinity desperately looking for a story that would put her back on top. A story about the Bone Artist. Now she was gone, and Josie didn't know if they'd get her back.

Life would go on for him and for Mila Kates but what about Trinity? What about Josie, Shannon, Christian, and Patrick? What about Nicci Webb? Her daughter and granddaughter? Had the Bone Artist taken her because Trinity had drawn him out? The faces of Monica Webb and little Annabelle flashed through Josie's mind. She had a job to do, she reminded herself. That didn't change, no matter how angry she was with Hayden Keating. Swallowing her rage, Josie asked, "Does the name Nicci Webb mean anything to you?"

He shook his head, the lines at the corners of his eyes tightening in look of puzzlement. "No, it doesn't. Who is she?"

Josie took out her phone and pulled up the photo of Nicci. The press hadn't yet caught wind of her murder. Their only focus was on Trinity. There was no way that Josie was giving this snake a tip. She ignored his question. "Do you recognize this woman?"

He stared at the photo. "No, I'm sorry, I don't. Who is she?"

Josie pocketed her phone. She stood up and Gretchen followed suit. "Mr. Keating, thank you for your time," Josie said. "If we have any more questions, we'll be in touch."

Hayden jumped up, knocking his chair back. He threw both hands up in front of him. "Wait, wait," he said. "Who is that woman? Is she connected to Trinity's abduction?"

Gretchen said, "We thought she might be, but she's clearly not. Like we said, Trinity was working on a lot of things before she was abducted, trying to develop a story, but not all of them panned out."

"Oh, okay," Hayden said. He scurried around the table and followed them to the door. "Please let me know right away if you learn anything," he implored them. "I worked side by side with Trinity for three years. Anything you can tell me would put my mind at ease." He smiled and Josie noted it was the same smile he used on air when he did cooking segments.

CHAPTER FORTY-TWO

In the car, Josie seethed. "That son of a bitch. He ruined my sister's life."

"I'm sorry, boss," Gretchen said, turning her key in the ignition. "You showed admirable restraint back there."

Josie's hands curled into fists in her lap. Through gritted teeth, she said, "He doesn't think Trinity's coming back. That's why he didn't care if we knew about him and Mila Kates."

Gretchen said, "We'd better get to finding her then. Getting her back alive would be big news. Big enough to make Mila Kates a distant memory."

Josie looked over at Gretchen and smiled, her rage receding a bit. "Yes," she said, loosening her jaw. "We'd better."

"Codie Lash got a letter from the Bone Artist," Gretchen offered.

"Absolutely," Josie agreed. "I don't think she told Hayden about it—or anyone."

"Why didn't she turn it in?"

"Maybe she got it after Hayden Keating received his, or maybe she didn't open it until after he received his. If you look in the Bone Artist file, the anchors at the other networks received their letters on different days but within the same week," Josie pointed out.

Gretchen pulled out of the Eudora parking lot and headed toward Josie's house. "The most likely scenario is that Keating got his and turned it in immediately. The meetings started with the FBI. They were going round and round about what to do—engage this guy and try to draw him out or ignore it."

Josie picked up her Komorrah's cup from the console and sipped what little was left, glad that it was still lukewarm. She was alarmed to find that she felt far more tired after that short interview than she should. Stopping herself from punching Hayden Keating in his smug face had taken a lot out of her. "Codie knew from the meetings that the network would never let them try to engage the Bone Artist," she said. "She didn't bother turning in her letter. To her, it wouldn't have mattered if she turned it in or not, since she and Keating both got exactly the same letter."

"Except that the letter was evidence," Gretchen said. "It should have been turned in so the FBI could analyze it at the very least."

"I agree," Josie said. "It was irresponsible for Codie not to turn it in. Then again, she was an anchor, not a police officer. Either that, or she thought she could be a hero and it wouldn't matter that she hadn't turned the letter in."

"I'm inclined to believe she was trying to be a hero," Gretchen said. "She probably hoped she could help solve the case somehow or draw this guy out just like Trinity. Regardless, we can't prove that she got a letter. Do you think it was in the personal effects that Trinity asked her assistant to dig up?"

"No," Josie said. "I think if something like that had been laying around after Codie's death, we would know about it. She probably destroyed it. But that doesn't matter."

Gretchen turned her head away from the road long enough to give Josie a raised brow. "It doesn't?"

"No, it doesn't. We only need to know if she tried to engage him or not. For that, all we need is network footage from the time that Keating received his letter through the time that Codie Lash was murdered. We can see if she said or did something that might have signaled the Bone Artist. Something Trinity might have seen."

When they arrived at Josie's house, Gretchen followed Josie inside, saying hello to Lisette and giving Trout a fuss. Shannon and Christian hadn't yet returned from the library. Another headache began behind Josie's eyes. She wanted to sleep so badly, but the thought of somehow getting closer to finding Trinity drove her. In the kitchen, she booted up her laptop and she and Gretchen searched YouTube for network footage of Codie Lash from a two-week period in 2014. Lisette shuffled in to make them coffee and then went back to watching television with Trout.

Shannon and Christian arrived with a Gregg shorthand dictionary and Patrick in tow. They ordered pizza and joined Lisette in the living room where Shannon paced on one side and Christian paced on the other. Patrick disappeared upstairs. After two hours of watching segments, Josie's eyes were dry, irritated, and painful. Her head pounded mercilessly, and her limbs felt heavy with fatigue. On the laptop screen, Codie Lash droned on. A piece about law enforcement using new DUI technology played and then the camera panned back to her and Hayden Keating. They made some commentary, smiles plastered on their faces.

"I think this is it," Gretchen said.

"What?" Josie asked.

Gretchen used the mouse pad to rewind the footage. The segment ended, the screen cut to the anchors and Hayden Keating said, "Technology is incredible, isn't it, Codie?"

Codie smiled widely at the camera. "It is certainly incredible, Hayden. In the hands of law enforcement, look what can be done! Police don't play games, do they?"

He gave her a strange look that lasted only seconds before picking up after her statement. "They get right to the job," he agreed. "Now—"

Codie cut him off. "They do their jobs and don't let criminals get the upper hand. They don't like to play games with suspects under any circumstances. It's just not possible."

Keating's expression was something between confusion and outright horror. "Right," he said stiffly. "As I was saying, now let's move on to a heart-warming story out of Iowa…"

They replayed it six or seven times. Josie said, "I think you're right. This was the first signal. She's telling him that law enforcement has his note and that the 'police don't play games'; in other words, they're not going to play his game."

Gretchen nodded. "She's definitely not just talking about this DUI segment."

"Right," Josie agreed. "Her words don't exactly fit the situation, do they? That's why Keating gives her that side-eye. Plus she went on a bit, didn't she?"

Gretchen bookmarked the video. She made a note of the date in her notebook. "If she signaled him here, it was about a week after Hayden got his note, but a week before she was killed—"

"And before Robert Ingram's remains were found," Josie interjected.

"He might have contacted her again."

"And she might have given him some type of signal again," Josie agreed.

"But what? We only knew this one because we knew what the Bone Artist's note said. If he communicated with her again and if she continued to engage him, how would we know?"

"We wouldn't," Josie said. "But it might be worth watching the rest of the videos from that week-long period. Something might jump out at us."

They trawled through more footage. Josie fought to stay awake as they watched different segments. As co-anchor, Codie Lash was on television for several hours a day. After the third cooking segment in three days of footage, Josie started thinking about the bottle of ibuprofen in her nightstand. She rubbed her eyes and shifted in her seat, trying to stay awake. The video continued into the day's final segment which was about cheap vacation spots.

Gretchen said, "Boss, I can do this myself if you want to get some rest."

The vacation segment ended, and the next video was Hayden and Codie kicking off the show by reading the day's top stories.

Stifling a yawn, Josie said, "No. I can do this. I need to see whatever Trinity saw—whatever it was that helped her make the Codie Lash connection. We've watched three days' worth of footage since she gave the Bone Artist his first signal. If there's anything else to be found, it has to be—" She lurched forward, fingers scrambling over the mouse pad to pause the footage.

"Oh my God," Josie said. "That's it. That's definitely it."

Filling the screen was Codie's face, her expression one of somber seriousness. In her short brown hair, on her right side, was a large, French-style bone-colored comb.

Josie's heart pounded double-time as she pointed to it. "There," she said.

They both stared for a long moment. Finally, Gretchen said, "Wow."

She took a screen shot and then tried to zoom in to get a better look at the comb. The photo blurred the more she zoomed in, but Josie could see that it was extremely similar to the one Trinity had received in Josie and Noah's mailbox. Gretchen wrote down the date in her notebook. "This is two days before Robert Ingram's remains were found and three days before Codie and her husband were killed. She played his game, and he killed Robert Ingram anyway. She must have been devastated."

"Look at the timeline though," Josie said. "Robert Ingram was probably dead before the Bone Artist sent the letters to the press. He never had any intention of letting anyone go, just like Drake said."

"But then the Bone Artist just stopped," Gretchen said. "He got a member of the press to play his game. Although she didn't mention his case specifically on television, she engaged with him. He got what he wanted. Why stop?"

"He didn't get what he wanted, though," Josie said. "Not really. He wanted attention, notoriety and the only way to get that was if the press did a story on him. Codie played his game but not in the way that he wanted. The only people who even knew they were playing a game were the two of them. Without press coverage, he wouldn't get to flaunt how smart he thought he was."

"Maybe it would have continued if she hadn't been killed," Gretchen mused.

"Maybe. Or maybe he was so angry with her for not making their game public, he retaliated against her."

Gretchen raised a brow. "That's a stretch, boss. Both she and her husband were killed in a mugging."

"A mugging that's never been solved," Josie pointed out. "It's worth looking into. Maybe Drake could get us whatever there is in the murder file. I mean, is it really that much of a stretch? A reporter makes contact with this guy and a few days later, she's dead? That doesn't bode well for Trinity, though, does it?"

Gretchen bumped her shoulder gently against Josie's. "We'll find her, boss. We won't stop until we do."

Josie stared at the screen where Codie Lash was frozen in profile, the comb tucked neatly into her hair. "Wait here," she told Gretchen.

She went to the bottom of the stairs and called for Patrick— which ended up drawing everyone else in the house. He jogged down the steps, pushing his brown hair out of his face. "What's up?"

Josie said, "Can you come into the kitchen and look at something for me?"

He followed her, as did Lisette, Christian, and Shannon. Even Trout trotted in, curious as to what all the humans were studying on the kitchen table. Gretchen played the Codie Lash segment, pausing it at the best angle for them to see the comb. Josie said, "Patrick, is this why the comb looked familiar to you? You'd seen it on television before?"

All eyes turned to him. He stared at the frozen screen for a long moment.

Christian said, "Patrick—" but before he could go on, Shannon grabbed his arm, silencing him.

Suddenly, Patrick's entire face went taut and pale with horror. "Oh my God," he gasped.

"What is it?" Josie asked.

He pointed to the screen. "No, no. That's not where I saw it."

"Then where?" Josie asked.

He took his phone out of his pocket, tapped and scrolled a few times.

"Son," Christian said but Shannon silenced him again.

When Patrick found what he was looking for, he turned the screen toward them. "It's Trinity's Facebook page," he explained. "She did this video for the network when she first got here six weeks ago. She was staying here at the time. The crew was still in town."

They crowded around the tiny screen. Trinity stood in front of the Denton PD headquarters, holding a microphone in hand. Her expression was all business. "It all started in this small town five years ago with the disappearance of seventeen-year-old Isabelle Coleman…"

Josie stopped listening, instead staring open-mouthed as she saw the reason Patrick had suddenly become so overwrought. In Trinity's hair was a comb just like the one Codie Lash had worn on-air six years earlier and just like the one Hummel had found tucked away in Trinity's suitcase after she was taken.

"When did you say this was recorded?" Gretchen asked.

"Six weeks ago," Patrick said. "A few days after she got into town. The network wanted her to do a story about the five-year anniversary of the missing girls' case and how it impacted the town. You guys didn't watch it?"

Josie stared at him. Quietly, she said, "Patrick, I lived through it. It was one of the most horrific experiences of my life. I know it's Trinity's job to revisit these things, but I can't do it. I'm sorry, I didn't watch it."

Gretchen said, "This was when she first got here to Denton. Before she moved out to the cabin. Josie, this was *before* she received the comb we found in her suitcase."

"So where did she get that one?" Shannon asked, pointing to Patrick's phone.

"From Codie Lash's things," Josie said. She walked back to the table and picked up her own phone, firing off a text to Jaime Pestrak. *Do you remember if there was a white French-style hair comb in Codie Lash's things when you sent them to Trinity?*

A few minutes later, Jaime replied, *I think so. There was some pretty ugly stuff in that box.*

Josie looked around, "Trinity's assistant believes there was a hair comb like that in Codie Lash's box of things."

Gretchen said, "Come on, boss. Let's go see the team."

CHAPTER FORTY-THREE

Two hours later, Josie sat at her own desk at the station house, thumbing through the Gregg shorthand dictionary that the Paynes had secured for her, trying to find the symbol she'd seen on the Bone Artist's truck. Page after page was lined with words in one column and squiggly lines in the column across from them. Swirls, dips, circles, lines... Josie didn't know how anyone could possibly make sense of this. All the shorthand words looked the same to her. She'd have to have Lisette give her a crash course when she got home. In the meantime, she used a pencil to make a light mark next to any symbols that seemed familiar.

"Any luck?" Noah asked as he came into the room.

"I think it might have started with an F. My grandmother said what I was drawing looked like it began with an F. I'll keep looking."

A moment later, Drake, Gretchen, and Mettner trailed in. Under Drake's arm was a laptop. "There is video of the attack on Codie Lash and her husband. It was captured from an ATM vestibule across the street from where it happened."

"I know," Josie said. "It was in Trinity's search history."

"Right but I made some calls and got a hold of the entire video—even the parts that weren't released to the press."

"But we're following Trinity's trail," Josie said. "I'm looking at things that she saw and trying to figure out how she got from knowing nothing about the case to making contact with this guy."

Drake smiled. "What makes you think she didn't see the entire video?"

Josie smiled back. "Who in the NYPD did she convince to let her see it?"

"I can't say," Drake replied. "I wouldn't want to get the poor guy in trouble. Anyway, she never got a copy of it. She just watched it under his supervision. Your sister can be… persuasive."

"I was thinking more along the lines of dogged," Josie said.

"I was going to say persistent," Gretchen chimed in.

"A pain in the ass," Noah said.

Josie and Drake both nodded. Josie said, "All of those are true. She must have had something over this NYPD guy to get access to this."

"She did," Drake admitted. "An affair that he doesn't want made public."

"How did you find out?" Gretchen asked.

Drake looked around at them. "She might have her ways, but I also have mine."

As Noah, Gretchen, and Mettner gathered around, Drake put the laptop in front of Josie and opened it, pulling up a black and white video of the attack. It was taken at an angle from slightly overhead across a small street. Streetlights illuminated the sidewalk. Codie Lash came walking down the street, arm in arm with her husband. Her skirt swished around her. She wore high-heeled boots. Her husband wore a trench coat over what looked like suit pants. They were in front of some sort of closed-down business with a security gate covering its entrance when a man came from the other direction. At first, neither Codie nor her husband looked at him. They were speaking to one another, her head tilted up and to the right toward his and him smiling down at her. The man who approached them was dressed in jeans, boots, and a dark-colored hoodie over a baseball cap. The cap was pulled low over his face and the hood kept his profile from being visible. He lifted a hand and then he must have said something because they stopped.

Josie counted off the seconds ticking by on the upper left-hand side of the video. Four seconds passed before anyone moved again. She wondered if they were speaking to one another. The man must have spoken to them. But from the angle of the video it was difficult to see any of their faces. Finally, the man stepped closer to the couple. Codie's husband stepped forward and held up both of his hands. Josie could tell by the way he gesticulated and the way his head bobbed that he was saying something to the man. Josie couldn't tell if the man was speaking back because his hat was pulled so low and his hood was swathed so tightly to his head. Codie's husband gently pushed her behind him, but she held on to one of his arms. Then the assailant reached out both hands toward the couple. Codie's husband turned and put his back against the security gate, pulling Codie along with him. They pressed themselves against the gate but still made no move to run. Codie's husband held his hands up as if in surrender. This was the entirety of the video that had been released to the public, Josie remembered, having watched it the other day.

For the benefit of the rest of the team, Drake said, "Now this is what the public hasn't seen."

The assailant's back was to the camera, but they could see him lift the brim of his hat. Codie looked into his face, and suddenly recoiled, wrenching away from her husband, but with nowhere to go, she merely pressed her back further into the security gate until it bowed a little. Her husband's eyes bulged and then he looked away, down toward the ground. Josie guessed the assailant was speaking to them because Codie continued to stare at him, transfixed, her mouth stretching back in a look of horror.

"I don't see a weapon," Mettner said. "What the hell is going on? Why don't they run?"

"They're too shocked," Josie said.

Gretchen said, "Well yeah, a lot of people freeze up in situations like these."

"It's not that," Josie said. "He's not a threat yet. No weapon. There's only one of him against two of them. There's plenty of room for them to get away from him. It's his face. Look at the way they're staring at him."

"What are you talking about?" Drake asked.

"Rewind it so you can see what happens when he lifts the brim of his hat and they get their first good look at his face. It startles them."

Noah said, "Because there's something wrong with his face. He's disfigured."

Josie glanced up at him. "Yes, I think so."

Drake rewound the video and they all watched it again.

"I see it," Gretchen said.

Drake said, "Disfigured like the guy who ran you off the road? You think *this guy* is the Bone Artist?"

Josie held his gaze. "Yes, I think this might be him. I think that he contacted Codie along with Hayden Keating. She didn't report it because she knew the network and the FBI wouldn't do anything with it. She thought she could play a game with this guy and save some lives. We know she didn't save anyone's life because Robert Ingram's remains were found right before this happened. Probably because the Bone Artist didn't get the press coverage he wanted. He didn't want the game to stay between the two of them. He wants the whole world to know that he's smart—smarter than the press and smarter than the police."

On the screen, the couple remained still, their arms locked together, their postures stiff. Codie's husband looked up slowly and stared at the other man's face. Then Codie began gesticulating angrily, pointing a finger at his chest as she spoke. The assailant stepped back a little. "What is she saying to him?" Mettner asked.

This time, Josie rewound the tape. "Noah?" she asked. He leaned in and she played it again. Noah said, "Looks like, 'you're a… psycho… psychopath and'… play it again." After three more attempts, Noah said, "She calls him a psychopath and a liar."

Drake reached across their bodies and set the video back, watching it once more. "How the hell can you tell that?"

"My ex-girlfriend was deaf. She read lips. I learned to do it as well."

"He's pretty good at it," Josie said.

Gretchen asked, "No one on the NYPD had this tape analyzed? Brought in a lip reader? This was a high profile case."

"Hold on," Drake said. As he walked off, he took out his phone, punched at it and pressed it to his ear.

"Let's see the rest," Mettner said, pressing play.

They let the rest of the video play. The assailant appeared to be speaking, based on the rapt attention Codie gave him. Her face fell. She said something else to him which Josie couldn't make out. "Is she saying 'robbery? Rob me? Why are you trying to rob me?'"

Noah played that part several more times before pausing it. "No," he said. "I think she's saying, 'Bobby? What do you mean, Bobby?'"

"That doesn't make sense," Mettner said.

"It does if she knew this guy," Gretchen put in. "She called him a liar which means she must know who he is."

"But if she knows who he is," Noah said. "Why is she so shocked by his face?"

"Because she's never met him in person," Josie said. "He's the Bone Artist. I'm telling you. He confronted them, they backed away, he showed his face, they were shocked. Then he started talking, and from whatever he was saying, she knew he was the Bone Artist. Robert Ingram's remains had just been found. She calls him a liar because he said he'd let a victim go if she played his game, and he didn't."

Mettner said, "So Bobby is Robert Ingram, then?"

"Seems that way," Gretchen said. She pressed play and they watched Codie sag against the security gate behind her. She said something else that was clear to all of them: "Oh my God." One of her hands reached to her forehead, her thumb and index finger rubbing either side of it.

Then everything went to hell.

Codie's husband ripped his arm from his wife's and lunged for the Bone Artist, wrapping both hands around the man's throat. Their bodies fused in a whirling dervish of limbs until they were on the ground, rolling around, each one fighting to be on top. Nearby, Codie screamed, and that, too, was very clear. "No!" She made some attempts to pull at one or the other of them, but their struggling bodies knocked her to the ground. Then one of the men went limp and the other man stood up. Josie saw that the man left standing was the attacker.

"Is that a knife in his hand?" Gretchen asked.

Noah paused the footage and zoomed in. "Yeah, I think it is. A small one, but lethal nonetheless."

He pressed play again, and they watched as the attacker walked over to Codie. On her back, she tried to scurry away from him, but he was too fast. Josie counted seven stabs, all delivered rapidly and efficiently, and then it was over. The assailant ran off, but the video continued. Sixteen seconds later, they saw why. He returned, patted down the husband's pockets and then reached into one to pull out a wallet. Then he tore Codie's small purse from her body and ran off again.

"That was not a mugging," Mettner said. "He came back and took their things so it would look like a mugging."

"This is why he stopped," Gretchen said. "He was caught on camera. Part of this footage was released right after Codie died. It was all over the news."

"Yes," Josie agreed. "He'd never been caught on camera before this. It was a point of pride with him."

"This shook him," Noah said. "Big time. But we can't even see him. The most you can get out of this video—at least the part that was released to the public—is maybe his estimated height and weight. There's nothing identifying about him."

"That's not the point," Josie said. "This is his first mistake, and it's not in keeping with—" She broke off, the very thought of it making her stomach turn.

"It's not in keeping with what?" Mettner coaxed.

"His work," she choked out. "He thinks of himself as an artist. He probably doesn't even consider himself a killer."

"Clearly not," Gretchen agreed. "If he specifically wrote to the press and told them he was the Bone Artist instead of the Boneyard Killer."

"He didn't and doesn't want to be associated with this," Josie said. "This is a mess. This is not up to his standards. I think he just lost it here. He lost control. Especially when the husband went for him."

They watched the video one more time without pausing it while they waited for Drake to return. A few minutes later, he did, holding a notebook in his hand. He read from his scrawled notes. "NYPD did get a lip reader. They said they believe that Codie called him a sycophant and a liar and that she also called him Bobby. They believed that this person knew the Lash couple. They checked out every person Mr. and Mrs. Lash knew. There were about five Roberts, but all of them had alibis for this particular evening. They didn't have DNA or prints from the crime scene so that's all they had to go on."

"Not a sycophant," Josie corrected. "A psychopath. She wasn't calling him Bobby. She was talking about someone named Bobby."

"Robert Ingram," Mettner said.

"The only context the NYPD had at that time was this video," Josie said. "It makes sense they looked for someone they knew by that name. That's exactly what I would have done. But now, knowing what we know about Codie Lash's contact with the Bone Artist, we have to view this in a different context."

Drake scratched his scalp. "All right, let's go with your theory. Codie Lash engaged this killer and she got killed. Trinity figured this all out. That's why she asked for Codie Lash's personal effects because she was looking for more of a connection."

"Which she found," Josie said. "With the comb. She used that to draw him out. She wore it during a segment and the next thing she knew, he delivered a second comb to her."

Noah asked, "How the hell did she draw him out in the first place, though? I mean, this guy hasn't been active for six years. It's not like he contacted her and told her to give him a signal of some kind. How did she get his attention to begin with? She had to have had his attention before she wore Codie Lash's comb, don't you think? She only did one report with that in her hair. What are the odds that he just happened to be watching that report on that channel at that particular time?"

Josie said, "She had his attention months ago. The network did. Remember, Drake said that they were doing stories on cold serial cases by geographical region? At some point, assuming this guy watches network morning television—and I think we can safely assume he does given that he contacted the network morning anchors for the three major networks in 2014—he would have come across this ongoing segment. He would have watched every week because he'd be hoping to make one of the lists. He would have been insulted if he didn't get on the list of cold northeast serial cases."

"I agree," Drake said. "That fits with the profile, with his thirst for attention, his desire to be admired and esteemed for his intelligence in evading capture all this time. Trinity walked right into it when she got into the argument with the correspondent. She actually used the word 'smart' in her argument. That would have caught his eye immediately."

"He would be fixated on her at that point," Josie said. "Then shortly after that she gets obsessed with the case, follows a convoluted path to Codie Lash and her hair comb."

Noah said, "She wore that comb on the air right after she arrived here. She probably hoped it would get his attention, but then a week went by and there was nothing. Remember, she had lunch with Patrick and told him that she thought she was onto a big story and it didn't pan out?"

"But then it did," Josie said. "Because a matching comb was delivered to our house for her."

Drake said, "So she figures out that Codie Lash was a part of this whole thing, gets lucky that Codie left her creepy serial killer comb in her office and someone packed it up and put it in storage, wears the creepy comb and gets herself abducted. In the process, this guy abducts some random woman from Central Pennsylvania, kills her, and leaves her in the place he took Trinity from."

Josie said, "He had to leave a display so we would know it was him."

Drake nodded. "I'll buy that."

"But why did he go off-pattern?" Mettner asked. "Nicci Webb was missing for only seventeen days before her remains were found behind Trinity's cabin. Why didn't he wait the full thirty days?"

Josie said, "Because Trinity's lease for the month was almost up. She rented the cabin for thirty days. She stayed for seven. There were only twenty-one days before the landlord or the next tenant would have shown up and found her abandoned car."

Noah said, "But he didn't want someone to find just Trinity's abandoned car. He wanted the whole world to know that the Bone Artist had been there."

"Yes," Josie said. "The staging of the remains was his signal that he was alive and well and still killing."

"He was announcing himself," Drake agreed.

"Right," Josie said. "But he took Nicci Webb after he took Trinity. Had he waited the full thirty days from Nicci Webb's abduction to staging her remains, he would have gone past the date that Trinity's lease was up. He would have missed his window for someone to find his sick display when they found Trinity's vehicle."

"But the Bone Artist wouldn't know that the cabin was a rental, much less how long the lease was," Gretchen pointed out.

"True," Josie said. "But it wouldn't take much effort or research for him to find out those details. He likely researched Trinity extensively before approaching her. He knew enough about her to know that her family lives in Callowhill. I'm sure he knew she has a residence in New York City. He prides himself on being smart, remember? He's a planner. He's careful. He had to have done some reconnaissance before going to the cabin. It would be easy enough to check property records—or even the internet—and find out that the Whispering Oaks cabins are rentals."

Noah said, "So he somehow figures out she's rented the cabin. He does enough recon to know she'll be alone there. He takes her from there. He's either found out ahead of time that her lease was only a month long or he finds out from her after he's taken her."

"Right," Josie said. "He had to plant Nicci Webb's remains early because he didn't have a full thirty days."

Drake nodded. "I'll buy that as well. Okay, we know what happened now and why it happened but how the hell does that help us find her or this killer?"

Gretchen said, "And why did Trinity write Vanessa in her car?"

Mettner said, "Why does she want you to read her diary? Presumably a diary she kept in high school if you're right about this trail of clues you've been following."

Josie closed Drake's laptop and put her head in her hands. "I don't know," she admitted. "I just don't know."

CHAPTER FORTY-FOUR

Hanna sat beside Alex in the courtroom. Beneath the table where they waited with his attorney, she reached over and found his hand. She squeezed it. The attorney went to the judge's bench to discuss finalizing the plea agreement. In Alex's ear, Hanna whispered, "Are you sure you want to do this?"

He nodded.

"You'll have to do community service. I don't know what that will be. The attorney said they would try to find something that would be a good fit. Maybe something outdoors."

"I understand," he muttered.

The attorney returned to the table with a document in hand. He told Alex to stand. The judge addressed him from across the room. "Son, this is a very serious matter."

"Yes, sir," Alex said.

"Your father is gravely injured and will need care for the rest of his life. I understand he has lost most of his faculties due to the head injury you gave him."

"Yes, sir," Alex repeated.

"But you're only sixteen. There's a chance that you could turn things around. Once you turn eighteen, your record will be expunged. You'll have a clean slate. I understand that things in your household have been less than ideal."

"Yes, sir."

"I'm also told that you are a very devoted son."

"Yes, sir."

"Do you have anything to say before I rule on whether or not to approve this plea deal your attorney has worked out with the district attorney?"

Alex remembered the words he and Hanna had come up with the week before. He recited them from memory. "I didn't want to hurt my dad."

They had decided that Alex should call him 'my dad', not 'my father.' It made it sound like Alex had had some affection for Francis. He had, once, a very long time ago. Before he knew what Francis really was.

"He was abusive," Alex explained.

The judge frowned. "Yes," he said. "Your mother has scars that bear this out."

"My mom tried to stop him. I thought he would hurt her. I love my mom very much. I was afraid for her life, so I intervened. I only meant to keep her safe, not to hurt my dad. If I could do it over again, I would have just called 911. But it was a very stressful moment. It happened so fast. I didn't make a good choice, and I am very sorry."

He felt Hanna squeeze his arm. The judge studied him for a long moment. Then, with a sigh, he said, "Very well. I'll approve the plea bargain. You'll have to perform one hundred twenty hours of community service. Rather than making you spend time in juvenile detention, I'm going to place you on probation and send you home to help your mother care for your father. She'll need your help now more than ever."

"Thank you, sir."

CHAPTER FORTY-FIVE

They were at a standstill. Josie's body ached for rest even though it was the last thing she wanted to do. When she could no longer stand the dizziness and pain throbbing in her head, she asked Noah to take her home. She took a hot bath and crawled into bed. Trout climbed up next to her and snuggled up against her side. Stroking his silky back, she fell into a deep sleep, not waking until the sunlight was streaming brightly through her bedroom windows the next day. She stirred. Beside her, Trout snored, deep in the sleep of total abandon. Josie thought about getting up, but she wasn't ready yet. Instead, she closed her eyes once more and let her mind circle all the things her team knew about the case, trying to connect the disparate elements, trying to see what Trinity had seen. She had followed Trinity's path so far, from her becoming obsessed with a case that her lover was lead investigator on to the Codie Lash connection to… what? What was Josie missing?

She had some kind of theory, Drake had said.

Which was what? And what did it have to do with some old diary she'd written in high school? What did it have to do with her past? Was the killer someone she went to high school with? Josie opened her eyes, reached for her phone, and fired off a text to Mettner, asking him to look into that angle. Without the actual diary, Josie had no idea what path Trinity had been trying to lead her down. As she drifted back into a near-sleep, various elements swept across the movie screen of her mind. The Post-it notes. *OCD? Symmetry? Mirror killings?* The combs—first in Codie Lash's hair and then in Trinity's. The search history on her laptop: Alphabet murders. Codie's mouth forming the words: *Bobby? What do you mean, Bobby?* The symbols. Male and female.

Mirror killings. Symmetry. Male. Female. Bobby.

No, not Bobby. Bobbi.

Josie's upper body levered up, startling Trout, who gave a little yelp and then shot her a dirty look. "Sorry, buddy," she told him. She threw her feet over the side of the bed but when she tried to stand, her body swayed. Quickly, she sat back down. Trout jumped down and stretched before her in front of her feet. He went to the bedroom door and nudged it open, waiting for her to stand. A few minutes later, a soft knock sounded from the other side of the half-open door. Trout's butt wiggled. Patrick stuck his head inside. "You okay?"

Josie smiled. "Fine. Just a little unsteady."

"Can I get you anything? Coffee? Juice?"

"My laptop," Josie said.

He rolled his eyes but laughed good-naturedly. "Oh right. I forgot. You're a Payne. Of course you'd want your laptop before sustenance."

"It's just that I think I—" Josie started.

He put up a hand. "I'm messing with you, Josie. It was a joke. I can actually get you your laptop *and* a coffee."

She grinned at him. "That would be perfect."

Five minutes later, Josie was leaning against her headboard with her laptop across her legs and a steaming cup of coffee on her nightstand. Patrick had taken Trout for a walk. Noah was at the station and Lisette, Shannon, and Christian were downstairs, "worrying," Patrick told her.

It took Josie four databases and a Google search to come up with what she was looking for. She downloaded an article from the *Pocono Record* dated two weeks after the Bone Artist had staged Robert Ingram's remains. The headline read: POLICE HAVE NO LEADS IN CASE OF MISSING WOMAN FOUND ALIVE WANDERING ROUTE 209.

Then she checked NamUs, spending another hour tracking down the reports needed to confirm her theory. She sent all of it to the printer in their home office. Then she called Noah. "Someone needs to come get me," she told him. "Is everyone there?"

"Just me," he said. "Mett and Gretchen went home to sleep. Drake is at his hotel, probably also sleeping."

"Wake them up," Josie said. "This is important."

A half hour later, the team and Drake were gathered in the station house conference room. Drake shot Josie daggers while Mettner continued to rub sleep from his eyes. Gretchen sipped calmly on a coffee, waiting to hear what Josie had to say. Noah sat next to Josie, holding the stack of report copies she had asked him to make. Josie nodded and he started handing them out to the rest of the team.

Josie began, "I think I know the theory that Trinity was working with. We know this guy likes symmetry. He has patterns, even if we haven't figured out what all of them are. We now know that his displays are based on a combination of the symbols for male and female. Trinity's notes—the few I managed to see before she packed up her stuff—mentioned something about mirror killings which made no sense to me at first. But then I thought about Codie Lash and what she had said to the Bone Artist the night she was murdered. She said, 'Bobby, what are you talking about? Bobby?' She already knew about Robert Ingram's murder. So why did she seem surprised? Unless she wasn't talking about Bobby as in Robert Ingram. Bobbi can also be a woman's name."

Gretchen said, "You think she was saying Bobbi with an 'i'?"

"Yes," Josie said. She picked up one of the reports she had printed. "Roberta Ingram, a twenty-seven-year-old dental hygienist from Bloomsburg went missing the day before Robert Ingram disappeared from East Stroudsburg."

Mettner stared at the NamUs report in his hands. "Holy shit," he said.

Josie waved the news article from the *Pocono Record* in the air. "Thirty days later Roberta, or Bobbi, Ingram was found wandering the woods in East Stroudsburg along Route 209, naked, badly dehydrated and completely disoriented, with what the news would only report were 'serious injuries'. She says she was abducted by a man with 'marks on his face.'"

Drake said, "Jesus."

Noah said, "We called East Stroudsburg PD. They confirmed all of this. They said that they worked hard on this one, but that they never developed any leads in the case."

Gretchen asked, "Did she recover from her injuries?"

Josie said, "The physical injuries, yes."

Noah said, "East Stroudsburg PD gave us her address. They said they thought she would be fine talking with us and offered to call her to give her a heads-up."

Mettner stood up. "Let's go then. Where does she live now?"

"She's in Danville now," Noah said. "About ten miles from Bloomsburg."

"There's one more thing," Josie said. "All the killings have mirrors." She spread out the reports from NamUs. "In 2008, a few days before the first victim, Anthony Yanetti, was kidnapped from outside of Newtown, Pennsylvania, a woman named Antonia 'Toni' Yanetti was abducted from King of Prussia."

"King of Prussia is where the Bone Artist left Anthony Yanetti's remains," Drake said.

"Let me guess," Mettner said. "Around the same time that Terri Abbott went missing in Pittsburgh, a man named Terrence Abbott went missing just outside of Pittsburgh."

"Correct," Josie said.

Gretchen supplied, "One or two days before or after Kenneth Darden went missing from Paoli, a woman named…" She studied the NamUs report. "Kendra Darden was abducted from Philadelphia."

"Yes," Josie said. "None of the mirrors—Antonia Yanetti, Terrence Abbott, or Kendra Darden have ever been found. The only mirror the Bone Artist ever set free was Roberta 'Bobbi' Ingram."

Noah said, "He let her go because Codie Lash was playing his game. She wore the comb on the air which is what he wanted."

"But he still killed her," Drake said.

"The husband attacked him," Josie said. "He lost control. Once he killed the husband in front of her, and she had seen his face, he couldn't exactly let her go."

"What does this mean for Nicci Webb?" Mettner asked. "Is there a Nicholas Webb out there who is also missing? One we don't know about?"

Josie shook her head. "I thought of that. I checked every database and news outlet I could think of and found nothing. There are three Nicolas Webbs in Pennsylvania."

Noah added, "They're all accounted for. Before you guys got here, I called the police departments in the towns they live in and had them do welfare checks."

Drake said, "So Nicci is the only one without a mirror? Why would he do that?"

"To throw us off?" Noah offered.

Mettner said, "We've talked about how off-pattern the Webb murder seems before. We're dealing with a serial offender. What would cause someone like this to change the way they do things?"

Noah said, "A stressor of some kind, maybe?"

Drake nodded. "A stressor could do it. Hey, what about Trinity? She didn't have a mirror. There's no male equivalent to Trinity, is there?"

Josie's skin felt cold. "No, but she actually does have a mirror. A literal mirror."

Drake's cheeks colored. "Right. Of course."

"That's why he tried to take you," Noah said looking at Josie. "It was off-pattern in terms of the timing since he waited so long after taking Trinity to try abducting you, but he did still try."

"Which makes Nicci Webb even more off-pattern." Gretchen said. "She's the only one without a mirror."

Mettner said, "Maybe she saw something she wasn't supposed to see. We should look more closely at her."

"I've been over the state police file," Noah said. "They did look closely at her and all of her activities in the days leading up to her abduction. They turned up nothing."

Drake met Josie's eyes. "Sometimes a fresh set of eyes makes all the difference. I'll get someone on my team to take another look at Nicci Webb."

"Thank you," Mettner and Josie said in unison.

Gretchen took a sip of her coffee and asked, "What does he do with the mirrors that he doesn't put on display? You don't think they're still alive, do you?"

Josie shook her head. "No, I don't. Perhaps the DNA from the combs will match DNA of one or two of the mirrors."

A visible shudder worked its way through Gretchen's body. She set her coffee cup back on the table.

Mettner looked like he might be sick, but he drew himself up and took a deep breath. "All right. We can't all go talk to Bobbi Ingram. Nothing like scaring the shit out of the poor woman with five of us showing up on her doorstep. I'll take the boss with me to talk to her. Now that we know about the mirrors, we have to go back and look closely at the circumstances surrounding their disappearances to see if the Bone Artist left any clues or evidence behind that we can use to track him down. Palmer—you and Fraley can work on those."

Drake said, "I'll stay here and help with that as well as the Webb thing. It won't hurt to have the weight of the FBI behind your inquiries to the police jurisdictions in which these mirror victims went missing."

"Let's get to work," said Mettner.

CHAPTER FORTY-SIX

Mettner fielded a call from the East Stroudsburg Police on their way to Danville informing him that Bobbi Ingram would be home that afternoon, and she was willing to speak with them. They arrived in Danville an hour and a half later. It was a small town on the Susquehanna and the home of the sprawling Geisinger Medical Center. Bobbi lived in a condominium in a development near the town's high school. Children played and rode their bikes up and down the street, which was lined on one side by condos and on the other by single homes. It was a beautiful, idyllic location. Bobbi greeted them at the door, wearing scrubs and toweling her hands dry with a dish towel. She was about Josie's height but curvier than Josie with wide hips and an ample bosom. Her brown hair was pulled away from her face and tied in a braid down her back.

"Come on in," she said, leading them down a small hallway and into a kitchen with a breakfast nook. Her home was neatly kept, and decorated in wood tones. A tabby cat stared at them from the top of the refrigerator as Josie and Mettner sat down at her kitchen table. Bobbi offered them drinks but they declined.

"You're here about what happened to me, they said."

"That's right," Mettner said.

Bobbi walked over to her fridge and whispered until the cat moved to the edge. She reached up and took it into her arms before taking a seat across from them. On her lap, the cat purred loudly as she stroked its head and back.

"Them police in East Stroudsburg were nice," she told them. "But they never found anything."

"That's what they said," Mettner replied. "We're sorry to hear that."

Josie said, "We have another case of a missing woman. We believe it might be related to your case. Anything you could tell us about what happened to you might be helpful."

Bobbi's face crumpled and she hid it in her cat's furry neck. The cat, unaffected, flicked its tail back and forth. A moment later, Bobbi looked up. Tears streaked her face, but she didn't wipe them away. Looking off into space , she sucked in a stuttering breath and began to speak. "I used to walk the fairgrounds in Bloomsburg before work every day. When there's no events going on, it's pretty dead there. A few people will drive over with their dogs and let them run. It was early March. It was freezing that day. Like, below freezing. I almost didn't go out, but I was trying to lose weight. I wasn't going to go out for long. I bundled myself up and set off."

Mettner asked, "Was anyone else out there?"

Bobbi gave a bitter laugh. "No. I was the only idiot. I only lived a few blocks away but by the time I got down there, I knew I had made a mistake. I turned around, started walking up Route 11 there before it turns into Main Street, near where the ramp to Route 42 going up to the mall is, and this truck was stopped there."

"What kind of truck?" Josie asked.

"I think it was a Chevy. I mean, I didn't notice at first. It was a white pickup. The police showed me about two dozen pictures of trucks afterward and the Chevy seemed the closest, but I couldn't say for certain. And no, I didn't get the tag. I didn't even look at the damn thing. It never occurred to me for a second I'd need to remember anything about that stupid truck or the driver."

Josie said, "We shouldn't have to remember such things. People shouldn't do bad things. What happened then?"

"Well, I was freezing my behind off walking past that thing. I saw the exhaust coming out and I thought, *Geez, I'd love to be in there.* Then the window rolled down and this guy leaned across the passenger seat and he said something like, 'I don't mean to scare you, miss.'"

"Why would he scare you?" Mettner asked.

"He had on a ski mask although I didn't think it was all that unusual. A lot of hunters wear those in the cold weather. They weren't uncommon in the winter around my area. I could see his eyes, they were brown, and there was a red mark going from his forehead down his nose. I didn't realize at first, not till I got closer. It was like a burn or a scar or something. He pointed to it and said it was on account of being burned with hot oil when he was a kid. He said it was embarrassing and that's why he wore a ski mask in winter sometimes. I wanted to tell him he could cover that with some make-up, but it didn't seem like the time."

Mettner was typing furiously into the note-taking app on his phone. "Did he tell you his name or where he was from or anything?"

Bobbi shook her head. "No. He just said he was from out of town and he was looking for the hospital. Said he was going to visit a friend. He had flowers on the seat there. I gave him directions and he thanked me. Then I walked on. He pulled up a few seconds later and said he was sorry for not offering me a ride after I helped him with directions. If it hadn't been so cold, I would have told him no."

Her fingers dug into the cat's thick mane as her eyes took on a far-off look. "But I said yes," she said, as if she were no longer talking to them but narrating some movie inside her own head. "I got in. Gave him directions. He drove right past my house. When I started to panic, he said, 'Calm down, Bobbi,' and I knew I was in real trouble cause I never told him my name. Next thing I know I'm screaming and he's plunging a needle into the meaty part of my thigh. I tried to stay awake after that, but I couldn't."

"Some kind of intramuscular injection," Josie said.

"Yeah," Bobbi agreed. "I was in and out of sleep after that. He drove and drove. Pulled into some long, gravel drive. It seemed like forever. I asked him a whole bunch of questions, but he never answered one of them. He pulled up to this old container."

"A shipping container?" Mettner said. "Like a metal one you see on docks?"

She nodded. "Or the kind they put on trains. It was big and metal."

"Windows?" Josie asked.

"No. But it wasn't bad in there. It was heated, at least. There was a mattress, a blanket, some water, a flashlight and a little camping toilet to relieve myself. He just left me in there. I screamed my head off in there for what felt like days, but he never came. No one did. He left me in there till all the water was gone and I was so hungry."

"What happened when he came back?" Mettner asked.

"I thought he was going to hurt me or something, but he wasn't interested in that. He brought me some food—snack food, pack-aged stuff like he'd got it from a mini-market or something—and more water. I asked him questions, but he never said anything. The flashlight battery ran out. That was the worst time."

Josie fought a feeling of claustrophobia imagining the utter darkness and sensory deprivation Bobbi must have experienced, all while stuck in an enclosed space. "I'm so sorry, Bobbi," she murmured.

"Thank you," Bobbi said.

"Did he ever harm you?" Mettner asked. "Hit you or anything?"

"No," Bobbi answered. "Other than to push me away when I tried to attack him. I was so weak, it was easy for him. He flicked me away like I was a bug."

"Did he drug you again?" Josie asked.

"Not the way he did in the truck. One day, toward the end, he came in and said he needed to take me somewhere. I said I wanted to go home. He said he was going to let me go. I didn't believe him, not really, because why else would he take me except to kill me? He said he needed something from me first. He blindfolded me, tied my hands behind my back, and marched me out into the cold. We walked and walked and walked. I was so weak, a couple of times he had to carry me. He slung me over his shoulder like I was nothing. Then we were in someplace warm. From under the blindfold, I could see it was light in there. I think it was a house. I heard doors opening and closing. Then he laid me down on something—a bed or something—and tied my arms and legs down."

She shivered.

Josie said, "Bobbi, we can take a break if you want."

Bobbi shook her head. Her cat rubbed the top of its head against her chin and she stroked it some more. "No. I have to keep going. It's okay. There's not much more. He put an IV in my arm." She pointed to the crook of her left arm. "Here. At least I think it was him. I always had this feeling like there was someone else in the room there, but I never heard anyone. It was just a… feeling. It felt like him putting in the IV. I could tell by the callouses on his fingers—when he tied my hands in the container, I felt them. Anyway, that's the last thing I remember. The next thing I know, I'm completely naked, wandering through the woods. It was freezing but not as cold as the day he took me, thank goodness. But the pain…" She set the cat down on the floor and it sauntered off, tail flicking. Bobbi pointed to the left side of her abdomen where her rib cage ended. "Here. It was excruciating. It got worse the more I walked. Any movement made it torture. There were these Frankenstein stitches and blood leaking out of it."

Josie swallowed as Bobbi lifted her scrub shirt to reveal a large, gnarled, six-inch scar. Mettner blanched before going back to his note-taking. Bobbi put her shirt back down, but Josie couldn't get the image from her head. Bobbi said, "It's okay. I know it's gruesome. When they found me and took me to the hospital, the doctors there said whoever did it had no idea what he was doing. They said I was lucky to be alive. I did get sepsis. Almost died. He sewed me up with actual thread."

"What did he want? Why did he do it?" Josie asked.

"A rib," Bobbie said. "He took my last rib. Broke it right off. I had to have surgery to repair the mess he made in there. They said it was a miracle he didn't damage any internal organs or anything."

Mettner said, "Can I use your bathroom?"

"Sure," Bobbi said. "Upstairs, second door to the right."

They watched him go. Bobbi said, "Men don't take it all that well. Women seem to handle it okay."

"Detective Mettner will be fine," Josie said. "I'm so sorry this happened to you, Bobbi. I'm glad you survived. Tell me, can you remember any other details about this man? Did you ever do a composite sketch?"

"No, I'm sorry. Every time I saw him, he was wearing his ski mask. I only ever saw his eyes and part of his forehead."

Josie had only seen his face for a few seconds. Not enough time for her to take in the kind of detail needed for an artist to create a sketch. She could definitely say that the red scar that Bobbie had seen ran from the center of his forehead, down the left side of his nose to the side of his mouth.

Bobbi went on, "The police thought he lived out where they found me. They checked out all these properties but never found a shipping container. They checked out lots of places near railroads but never found anything."

"Why railroads? Because of the container? Or did you hear trains when you were in the container?"

"Not trains," Bobbi said. "But I heard this ringing. Not like a bell, exactly, but sort of. It wasn't all the time, only sometimes. It would happen a whole lot and then stop for days. It sounded like metal but not metal. I can't explain it. The closest I could come was the sound that railroad workers make when they hammer in rail ties."

Mettner returned to the room, taking his seat again with a muttered apology. Josie caught him up on what he'd missed, and his thumbs scrabbled across his phone screen, taking down notes.

When he finished, he asked, "Did you ever hear any other noises while you were in the shipping container?"

Bobbi's eyes drifted away from Josie and Mettner again, taking on a glassy look once more. "Birds," she said. "Lots and lots of birds."

CHAPTER FORTY-SEVEN

Drool dripped from Francis's mouth onto his already saturated bib. His body leaned to the side, one arm hanging down over his wheelchair. Zandra had turned him to face the living room wall again. She sat on the couch, flipping through a magazine and eating from a bowl of popcorn. She didn't even acknowledge Alex. But Francis knew he was there.

"Ahhhmmaax," he cried. "Ahhhmmmaax."

Alex walked across the room and gripped the handles of the wheelchair. "Don't," Zandra said. "He's enjoying the wall. Aren't you, Francis? You like staring at nothing all day, don't you? It's entertaining, isn't it?"

Francis made the sound he made when he began crying, which he did a lot of now.

"Ahhmmaax," he tried again. "M-m-max."

Zandra laughed. "He's trying to say Alex, but it keeps coming out Max. That's what I'm going to call you from now on. Max."

Hanna sailed in from outside, cheeks flushed, grinning from ear to ear, and holding an envelope in her hands.

"Mother," Zandra called. "We've decided to call Alex 'Max' from now on."

Francis gave a strangled, "Aahhmmmaax," and Hanna and Zandra laughed together.

Hanna plopped onto the couch. She patted the cushion next to her. "Come, 'Max.' Join us."

Alex sat beside her. "What's that?" he asked.

She took some pages out of the envelope. "It's the deed to the one hundred acres of land behind us. I bought it outright. It's yours. After I'm gone, you'll have it."

Zandra wrinkled her nose. "I would rather have the money. What are we supposed to do with a bunch of land?"

"It's a blank slate, Zandra." Hanna put a hand to Alex's cheek. She stared meaningfully into his eyes, her own brimming with unshed tears. "It's a blank canvas, my love. All for you."

CHAPTER FORTY-EIGHT

Back at the station house, they assembled in the conference room once more. Drake started. "There was no railroad construction in the East Stroudsburg area in March of 2014."

Josie said, "We don't know that what she heard had any connection to a railroad. She never heard any trains."

"What else could it be?" Drake asked.

"I just don't know yet," Josie said.

Noah said, "We don't know for sure that he was keeping her near East Stroudsburg, either. That's just where he let her go. He let her go in the same town as he kidnapped Robert Ingram. That's part of his pattern. That doesn't mean he lives in any of the places he's either abducted people from or displayed their remains."

"He's right," Josie said. "We need to expand the search if we're going to look at railroads."

Drake hung his head. "Do you have any idea how many miles of railroad there are in this state? That could take years to run down."

Mettner said, "Start with the eastern edge of the state. That's where most of this guy's activity seems to be concentrated. Where are we with the mirror victims? What have you found out?"

Gretchen flipped open her notebook. "It's more of the same. Each person seemed to vanish into thin air, leaving everything behind. No clues. No video footage. Nothing. In 2008, thirty-five-year-old Antonia Yanetti went for an early morning jog in a park near her King of Prussia apartment. Never came home. Her live-in boyfriend reported her missing. Her phone and ID were found in the brush in the park. No witnesses. She was never heard from again. In 2010, fifty-three-year-old Terrence Abbott left his job bussing tables at a downtown restaurant at eleven-thirty at night to go home to his apartment and never made it there. His wallet, watch, phone, and cigarettes were found in the courtyard of his apartment building. No cameras. He was an ex-con. Only his mother kept in touch with him. When she didn't hear from him for a week, she filed a report. In 2012, twenty-six-year-old Kendra Darden, a deli worker, went for a walk in Fairmount Park and was never seen again. Her purse was found near the Wissahickon Creek—her phone was inside. She lived with her grandmother who filed a missing person report."

"This is great work, but it doesn't help us find this guy," Mettner groused.

"True," Josie said. "But we have uncovered a lot of his secrets. He's not as smart or as savvy as he thinks he is. We have to exploit that somehow." She turned to Drake. "I was looking through the file when I was in Callowhill. There's a handwritten note on the psychological profile that says something like, 'employ Supercop strategy.' What was that?"

Drake sighed. "My contact in the Behavioral Analysis Unit suggested it. It was a strategy developed and rolled out by John Douglas and the BAU in the 1980s to catch certain offenders, in particular, serial offenders they believed it would be most effective on. The idea is that we choose one member of law enforcement to get out in front of cameras and address the killer directly and really get into his head. It would be someone the killer would identify with and come to think of as a main point of contact with police. The Supercop would try to build a rapport so the killer will make contact and thus, make mistakes."

"Build a rapport?" Noah asked. "How do you build a rapport with a killer? On camera?"

Josie said, "You let him know that you think he's smart—that you know he's smart—but that you're just as smart. You let him know you've figured out some of his secrets, that you're onto him. Then he believes you're a worthy opponent. He won't be able to resist playing his little game. Then he'll make some stupid mistake and get caught."

"You can't guarantee that," Mettner said. "Look what happened to Codie, and—sorry, boss—but Trinity."

Josie said, "You're missing something, Mett. Codie Lash was one person carrying out secret communications with this guy. Trinity was one person trying to draw him out. We're a team, and we've got a ton of resources at our disposal. The more communication we have with him, the greater the chances are of him screwing up and showing his hand. Do any of you have a better idea? I'd love to hear it because my sister's life is at stake."

No one spoke for a long moment.

Then Noah said, "Are you proposing that we use you as the bait?"

"He already tried to take me once," Josie said. "I'm Trinity's literal mirror. Why else would he try to take me? I'm telling you—call a press conference. Put me in front of the camera and let me talk to this guy."

"What would you say?" Drake asked.

"That this case is personal. That I know he has my sister and that I'm going to find him if it takes the rest of my life. That will speak to his inflated sense of self—the fact that I would devote my life to figuring him out and finding him. But what I say isn't going to be as important as what he'll see."

"You need props," Noah said. "Like the comb."

"Trinity's comb has already gone to the lab," Gretchen said. "We can't get that back."

"We don't necessarily need a comb," Josie said. "We'll have all of you standing behind me at the press conference—so he sees there's a crowd. It will make him feel important and seen. Then we'll get Bobbi Ingram to stand among you—if we can get her to agree."

Drake said, "I'd also suggest getting Hayden Keating to stand with us, maybe wearing some token that evokes Codie Lash."

"Yes," Josie said, even though the thought of being near Hayden Keating again made her stomach turn. "We want him to know that we've found out a lot more than we're letting on. The press won't know what these things mean, but he will. He'll see we're taking him seriously. Playing the game he's wanted to play all along. Giving him the attention he craves."

"What about having Monica Webb there with us?" Mettner suggested.

"Yes," Josie agreed. "We'll have to bring her in and tell her what's going on. I'm sure she would agree."

Noah said, "Then what?"

"Then we wait," Drake said. "This guy will come out. He'll make contact somehow."

"I don't like the idea of Detective Quinn being used as bait," Noah said. "I don't think anyone here is on board with that."

Gretchen and Mettner nodded.

"Not *bait*," Josie said. "I'm not going to be waiting around to be kidnapped by this guy. We're only looking for contact. We want him to deliver something to us—a letter or a package."

"I don't think anyone wants another one of his creepy packages," Gretchen commented.

Drake said, "Yeah, but right now we've got nothing. We need to force his hand a little."

Josie turned to Mettner. "You're the lead, Mett. What do you say?"

Mettner rubbed his chin. "I'd have to discuss it with the Chief, get his approval on something this big. Once we blow the lid off this thing by telling the whole world that we know the Bone Artist has Trinity, we can't get that lid back on. We need to be ready for whatever comes after that."

"Fair enough," Josie said.

Mettner looked around. "Now, why don't all of you go get some rest? Noah, you can relieve me in about four hours. Then Gretchen. We'll rotate. I'll talk to the Chief, and we'll discuss this again tomorrow."

CHAPTER FORTY-NINE

The next day the station house was abuzz with nervous energy. Officers moved to and fro, setting up podiums, microphones, and other equipment for the news conference which they intended to hold out front of the police station. Mettner had gotten Chief Chitwood to agree to it and had notified the press that morning that they'd be delivering news about Trinity Payne's disappearance. He'd also contacted Bobbi Ingram, who was game to appear on camera, and sent someone to pick her up. Josie had spoken at length with Shannon, Christian, and Patrick the evening before about their strategy. They, too, had agreed to appear on camera in the background while Josie spoke.

Josie stood in the Chief's office on the second floor of the station house, watching the press assemble on the street below. Her stomach felt as if it were filled with butterflies. She heard someone's footsteps behind her and braced herself for the Chief's ire for having invaded his space. Instead, she heard Noah's voice. "Are you almost ready?"

Josie turned and managed a tight smile. "As ready as I'll ever be."

He stepped further into the room. "It's almost time."

She took his arm when he offered it and together, they walked down to the lobby. Chief Chitwood, Mettner, Gretchen, Drake, Shannon, Christian, and Bobbi Ingram had all gathered there. Hayden Keating stood slightly apart from the others, scrolling away on his phone. He wore a subdued gray suit with a shiny lapel pin bearing the initials *CL*. Josie walked over and greeted him, taking a closer look at it. He pointed to the pin and said, "The network had these made after Codie was murdered. We all wore them for a year after her death. Is this sufficient?"

"It's perfect," Josie said. "Thank you."

Josie felt a light tap on the shoulder, a welcome interruption. She didn't want to talk to Hayden any more than she absolutely had to. She turned to see Monica Webb, dressed smartly in pressed black slacks, two-inch heels, and a form-fitting purple blouse. Josie could see the smears beneath her eyes where she had cried and then tried to clean her runny mascara. State Police detective Heather Loughlin had brought her to the station several hours ago while one of her friends watched young Annabelle. Josie and Gretchen had sat down with her and broken the news that they believed the Bone Artist had killed her mother. As she had done at her home in Keller Hollow, she'd excused herself, gone to the bathroom to have a cry, and returned with a determined tilt to her chin. "I'll do anything I can to help you catch this bastard," she had told them.

Now, standing before Josie, she looked much older than twenty-one. "How are you holding up?" Josie asked.

Monica's gaze swept toward the floor. "Not great," she admitted. "But it's better being here." She waved a hand around them. "Everyone is so busy. It makes me feel like something is getting done to find my mom's killer."

Josie touched Monica's arm. "It is," she said. "We're doing everything we can, and it's a big help having you here."

Monica met Josie's eyes. She held her hand out and uncurled her fist so Josie could see a large brooch in her palm. It was a dark blue, oval-shaped polished stone with multiple striations all through it. Cradling it was thin copper wire, twisted into various whorls, much like the larger wire Josie had seen in Nicci Webb's back yard. "My mom made this," Monica said.

"It's beautiful," Josie breathed, leaning in for a closer look.

"I thought you could wear it," Monica told her. "During the press conference."

"Oh," Josie said, standing up straight and putting a hand to her chest. "I'd be honored."

Monica pinned the brooch to Josie's lapel. Noah walked over. "Where's Patrick?" he asked.

Josie panned the room. "Has anyone seen Patrick?" she asked.

Everyone else looked around as well. Shannon said, "He's not here yet?"

Christian took out his phone. "I'm going to throttle this kid." Just as he began to punch in his passcode, the front door opened. A whoosh of air burst into the room, followed by the cacophony of the press outside anxiously waiting for Josie to emerge. Patrick stood there, wearing khaki pants and a navy blue polo shirt instead of his usual jeans and sweatshirt. His normally shaggy hair was combed neatly to the side. Josie had a sudden flash of what Trinity would say if she saw him like this—she'd make fun of him, for sure. Probably ask him if he was getting his school picture taken or something like that. In his hands was a cardboard box.

"Where the hell have you been?" Christian demanded.

Ignoring their father, Patrick walked over to Josie and handed her the box. "I made something for you. I thought about all the stuff you told us last night and about your plan. I thought this might help."

She opened it, gasping and nearly dropping the box when she saw what was inside. "Jesus, Patrick, where did you get this?"

Noah took the box and stared at the bone-colored, French style hair comb inside of it.

Patrick grinned. "It's not real, you guys, but from your reaction, I can tell you thought it was. Sorry, I know I should have told you first, but I had to see your authentic reaction. If you guys thought it was real in person, then the Bone Artist will think it's real on television."

Noah passed the box around and they each took a look inside.

Shannon's hand shook as she handed the box off to Drake. "Pat, where did you get that thing?"

"I made it," he said proudly.

Josie thought she might be sick. "You... made that?"

When he realized the entire room was looking at him in horror, Patrick threw his hands up in the air. "I made it with a 3D printer!" he exclaimed. "Here, I'll show you." He took out his phone and brought up a video he had made. Josie could see that he had edited it to show them the highlights. It showed him at his computer, using some kind of software to virtually design the comb. "The software I used for design is called Maya," he explained. "There are a few other steps to get it to go to the printer, but you can see here, the printer uses plastic filament to create my design."

On the screen, a time lapse showed a machine printing the comb in layers. It started with just a few lines of filament and slowly filled in and built up until the comb appeared. "That's why I'm late," Patrick explained. "It takes hours for the printer to actually print it out. Then I had to get a buddy of mine to paint it so it would look real and not like plastic. Then it had to dry."

At the end of the video, another college student appeared with the plastic comb in one hand and a paintbrush in the other. Another time lapse video showed him using various brushes and paints to make the comb look like real bone.

Josie threw her arms around him. "Patrick, this is brilliant!"

She released him and took the box back from Mettner, who now held it, taking the comb out and admiring it. "I'll use it on my right side to hold my hair back. My scar will be visible that way. It's another way of mirroring this guy."

She looked up to see Christian staring at his son in what could only be described as awe. In a husky voice, he said, "Good job, son."

A teary-eyed Shannon took Patrick in her arms. Gretchen helped Josie fix the comb in her hair so that her scar was visible. At three p.m. sharp, they all shuffled outside, assembling behind the podium just as Mettner and Josie had directed, all lined up, a wall of support for Trinity. A handful of uniformed officers followed them and flanked them, adding to the display. Family, colleagues, and law enforcement. Only Monica Webb and Bobbi Ingram were out of place, but Monica's presence would soon be explained, and Bobbi, in her tasteful coffee-colored pants suit, merely looked like a producer from the network. They had placed her beside Hayden for that reason. She could also pass as a public relations liaison for one of the branches of law enforcement or even some kind of intern. Josie was quite certain that no one in the press was going to care all that much about who stood behind Josie. Not once they heard what she had to say. A national network news anchor abducted by a serial killer? It didn't get more ratings-worthy than that.

Josie stepped up to the thin podium and leaned into the bank of microphones the various members of the press had set up. Immediately, she began to sweat under the glare of the camera lights. Reporters shouted questions before she even began, but she cleared her throat and waited for complete silence.

"My name is Detective Josie Quinn," she announced. "I'm a member of the Denton Police Department. Earlier this week, the remains of forty-five-year-old Keller Hollow schoolteacher, Nicci Webb were found in Denton. Specifically, they were found near a cabin which my twin sister, Trinity Payne—who most of you know as the co-host of a major network morning show and a colleague—was renting. At or around the time that Mrs. Webb's remains were found, my sister was discovered to have disappeared. As was reported initially, her vehicle, purse, and phone were found abandoned at the cabin she had been renting. There were some personal effects missing. We're prepared to disclose to you now that those personal effects consisted of personal notes and files Trinity had amassed while she worked on a story about the Bone Artist.

"For those of you who don't remember or are not aware, the Bone Artist is a serial killer based here in Pennsylvania who was active between 2008 and 2014. He has been inactive, as far as we know, for the last six years. It is our belief that Trinity's work on the piece she was preparing on the Bone Artist brought her into contact with the killer."

A gasp rippled through the crowd. Josie kept her eyes up and straight ahead, looking into the cameras. "It is also our belief that the remains of Mrs. Webb were left at Trinity's cabin by the Bone Artist. We believe he is responsible for her murder. Our investigation has also revealed that Trinity Payne was abducted by the Bone Artist. Here is what we know: we are looking for a Caucasian male between the ages of thirty and forty, about six feet tall with brown hair, brown eyes, and a red scar running down the left side of his face."

Slowly, Josie traced her own face, beginning at her forehead and running her finger down her nose and to the left, over her cheek and to her mouth. "He may be driving a white Chevy pickup with front-end damage. We believe that he is holding Trinity somewhere in eastern Pennsylvania. We are actively working with the FBI to locate and apprehend him."

Josie turned and beckoned Drake forward. She introduced him and he said a few words about the case before giving the microphone back to Josie. She stepped back to the podium and leaned into the microphones, staring out at the eyes of the cameras, her face fixed in a grim look of determination. "To the Bone Artist, I would like to say that if it takes me the rest of my life, I'm going to find you and get my sister back. I will not rest until you are caught. I will not stop. This is my life now, do you understand? I will get Trinity back. I will put you away." She paused for dramatic effect. She could practically hear the collective silence of the reporters holding their breath. Leaning in a little closer to ensure that her words were heard loud and clear, she said, "Let the games begin."

Then she turned on her heel and strode back into the police station, the rest of the team moving in a somber but proud procession behind her as the press shouted questions at their backs.

CHAPTER FIFTY

Josie felt wiped out from the press conference. At home, she swallowed three ibuprofen and curled up on her couch with Trout. She closed her eyes and listened to the sounds of her family moving through the house. Lisette, Shannon, Christian, Patrick, and Noah. Trinity's face flashed through her mind. Please be alive, Josie thought. Please still be alive. I'm going to bring you home.

"Josie," Noah said. She opened her eyes and he sat beside her on the couch, using the remote to turn on the television. "Hayden Keating is on all the networks being interviewed. He's doing exactly what we told him to do."

As the television flickered to life, Hayden Keating's face filled the screen. He wore his most morose expression as he discussed that the police had many leads they could not divulge but that he believed they were very close to solving the Bone Artist case. His *CL* pin sparkled as he went on to highlight the high-profile cases that Josie had solved in her career, touting her as the best person for the job. Josie hated seeing his face, hated hearing Trinity's name come out of his mouth, especially after his betrayal, but she understood that he served a valuable purpose in their manipulation of the Bone Artist. He was a means to an end, she reminded herself, and that end was getting her sister back.

A CNN reporter asked Hayden, "Does the FBI have any concerns that Detective Quinn's personal involvement in this case could be a liability?"

"While it's true that normally a law enforcement officer would not be allowed to assist on a case this personal to them, the FBI believes that Detective Quinn's unique insight into her sister and her experience solving some of Pennsylvania's highest profile cases outweigh any negative impact her emotional connection may have to the case."

It was complete bullshit, but Hayden sold it well.

"Do the police believe that Ms. Payne is still alive?" the reporter asked.

"That was not discussed," Hayden answered. "But we all hope and pray that she is. Regardless, you heard Detective Quinn. She will not rest until this killer is in custody."

The coverage went on. Noah flipped channels only to find that Hayden was on most of them. "How many interviews do you think he's given in the last couple of hours?" Josie asked.

"At least a dozen. At least he's toeing the line. You think this will work?"

"I don't know, but it's our best chance."

Trout's head popped up when Lisette came shuffling into the room, pushing her walker. He jumped down and ran over to her, sniffing her feet excitedly. She gave him some attention and settled herself onto the couch on the other side of Josie. From the pocket slung over the front of her walker, she pulled the shorthand dictionary that Shannon and Christian had taken out of the library. Yellow Post-it notes stuck out of its pages. "I think I figured out what you were trying to draw, dear," Lisette said.

She opened the book in her lap and flipped to the Fs, paging through until she came to page eighty-three. The first word in the first column was 'formaldehyde'. Lisette ran a finger across to the third column and down to the word 'free'. "Here," she said. "Maybe she was trying to write some variation of the word 'free'? 'Freedom'? 'Free her'?"

Josie studied the shorthand, studying each word in the column. "No," she said. "Not 'free'."

"Are you sure?" Lisette asked. "What you drew looks like the word 'freedom'."

Josie studied it. Indeed it did, but she'd only seen the symbol for a second and then been concussed in a car accident and nearly abducted by a serial killer. Her brain had been understandably clouded when she'd tried to recreate the word. Besides that, why would Trinity write the word 'freedom'? She would have known that Josie would come after her and try to free her. There was no need to telegraph that to Josie. Trinity must have had only seconds to trace that one symbol onto the passenger's side door of the truck. *How* she had done it was easy to figure out. All she would have had to do was feign falling and trying to claw her way back up when the killer dragged her out of the truck. *Why* she did it at all still baffled Josie. How could she have known that Josie would see it?

Because she knew he was coming after Josie. She knew about the mirror killings. She knew more about the Bone Artist than any other person ever had. Josie had no idea if Trinity was still alive, but she knew her sister would have used everything she knew about the killer to convince him not to kill her. She would have talked to him—at him—relentlessly. She would have done everything possible to draw him out, engage him, get him talking.

"She knew he was coming for me," Josie said. "Whether it was because I was her mirror or whether it was because he told her he was going to come for me, she knew. Either he moved her from one location to another and gave her an opportunity to draw this symbol on the truck or she talked him into getting her back into the truck for some reason."

"What she wrote was a warning, then?" Lisette asked.

"I don't know," Josie said.

Noah looked over and pointed to the next word below the variations of 'free'. "Freight?" he asked. "Bobbi said she was held in a shipping container. Maybe that's what she was trying to tell you? To look for a freight container?"

Josie shook her head. "No, that's not it."

The next three words were 'frequent', 'frequency', and 'frequently'.

Josie's heart thundered against her sternum as the meaning sunk in. "Oh my God," she said. "That's it."

She jumped up from the couch. "Shannon," she yelled.

Lisette and Noah stared at her. "Josie?" Lisette said.

Josie ran to the foyer. "Mom!" she hollered. "Dad!"

Shannon came sprinting from the kitchen and Christian came running down the steps. He said, "Josie, what is it? What's wrong?"

"I know where the diary is," she said. "We need to go back to your house. Back to Callowhill. I need to get into the attic."

"Right now?" Shannon said. "It's five o'clock. I was going to make everyone dinner."

"We'll get a pizza on the way or something," Josie said. "Right now we need to get to Callowhill."

CHAPTER FIFTY-ONE

Two hours later, Josie, Noah, Shannon, and Christian were deep inside the Paynes' attic in Callowhill tearing through the boxes that Shannon had so painstakingly put back together only days earlier.

Noah used his forearm to wipe the sweat from his brow. Then he opened a new box. "What are we looking for again?"

"It's a movie," Josie said. "Called *Frequency*. You're looking for the collection of VHS tapes that Trinity had—it will be with those."

"I don't understand why we have to find this movie," Christian said from behind a pile of old clothes and purses. "Can't you just watch it? I'm sure you can stream it by now."

"That's not it," Josie said. "It has the diary. I'm sure of it."

"How could a VHS tape have a diary?" Christian asked, a tinge of frustration in his voice.

"Just look for the damn tape," Shannon snapped.

"Don't snap at me," Christian shot back. "I'm just going to say what no one else will: this is absurd. This is a wild goose chase."

Shannon stood up straight from where she'd been leaning over a box, riffling through it. She glared at her husband. "Shut up, Christian. Just shut up. Just do what we ask."

He froze, a cosmetic bag in hand, and shot a dirty look right back at her. "Shan, this is ridiculous. No offense, Josie, but I think this is going nowhere."

Josie had never seen Christian this way—frustrated to the point of lashing out—but now she could see where the tension between him and Patrick stemmed from. She could also see where both she and Trinity got their punchier sides. She said, "I don't need you to think it's going somewhere. I just need you to help me look."

Shannon pressed a hand to her chest. "I trust our children, Christian. If Josie says she needs that tape, she needs it."

Wordlessly, he bowed his head and resumed searching. Five minutes later, Noah yelled, "Got it!"

He held the tape in the air. Josie jumped up and ran across the attic, leaping over the mess of items her parents had left all over the floor. She tore the tape from Noah's hands and turned it over so she could see the base where the tape slid out. The black plastic piece was there, just like all the other VHS tapes had, except when she tried to slide the tape out, it wouldn't budge. She ran a nail inside the edge of the cardboard and dislodged the plastic. It flipped out—not attached to a tape, just taped to the inside of the box. Josie pulled the piece off and shook out a small brown book.

"Holy shit," Noah said.

Josie opened the cover and it nearly fell off in her hand. Inside, the lined pages were filled with Trinity's shorthand, scrawled in black ink. Josie thumbed through them. "Wow," she said.

Noah said, "That's going to take forever to get through."

Christian walked over and picked up the discarded cover, reading the back of it. He looked up at Josie. "How did you know?"

Josie clutched the diary to her chest. "If you had a chance to go back in time and change something, would you?"

Tears welled in Christian's eyes. He put out a hand and Shannon stepped up to his side to take it. "You know what we'd change, Josie. You would have stayed with us. We never would have been separated."

Just like that, Josie knew the worst thing that had ever happened to her sister. Cradling the diary, she said, "I need to get this to my grandmother."

*

They drove back to Denton. Lisette had the coffee ready and the kitchen table cleared. She and Josie sat side by side, Josie with a blank notepad and Lisette poring over the diary. Occasionally she had to look something up in the dictionary. Slowly, she began to read the pages out loud.

Vanessa:

Mom and Dad made me see this stupid therapist. They think I'm all crazy and psychotic because I told a couple of the girls at school that you were real. I mean, you were real. You're just dead now, like Nana. But it's not like you were never here. I like to think you're out there somewhere, looking over me, the same way Nana promised she would be. Maybe you two are together now. Anyway, the dumb old therapist made me write these letters to you except that she wanted to read them. Holy invasion of privacy. I wrote them but I didn't write what I was really thinking or what I really want to say to you. If you were here with me, I'd tell you everything. We'd stay up late at night and talk about everything. We'd always be together. Things would be better. That's the thing Mom and Dad and Dr. Who Cares What Her Name Is don't understand. I know they think I'm really messed up. They say I have an unhealthy fixation on you. But am I really supposed to pretend that my life would have been this shitty if you were still alive? I don't believe that. If you were here, I'd at least have one friend. Sometimes I need to imagine that you're here or that maybe you still exist in spirit or in some other dimension or whatever. Sometimes I need to think you can hear me or else I'll go crazy for real. No one knows what it's like for me. What it's really like. Being alone all the time. Picked on, teased constantly.

"Stop," Josie choked out. A sob rose in her throat. *I was here the whole time*, she wanted to tell her fourteen-year-old sister.

Shannon stood in the doorway with tears streaming down her face. Lisette adjusted her reading glasses and turned some more pages. "Let me just look and see," she said. "Maybe I can figure out what it is she wanted you to read."

"No," Josie said. "I want to hear it. Please. Go on."

Shannon walked over and sat beside Josie. As Lisette read on, Shannon inched her chair closer to Josie's until they were touching. Josie leaned into her mother, letting her head rest on Shannon's shoulder as Lisette read well into the night. The details were heart-wrenching. Trinity's high school experience was far worse than even Shannon and Christian knew. The bullying was so relentless that eventually, Trinity began eating lunch in a bathroom stall. Her locker was vandalized on an almost daily basis—usually with something that smelled so that she'd have to walk around all day with one or more of her books stinking like urine or dog feces. She couldn't even get partners in her classes when teachers assigned group projects. In biology class when she was supposed to be working with a partner, she cut class instead, too embarrassed to work alone. With each new revelation, anger flamed brighter in Josie's core.

Then an entry struck a more hopeful tone.

Vanessa,

I met you today. Okay, well not you, but what I imagine you'd be like if you had lived. Actually, the girl I met looked a lot like me only she had this bright teal scarf around her neck that didn't really go with her outfit. Like I would never wear that scarf with a coral shirt, but that's not the point. The point is that I couldn't help imagining that she was you. Sometimes I like to pretend you didn't die in the fire at all, but that we were separated at birth instead. If we had been separated at birth and you were alive, you'd definitely be like the girl I met today. By the way, I got in serious trouble, but I don't even care. I didn't get her name which is okay because I like to think it was you. We were on that stupid school trip I told you about. The one I didn't want to go on. We went to a deer farm and pumpkin patch which is just dumb. What is this? Kindergarten? I had to sit by myself on the bus of course and that bitch, Melanie, messed with me the whole time. She even threw gum at me and it got in my hair. Then everyone laughed hysterically. Longest bus ride ever. We got to the farm and everyone went off on their own. I was actually glad to be alone for once. I wanted to try to get the gum out of my hair but all they had were portajohns. So gross.

Anyway, there were a bunch of other schools there. At the end of the day I was walking back to the bus when I heard Melanie and her bitchy friends talking behind me. At first, I didn't think they noticed me. Then this group of girls from some other school were walking past me in the other direction and I felt Melanie shove me right into the other girls. I know it was her. I fell right into one girl and knocked her down. She was pissed. Crazy pissed. She got up and started yelling at me. Before I could explain, she shoved me. I could hear Melanie and her friends laughing. I just lost it. I started shoving the girl back and the next thing I knew we were rolling around on the ground. I was trying to hit her, and she was pulling my hair. It hurt like hell. Then the girl ended up on top of me, and Melanie was standing behind her yelling about how she saw me knock her down and that she should kick my ass. Which she started to do. I'm ashamed to say it but 'losing it' didn't get me very far. To tell you the truth—and I would only tell you this, no one else—I'm really pathetic. The worst part was when I started to cry.

Then, out of nowhere, you were there. I thought I was hallucinating. Okay, so it wasn't you. It was that girl I told you about with the bright teal mismatched scarf. I have no idea who she was or what school she was from, but she kicked that crazy girl right off me. She must have known her because she called her Beverly. She said, "Beverly, get off her." Then she elbowed Melanie right in the face. It was amazing. I only wish she had broken Melanie's nose. She made her bleed, but apparently it wasn't broken. Then she dragged Beverly right up by her hair and told her to leave me the hell alone. Beverly told her to stay out of it but she said, "There's nothing to stay out of cause you're going to leave her alone or I'm going to make you sorry you got out of bed this morning." Then she gave Beverly this glare. It was insane. I never saw anything like it. Beverly looked like she was going to piss herself. Meanwhile, dumbass Melanie was fake crying and got the attention of some teachers. They started running over and I knew I was screwed but I didn't even care. You didn't even care. You tossed Beverly aside and put your finger right in Melanie's face. She even jumped back. You told her you'd make her sorry, too. Then you said if she wanted to keep her teeth in her mouth, she'd stop messing with me, too. By that time, the teachers were there. I told you to go so you wouldn't get in trouble. You didn't even seem like you cared. You gave Beverly and Melanie this warning look and then you walked off, all slow, like you knew neither of them would tell on you—and they didn't. We all got in trouble, but no one said anything about you. Best of all, Melanie left me alone the whole bus ride home. I can't wait to see her face at school tomorrow!

Josie's heart was a freight train trying to burst out of her chest.

When Lisette stopped reading, Shannon said, "She never told me that. All she ever said was that she got into a fight with a girl from another school and that she accidentally hit Melanie. All three girls got in trouble."

"That's when she had to do community service," Josie whispered.

"Yes."

Josie felt Lisette's eyes on her. She knew. Somehow, Lisette knew. Of course she did. Josie had been living with Lisette by the time she was in high school. She said, "Josie."

"Not now, Gram."

"What?" Shannon asked, looking from Josie to Lisette and back.

"Nothing," Josie said. "Just something I need to tell Trinity when we find her."

Lisette smiled. She turned a page, and began reading again, but was soon interrupted by Noah. "Josie," he said from the doorway. She looked up to see that his face was flushed. She jumped up. "What is it?"

"The Bone Artist just made contact."

CHAPTER FIFTY-TWO

Dawn was breaking in a splash of pink and purple on the horizon. Lisette and Shannon promised to continue working on the diary while Noah and Josie drove to the station house. Gretchen, Mettner, and Drake were already there, looking as though they hadn't slept in a week which, essentially, they hadn't. They met in the great room, all gathered around the detectives' desks. Chief Chitwood was there as well, his arms folded over his thin chest.

"What's going on?" Josie said.

Gretchen said, "The Bone Artist left you a package at Moss Gardens Trailer Park."

Josie stared at her for a long moment, not sure she was hearing Gretchen correctly.

Drake said, "There are no cameras there, which works out perfectly for this guy, but your team says that the park has special meaning for you."

Josie nodded slowly, her mind working. "I was raised there. That's where Trinity and I were when we first talked about the fact that we were probably sisters."

"The only way that the Bone Artist would know about the significance of the trailer park…" Mettner began but trailed off. None of them wanted to say it. It was as if saying it might jinx it somehow. But Josie knew what they were all thinking: Trinity might still be alive.

Josie said, "Take me to the trailer park."

They rode in a caravan of unmarked vehicles. There was no need for their emergency lights as the traffic was almost non-existent that early in the morning. Moss Gardens sat on top of a hill behind the city park, a collection of about two dozen trailer homes. At the entrance, a wrought-iron archway announced the name of the park in large, ornate letters. Beyond it were brightly painted, well-kept trailers, their small yards cheerily decorated. It was a far cry from the dreariness of her youth. The caravan passed the lot where her childhood home had once been. The trailer she'd lived in with the people she'd believed to be her parents had been torn down long ago after a fire destroyed most of it. The last time Josie was in the park, the lot had held nothing but a few pipes poking from yellowed grass. Now there was a new trailer with cream siding, its windows trimmed in burgundy. The driveway was freshly blacktopped, and the tiny yard in front of it had been turned into a large flowerbed boasting a large array of vibrant colors.

Josie watched it pass by as the caravan headed toward the back of the park where a paved one-lane road ran alongside a wooded valley that lay between the trailer park and one of Denton's working-class neighborhoods. The vehicles stopped in a line along the woodland side and they all got out.

Josie asked Mettner, "Does the Price family still live here?"

He nodded and gave her a grim smile. "That's who called us."

Three years earlier during a different investigation, Maureen Price and her two boys, Kyle and Troy, had been instrumental in helping Josie and her team resolve a difficult case. The last time Josie had seen them, Kyle was twelve and Troy was eleven. Walking toward their trailer, Josie barely recognized Kyle, now fifteen, and taller than her. He was still thin, with thick brown hair that fell just above his eyes, but he looked much older. More like a college student, Josie thought. He stood at the edge of the Price driveway, dressed in jeans and a gray T-shirt with the periodic table on it and beneath that, the words: "I wear this shirt periodically". He smiled when he saw her. "Detective Quinn."

"Just Josie to you, Kyle," she said. "How are you? How's your mom and Troy?"

"Pretty good," he replied, bobbing his head. He pointed to an area from their yard to the street that he had cordoned off using hockey sticks. In the center of it was a cardboard box, slightly bigger than the one Trinity had received at Josie and Noah's house. On the top of it, large block letters spelled out Josie's name. Kyle said, "I saw you on the news last night. I'm sorry about your sister."

"Thank you," Josie replied. Turning to Mettner, she said, "Call Hummel."

"Already did," he said. "The ERT is on the way."

"And Dr. Feist," Josie said.

"What?" Mettner said.

Josie turned to see all three members of her team and Drake staring at her. "There's only one thing that could be in that box," she said. "Remains. Let's just hope they're not Trinity's."

No one spoke.

She turned back to Kyle. "Did you see who left this?"

He shook his head. "No, I'm sorry. My bedroom is on this side of the trailer. Near the road. A noise woke me up. Like a low rumble. Took me a few minutes to realize it was a car or a truck idling. Probably a truck by the sound of it. By the time I got up to look out the window, I heard the sound of screeching, like tires burning rubber to get the hell out of here."

"We'll canvass the park," Gretchen said. She, Noah, and Drake walked off.

Kyle continued, "I saw taillights, that way, but I couldn't make out a plate or anything. Looked like a white pickup to me, but it was really dark. I'm sorry."

"It's okay," Josie said. "You did great."

"I grabbed a flashlight, came out here, and looked around. I checked to see if our bikes were still here. That's what I thought— that someone had come to steal our bikes, but they were fine. Then I looked at my mom's car, thinking maybe someone was back here vandalizing stuff. That kind of thing happens around here, unfortunately. Car was fine. I was just shining the light around to see if anything was messed with and I saw the box. When I saw your name on it, I had a real bad feeling. I knew something was up cause, like I said, we saw you on the news last night."

"I appreciate you calling us," Josie said. "Did you put the hockey sticks out?"

"Yeah, I didn't want anyone to walk by and try to touch it or step on it or anything. I've been out here the whole time. My mom got up and drove around, trying to see if she could find the truck but it was gone. Then she had to take my brother to school and go to work. I figured it was okay if I was late to school for something like this."

Josie smiled. "I'm sure I can work it out with your principal. What you did was very smart."

The sun peeked over the horizon by the time Hummel and his team arrived to process the scene. Josie and Mettner conferred with Noah, Gretchen, and Drake while the ERT got to work. Unfortunately, no one else in the trailer park had noticed a white pickup or anything else unusual. The Bone Artist had escaped into the night like a ghost. Again.

"Boss," Hummel called.

Josie walked over to the area Kyle had marked off where Hummel now knelt. In his gloved hands was the box, its flaps now open. Inside, in a bed of what looked like paper towels, lay a small curved bone about three inches in length. Josie knew immediately what it was, and her throat filled with bile. She thought of Bobbi Ingram's ghastly scar and hoped the rib bone she was looking at didn't belong to Trinity.

"I'd like Dr. Feist to have a look at it, see if she can glean any information from examining it. Then it needs to be sent to the FBI lab immediately for expedited processing," Josie said, trying to keep her voice steady. "There was no note?"

"Only this," Hummel said. He turned one of the cardboard flaps all the way out and pointed to two words written in black Magic Marker. 'Your move.'

Josie felt a crush of bodies behind her and moved aside so the rest of the team could have a look. She took a few steps toward the street. Jenny Chan, a newer member of the ERT, knelt in the road. "Detective Quinn," she said. "It looks like the killer left something behind."

Josie dared not get excited as she moved closer to Chan and peered down at the asphalt. "Here," Chan said, pointing to a small amount of mud on the otherwise pristine road. "Look what it's in the shape of."

Josie's heart gave a little flutter. "A tire tread."

Chan nodded. "From a truck, judging by the size of it. We'll get it off to the lab and see if the soil can tell us anything about where this guy came from."

Josie knew this was unlikely, but it was more than the killer had ever left behind at any scene before. "Thank you, Officer Chan."

CHAPTER FIFTY-THREE

"I think I've found what Trinity wanted you to read," Lisette said when Josie and Noah returned to the house. "Sit."

Exhaustion clouded Josie's mind, but she sat at the kitchen table anyway. Her head pounded harder than ever. She knew she needed to rest but not until she knew what else was in the diary. Noah made more coffee. Shannon had gone to bed, while Christian and Patrick sat in the living room. Christian had dozed off, and Patrick scrolled on his phone. Once Noah had supplied both Josie and Lisette with fresh cups of coffee, Lisette began to read again.

Vanessa:

Oh boy, did I ever get in trouble. All for being pushed into a girl and then getting my ass kicked by her. It hardly seems fair, but whatever. The good news is that Melanie got in trouble, too. Big time. Well, we both got suspended. I'm in worse trouble than her though because she told everyone I was the one who elbowed her in the nose. I promised I wouldn't tell on you—okay, well on the girl who actually hit her—so I'm taking the blame. Her mom pressed criminal charges against me. Can you believe that? I wonder if she knows what a mean, lying, manipulative cow Melanie really is. Mom and Dad got me a lawyer though and he made some kind of deal with the judge or the DA, or whoever, so I only have to do community service. I thought they'd make me pick up trash on the highway or something but instead, I have to go to this nature preserve and help out there. It's mostly picking up litter and helping to clean out the animal enclosures. That might sound great—Mom said, "Oh, how fascinating"—but it's disgusting. I never knew there were so many different kinds of poop. (Gag.)

The good news is, there are a couple of other kids volunteering there who are around my age and they're all pretty nice. Other teenagers who don't treat me like garbage. Imagine that! I don't think any of them are there because they have to be, though. They all seem pretty into nature and stuff. They get to do cool stuff, like give tours to people and do crafts with groups of kids who come to visit, like from daycares and schools and stuff. There's this one kid, Max, who might be there on probation like me. He's a little creepy but I think it might just be the way he looks. He's got some big red scar running down the middle of his face. He must get crucified at whatever school he goes to, if the kids there are anything like the kids at my school.

"Oh my God," Josie said.

"Do we know the name and location of this nature preserve?" Noah asked.

"Go get Christian and see if he remembers. If not, wake Shannon and find out."

Noah raced into the other room.

"Keep going," Josie told Lisette.

Lisette said, "Many of these entries are just about the disgusting work she had to do at the preserve. She talks about Max but mostly just about how mysterious he is and how he never talks to anyone. But this one… here, listen to this one."

Vanessa:

I finally got Max to talk to me today. Turns out he's sixteen. He claims he's not there for community service. He laughed when he found out that I was. I was a little offended at first but then he said it was hard to imagine someone like me getting into enough trouble that I'd have to do community service. I wanted to ask him what he meant by 'someone like me' but I didn't have a chance because then we got sent over to clean out the cages where they keep the raptors who are recovering from injuries. There's a red-tailed hawk and two owls in there right now. They're kind of cool. Max didn't like them much but he knew a lot about them. Turns out his dad is some kind of professional bird watcher or something. Works at a college. Or he did, I guess. The way Max talked, I wasn't sure if his dad was still alive or not. He got real weird when I started asking him about his family so I stopped.

"An ornithologist," Josie muttered. "Or a biologist. Hang on, I'll ask the others to run this down." She fired off a text to the rest of the team.

Shannon, Christian, and Noah came into the kitchen. Shannon rubbed sleep from her eyes. "Noah told me what's going on. We don't remember the name of that place, but it was an hour from Callowhill."

"Is it still there?" Josie asked.

"I don't know," Christian answered.

Josie opened her laptop and spun it around to face them. "Do you think you could find it on Google Maps?"

"We can try," Shannon said. They sat side by side in front of the computer while Lisette kept reading.

Vanessa:

My time at the nature preserve is almost up. I'm kind of bummed, which is weird, right? I hate the work but everyone is nice to me and leaves me alone. Even creepy Max. He kind of stopped talking to me after I asked about his dad. I'm dying to know about his scar. I heard one girl ask him last week—she just came right out and asked. Just like that. He looked kind of annoyed and mumbled something about cooking and hot oil or something. I couldn't quite make it out from where I was. I wanted to ask her after he left but

I don't want to be that person. I've tried to talk to him again but he's never near where I'm working. Lately he's just in the woods all the time. I don't even know what he's doing out there.

Lisette stopped reading and turned some more pages. Across from her and Josie, Noah leaned in between the Paynes to study the computer screen.

Josie said, "Is there anything more, Gram?"

Lisette looked up from over her reading glasses and said, "Oh, one more you might be interested in."

Vanessa:

I saw Max in the woods today. I don't know if I should say something to the preserve director or not. It was so weird. It's not like he was really doing anything wrong. I was out collecting litter and I saw him on one of the other trails. He was messing with this dead animal. I mean, it's not unusual to find dead animals in the woods. I've seen more dead animals working at this stupid preserve than you can even imagine. Anyway, not the point. It was small—like maybe a rabbit or something—and already skeletonized which also is not unusual cause any dead animal in the woods gets picked clean by the scavengers. Basically, other animals. Circle of life, food chain, something like that. This is stuff I have to write about for the judge when I complete my community service. Max was arranging the bones, making different shapes with them. I watched him for a long time. I have no idea what he was trying to do but the whole thing was making me sick. I didn't say anything to him. Finally, he just threw the bones into the woods, all scattered around and walked back to the main building. Really bizarre, right? I thought about telling on him, but what would I say? Max found some old bones in the woods and played with them? So what? It's not like he killed the animal. He didn't keep the bones. Plus, he's a boy and boys are freaks. I mean, this boy at my school takes his little sister's Barbie dolls, burns their private parts off, and brags about it, but no one cares about him. So what if Max touched some animal bones? The whole thing gives me the heebie jeebies.

Shannon, Christian, and Noah were all staring at Lisette by the time she finished. Noah said, "No wonder she became obsessed with the case. She *knew* this guy."

Josie said, "She didn't know him, though. Not really. He was a weird boy she met when she was fourteen. But I think the deeper she got into her investigation, the more she suspected that the bizarre guy she worked with at the nature preserve when she was a teenager might be the Bone Artist."

Noah said, "She would have recognized him when he pulled up to the cabin. Especially when she saw his scar."

"Sweet Jesus," Christian said.

Shannon touched his arm. "Come on, we have to find the preserve. Keep looking. Lisette, you can keep reading."

Nodding, Lisette turned a few more pages. Then she started to read once more.

Vanessa:

I haven't written in a few days because everything has been crazy. I'm done at the nature preserve now, finally. I was feeling bad about leaving, but the last week there really freaked me out. I found human bones! Like a dead body! It was so weird and nothing like I thought it would be. It didn't even smell or anything. I guess because the guy was dead for so long. Turns out it was this hunter who went missing last year. An elderly guy. It was very sad. Anyway, I was out clearing debris from the hiking trails but what I was really doing was looking for Max. I couldn't stop thinking about him and those bones. I was wondering if he went out all the time searching for bones. I think I was right because I found him standing over that hunter's body with the skull in his hands. Can you believe that? He touched a dead person's skull!!!! Gross doesn't even begin to describe it. He saw me, and I must have looked super shocked cause he said he was out taking a walk and just found them. I got a closer look at them and it looked like someone curled up on their side and went to sleep or something. The police already said there was no 'foul play'. The guy got lost and froze to death. Anyway, I asked Max why in the hell he would touch a dead person's skull?!?! He looked at me and said something like, "Haven't you ever wanted to see a person without their skin?" I was so skeeved out. I told him I was going to get the director so she could call the police. When I got back out there with her and the police, Max was gone. I never saw him after that. Mom and Dad didn't let me go back after that although they did let me do some TV interviews about finding the guy.

"Here it is," Shannon said. "Quail Ridge Nature Preserve. Looks like it's still in operation. A little over an hour from here."

Noah took his phone out again. He looked at Josie. "I'm calling Mettner. Let's go."

CHAPTER FIFTY-FOUR

Cheyenne Thomas was the current director of the Quail Ridge Nature Preserve. Josie estimated her to be in her mid-twenties. She'd only held her current post for two years so she didn't remember Trinity or Max or the dead hunter who had been found there nearly twenty years earlier. She was, however, extremely helpful and allowed Josie's team, as well as several FBI agents, to search the preserve without a warrant while she checked their employment records. Unfortunately, they didn't go back that far. There were also no employees currently on staff who would have been there when Trinity and Max were there.

Mettner drove their team back in a department issue SUV while Drake followed behind with several of his agents. Josie sat in the front seat, her mind fighting fatigue and fogginess. "High schools," she said. "He was sixteen. He would have been a junior at one of the local high schools within an hour from the preserve."

From the backseat, Gretchen said, "I'll get on that."

Noah said, "How many guys named Max are there in the state, anyway? We know his age. We should try searching that way, too."

Mettner said, "As soon as we get back, someone needs to start contacting colleges within an hour or two of the preserve and see if we can track down an ornithology or biology professor with a son named Max."

Josie leaned her head back against the seat and closed her eyes. They were getting close. Noah, Gretchen, and Mettner kept talking. Gretchen called Drake on his cell phone and put him on speakerphone so they could coordinate with him. They'd hit the ground running as soon as they got back to Denton. As the car sped down the highway, Josie couldn't fight her exhaustion any longer. She drifted off to sleep, sending a psychic message to Trinity. *We're getting close. Just hold on a little longer.*

When she woke, the sky was dark. The dashboard clock read seven thirty in the evening. They were outside her house. Noah shook her shoulder lightly and she looked around bleary-eyed. "No," she said. "This isn't right. I'm going to the station house with you guys. I have to help."

From the back seat, Gretchen said, "You have to sleep, boss. You're concussed and sleep-deprived."

"When's the last time you ate?" Noah asked pointedly.

Mettner added, "None of us will go home yet, okay, boss? We're going to work on this until we find Trinity. You get some sleep. When you come back in, one of us will rotate out. It will be all hands on deck, I promise."

Josie looked at them one by one. She knew she was truly at a new level of tired when tears leaked from her eyes. She couldn't remember ever crying in front of her team. "Thank you," she told them and let Noah walk her into the house.

She slept for twelve hours and woke in a full-blown panic. She'd only meant to sleep for two or three hours at most. She checked her phone but no one on the team had called her. Downstairs, her family wandered around the house at loose ends, passing the time by playing and cuddling with Trout. None of them had heard from Noah or anyone else either. Josie was ready in fifteen minutes. Christian dropped her off at the station house. In the great room, Mettner was slumped over his desk, drooling on a pile of what looked like background checks. Across from him, Gretchen was obscured by a stack of what appeared to be high school yearbooks. She leafed through one, turning the pages slowly.

At his desk, Noah spoke on the phone. "He would have been on your faculty sometime around the year 2000, perhaps earlier than that? Specializing in ornithology, zoology, or biology? Maybe a subspecialty in raptors?"

Gretchen offered Josie a smile. "Good to see you, although I wish we had better news."

Josie's heart sank. "Nothing yet? Nothing at all?"

Gretchen closed the yearbook. "Sorry, boss. He's not in any of these yearbooks. It's possible he was home-schooled, especially with his scar. Maybe his parents didn't want him in school or maybe he had too difficult a time with bullying."

Josie sighed and plopped into her chair. Noah hung up. "We struck out with colleges."

"How is that *possible*? There have to be over fifty colleges within an hour of that preserve."

"Only a handful of those have ornithology or zoology programs," Noah said. "Drake took his guys to check those out in person. They got nothing. Then we started working down the rest of the list, checking colleges with departments of biology. The FBI took half and we took half. We can't find anyone who fits the bill."

"Because it's too vague," Josie said. "What we're looking for is too vague. A professor maybe of ornithology or maybe of zoology or perhaps biology who worked there in the late nineties, early two thousands with a teenage son named Max who has a scar? Departments don't keep records of their faculty's personal lives."

Gretchen said, "We've got a name now. A thirty-five-year-old white male named Max with a red scar down the middle of his face. We should get you back out in front of the cameras."

"No," Josie said. "He'll disappear again. I want him to know we're on to him, but I don't want him to know we're struggling. If I go out there and say his name is Max and that's all we've got, he's going to know he's winning. It's my move. I'm not ready to make it yet. We need something more."

Noah looked over at Mettner. A line of drool leaked from the side of his mouth onto the page beneath his head. "Mett!" Noah shouted.

Mettner's head sprung up, sending pages flying across all their desks. "I'm up," he said.

They gave him a minute before Noah asked him, "You get anywhere with the Maxes in the state?"

Mettner sifted through some pages. "There are a bunch of guys named Maxwell, Maximus, Maximillian. Plenty of them in the age range. I looked up all their drivers' licenses. None of them are scarred down the middle of their face."

Josie shook her head. How could they have gotten such a huge break but not be any closer to finding him? "No tips from the news conference?" she asked. "No one called in about the scar? It's pretty distinctive."

"Sorry, boss," Mettner said. "Nothing that's panned out. Drake's guys ran down a few leads, but they were no good."

"We have to be missing something. His middle name is Max or maybe his last name is Maxwell. Dammit. He's right under our noses. What about the truck? Have we checked for any white Chevy trucks registered to someone with Max in their name?"

Gretchen said, "I can check on that."

Josie held out her hand to Mettner. "Let me see your notes. I want to go back over this."

Noah stood up. "I'm going to track down Drake and see if we can double-check all the professors we already checked out, or maybe expand the search radius."

"Please," Josie said. "He's here somewhere. He's not a ghost. He's real, and we have to find him before he kills my sister—if he hasn't already."

CHAPTER FIFTY-FIVE

No one attended Hanna's funeral except for Alex and Zandra. Even after her illustrious art career, which took off even more after Francis's accident, in death she was alone. They buried her on a Tuesday, in the rain, in a cemetery she had chosen. She had had time to decide what they were to do with her remains. She had had time to instruct them on how they could continue to live the small life they'd carved out in the old house since the accident. They didn't know much else. Only Alex had been out in the world. Zandra had only left the property a few times. She had said she wanted to leave but once Hanna took her out into the world, she no longer wanted any part of it. Alex, however, was fascinated with it. There were new adventures, ones he could embark on by himself and without Francis's censure. People were a lot like the raptors Francis loved so much. Not all of them, but many of them.

Without Hanna there, his bad thoughts emerged like animals waking from hibernation. He didn't have to watch Zandra anymore or keep her in check. He felt free for the first time in his life, and he realized how much of a prisoner she had made him when they were growing up. His entire life had revolved around policing her and her urges so she didn't hurt or even kill their mother. He had suffered because of her, been put out in the cold because of her. Perhaps she sensed his growing anger toward her because after Hanna's death, Zandra kept herself locked away most of the time.

She did come out to see his first art installation, which he'd created on a remote part of the land Hanna had left them. The foundation of an old building still stood beneath a cluster of trees.

He had spent months building it up, little by little, until it provided enough cover for him to do his work. He didn't even know that Zandra was aware of what he was doing until she showed up one day with no warning.

"I'm almost finished," he said, smearing paint across the floor with one hand.

She looked around, her eyes taking in every detail. "This is disgusting," she said.

He stopped painting. "No, it's not. This is art. Our mother left us a blank canvas."

"You think you're some kind of artist? Like she was?"

He said nothing and resumed painting.

"You know this isn't art, right? No one is going to think this is art. I'm pretty sure you'd go to prison for this. I mean, how dumb can you be?"

"You don't need to be here anymore," he muttered.

"What the hell does that mean?"

"You could leave."

"No, I can't," she said. "You need me. You've always needed me."

He laughed. "You're so selfish."

"You son of a bitch," she spat. "Is that really what you believe? Do you honestly think I'm the selfish one here?"

He didn't answer. His hand worked harder to rub in the paint. He put his entire body behind it until he was gasping with the effort. When he was satisfied, he sat back on his haunches and wiped his brow with a forearm. Zandra was still there.

"I'm going to kill you one day," he told her.

She said, "I know."

CHAPTER FIFTY-SIX

The search for Max went on for a week. Between Denton PD and the FBI team, they worked around the clock to try to locate him. Hours were spent behind computers, sifting through documents, driving out to residences and properties, questioning people. Sitting at her desk, sifting through drivers' license photos of all the males in Pennsylvania between thirty-five and forty with Max in their name for the hundredth time, Josie couldn't stop the questions or the sense of desperation she felt. Trinity was slipping away. The entire case was in danger of disintegrating into dust. She was beginning to think she was crazy. Or maybe they'd been all wrong about the diary. Maybe Trinity had been all wrong.

But the scar, she reminded herself.

Which led to her next question: how was this guy going unnoticed by everyone in the state, it seemed, when he had a scar running down the middle of his face? How was that possible when Trinity's abduction by the Bone Artist was the top story every single day? She remembered what Bobbi Ingram had said; that he could cover it with make-up. Josie had had a flash of his face in the truck the day he'd run her off the road. It had only lasted a second, maybe two, but she'd seen it. It was true, make-up would help. It might not entirely cover the scar, but it would certainly minimize it. It was an easy thing for him to hide his truck and put on some foundation whenever he went out.

But where the hell was he?

"Quinn!" Drake strode into the room, waving a piece of paper. He looked around. "Where is everyone?"

"Gretchen and Noah are at home resting. Mettner's down in the break room. Why? What've you got?"

He smiled. In the two short weeks she'd known him, she hadn't seen a smile that went all the way to his eyes. Until now. Her heartbeat picked up pace. She said, "Don't smile like that unless you have a real lead. An actual, honest to goodness lead. Please."

He placed the paper in the center of her desk and tapped an index finger against it. "Remember your ERT took a sample of mud from the trailer park? From the tread of the killer's truck?"

Josie leaned over, studying the document. It was a lab report of the soil composition from the sample that Jenny Chan had taken. Denton's ERT had collected the evidence but it had been turned over to the FBI labs for processing. The DNA testing from the combs and the rib found in front of the Price family's trailer would still take weeks, if not months, but Josie knew soil samples could be processed in as few as seven days. She ran her finger down the list of the test results until she found the reason that Drake was smiling.

"Eastonite," she said.

"It's a mineral," Drake said. Josie looked over to see him bouncing up and down on the balls of his feet.

"I know," she said. "It's only found in two places in the world—a small locality in Norway and Easton, Pennsylvania."

He stopped bouncing, staring down at her with a disappointed expression. "How the hell do you know that?"

Josie smiled. "Noah's sister runs a number of quarries in Pennsylvania. I picked some things up. But it doesn't matter how I know that. What matters is that we've got a search area! Let me get the rest of the team."

Four hours later, they all sat at the conference room table with laptops open in front of them. A half-eaten box of pizza lay in the center of the table. Empty coffee cups and soda bottles littered the rest of the table. The energy they'd started with was now a distant memory. No one spoke. Occasionally, someone would grunt or issue a heavy sigh. An acute ache bloomed behind Josie's eyes as she studied property records within Easton, Pennsylvania and the areas surrounding it that she'd already been over a half dozen times. She rubbed her eyes and stretched her arms over her head. "I've got nothing," she said.

"Same here," Gretchen grumbled.

Drake said, "There are people in Easton named Max, property owners named Max—first and last names—but no one is matching up either age-wise or by driver's license."

"It can't be this hard," Noah said.

"We're missing something," Mettner agreed. "I even struck out with the colleges again. There are two in Easton—Lafayette and Aubertine—and neither of their biology departments believed anyone on their faculties in the late nineties or early two thousands had a son named Max or a son with a scar on his face or a faculty member with a particular interest in raptors."

Noah said, "Maybe we need to stop looking for Max and look at actual properties. Some place with a lot of land, enough land where a group of twenty to thirty black vultures gathering wouldn't be all that noticeable."

"Maybe somewhere near a railroad," Gretchen said. "Has anyone looked at the satellite images? Maybe we can spot a large property with one or more shipping containers on it."

"I did," Mettner said. "Nothing stood out, but the shipping container could be obscured by tree cover. Or the satellite photos could be out of date. Bobbi Ingram was held in one six years ago."

"Noah has a point, though," Josie said. "We're focusing too hard on the name. We're focusing too hard on trying to assemble all the pieces. Maybe we only need one to point us in a direction."

Drake huffed. "Which one?"

Josie clicked out of the property records and pulled up her internet browser, using it to pull up Google satellite images of Easton and its surrounding areas. "I don't know," she said. "We'll know it when we see it. Let's keep looking."

Noah said, "You've got the aerials?"

She nodded. He rolled his chair over, around Mettner's, and next to hers. Together they studied the overhead view, zooming in and out and moving from area to area. Josie kept coming back to a small, almost circular area of what looked like boulders that stood out among the trees surrounding it. She zoomed in on them. It was impossible to say how big an area they covered but they were grouped closely together with no room for vegetation.

"What is it?" Noah asked.

"Boulders," Josie said. She zoomed back out, noting that the several acres around them were green. There were lots of trees and then an area that looked almost like a farm or the grounds of a large estate. She pointed to it. "What is this?"

"Let me see." He used the mousepad to manipulate the images on the screen and then pointed to a large group of buildings. "Well, this right here is Aubertine College. Maybe it's part of the campus."

Josie looked again. "But there's nothing there but land."

Noah backed up so Mettner could get a look at the screen. She pointed to the area they were studying. Mettner said, "It could be an arboretum. Gretchen, look it up and see if Aubertine College has an arboretum."

"On it," Gretchen said, tapping away at the laptop before her. A moment later she said, "They do. The Agnes Hill Arboretum. It's owned by a private foundation which was founded by a former alum back in the 1800s but it's operated by the college. It's fifty-five acres and it has been home to many raptors native to Pennsylvania which Aubertine students majoring in biology or zoology have access to for their research."

Josie zoomed out once more, staring at the stones again. Noah said, "What is it?"

"Give me a minute," she told him. The stones. What was it about the stones?

Drake and Gretchen stood and came over to study the screen. Drake said, "There's no railroad nearby. Bobbi Ingram told you—"

It clicked into place. Josie jumped out of her seat, nearly knocking Drake and Gretchen into the wall behind them. "That's it!" she said. "That's where he is!"

They all stared at her. "Boss," said Mettner.

Josie said, "The sounds that Bobbi Ingram heard were not people hammering in rail ties. They were ringing rocks."

Gretchen said, "The ringing rocks are in Bucks County. They're in a state park—a huge tourist attraction."

Drake said, "What the hell are ringing rocks?"

"They're lithophonic rocks," Josie explained. "They resonate like bells when you strike them. In Bucks County, they call it 'the field of boulders', I think. You take hammers, and you can go out among the boulders, strike them and make music. Well, it sounds like bells. Or like the sound of rail ties being struck. There are some in the UK and in Australia, too."

"But boss," Mettner said, "isn't Bucks County the only site in Pennsylvania?"

"No," Josie said. "It's not. There are some smaller sites and some of them are on privately owned property. These are ringing rocks. That's what Bobbi heard when she was captive."

"I don't see any shipping containers on this land," Drake pointed out, reaching across and zooming in on the property.

"Like Mettner said, it could be under tree cover or it might not be there now," Josie said. "Hear me out. In the diary, Trinity said that Max's dad worked for the college. Not that he was a professor there. No, he 'worked' there. Maybe he was the caretaker. It would make sense. He'd be familiar with the raptors there. He may have even had an interest in ornithology. Maybe Max took over his duties or maybe Max works with him there."

Gretchen said, "And the reason we can't find the truck is because it's not registered to anyone named Max, it's registered to either the college or the foundation."

Noah had moved over and was now clicking away on his own laptop. "And they've got an animal sanctuary there with a staff veterinarian."

"Which means they have medical supplies and a place to operate," Gretchen said.

Mettner grimaced. "With fifty-five acres, he could probably find a spot to leave his victims out for the black vultures without drawing too much attention."

Josie nodded. "This area to the north is adjacent to some large tracts of land. Doesn't look like there's anyone or anything there. It looks like maybe a tributary of the Lehigh River, maybe a waterfall here."

Noah said, "The caretaker would have his own quarters on the land."

Gretchen added, "Which would also technically be owned by either the university or the foundation, so searching property records for someone named Max would be useless."

Josie said, "Let's make some phone calls, do some recon, and firm this up."

Drake met her eyes. "Then we'll go get Trinity."

CHAPTER FIFTY-SEVEN

The air in the building seemed suddenly energized. Everyone was jittery. An hour later, they had the information they needed. Chief Chitwood stood in the center of the great room while they briefed him. Mettner began, "The caretaker of the arboretum from 1980 until 1996 was a man named Francis Thornberg. He lived in the private quarters with a woman named Hanna Cahill."

"Cahill," Chitwood said. "That sounds familiar."

Josie said, "It was Nicci Webb's maiden name."

"The Bone Artist *knew* Nicci Webb?" Chitwood asked incredulously.

Gretchen said, "In 1975, Hanna Cahill gave birth to Nicolette Cahill in Philadelphia. There is no father listed on the birth certificate."

Noah said, "Then in 1985, she gave birth to a son, Alexander Thornberg. She gave him Francis's last name, but Francis is not listed on the birth certificate."

Mettner added, "Hanna was a pretty famous and successful artist in the nineties. Then, for some reason, she faded into obscurity."

"Francis and Hanna weren't married?" Chitwood asked.

"No," Gretchen said. "We couldn't find any record of them having married."

"Were there any other children?"

Mettner said, "We couldn't find any evidence of other children. But we did find that Hanna dedicated one of her last art shows to—" he looked down at his notes. "*My darling Alex and Zandra.*"

"Who is Zandra?" Chitwood asked.

"We don't know," Mettner said.

Josie said, "We thought it might be short for Alexandra."

Drake said, "As in Alexander and Alexandra—creepy twins, perhaps? But there is no evidence at all that Hanna Cahill had twins. There is no Alexandra Thornberg or Alexandra Cahill. There was only Nicolette and Alexander."

Josie said, "I asked Monica Webb about Nicci's childhood. Nicci told her that her mother died when she was fifteen, and that she left home. That would have been in 1990."

"But Hanna Cahill didn't die until 2005," Mettner put in.

"Which means Nicci lied to her daughter about why she left home," Noah said. "At least, that's our assumption."

Chitwood said, "Why would Nicci Webb lie about her mother? Why wouldn't she tell her daughter about Alexander? That's Monica Webb's uncle."

Josie said, "There's no way for us to know for certain, but I'd guess there was some kind of abuse going on in the household. Nicci fled, and her little brother Alex turned out to be a serial killer."

Gretchen said, "After Nicci left, Alex was home-schooled, evidently, and at some point in the late nineties, the entire family became recluses."

"Is the dad still alive?" Chitwood asked.

"We don't know," Josie responded. "There's no death certificate for him, and he still draws a salary from the college for caretaking. Alex Thornberg became an official employee of the Foundation in 1998 when he turned eighteen. He, too, is listed as a caretaker."

Chitwood patted down the hairs floating over his head. "What else?"

Drake said, "My team is going to take point on this. It's a lot of area to cover—fifty-five acres of land in the arboretum. There are five structures."

"And," Josie said, "the land to the north, adjacent to the arboretum, was purchased by Hanna Cahill in 2001. One hundred acres. No structures on record but plenty of land."

Chitwood shook his head. "You're telling me that this guy has had a hundred-acre playground for over twenty years?"

"Well he would have been sixteen when Hanna bought the land," Drake said. "But yeah, the land passed to him when the mother died. Well, it would have passed to Nicci Webb in part as well, but since she wasn't around, it was a non-issue. The deed was never changed over anyway. Property taxes were always paid on time, so no one cared about the title to the land. Oh and a shipping container was removed from the property three years after Bobbi Ingram was released."

"No shipping containers now?"

"No," Drake answered. "Which means he has to be holding Trinity in his private residence."

"How about our guy, Alexander Thornberg?" Chitwood asked. "He have a driver's license?"

Noah took a sheet of paper from his desk and held it up for Chitwood to see. The sight of it still chilled Josie. There he was—the man she had seen in the truck, who had later tried to take her. In his driver's license photo, the scar was barely visible. He must have used make-up to cover it before getting his photo taken. But still, she could see its faint mark.

Chitwood studied it. "Does he have a criminal record?"

Josie answered, "No. Not as an adult. It's possible he had one as a juvenile, but we wouldn't have access to that, or it would have been expunged by now."

"Okay," Chitwood said. "You've got this guy, probably holding Trinity in the caretaker's residence. Of the people living there after Nicolette Webb left, his mother is deceased, but the dad is unaccounted for, which means he could still be on the property."

"Right," Drake said.

Chitwood said, "You've still got a lot of ground to cover. A lot of places this guy could hide if you don't get him. Your team have a plan in place to end this thing?"

Drake said, "We're working on it now."

CHAPTER FIFTY-EIGHT

The reporter was a curious creature. Alex had never seen anyone so beautiful in person. She was also insufferable, with her incessant demands and nonstop talking. He'd never met anyone who talked as much as she did. For a long time, he wished he had kept the storage container. Then he wouldn't have to hear her whine about going home, about her sister, the cop. Trinity didn't know it, but he'd watched her twin on television. He'd seen the clues she had planted, the tableau she had prepared especially for him. He had felt a stirring he hadn't felt in a long time. He should have taken her when he had the chance. He'd been too cautious.

From the upstairs bathroom came pounding on the pipes. Trinity again. Alex trudged upstairs and listened at the door. He felt her throw herself against it. "I know you're out there!" she shouted.

"How many pages do you have today?" he asked.

"I ran out of... tape or ribbon... or whatever the hell this is. Please, I need a laptop. I can't do this on a typewriter."

"You think I'm stupid," he answered. "I know you'll be able to use a laptop to access the internet somehow."

"No, I promise," she cried. "I wouldn't do that."

Her sister wouldn't have lied to him. She would not treat him as if he was stupid. She knew how smart he was. She was, possibly, the first person who had ever understood the depth of his intelligence. She hadn't made a move since his last communication. He was beginning to worry that she had figured out more than she let on. Of course she had. She wouldn't show him her hand. She wasn't going to make it easy for him. He didn't want to, but he liked her.

"I'll get you more ribbon," he promised Trinity.

"I don't need more ribbon. I *need* a laptop."

"No," he said. "I can get you ribbon, but you must finish."

"I can't finish this without talking to Zandra. I want her side of the story."

He sighed. "You can't meet her. I told you, she went away a long time ago."

There was silence. He waited for more demands, more questions, more complaining, but there was nothing.

Alex said, "I'm going to get you more ribbon now so you can finish. We don't have much time left."

Her voice came again, more high-pitched this time. "Much time? What are you talking about? What's going to happen? What are you going to do with me?"

"The raptors are coming," he said. "I need to be ready."

CHAPTER FIFTY-NINE

It seemed like days later, but in reality it was only hours by the time they arrived on the outskirts of Easton. Josie, Noah, Gretchen, and Mettner suited up in tactical gear but sat out of the raid on the caretaker's residence at the back of the arboretum property. They waited outside the FBI's perimeter, near the college. Drake had decided to go in just before dawn, when the rest of the staff and students who normally used the arboretum would be absent and they could creep in under the cover of night, approaching the house just as daylight crept in. As much as it killed her to sit out, Josie knew she had no choice. She and her team stood outside their vehicle, listening to the comms as the FBI carried out the raid.

When Josie heard the words, "Suspect is in custody," her knees went weak. She waited for some chatter about Trinity, but there was none. Instead, came a report of an "unknown male in one of the upstairs bedrooms, elderly, disabled and in need of medical care." Over the comms she heard a horrific sound, like a rabbit caught in a bear trap. "Aaahhmaaxx!"

She looked around to see Noah, Gretchen, and Mettner all wince at the same time she did. "What the hell is that?" Noah asked.

It came again over the comms, this time abbreviated. "Mmmaaxx."
Max.

One of the ambulances on standby in the nearest college parking lot sped past them and off onto the narrow drive through the arboretum. Then came calls of "all clear" from various agents.

"No!" Josie said.

"Boss," said Gretchen, reaching for Josie's arm, but she swatted her away and started marching into the arboretum. They'd studied maps of the place extensively prior to the raid so Josie knew exactly where she was headed although even if she hadn't, she need only follow all the FBI vehicles. A light sweat broke out all over her body by the time she reached the back of the property. A large, stately old house with pillars at the entrance, it stood beneath a copse of tall trees.

The pickup truck sat next to it, partially covered with a blue tarp. The ambulance was parked just feet away from the front door. As she pushed her way through heavily armed FBI agents, she saw the paramedics maneuvering a gurney out of the house. On it, a shriveled husk of a man lay on his side. He wore a T-shirt and adult diaper. His arms and legs were permanently bent and curled into his body. His eyes bulged from his head, and his skin pulled tightly against the bones of his face. He didn't even look like a living thing.

"Francis Thornberg," she said when Drake met her in the doorway.

"We believe so, yes."

"Where is my sister?"

Drake's mask of professionalism slipped, and in that moment, Josie saw a number of emotions: rage, frustration, panic, and sorrow.

"Drake," Josie said quietly. "Just tell me."

Rip the Band-Aid off, she thought. We're too late.

He looked behind him into a large foyer. "She's not here."

Josie looked around. "She's not in the house, but she has to be here. We just need to look."

"I already dispatched search teams onto the rest of the arboretum property and Hanna Cahill's hundred acres behind us."

Josie put a hand on her hip. "Where is he?"

"Detective Quinn—"

"Where is he?" she repeated, her voice rising to a shout.

He stepped aside and she moved past him, into the house. "He's already been read his Miranda rights," Drake called after her.

Drake's agents held him in the kitchen, which didn't look like it had been updated since the early eighties. The walls were dark wood paneling and the cabinets looked almost identical. The faux-brick tile floor was worn and chipped. Alex Thornberg sat in a chair with his hands cuffed in front of him. Leaning forward, he rested his elbows on his knees and his chin on his fists. When Josie entered the room, he sat up straight. She thought she saw a smile, or at least the beginnings of one. It took everything in her not to punch him right in the face.

Three agents surrounded him, but when they saw the look on her face, they backed away, giving her room. She pulled one of the other chairs over and pushed it as close to him as she could get it and still have room to sit down. A look of surprise lit his face as she took her seat, her knees between his, her face inches from his. He had no choice but to back up slightly, holding his bound hands up between them.

Josie used one hand to gently push them down into his lap. "Your father calls you Max," she said. "Because he can't say Alex, isn't that right?"

Confusion creased his face. "Yes," he murmured.

"You left your sister's bones behind Trinity's cabin."

"No, I—I left a piece behind Trinity's cabin. You needed to know it was me."

"The 'piece' you left behind the cabin was made up of your sister's bones."

"That's not possible."

Josie stared at him. What was he trying to accomplish by denying that Nicci was his sister? This made no sense. She tried again, drawing out her words. "Nicolette Webb was your biological half-sister."

His head reared back ever so slightly. He blinked. Then he leaned back in toward her and said, in a voice that was almost childlike, "We don't say her name. Not ever."

"What about the name Zandra? Can we say that name? Where is Zandra, Alex? Is she here?"

His chin dropped to his chest. "She went away a long time ago. I made her. She did bad things. Worse things than me."

Behind him, Drake lingered in the doorway. Josie met his eyes and he shrugged and shook his head. His team had cleared the house. There was no one else there.

Josie looked back at Alex. "Does Zandra have Trinity?"

He didn't answer. Josie kept her expression carefully blank even though she was baffled by his behavior. "Alex," she said loudly, firmly.

He looked up just in time for her to see something in his dark eyes shift. It was barely perceptible but Josie saw it. The childlike moping was gone, replaced by the keen intelligence that had been there only seconds earlier. She asked, "Does Zandra have Trinity?"

He sighed. "I told you, Zandra is gone. She has nothing to do with this."

"Then where is Trinity?"

"Do you think I'd tell you that easily?"

"I think this game is over, and I won. You can tell me where she is, and I can pull whatever strings are available to me to make the judicial process easier on you—maybe argue against the death penalty. Or you can not tell me and rot in hell, because whether I know where she is or not, I'll be free and you'll die in prison, and every single day of my life I will work to make sure that people like you don't hurt people like my sister ever again. I'll track down Zandra and find out just how much she knew about your crimes, and if I have to, I'll send her to prison as well. So what's it going to be, *Max*?"

"Detective Quinn, the game's not over."

Josie tapped on the cuffs circling his wrists. "I think it is, Alex."

He smiled. "No, it's not over. It's your move."

CHAPTER SIXTY

"Detective Quinn," Drake called. "Upstairs!"

Josie struggled to keep from jumping out of her chair and sprinting into the foyer. She slid her chair back slowly, placed it back under the kitchen table, and walked calmly out of the kitchen, head held high. She made herself walk slowly up the steps so Thornberg wouldn't hear her footsteps pounding on the stairs. Drake stood outside the bathroom. "He was keeping Trinity here."

Josie peeked around him and saw a large clawfoot tub with a blanket inside it. On the floor was a pair of Louis Vuitton heels. On top of the sink was an old typewriter. A stack of paper sat beside it. Josie snapped on some gloves and went over to peruse the pages. "This is his story," she said. "He was making her write his story."

Drake rubbed a hand over his face. "She could still be alive."

"But where?"

"We'll get dogs," he said. "If she's here, we'll find her. Also, I'm going to have my people comb through every one of these sickos' backgrounds—Hanna Cahill, Francis Thornberg, and Alex—to see if we can find this Zandra person. She could be an accomplice, for all we know. She could have taken Trinity. We can't believe anything this psycho says."

"Zandra could well be another victim," Josie said. "You'll also need to search both the arboretum and the Cahill property for the remains of the mirror victims."

*

Alex Thornberg was transported to Denton where he was booked and put in their holding area, which was a little-used group of cells in the basement of police headquarters. It was mostly reserved for rowdy college students and drunks who needed to sleep it off. They'd only be able to keep Alex there for a day, two at most. Once he was charged, he would be transferred to the county's central booking office which was roughly forty miles away. It was much more secure, manned twenty-four hours, and the sheriff supplied transportation of prisoners to and from court. There he would be arraigned and held until it was time for his trial.

After Drake dispatched a separate team to try to track down the mysterious Zandra, Josie, Noah, Gretchen, and Mettner joined the FBI, state police, and Easton police department in an exhaustive search of the arboretum and the property behind it. Josie's team worked in twos. She and Noah searched for six hours while Mettner and Gretchen slept in the vehicle. Then they traded off. Noah fell asleep instantly, reclined in the passenger's seat. Despite her overwhelming exhaustion and the headache that just wouldn't quit, Josie forwent rest to read the pages that Trinity had typed while in captivity. The narrative was choppy, with many typos, and sometimes it didn't make sense at all. Trinity must have been typing as Alex spoke, trying to get everything down. There were references to Zandra, but Alex didn't identify exactly who she was—Trinity had typed *his sister???* in parentheses the first few times Alex talked about her. There was no mention of Nicolette at all.

From what Josie could gather from Trinity's stab at the Bone Artist's biography, Hanna had been the more loving and stable of the two parents in this reclusive family, which wasn't saying a lot considering she let Francis do anything he wanted—including making Alex sleep in the shed for several years from a very young age. By Alex's account, Francis was cold, manipulative, and mean. If there was serious traumatic abuse beyond the burn on his face,

Alex had not confessed it to Trinity. He had, however, noted that Zandra frequently harmed Hanna, and that it was a source of great contention in their family. Although after Francis's "accident" the attacks seemed to stop. Zandra wasn't mentioned much after that, and yet, Alex seemed to blame her for all his woes.

Who the hell was she? Josie wondered. Had he killed her?

She didn't have time to puzzle over it since Mettner and Gretchen were back, and it was time for her and Noah to join the search once more. They spent another six hours on the two properties with dozens of other searchers.

But Trinity wasn't there.

Nor were the remains of the mirror victims. Or any human remains, for that matter.

Even the trusty K-9 unit failed to find anything. The search and rescue dogs followed Trinity's scent to the truck. The cadaver dogs gave several passive indicators on the Cahill property behind the arboretum, lying down when they detected the scent of human remains, however, after digging up several areas, no human bones were found.

"That doesn't mean someone wasn't here," one of the handlers explained. "If someone decomposed in these places where the dogs are indicating, there could be cells or other decomp materials that have leeched into the soil. What's most likely is that there were bodies in these places, and they were moved."

Josie trudged back to the caretaker house where Drake dealt her another blow. "There is no one named Zandra. My team couldn't find any evidence that she even existed. They interviewed staff and faculty from the college going back thirty years. Several people remember Francis and Hanna. They remember them having a little boy, but that's it. Two people even remembered Nicolette and confirmed that she ran off one day and never came back. The only possibility is that Hanna gave birth to Zandra at home. That's the only thing that would explain why there is no record of her."

Josie swiped at her brow with her forearm. She badly needed a shower. All of them did. "Maybe," she conceded. "But if that's the case, we have no way of knowing if she's alive or dead. Either way, she's not here. No one is here. No bodies, no Trinity. Drake, he took her somewhere. He would have known all we'd have to do is get the dogs out here and we'd find her."

"All right, let's say he figured out that we might be onto him or he simply decided to take precautions in case we showed up on his doorstep, which meant moving Trinity," Drake said.

"He moved her, but he stayed even though he suspected we were coming for him," Josie added.

"Why?"

"Because we're still playing his game," Josie said. "And it's my move."

"But why?" Drake asked. "Why continue when he's caught? He gets nothing out of this now. I guess—I guess unless she's dead. Then he has the satisfaction of you figuring out his cryptic, sick little game, knowing that you'll be devastated in the end. Or he gets the satisfaction of this Zandra escaping forever because she technically doesn't exist."

Josie shook her head. "No, Zandra isn't part of this game."

"What makes you say that?"

"The way he talked about her—"

Drake shook his head. "You can't believe anything this guy says. You know that, Quinn."

"Not the way he talked about her when I spoke to him. The way he talked about her to Trinity when she was taking down his story. Zandra wasn't nice to him. She didn't believe in him. She was a thorn in his side. I don't know what happened to her, but she's not part of this game. I still need to find my sister. We need to maintain focus on that goal."

Drake threw his arms in the air. "What the hell do you think I've been doing for the last forty-eight hours, Quinn? You think I like slogging through almost two hundred acres of mud and bird shit looking for human remains? You think I'm here for a damn vacation?"

"Calm down," Josie told him.

But the cool façade of professionalism had cracked. Drake whirled and kicked at the front door. Grunting, he kicked and kicked until the wood splintered.

"Drake," Josie said.

"I'll calm down when we find her," he shouted. His fists pummeled the door at lightning speed. Sweat poured from his hairline. The tendons in his neck pulled taut. Smears of blood dotted the front door. His knuckles bled.

"Drake!" Josie shouted. She tried to grab at his arm but nearly took an elbow to the face. In his frenzy, she had no chance against him. He was too big, too powerful.

She looked around for another FBI member, or any other law enforcement colleague, but there was no one. She thought about calling someone from her own team, but they would take at least ten minutes to get here and the blood on the door had gone from smudges to streaks. Drake was seriously going to hurt himself.

She jumped on his back.

He spun, once to his right and once to his left, but Josie hung on, applying a light choke hold on him as she spoke into his ear. "Dammit, Agent Nally. Stand down. Stand. Down!"

She felt him heaving beneath her, but his fight with the door had ceased. He stumbled down off the stoop, taking a few steps onto the grass in front of the house. When he stopped moving, Josie dropped off him. With mangled hands, he rubbed his throat.

"I'm sorry," Josie said. "For choking you. But you were... I mean, you freaked out. Drake, you can't—"

He didn't look at her, his gaze on the grass, but he cut her off. "I know," he said. "I'm sorry. I just—I just lost it." He looked at his hands. A large splinter protruded from the middle knuckle of his left hand. He shook his head. "Quinn, I think I love her. I'm in love with her."

Emotion threatened to bubble up, but Josie pushed it back down. Focus. She had to focus. "You need to stow that, Agent. Put it away. Right now."

He met her eyes finally. "Is that what you do? Is that how you do this?"

"I have to."

"I used to be able to," he said. "I never had a problem before…" He waved his bloodied hands. "Before this. I'm sorry."

"No need to apologize," Josie said.

Drake laughed. "She's your sister! How are you handling this better than I am?"

Josie put a hand on her hip. "I've had to do this since I was a child," she admitted. "Compartmentalize. Maintain focus on one thing. It helps in my job, but it used to be a matter of survival."

"You survived a lot," Drake noted. "From what Trinity told me."

"She told you? About my childhood? Wait till we find her. She's going to be sorry. I'm going to throttle—oh my God."

A realization hit her like a thunderbolt. Every fine hair on her body stood on end. Her vision tunneled momentarily and then came back into focus. Drake said, "Hey, are you okay?"

"I know how to find Zandra," she said.

CHAPTER SIXTY-ONE

Eight hours later, Drake stood with Josie and her team in the CCTV room next to Denton's interview room one where two weeks earlier Mettner and Gretchen had questioned Jaime Pestrak. Now, Alex Thornberg sat calmly at the same table, waiting for his court-appointed attorney.

Drake said, "Quinn, if you do this, you're going to blow this whole case."

Noah raised a brow. "That's a little dramatic, don't you think?"

Drake pointed to the television screen. "If you do this, you're presenting this guy with a defense that could not only keep him off death row, it could even keep him out of prison. The best case scenario is that the case spends years in litigation because he'll be deemed not competent to stand trial."

From her seat at the table, Gretchen said, "That's what trial experts are for—exactly these issues. The prosecutor will get a psychological expert to bolster their case. After everything this guy has done—everything he's already admitted to doing—there's no way he's walking."

Mettner added, "If the boss is right, it's going to come out eventually. If I'm the defense attorney and I get even an inkling this guy has a psychological problem this deep, I'm milking it for all its worth. If the defense attorney doesn't figure it out, and it comes out during trial, you've got a mistrial."

Josie stared at Drake. "They're right. I'm not jeopardizing the case. I'm trying to find my sister while there's still a chance that she's alive. His lawyer will be present. No funny business. Nothing out of bounds."

A knock sounded on the door and Chief Chitwood popped his head inside. "Kids," he said. "Thornberg's lawyer is here. Shut down the CCTV and vacate this room while they consult."

They turned off the CCTV apparatus and filed out of the room as Alex's public defender entered the interview room. They went back to the great room where they waited in tense silence until she came to get them. "My client is willing to talk to Detective Quinn," she said. "Detective Quinn only."

"Thank you," Josie said and followed her back to the interview room.

She waited a long moment until she knew her colleagues were in the CCTV room and saw the red light beneath the camera come on, indicating that the interview was being recorded. She noted the date and time as well as the names of all present for the camera before she looked at Alex.

"I need to talk to Zandra."

His attorney raised a brow. "I'm sorry, but who is Zandra?"

"Alex knows who she is, don't you Alex?"

He stared at her.

His attorney said, "Alex? Is there something we need to discuss in private?"

Ignoring her, he continued to stare at Josie. "I told her not to come back. She only ever caused trouble."

"I don't think that's true," Josie said.

He leaned forward, eyes wide. "It is true. She was the one who hurt Mother."

"Because she was angry with your mother, Alex. Your mother let Francis hurt you. Zandra knew that none of you—not you or her or your mother—could hurt Francis back, so she took things out on your mother."

"No, I—that's not—she did hurt Mother but Father, he didn't—he never—"

"He did hurt you, Alex. You must know that. Where do you think Zandra came from? She arrived after Nicolette left, didn't she? Nicolette was bigger than you, older than you. She tried to protect you from Francis, but it was a losing battle, wasn't it?"

He gave her a pinched expression.

Josie went on. "Nicolette couldn't handle what was happening in your house. She was just a kid herself. She had no resources. Her own mother failed to protect you from Francis. She had nowhere to turn, no way to keep you from getting hurt. So she left. One day she was there and the next, she was gone, and you were left with a monster. You were vulnerable, helpless, defenseless, and—"

Alex's eyes dropped to the table, and something rippled over his face. The skin of his forehead loosened, and his lower lip jutted out in a pout. Josie dipped her head so she could see his eyes, which glistened with tears. "We're not supposed to say her name ever," he said in the childlike tone he'd used at the caretaker's home when Josie first talked to him.

"Alex," Josie snapped.

The attorney jumped. "Detective Quinn."

He looked up at her again, his features sharper, his expression confident. "This is not part of the game," he said.

"Zandra's not part of the game?" Josie asked. "That hardly seems fair. She's been playing all along."

The attorney said, "Maybe we should stop. I'm afraid I don't understand what's going on. Alex—"

"Shut up," he told her. To Josie he said, "You don't know what you're talking about."

"Don't I? Who killed Nicci, Alex? Was it you?"

"Of course not."

"Who killed Codie Lash and her husband?"

"I didn't do that," he said. "It was a mistake."

"Your mistake or Zandra's?" Josie asked.

A low growl vibrated in his throat. "That bitch. I spent my whole life keeping her out of trouble. She ruins everything."

"No," Josie said. She thought about the exchange between Alex and the Lash couple. Even before Mr. Lash had gone after him, Codie had been berating him. She had pushed him. Pushed and pushed until he was at a breaking point.

"She does!" Alex insisted.

"No, she doesn't," Josie argued. "Her job has always been to protect you because you're a psychopath."

"That's enough, Detective Quinn," the attorney huffed.

Alex put his hands over his ears. "I said shut up," he hollered.

Josie pointed a finger at him just the way Codie Lash had and said, "It's true. You're a psychopath and a liar. Everyone knew it, didn't they? Your mother knew it, Francis knew it. That's why you weren't allowed to go to school, because you're mentally—"

The attorney stood. "Really, Detective Quinn. That's enough. This interview is over. You're out of line. I didn't come here so you could berate my client and call him names."

Alex lunged across the table and wrapped his hands around Josie's throat. The attorney screamed. Josie fell backwards as Alex's full weight descended on her. She used their momentum to roll him over so that she straddled him. His hands loosened, and she whipped them out of the way, turning him swiftly onto his stomach and pinning them behind his back. She used the cuffs on her belt to restrain him. Her breath came fast, but she was relieved to see that her team had followed her instructions and not come racing to her rescue immediately.

"We're going to stand up now," she told him.

Alex's attorney helped Josie stand him up and sit him in the nearest chair. He shook his head as if he were flipping long hair out of his face. His eyes narrowed and he glared at Josie. His voice sounded different when he spoke. Petulant and higher-pitched. "He doesn't remember any of that shit, you dumb bitch."

Josie's heart skipped two beats. She tried to keep the tremble out of her voice when she said, "Zandra?"

Alex rolled his eyes. "Who the hell else were you expecting? I mean, you were trying to get me, weren't you?"

Josie looked at Alex's attorney, but she didn't object. She nodded for Josie to continue. This was what Drake worried about. A client with Dissociative Identity Disorder was his own defense.

To Zandra, Josie said, "You did the killing, didn't you?"

"Of course I did. You think little baby Alex could have done it? You think *sensitive artist* Alex could have done the dirty work?"

"He had to know that you were doing it," Josie said.

Another eye-roll. "He knows what he wants to know. He hears what he wants to hear. He listens to me when he feels like listening. I don't care what he says about me or how much he resents me, he knows I took care of him. He knows I've always taken on the bad parts, the parts he couldn't handle. So yeah, I went into that locked bedroom with Francis every time. I did that so little baby Alex wouldn't have to. I killed the people he took, the people whose bones he wanted to use for his art and his games. He tried to make me go away so many times. He's wanted to kill me for so long, did you know that?"

Josie said, "Yes. I did. Do you know why?"

"He thinks you're so smart, but you seem pretty dumb to me," Zandra said. "Didn't you hear anything I just said? I take the bad stuff so he doesn't have to. If he kills me, all those memories die with me."

"Then why are you still here?" Josie asked.

"Because unlike that worthless bitch Nicolette, I will never leave him. No matter how bad things get. No matter what happens. I will never abandon him. I'm his real sister. I'm the one who was there for him."

"You're his mirror," Josie said. "It's not Alex choosing the victims, is it? It's you."

"Duh," Zandra said. "I choose them and he takes them. I kill them and he makes art out of them."

"You always choose two people who reflect each other in some way," Josie went on. "That's why their names are similar. Terri and Terry, Kenneth and Kendra, Tony and Toni. Male and female."

"He likes it that way," Zandra explained. "No one is ever alone, not even in death. That's how he prefers it. I told you, he's a baby. He doesn't want anyone left alone the way that shitbag Nicolette left him. I told you, I'm a better sister than she ever was."

"Why does he only display one of them, then?" Josie asked.

Zandra shook her head. "You're really thick, aren't you? Because he knows I'm supposed to be a secret."

Josie remembered that Hanna had dedicated one of her shows to 'my darling Alex and Zandra.' "But your mother knew about you."

"Why do you think she made us stay in that godawful house? She couldn't let us out into the world. The first time she sent that little baby to school, I would have made him go away where he was safe and told the teachers what Francis was doing to him. Then they would have taken us out of there and put Francis in jail. No way were either of them going for that."

"They both knew that Alex had alters?" Josie asked.

She had researched Dissociative Identity Disorder before this interview. She knew that there was still some discord in the field of psychology where the disorder was concerned. There were many camps that didn't believe it existed at all. But the experts who studied it most extensively were unified on several characteristics: it was usually the result of extreme trauma, often in childhood. The affected person's psyche developed what were called alters, meaning entirely different personalities or people within their fractured psyche. Some alters, like Zandra, emerged for the very purpose of bearing the brunt of abuse. There didn't seem to be any limit as to how many alters a person with DID could have but most experts agreed that there was always a main alter—one who showed him or herself more than the others and had a great deal of influence. There were some patients with DID whose alters spoke to one another and other people with DID who simply had amnesia for the time periods during which their alters took over. Alex appeared to have a little bit of both. He was well aware of Zandra, and based on the pages that Trinity had typed up, he had often engaged in dialogues with her, but he didn't remember all of the things that happened when Zandra was firmly in control.

Zandra said, "They both knew—about me, anyway. There are a couple of others they never met. We didn't have many friends."

"Why did you kill Nicci?" Josie asked.

"Because he took the reporter," Zandra replied. "He didn't want her for her bones, you know. He wanted her to tell his story. Like it's some big epic story. He really thinks he's the smartest thing ever, you know, and this art obsession of his—he's even worse than our mother. She thought she was hot shit, too. Anyway, he was keeping the reporter so she'd tell his life story, but how could his story be complete with that nasty woman still out there, living a perfectly normal life? She had to go. I had to prove to him that I'm a more important part of his story than she ever was. She's dead and I'm still here. Just like I told him I always would be."

"What happened to the reporter?" Josie asked. She felt light-headed waiting for the answer.

Zandra smiled. "Oh, you think I'm just going to tell you? I'm not him, dumbass! You have to ask him what he did with her."

"I did," Josie said. "He wouldn't tell me."

"You think I will?" Zandra shook her head. "No, that's not how this works. You have to play his game, Detective."

CHAPTER SIXTY-TWO

Josie felt as though she had run a marathon. Back in the great room, she sat at her desk while her team and Drake stood staring at her.

"I feel sick," Drake said. "You know his attorney is having a field day right now. It's like winning the lottery for her, and we're no closer to finding Trinity."

Noah said, "Hey, that's enough. Let's keep our focus on Trinity, okay? So we didn't get her location from… Zandra or whoever the hell was talking in there. We need to keep trying other avenues."

Mettner said, "Was that even real? What if it's all an act?"

"It wasn't an act," Josie said.

"Boss is right," Gretchen agreed. "I dealt with some criminals with DID back in Philadelphia. It's a real thing. Complex and complicated. But that's not our problem. That's for the attorneys to hash out before trial. Right now, we need to get into the head of one person and that's Alex Thornberg. He's the Bone Artist."

"This is his game," Josie agreed. "Just like Zandra said."

"Okay," Noah said, beginning to pace. "Then what is he after? Every game has a winner and a loser. He wants to win. How does he do that?"

"Press coverage?" Mettner suggested. "He's always wanted that, so people would know how smart he is—although he's already going to get all the press he could possibly want now that he's been caught."

"It's not just about him wanting people to know how smart he is," Josie said. "This is about him trying to prove something."

"Prove something to who?" Drake scoffed.

Josie rocked in her chair. "To the only person he left alive."

"His dad?"

"Yeah, did you read any of the pages that Trinity typed?"

Drake grimaced. "Of course I did."

"He thought Alex was stupid. Alex wanted to be an artist, like Hanna, but Francis squashed that."

"So what? What does this have to do with Trinity?" Mettner asked.

"She's his historian," Gretchen said. "Zandra just told us that. His biographer. She knew everything there was to know about his case before he took her."

Josie added, "Including the fact that for every victim he put on display for the world to see, there was one we never found. One no one even knew about. We still have to find those victims. He would have used their bones. He must have because they're not anywhere on the properties. Wherever he took Trinity, it's the site of his final piece."

Drake raised a brow. "Piece of what?"

"Art!" Josie said. "Remember—he thinks of himself as an artist. Somewhere in this state is his final work of art. If we find that, we find Trinity."

"Are you listening to yourself? Where in the hell could this guy put on a goddamn art installation made of bones and a famous reporter and not have the whole damn world freaking out?"

Josie looked around at all of them, working through everything she knew in her mind. She kept coming back to Alex's relationship with Francis. She turned her chair around until she was facing Chief Chitwood's office. His door was open. He had gone to a meeting with the District Attorney. Josie stood up and walked into his office, looking out the window. She heard the footsteps of her team and Drake following her. Then Gretchen's voice. "Boss?"

Josie looked across the street to the trees lining the sidewalk. Then her gaze drifted upward to the blue sky where a large bird glided past. A hawk or an osprey. She couldn't be sure. Not a carrion bird.

"Raptors," she blurted out.

"What's that?" Noah said.

She turned and looked at them all crowded inside the Chief's door. "Raptors kill for their food. They snatch living creatures out of their natural habitats. They roost up high, don't they?"

Drake shook his head. "Have you lost your mind? Is this what a nervous breakdown looks like?"

"I'm serious," Josie said. "Many raptors roost in treetops or the tops of buildings or telephone poles, don't they?"

"How the hell would I know?" Drake snapped.

"Francis's favorite birds were raptors," Josie said. "In the pages that Trinity typed, that was mentioned. Also, Trinity wrote in her diary that the subject of raptors came up between her and Alex—well, Max—and he was uncomfortable. He knew all about them from his dad, but he didn't like them. He does, however, like scavenger birds."

"Does he like them or does he just like the fact that they accelerate skeletonization?" Noah asked.

"It doesn't matter," Josie replied. "Alex's entire life has been about proving to Francis that he is smart, that he is worthy; that he is as talented an artist as his mother."

"I'm pretty sure Francis knows that Alex got the last laugh in this situation," Mettner argued.

"Sure," Josie said. "But we're not talking in the literal sense right now. We're talking about Alex's body of work as an artist. The symbolism. His last, great piece would be in a place that symbolically, Francis would see. Francis is a raptor."

"And Alex is a scavenger," Gretchen said.

"Raptors have great eyesight." Drake said with a sigh. He walked over to the window and looked up, spotting the raptor Josie had seen moments earlier catching thermals above them. "Would you say they spend more time in the sky than perhaps a scavenger bird does? Since scavenger birds will spend a great deal of time on the ground feeding once they find a food source?"

Josie said, "I would. Drake, she's on a roof. Trinity is on a roof somewhere. Some kind of raised structure—a bell tower or clock tower. Somewhere high up in the air."

"But where?"

"We have to follow the pattern," Josie said. "The mirror victims. I was supposed to be the mirror victim in this case."

"The mirror victims were male and female," Mettner reminded them. "They had the same names: Anthony and Antonia, Kenneth and Kendra, Terrence and Teresa, Robert and Roberta."

"Like him and his sister—well, his alter," Noah added. "Alexander and Alexandra."

"To him, Zandra was his sister in a much more real sense than his actual sister ever was," Josie said. "So yes, him and his sister. I can be the mirror because I'm Trinity's sister. He always leaves his display in the place where he took his mirror victim from."

Drake said, "But he didn't take you."

"No, but he tried. Near Callowhill, where Trinity grew up."

"So what? You think she's on the roof of your parents' house or something?" Mettner asked.

"No," Josie said. She thought about Callowhill. She'd been almost an hour from her parents' house when he crashed into her. "The preserve."

CHAPTER SIXTY-THREE

They got to the preserve in less than an hour, rolling up to the main building in a caravan of police vehicles. It was late afternoon but there was still plenty of daylight. Cheyenne Thomas and a few of her staff came running out of the building, panicked. When Josie explained to her what was going on, she said, "I'm sorry, but we've had no unusual activity. As you can see, we've only got this small group of buildings and none of them are particularly high. We've got some ladders if you'd like to get up there and have a look."

Josie panned the area. Disappointment rounded her shoulders. Noah walked up beside her. "Maybe she's not here."

"No," Josie said. "This is the place. I'm sure of it."

Mettner jogged over. "I'll call the K-9 unit in this county and see if I can get them down here. We've still got stuff from her suitcase we can use to scent her."

"Thanks, Mett," Josie said. She turned to Cheyenne. "Do you have any old maps of this place? There was a hunter who went missing and whose remains were found on the preserve back in 2000. Do you know if he had a deer stand nearby?"

"I'm sorry. A what?"

"A platform or a small structure up in a tree that he could sit in and hunt from," Josie explained.

"Oh, I don't know, but we had a recent survey of the land the last time we applied for a grant. There might be something on those maps."

It took a half hour to find what they were looking for. On the maps that had been prepared in the last year, the surveyor had marked a "tree platform of unknown origin" at the southernmost point of the preserve property. His notes indicated that there was some uncertainty as to whether the platform was actually part of the preserve premises or if it was part of the privately-owned land adjacent.

Josie didn't care.

It took them another half hour to find the elevated deer blind which looked like a small shed affixed to the side of a tall tree. Wooden footholds had been nailed into the tree from the ground to the hatch on the bottom of the structure. Before anyone could stop her, Josie started climbing.

"Josie," Noah called. "We should get you a harness."

She was already halfway up. She stopped and looked down. From this height, a fall wouldn't kill her or break any of her bones, but at the height of the stand, she'd definitely die if she fell. "Too late," she called. Without looking back, she scrambled to the hatch and pushed it open. Her head swiveled around, taking in the Bone Artist's final creation. She nearly fell as her brain processed what she was seeing. The entire inside had been painted in a psychedelic swirl of pinks and reds. Hundreds of bones had been affixed to the floor and walls, and there, along the right-hand wall, cocooned in some kind of netting and tied to a square post that Alex had obviously installed, was Trinity, her body limp, head lolling on her chest. Her black hair hung across her face. He had screwed eyehooks into the ceiling and woven several threads of fishing line through them. He had looped the bottom of the fishing line around Trinity's wrists, extending her arms from her sides. Behind her, on the wall, were thousands of different kinds of feathers.

She was spreading her wings.

Tears streamed down Josie's face as she climbed into the small blind, careful not to disturb any of the remains at her feet. She heard someone below, climbing up the tree. She looked down to see Drake halfway there.

"Not yet," she said.

"Is she alive?" he shouted.

"Please," Josie muttered.

She walked over to Trinity, afraid to touch her and find her cold and completely still. "Trin," she said, voice cracking.

No movement.

Josie's hand shook as she reached out and pushed a shank of Trinity's hair out of her face and behind her ear. She touched Trinity's cheek, alarmed by the icy feel of it. Then Trinity's body jerked, her head lifted, and she howled. Josie was so startled, she fell backward, landing flat on her back, and knocking bones everywhere. She heard the floor beneath her splinter and give way. As she went into freefall, her hands reached out, searching for anything to hold onto. A jagged piece of wood shredded her palms, but she held on.

"Josie?" Trinity hollered.

Josie looked up to see that she had fallen through a rotted piece of wood at Trinity's feet. Trinity had broken the fishing line on one of her arms. She tugged hard with the other arm, trying to free it. After several tries, it broke loose, but her lower body was wrapped tightly in netting, immobile. Josie was aware of shouting from below and Drake hollering nearby. As her legs dangled, she craned her neck to look behind her, but he was too far down to help her.

Trinity said, "Can you climb up? Grab my hand."

Josie grabbed onto Trinity's feet, clawing until she lifted her upper body far enough to wrap her arms around Trinity's calves and the post behind them. Trinity's hands scrabbled in the air, trying to reach her. Josie shimmied up a little more until Trinity was able to slip her hands under Josie's armpits and into an awkward embrace. Above the cacophony below, Josie could hear Noah's voice telling her to hang on. She closed her eyes and released some of the tension in her upper body for a few precious seconds, letting Trinity take the weight. Then she pulled herself up further until they were face to face.

"Hold on to me," Trinity said.

They wrapped their arms around one another. Trinity's cheek was freezing against Josie's. She felt sobs wracking Trinity's body. Her own body responded in kind until they were both weeping.

From somewhere below, Drake hollered, "Quinn! Stay where you are. This whole thing is unstable. Don't move. We're getting ladders. Just hold on."

Into Trinity's ear, Josie said, "I'm sorry for the way we left things when you walked out of my house."

"Me too," Trinity said.

"I know what the worst thing that ever happened to you was—it was me being taken as a child."

Trinity's arms tightened around her. "Yes," she breathed.

"I know what the best thing that ever happened to you was—it was when we were reunited."

Trinity laughed. "You're wrong," she said.

Josie heard the clang of an aluminum ladder against the tree and felt its vibration near her feet.

Trinity said, "You rescuing me from a serial killer is the best thing that ever happened to me."

CHAPTER SIXTY-FOUR

Trout chased a tennis ball across Josie and Noah's yard. Once he retrieved it, he weaved through the crush of bodies on the patio and found Patrick, depositing the ball into Patrick's lap. Laughing, Patrick tossed it again. This time, after he caught it, he searched out Josie, sitting in a folding chair at one of the card tables that Noah had set up in their backyard. He put the ball between her feet and nudged one of her hands with his head. Josie scratched between his ears. Across from her, Trinity raised a brow. "I don't think Trout likes me. He hasn't brought that ball over to me once."

Josie laughed. "He's food-motivated. Give him some of that hamburger you've got there, and you won't be able to get rid of him."

Trinity used a fork to carve out a small piece of her hamburger which she dangled beneath the table. Trout ran over and swallowed it without even chewing, making Trinity laugh. Trinity looked down at him. "Oh you're right. He's looking at me like he wants to get married."

"Told you," Josie said.

They sat in silence, looking around at their friends, family, and colleagues eating, drinking, and celebrating Trinity's safe return. They'd been lucky to get warm weather. Noah manned the barbecue, doling out food. Nearby, Gretchen and Mettner ribbed one another. Even Bob Chitwood had come. He stood listening to something Lisette said. In another corner of the yard, Drake held Shannon and Christian's attention.

Trinity said, "This is nice."

"Yes," Josie agreed. "It is."

"I'm going to ruin it by talking about the case but I have to know—did the DNA from the combs match any of the known victims?"

Josie nodded. "Yes, both were from mirror victims. All of the mirror victims' remains were found in the tree blind where he had tied you up."

Trinity hugged herself. "Were there any more victims? Any no one knew about?"

"No. The arboretum property as well as the hundred acres that Hanna Cahill left Alex were searched very thoroughly. We don't believe there are any other victims. All of them are accounted for; the identities of the mirror victims have been confirmed; and soon their remains will be returned to their families."

"That's good," Trinity whispered. "I'm glad that their families will have closure, at least."

"Did you know about the mirror victims when he took you?" Josie asked.

"Yes, I'd figured it out. I had handwritten notes on them. They were in the boxes. I was hoping he'd leave them so you'd see the trail that led to him, but he took all my notes, all my materials on his case."

"When did you know that the Bone Artist was the boy you met at the nature preserve when you were fourteen?"

"I didn't truly know until he drove up the driveway to the cabin and got out. When I saw his face—his scar—I knew immediately it was Max."

"But you suspected," Josie said. "Is that why you became so obsessed with the case?"

Trinity looked away for a moment, her gaze drifting over toward Drake, a flash of regret sweeping across her features. "It was dumb luck. I had an argument on air with a correspondent about the Bone Artist. She said he was dead and that's why he stopped killing. I didn't believe that. I was venting to Drake about the whole thing over dinner later that night. That's when he told me it was his case. It wasn't hard to get him to discuss it. Pretty soon, I convinced him to show me photos of the crime scenes. Photos no member of the public had seen before."

"The way the bones were arranged made you remember Max?" Josie suggested.

Trinity looked back at her. "It wasn't that simple. Not exactly. It wasn't like I had this big epiphany. There was just something about the way the bones were displayed that got under my skin. I felt like there was something important that I was missing, something I should remember. I had no idea what it was or why I would feel that way about a serial killer case I knew so little about."

"So you started digging through Drake's files."

Trinity frowned. "I know I shouldn't have done it. It was so wrong on so many levels, the least of which the fact that we were lovers and I betrayed his trust." Again, her gaze shifted to Drake, a wistful look on her face. He must have felt her eyes on him because he looked up at her. A grin broke across his face.

"I think he's forgiven you," Josie said.

Trinity sighed. "He's too good for me."

Josie reached across and touched her sister's arm lightly, drawing her focus back. "Or maybe he's just right. Once you had the files, then what?"

"I followed the path: the killer's need for symmetry; the male/female symbols; the Codie Lash connection; the Bobbi/Robert Ingram clue; then the mirror victims. When I read the report about the avian scavengers, it all clicked into place for me. That day in the woods when I saw Max messing with the bones—he'd been trying them out in different arrangements. I'd seen him make those symbols. And I realized he might be the Bone Artist. On the one hand, it seemed like such a long shot, but on the other, if I was right, it could be the biggest story of my career."

"So you tried to make contact with him by wearing Codie Lash's comb in your hair? How did you know he'd be watching?"

"I didn't. It was a shot in the dark. I thought it was a lost cause. I wore the comb in that piece on the missing girls case, a week went by, and nothing happened."

"That was why you told Patrick that your big lead had fallen through."

"Yes," Trinity agreed. "But then the comb arrived here at your house. I had to get out of here. I couldn't put you and Noah in jeopardy. So I left and rented the cabin."

"You could have told us," Josie said. "We would have helped you."

"By taking over. You would never have let me try to make contact again."

"By keeping you safe, Trinity. You don't always have to put your life on the line for a big story." Before Trinity could protest, Josie continued, "The comb arrived here. You left and rented the cabin. You stayed there for a week, and then you decided to go back to New York? Why?"

"I thought he wouldn't be able to find me. I thought if I went back to New York, he would know where to find me. But as I was leaving, he pulled up into the driveway. I was already in my car. Ready to drive off. Then he was there. As soon as he got out of the truck, I knew I had been right about him."

"Did he threaten you?"

"No," Trinity said. "He told me he wanted me to tell his story."

"He didn't drug you?" Josie asked.

She shook her head. "Only once… I knew that he always kidnapped a mirror and he had been asking me questions about you during our 'sessions'. I suspected he was going to take you. I tried to escape…"

"How?"

"I acted really sick. I told him he had to get me help. He told me there was a small veterinarian hospital on the property and it had medicine. He wanted to take me there. I just had to get out of the house. I acted weak, like I had to lean on him just to walk. As soon as we got outside, I ran. I went right for the truck but he caught up with me. He must have known that I might have been faking because he had a needle in his pocket. He stabbed it into my leg and I started to feel woozy. I went right down. There I was lying next to the truck—I wasn't even on the damn driver's side—and he was pacing back and forth talking about how he needed me to write his story and how I shouldn't run because he hadn't done anything to hurt me. I knew I was going to pass out, and I looked up and saw someone had written *Wash Me* on the door of the truck. That gave me the idea to write my own message."

"But you couldn't write words," Josie said. "He would have noticed that right away."

"Yes," Trinity said. "I had to use shorthand. I had already left you the message to read my diary because I thought if you had his name and age, you'd be able to find him. But I didn't know if you'd be able to find the diary. I was on the verge of blacking out so I just scrawled the movie name on the door. I hoped that when he came for you, you'd see it somehow. I had no way of knowing if you would or not or if you'd even get away from him. I'm so sorry, Josie."

Josie smiled at her. "That was smart. You did well."

"I was an idiot, Josie," Trinity argued. "I did so many stupid, reckless things. I want you to know that I'm truly sorry. For everything. I shouldn't have gone off on my own. I should have asked for help. I—"

"Stop," Josie said. "You don't need to apologize."

Trinity's brows shot up. "Really? Cause what I did was messed up and dangerous and irresponsible and—"

Josie reached across the table and covered one of Trinity's hands with her own, silencing her. "I will always come for you, do you understand?"

Trinity's eyes filled with tears. They'd both been crying a lot in the last week. "Josie," she whispered.

"I will always follow you into any hell that you get yourself into, do you understand?"

Biting her bottom lip, Trinity nodded.

"There's something I need to tell you. I read your diary."

"I know," Trinity said. "You were supposed to. It's okay."

Josie smiled. "Yes, but there's something you need to know. Remember the fight that got you into trouble? The one that landed you in community service?"

"Oh, yes, at the school trip? I know, I sounded crazy, saying that I met you. You have to understand how messed up I was then. My nana had just died. I was getting bullied mercilessly at school. I just needed something to hold onto. The idea of you—it was just—"

"That *was* me," Josie said.

Trinity's face lost two shades of color. "Wh-what?"

"It was me. I dragged Beverly off you and elbowed Melanie in the face."

"But how?"

"There were schools there from all over, remember? I was there with a bunch of freshmen from Denton East that day. Beverly was a notorious troublemaker in our class. Believe me, it wasn't the first time or the last time I got into it with her. Lisette can vouch for that. She moved away right before senior year, thank God. In fact…" Josie stood and wrestled a long piece of fabric from her jacket pocket. She deposited the teal scarf onto the table between them.

"Oh my God, Josie." Trinity touched it reverently.

Josie said, "Lisette gave it to me shortly after she won custody of me. I used to wear it all the time—even when it didn't match my clothes. Then, during sophomore year of high school, I spilled something on it and decided to put it away so I didn't ruin it."

Trinity looked up at her. "Josie, this is—I can't believe this—this means that—"

Josie smiled. "You did meet me that day."

Trinity wiped more tears from her eyes. "You were there. You were there when I needed you."

"I was there."

A LETTER FROM LISA

Thank you so much for choosing to read *Find Her Alive*. It was such a pleasure to bring you this adventure with Josie, particularly because it explored Trinity's past and their relationship as sisters. If you enjoyed it and want to keep up-to-date with all my latest releases, just sign up at the following link. Your email address will never be shared, and you can unsubscribe at any time.

www.bookouture.com/lisa-regan

I have to take creative liberties with many things for purposes of plot and pacing. Aubertine College and its arboretum are complete fictions. Denton is a made-up city. Keller Hollow is a made-up town. You should know that there really was a study done regarding avian scavengers at a body farm in Texas showing that black vultures could reduce a body to bones in a matter of hours. The paper is called *Spatial Patterning of vulture scavenged human remains* by M. Katherine Spradley, Michelle D. Hamilton and Alberto Giordano and it was published in Forensic Science International in 2012. Ringing (lithophonic) rocks and Eastonite are real things.

I love hearing from readers. You can get in touch with me through any of the social media outlets below, including my website and Goodreads page. Also, if you are up for it, I'd really appreciate it if you'd leave a review and perhaps recommend *Find Her Alive* to other readers. Reviews and word-of-mouth recommendations go a long way in helping readers discover my books for the first time. As always, thank you so much for your support. It means the world to me. I can't wait to hear from you, and I hope to see you next time!

Thanks,
Lisa Regan

📘 LisaReganCrimeAuthor

🐦 @LisaIRegan

🖥 www.lisaregan.com

ACKNOWLEDGEMENTS

Wonderful readers and devoted fans, I cannot thank you enough! Your relentless enthusiasm and desire to continue reading this series is the greatest gift an author could ever imagine. This has been such an amazing journey and I'm so grateful to share it with all of you. You are truly the best readers in the world! Thank you, as always, to my husband, Fred, for your support and patience as well as for keeping me fed and caffeinated and doing whatever needed to be done in order for me to finish this book. Thank you to my daughter, Morgan, for all your patience and for going so many hours without my attention. Thank you to my first readers: Dana Mason, Katie Mettner, Nancy S. Thompson, Maureen Downey, and Torese Hummel. Thank you to my Entrada readers. Thank you to Matty Dalrymple and Jane Kelly for helping me work out plot issues over and over again and not batting an eye while we discussed the Bone Artist's habits over brunch! Thank you to my grandmothers: Helen Conlen and Marilyn House; my parents: William Regan, Donna House, Joyce Regan, Rusty House and Julie House; my brothers and sisters-in-law: Sean and Cassie House, Kevin and Christine Brock and Andy Brock; as well as my lovely sisters: Ava McKittrick and Melissia McKittrick. Thank you as well to all of the usual suspects for your incredible support and love and for always spreading the word—you know who you are! I'd also like to thank all the fabulous bloggers and reviewers who read the first seven Josie Quinn books or who have picked up the series somewhere in the middle. I really appreciate your continued enthusiasm and passion for the series!

Thank you so very much to Sgt. Jason Jay for answering all my law-enforcement questions at every hour of the day and night with such patience. I am so grateful for your support and your willingness to help!

Thank you to Oliver Rhodes, Noelle Holten, Kim Nash, and the entire team at Bookouture for making this fantastic journey both possible and the most fun I've ever had in my life. Last but certainly not least, thank you to the absolutely amazing Jessie Botterill for rescuing this book and helping me turn it into something that makes me really proud. I don't believe that anyone else in the world could pull the kind of work out of me that you somehow manage to do every single time. I'm astounded by your brilliance and eternally grateful for your vision, your support, and the fact that you always manage to calm me down when I am most anxious! Thank you, thank you, thank you!